Real Men Last All Night

Real Men Last All Night

Four Novellas of Super-Hot Romance

LORA LEIGH

LORI FOSTER

CHEYENNE McCRAY

HEIDI BETTS

 St. Martin's Griffin ⚶ New York

This is a work of fiction. All of the characters, organizations, and events portrayed in these stories are either products of the authors' imaginations or are used fictitiously.

www.stmartins.com

Library of Congress Cataloging-in-Publication Data

Real men last all night / Lori Foster, Lora Leigh, Cheyenne McCray, and Heidi Betts.— 1st ed.
    p. cm.
  ISBN-13: 978-0-312-38779-2
  ISBN-10: 0-312-38779-2
  1. Erotic stories, American.   I. Foster, Lori, 1958– Luring Lucy.   II. Leigh, Lora. Cooper's fall.   III. McCray, Cheyenne. Edge of sin.   IV. Betts, Heidi. Wanted: a real man.
  PS648.E7R433 2009
  813'.01083538—dc22

2009007375

First Edition: July 2009

10 9 8 7 6 5 4 3 2 1

Contents

Real Men Last All Night

Cooper's Fall

by

Lora Leigh

For our men and our women who fight so hard to protect us. And for those here at home who give so much of themselves to make certain our soldiers know they are remembered and appreciated.

A special acknowledgment and dedication to both Kelly Granzow, with the SOS (Support Our Soldiers), and Diane Smith, who both work tirelessly to provide for the soldiers they can reach.

For all of you, our protectors in the military and at home, and those of you who give of your hearts, your hands, and your generosity to send the letters and packages to show your love. You are an inspiration to us all. And to those of us who enjoy the freedoms our soldiers provide, you are our Godsend. God bless you every one.

And a special thank-you to Sair, my wonderful Aussie friend. Hope to see you again sometime soon.

1

Ethan Cooper stared out the window, his expression bland. He knew it was bland. He could feel it pulling into lines of complete blank shock.

Fascination.

Lust.

He should move. He told himself to move as he clenched his fists and pressed them into the wall beside the small attic window.

He was going to move.

In just a minute.

Just as soon as he came in his jeans from the sight that met his bemused eyes.

It wasn't his fault.

He was excusing himself and he damned well knew it. He was just too . . . shell-shocked. Yeah, that was the word. Too shell-shocked to move a single muscle and drag himself away from the little window with a bird's-eye view into the neighbors' secluded backyard.

Pervert! he railed at himself.

That didn't stop him. He was transfixed. His cock was in hell. He was practically drooling on his dusty attic floor as he watched shy little priss, Miss Sarah Fox, naked as God created her.

Glistening beneath the sun, slender hands moving.

He closed his eyes. Swallowed tightly. She thought she was in the privacy of her own home. She thought that sheltering fence she'd paid a fucking fortune to have built around her pool was tall enough to protect her. That no one could see her. That she was safe.

He opened his eyes.

He felt sweat bead on his forehead and roll down his temple as she smoothed her hands over her breasts. Cupped them. Rolled her nipples.

"Christ," he wheezed. There was a flash of gold.

Holy hell.

He felt his cock get impossibly thicker. Felt his balls tighten. His balls? Damn. He could barely breathe.

Prissy Miss Fox had nipple rings. Fucking nipple rings. Beneath those staid blouses and too-long damned skirts she wore, she was wearing fucking nipple rings?

His fists tightened as he pressed them into the window frame. He blinked back sweat, and he couldn't drag his eyes away from her.

Long nut-brown, riotously curly hair fanned around her. A hell of a lot longer than he had imagined it was. And she was curved. Curved where a woman should be curved.

And her fingers.

He tried to swallow. Her fingers were pulling at the little gold piercings in her nipples, and her expression was filled with pleasure.

Her entire body was sheened with oil. He forced his eyes from her nipples. Down.

"God have mercy." He was breathing fast, hard.

Fine. He was a fucking pervert. He unzipped his jeans, dragged free his dick, and curled his fingers around the shaft, palming it, stroking it.

Because, she was moving again. The fingers of one hand were trailing down her stomach, to her bare, waxed, glistening . . .

He leaned his forehead against the little circular window, stared, fought to breathe. There was gold there, too. Just a flash. Just enough to assure his very trained eye that Sarah Fox had a piercing at the hood of her clitoris.

And she was playing with it. Pulling at it. Stroking her clit with glistening fingers.

She didn't writhe. She wasn't arching or giving him a show. She was a woman, lost in her own fantasy, her own touch. Her teeth clenched her lower lip, perspiration beaded her skin. Oil shimmered on it. And she was stroking herself. Slowly. Enjoying it. A woman who liked to be teased. Who liked the buildup. A slow hand.

He timed the strokes on his cock with the slender fingers moving between her thighs. Fine, he was fucking hard-core into watching the coolest little piece of flesh in town touching herself.

Damn. It was good. Who knew?

He stroked his cock, feeling her fingers on his flesh, slick, oil slick. He palmed the thick crown, feeling the steel that pierced the head of his cock, stroked down the shaft, and felt his chest tightening with the release building inside his balls.

And still she played.

His gaze narrowed on her. Her expression was almost distressed. Her fingers were moving faster now, stroking. His fingers stroked.

His thumb raked over the curved steel beneath the head of his cock as he imagined the piercing in her clit.

Ah hell. Damn. He couldn't handle it. He watched. Her fingers, her face, the sweat that ran into her hair and then he blew. He felt the ragged growl that tore from his throat, the blistering curse as his come exploded from his balls, splattering against his fingers as Sarah's hips arched and her expression twisted.

In disappointment.

Her hand slapped the cement beside her. She sat up, pushed her fingers through her hair, then jerked to her feet and stalked back into her little house as Cooper stared at her in shock.

His come was cooling on his fingers and Sarah had been left disappointed?

He blinked down at the pool area as he absently grabbed an old T-shirt and wiped his fingers clean of his release, then his still-hard cock.

Fixing his jeans he stared out the window, narrowing his eyes. Most of the houses in the area were single story, with privacy fences built around them. It just so happened Cooper's was just a little bit taller than most to allow for a taller attic. Just tall enough, the window positioned just right to look down into her pool area.

For some unknown reason, there were few of the houses built on the same line in the little Southern Texas town. Just so happened, his was built just right.

He grinned at his luck. Then he frowned as he readjusted his jeans and moved to the door of the long attic and down the spiral, metal stairs that led down to the kitchen. Damn if Miss Fox hadn't just given him the release of the year or something.

The thought of her—disappointed. Wet. Pierced.

Fuck. Pierced. Sarah Fox. The woman he assumed was a staid

little virgin. At least, that was the rumor. Virgin? With those piercings? Not likely.

Satisfied was another thing entirely, and as much as he would have liked to, helping Miss Sarah find her release wasn't going to become his aim in life.

Ethan Cooper was the bad boy, and he knew it. He owned the local bar, a sometimes biker hangout and generally ill-reputed establishment. And he liked it that way.

He was ill-reputable. The local troublemaker turned bar owner after returning from the Army where he'd served more than eight years. A bullet to his knee had put him out of the Rangers, but it hadn't put him out of life. A few scars and heavy pins in a reconstructed knee weren't enough to kill that untamed, sometimes dark core inside his soul.

The Army had honed it. The Rangers had sharpened it. Life itself may have darkened it further. But it was still there. He was still dangerous. He was still dark. He was still footloose and fancy-free. And he intended to stay that way.

Sarah threw the towel on her bed, pouted, and stomped to the shower. She washed the tanning oil from her body beneath the spray and sighed in exasperation at the need that still throbbed between her thighs.

Twenty-four years old. She was twenty-four years old and still a virgin. And as though everyone in this little town she had moved to knew it, she was still known as Miss Sarah. And she was tired of it.

She washed quickly, dried her hair vigorously before combing through the tangles and leaving the long, loose ringlets hanging to the middle of her back before moving back to the bedroom and breathing out roughly.

She'd tried everything to make herself fit in here, in this little Texas town.

Well, everything but walking into a bar and just picking up a man and she just couldn't bring herself to do that. Just as she hadn't been able to bring herself to let one of the drunken frat boys from college heave and moan over her.

She grimaced at the thought of the parties her sorority sisters had dragged her to while in college. There had been a few boys who hadn't been drunk. Who had flirted with her, seemed interested. In a quick little screw.

She sat down on her bed and glared at her bedroom wall. She should have moved to a larger town. She made a damn good living as a Web designer and computer programmer. She worked for an excellent company. She had good benefits. She'd been damn lucky. She didn't have to do the nine-to-five rush and could relax. She could afford to move to Houston or Dallas. The thought had her breath trapping in her throat. So many strangers. So much noise and fear. It was quieter here in Simsburg. A little, almost unknown, town outside of Corpus Christi. She could relax here.

Hide away.

Shaking her head, she rose from the bed and headed to the closet. She pulled one of the sleeveless dresses from the closet and slipped it over her head before buttoning it nearly to her neck.

She went back to the bathroom and stood in front of the mirror. She unbuttoned the dress, spread it back from her chest and stared.

The faint white lines were still there. She should stay out of the sun, she told herself as she let her fingers trace over the thin white scars. Tanning made them worse, she reminded herself. Made them easier to see. Harder to hide.

She let her fingers trace over them. There were half a dozen, long, narrow, very thin. But they were there. They had been there since she was sixteen years old. Sixteen and stupid.

She rebuttoned her dress before moving back to the bedroom and pulling on the bronze lace panties she took from her dresser. She slid her feet into sandals, twisted up her hair and secured it in a smooth twist at the back of her head before heading to the kitchen for her purse.

She locked the house quickly but securely as she stepped out on the front porch a few moments later. Even here, in the quaint little town, amid the little houses and friendly citizens, she didn't take chances. She kept her doors locked. Her windows locked. She kept her car locked.

Head down, she dug her keys out of her purse, raising her head just in time to see her neighbor driving into the driveway right beside hers.

The powerful steel-gray four-by-four rumbled with power as he drove into the driveway. Parking, he moved from the vehicle, then stopped and stared.

God, he was a poster boy for big, bad, and dangerous. Six four. Jeans and boots. A T-shirt that did nothing to hide the snake tattoo wrapping around his bicep.

And he was staring at her. He stopped by his pickup, folded his arms on the top of it, and just stared. Hooded dark eyes, thick lashes. Black hair, dark flesh.

She stared back, feeling her chest tighten as it did every time she saw him. She could feel her breasts suddenly swelling, her nipples pressing against the thin material of her dress. She could feel heat skimming over her body, as she felt pinned in place, held by his gaze.

His lips quirked. The lower lip was a little fuller than the upper. It was sexy, sexual. It was a wicked smile that promised he knew her secret fantasies. And knew he starred in them.

Sarah felt held. Caught. Her fingers gripped her keys, and as a breeze whispered around her, she was sure she felt his gaze like a caress. Licking over her bare legs. Up her dress.

Her breath caught.

"Miss Sarah, how are you doing today?" His voice rumbled and stroked her senses with wicked fingers of desire.

God, he was incredible.

"Just fine, Mr. Cooper. And your knee appears to be doing quite well."

He had returned from the military wounded. Sarah had done the neighborly thing for a year. Fixed soup and cookies, and a few times made certain to pick up fresh vegetables or light snacks from the store for him to eat.

He was appreciative. He always thanked her nicely. But damn if he had ever invited her to share a meal. She had done everything to make certain he was in fit, healthy shape, and he still called her Miss Sarah.

"The knee is as good as it's gonna get." He flashed her that bad-boy smile and her heart raced as though he had actually touched her.

"I'm glad you're doing better."

He made her feel jittery. He made her feel flushed and hot.

"I'm doing just fine." He tilted his head, lifted a hand, and touched two fingers to his forehead in a gesture of farewell before striding to the front door of his house, unlocking it and moving out of sight.

Damn.

She drew in oxygen with a ragged breath, clenched her keys, and forced herself to the car. Hitting the auto door lock, she got into the sweltering confines of the car and started the engine with a hard turn of the key.

He couldn't know her fantasies. She kept all her fantasies safely locked away, along with her nightmares.

He would never know that when she touched herself, she thought of him. That when she thought of being bad, being naughty, she always thought of being naughty with him. He would never know that she had come here because of him. Because of his actions on a dark, shadowed Dallas street and her fascination for the man who her uncle had saved.

Ethan Cooper had been one of the first people she met when the realty agent showed her the little house. He had been outside, cutting the grass in his front yard, pausing to watch as she drove into the driveway with the Realtor.

He had smiled and lifted his hand in greeting before going back to his yard work. Shirtless. In jeans and boots. Dark flesh gleaming. Sweat running in narrow rivulets down his back and shoulders. Black hair laying damp along his nape.

Then he had turned his head back quickly, and grinned and winked at her while the Realtor wasn't looking, which made her respond as though he had actually touched her.

She had gotten wet instantly. Hot and wet. And she had practically been panting as she walked up the drive to the little house. As though it had been a sign, that the dreams and fantasies she had woven around him could have a chance.

He was big, tall, broad, and dangerous-looking. The Realtor said Mr. Cooper was in the military. He had disappeared several weeks later and his house had sat empty, except for the occasional motorcycle-riding thug-looking type who came, checked over things, and then left.

A year later, Ethan Cooper had returned limping. She'd heard he'd been wounded in action. She'd watched as he worked out in the enclosed acre he owned behind his house. Weights, push-ups, sit-ups, stretches. God, he had made her crazy that year. She'd nearly killed herself trying to ease the cramp of arousal in her stomach.

During those months, she'd had a chance to get to know him. When she took him cookies or soup, he always chatted, always laughed with her. And she always came home, desperate to be touched.

She was tired of masturbating. She was tired of being alone. And she was tired of aching for that tall, broad bar owner with the sexy grin.

Perhaps it was time to do something about this, she told herself. After all, covert looks and wishing weren't going to get her anywhere. It was time to do something about it. If she was going to get Ethan Cooper to fall into her bed, then she was going to have to take the initiative.

2

He couldn't get it out of his mind. Sarah Fox, spread out on the cement by her pool, long heavy ringlets fanned around her head, her curvy body slick and hot and oh so aroused.

He jacked off to it after he got back in the house. Hell, as if he could help it. The more he thought about it, the harder he got. He hadn't been so damned hot for a woman in years. Not since his first woman, in fact.

Who would have thought it? Timid little Miss Sarah.

He shook his head again before grabbing a beer and heading to his back deck. Sarah's privacy fence was over seven feet tall and extended around the full half acre of land behind her house. His white wooden fence connected with hers at a corner and extended almost double her area.

He didn't have a pool, though. He narrowed his eyes at the backyard and considered it before grinning and lifting the beer to his lips. He'd just end up in trouble. He'd never be able to keep his buddies out of it. It was hard enough keeping them out of his house.

He grinned, wondering if Miss Sarah would let him use her pool. Maybe while she was tanning herself beneath the hot Texas sun. All ripe and wet.

He grimaced at the thought of that. Piercings aside, luscious sweet little body aside, Miss Sarah Fox wasn't for the likes of him.

He finished his beer before heading into the bathroom to shower and change. Owning one of the roughest bars in the area could get dicey at times. He liked to be there before too late in the evening.

He was leaving the house, locking the door behind him when Sarah's compact, boring-looking little sedan pulled into her driveway.

He felt the hot lick of her gaze for just a second before the car shut off and she was moving from the vehicle. She kept her head down.

Cooper couldn't help but watch as she rounded the back of the car and opened the trunk. She pulled out a canvas bag—groceries, he assumed—and strode quickly up the drive to the house.

Ignoring him.

"Hello, Miss Sarah," he called out as she stepped up on her porch and came to a hard stop.

Her head lifted, eyes widened. "H-hello." A small smile, not hardly a smile, tipped her lips. Pouty lips. He liked pouty lips.

Cooper stepped across the drive. There wasn't much distance that separated their particular houses. The two homes had been built by two sisters, close together. The property extended out behind and beside one side of the houses, bunching them close while other neighbors were kept at a distance.

Cooper couldn't even explain why he was pushing this, except he'd already jacked off twice today because of her. He gave her one of his trademark slow smiles and watched the little flush that filled her cheeks.

She watched him carefully, making no move to unlock the door, holding her keys carefully with one hand, the canvas bag with the other, as though she hadn't known him for two years. Wary, pausing to be careful. Miss Sarah wasn't a casual person by any means.

His eyes almost narrowed. She was in a carefully disguised protective stance. Keys to slash out with, bag to hit out with. Her body was balanced, ready to flee at a moment's notice. Now, why the hell would something that tiny, that damned shy, be on guard against a neighbor?

"Can I help you, Mr. Cooper?" she asked carefully as he leaned against the side of her house.

He let his smile widen. "Yes, ma'am, you sure can." He nodded. "You can tell me why a pretty little thing like you is all alone on a Friday night. There should be a law against it."

"I'm sure there should be." There was the barest hint of cynicism in the look she gave him.

"Boys around here didn't use to be so dumb." He shook his head. "Leaving a pretty girl like you twiddling her thumbs."

"I'm into men, Mr. Cooper, not boys," she told him coolly. "And I've been a woman, not a little girl, for a long time now. Is there anything else I can help you with?"

There was no fear in her. None he could detect. Wariness, suspicion, a whole lot of arousal, but not fear.

"No, ma'am." He finally shook his head and eased back.

He wasn't going there, he decided. There was something about

Miss Sarah Fox that had every male instinct inside him rioting. And he wasn't the man this delicate woman needed. No, Miss Sarah needed a forever kind of guy, and Cooper just wasn't the forever kind. "Good evening, Miss Sarah."

"Mr. Cooper." Her voice stopped him.

He turned back to her, his brow arching at the confidence, the sudden look of a woman who sees more than she ever shows the world.

"Yes, ma'am?"

"My name is Sarah. Not Miss Sarah. Or Miss Fox if you prefer. But after two years, uncounted plates of cookies and bowls of soup, I think you can call me by my name."

There was no censure in her voice, just quiet command. That quiet command almost had him chuckling. She wasn't a pushover and she was finally letting him know it.

"Yes, ma'am." He nodded back to her. "I'll see you around."

" 'Ma'am' wasn't one of the choices," he heard her mutter as the scrape of the storm door told him she was going into the house.

It slammed behind her as he stepped into his truck and let a low burst of laughter pass his lips. Damn if she didn't have spirit. Maybe Miss Sarah wasn't the timid miss everyone had grown to believe she was since moving here. Seemed to him, she just might have a little fire in her.

Hell, he knew she had fire. Too much fire for a man to step into without giving it a hell of a lot of thought first. And for a man like Cooper, it took more than just thought on his part. More than just fire on her part.

Too damned bad. He wouldn't have minded sharing her bed, her pool, and anything else she wanted to give up to him. For a little while.

Sarah closed the door to her house and leaned back against it to let out a long, slow breath. Oh Lord, that man was seriously hot. She dropped her keys to the side table, dropped the bag of groceries to the floor, and waved her hands over her flushed face.

Those jeans were snug. They cupped his ass. His T-shirt highlighted a six-pack that would make any woman's eyes bug out. And those arms, serious biceps; that face, rugged and tough. He wasn't a pretty boy. He looked dangerous and hard and so hot that he made her perspire.

Damn.

Just the sound of his voice had her creaming her panties. And that was so not fair, because she still just hadn't gotten the hang of masturbation. She could get to a certain point, she'd get almost there, but only sometimes did she actually manage to go over.

She had all the books. And she practiced. There had to be a trick to it. And she really wished she could find that trick, because her neighbor made her so hot she was changing panties several times a day and driving herself crazy with the arousal.

She picked up her canvas bag, slid off her sandals, and padded barefoot through the house to the large, airy kitchen in the back. There were a lot of windows spaced around the room, making it seem as though the backyard was a part of the room.

The pool had been the selling point. She loved the pool. She loved the way the sun spilled in the kitchen at dawn and how cozy and warm she felt in the house.

And it was all hers.

She put away the milk and eggs, the bag of coffee, the sugar and cream. A pack of cookies and some sweet rolls went on the counter, a carefully wrapped steak went in the fridge, with the wine and a baking potato on the counter.

Dinner.

One steak, one potato, one glass of wine, perhaps on the deck.

She stared out at the deck, bracing her arms on the counter and watching the water in the pool as she frowned and considered her neighbor Ethan Cooper. He'd introduced himself right after she moved in. Told her if she had any problems to let him know. And if any of his friends who came over sometimes bothered her or offended her, then he definitely wanted to know. And he'd been serious.

His friends weren't that bad though. They were rough-looking, funny, and always joking with her. She thought perhaps they talked to her more than Ethan had over the years. But they never flirted with her, they never came on to her. She could be everyone's kid sister for the way they treated her.

Not that she wanted his friends. She wanted Ethan. But, she glared at the pool, it was enough to make a woman wonder if perhaps she was completely unattractive to the opposite sex.

She pushed back from the counter, stared at the potato, and sighed again. A meal alone. On a Friday night. She'd lived here for two years and had never noticed how really little other people wanted anything to do with her, until now.

And she went out every day, she made sure she did, if only to buy her dinner. She was friendly, wasn't she?

She was lonely. She trailed her fingers over the wide kitchen island, drifted through the house, and frowned at the odd feeling. She hadn't been lonely in a very long time. She'd been too busy, too concerned with surviving to worry about loneliness.

Her hand lifted to her chest as she stopped in the middle of the living room and stared at the floor. She rubbed at the scars, almost as though she could feel the horrendous fear and pain that she had felt when they had been made.

She shook her head. No, she wasn't thinking about that. She had pushed it to the back of her mind and it was staying there. She had dealt with it. She had survived it. That was all that mattered. Wasn't it?

But had she survived it, really? She was still hiding. She was still keeping herself locked in her work as though each minute meant success or failure. And it didn't. Not anymore.

She had built a life for herself. In the past two years, she had picked up some great contracts within the business she was in. She didn't have to worry about going hungry, and she didn't have to worry about losing her home—her uncle Martin had made certain of that. She never had to worry about that again.

So why was she standing here like a lost puppy?

Because she didn't know how to have fun. She'd been to the bar before, but no one even asked her to dance. She had joined the business club in town, but they only met once a month and they rarely did anything but talk about how small the community was, and how high taxes were, and how the good jobs were closer to Corpus Christi.

Maybe a small town really was a bad idea. She had thought she would find it easier to fit in here; she hadn't expected it to be harder.

It was Friday night. She had a steak and a potato waiting. At least she had a few good books to go with it.

Cooper strode around the bar a week later, his eyes narrowed against the smoke and gloom, watching for drugs more than anything else. He had only a few hard, firm rules in his place. They fought in the parking lot if they wanted to use their fists. No one hit a woman, whether she was a lady or not. And no one, but no one, dealt in his place.

His bartender, an ex-Ranger like himself, was holding down the bar with the help of one of the local college kids. The boy was a hard worker, eager to learn. There were two other bouncers, ex-Rangers as well, and as hard and tough as any Cooper knew, despite their medical discharges from the service. They were all termed "disabled vets." But his men were as hard and as efficient as they had ever been in the military. Maybe just not as fast, he thought with a grin.

The Broken Bar was one of the most popular spots in the area and the only bar. Most weekdays were busy, but the weekends could turn into a madhouse if they weren't careful.

The band on the other end of the cavernous building was belting a slow country tune and couples were circling the floor. There was the usual assortment of bikers, college kids, and general barhoppers.

Motioning to the closest bouncer, he indicated the other man should take his spot as Cooper headed back toward the bar. As he did, he nearly came to a full-blown, hard stop.

Hell. No, he didn't need this. Not after seeing her naked, aroused, and unsatisfied.

There, standing in the doorway like a wary angel, was his intrepid little neighbor. And she wasn't wearing a dress. Or a skirt. She was wearing jeans that made her legs look like the best wet dream a man could have. Low on the hip, belted over a sleeveless blouse that was buttoned damned near to the neck, and over boots.

And her hair was down.

He felt a hard strike of jealousy at the sight of the men whose eyes found her, lusted for her, worshipped those long, wild curls.

Shit. How the hell was he supposed to get her out of here this time? This was not the place for Miss Sarah.

Pushing the fingers of one hand through his hair in irritation, he moved toward her, cutting through the room on a diagonal path as she headed for the bar.

Didn't she know the scum she could find in a damn bar? What the hell was she doing here?

And it should be damned illegal for a woman to move like that in a pair of jeans. Like they were loving every step she took in them. Like they were hugging her shapely little ass with possessive hands.

Son of a bitch.

"Hi." She smiled at his bartender. Jake damned near dropped the bottle of whiskey he was holding. "Could I have a whiskey, straight?"

Jake's brown eyes flickered over her. Yeah, she didn't look the whiskey type.

"I have some wine coolers back here," Jake offered. "Fruity ones."

Cooper almost laughed at Jake's floored expression.

"No." She shook her head and Cooper caught her expression in the mirror behind the bar. She was one determined lady. "Just the whiskey, please." Then she named her brand. "If you have it?"

Damned expensive. Oh yeah, they had it.

Cooper moved to the end of the bar, next to the stool she had snagged, leaned his forearms on it and stared at her silently as she turned to him, her eyes widening just a little bit.

"Mr. Cooper." That little hint of a smile. A little bit of dimple.

"Just Cooper." His lips quirked as he stared back at her, watching as her gaze slid to the tattoo curling around his bicep.

She let her teeth rake over her lip before meeting his eyes again. Jake chose that moment to sit the shot of whiskey in front of her.

Cooper arched his brow as she lifted it, sipped as delicately as a lady would a glass of wine, then sat the shot glass back on the bar without a grimace.

"It's a busy bar." She looked around. "It's been like this every time I've come. Even during the week."

Her voice lifted as she turned away. When she turned back, that little dimple peeked out again. Her smile was careful, as though she didn't quite know what to do with those pretty lips.

Cooper lifted his hand and propped his jaw in his palm as he just stared at her.

She fiddled with the shot glass for a moment, then surprised him when she lifted it and took the half shot back without a single choke or cough. Her lips tightened and he imagined the burn that hit her, his body tightening as her expression took that relaxed, slightly pleasurable look of a woman relishing the sizzle.

Now that was a look he had never seen on a woman's face, and it made him hard. Hell. Harder. He'd been hard for her for over a week now.

"Another?" he asked, glancing at the shot glass.

"No, thank you." She shook her head, a hint of vulnerable, self-consciousness entering her eyes as she stared around the bar.

She turned her gaze to the band, the dancers, her profile faintly wistful as she watched them.

"I've been here several times." She turned back to him, those wide pale blue eyes stroking over his face. Hell, it was almost a caress.

"I've seen you." He nodded.

She looked down at the shot glass, played with it for a moment, then stared back at the dance floor as the band slid into a rousing dance tune.

Damn, the look on her face. She wanted to be out there. He could see it, feel it. So what the hell was holding her back? Each time she had come into the bar, she had sat at one of the back tables, alone. She had watched, drank a soda or wine cooler or two, and left.

She had never come to the counter. She had never drank his finest whiskey with a curl of pleasure tightening her face. He would have noticed. He always noticed Miss Sarah.

"Miss Sarah . . ."

"Sarah." Her head swung around, those wild curls feathering over her shoulder, and there was that little dimple again. "I'm not that old, Mr. Cooper."

"Cooper," he murmured, his jaw still braced on his palm as he watched her.

"Cooper." There was the slightest edge of delight in her gaze then. "Please call me Sarah."

"Yes, ma'am." He smiled back at her, just to watch her eyes flare in irritation.

She lowered her eyes again, played with the shot glass again, then lifted her gaze back to Jake and indicated another shot.

Cooper almost laughed out loud. Jake gave him a hard, disapproving glance, as though he thought Cooper could keep her from drinking.

And Miss Sarah caught that look. For a moment, Cooper saw a shattered, weary pain flash in her eyes. Then a tight smile twisted her lips.

"Forget it." She fumbled in her jeans pocket, pulled out a few bills, and slapped them on the bar. "I shouldn't have come here."

Fuck!

Cooper straightened as she slid off the bar, head held high, and all but ran toward the door. What the hell?

Following her, Cooper felt something tighten in his gut. A strange, almost tender amusement mixed with confusion. Damn it. She looked like she was going to cry when Jake didn't want to serve her the whiskey. As though somehow, she had been rejected.

"Hey, whoa. Sair. Come on, hold up." He caught up with her in the graveled parking lot, his fingers curling over an arm so damned soft it felt like heated silk. He had shortened her name. Not Miss Sarah, or Sarah. His Sair.

She jerked away from him, turned on him, her face flushed, eyes glittering. And those *were* tears.

She blinked them back furiously.

"I got the message, Mr. Cooper," she snapped. "Don't worry, I won't come back into your bar again."

"Whoa. Sair." He moved in front of her, staring down at her. "What message did you get exactly?"

Sarah stared back at him, battling her tears. "That makes half a dozen times I've been in that damned bar." She swung her arm to it. "The only bar in driving distance, mind you. Each time, I order whiskey. Each time, I get some damned kid's drink. The last time, I got a soda. Now I have to have your permission to drink whiskey in there? When the hell did you decide to ostracize me from this town?"

He blinked down at her. "When did I decide to do what?"

Cooper decided he was in shock. He hadn't wanted her ostracized, just protected. Nothing more.

"I walk into that bar and no one asks me to dance," she informed him frostily. "If anyone seems to be coming close to me, your bouncers waylay them and suddenly no one is speaking. And now your bartender won't serve me whiskey?" She sniffed.

Ah hell. She couldn't cry on him here. Not in the damned parking lot.

Cooper rubbed the back of his neck as he stared down at her furious little face. She had guts, he had to give her that.

"That's not what it is," he finally said, grimacing.

Her arms were crossed over her breasts, her hip cocked. Damn. He was going to end up fucking her on the hood of a car if she kept this up.

"Then what, Mr. Cooper, is your problem? I'm over twenty-one. I don't believe I'm a total hag, but last I heard, even ugly women were allowed to drink whiskey."

"That's not it." He hardened his voice. Hell if he wanted to explain this here.

"I just wanted to dance," she whispered, the moonlight striking her eyes, making them deeper, darker. Damn, he wanted to fuck her. "To have a drink. I just wanted to be a woman, Mr. Cooper. I'm sorry if I inconvenienced you."

She jerked her keys from her jeans pocket and turned to stalk to her car as though it were over. Son of a bitch. He should let it go. He was fucking stupid. Insane.

He caught up to her, slamming his hands against the top of the car as she reached the door, pinning her in, watching her start, feeling her sharp intake of breath as he leaned in close to her.

"This isn't a nice place," he told her softly. "This is a bar. The men who come here only want a fuck, Sair. They're not all nice, and they're sure as hell not here to share a drink and a dance and go quietly home."

He could smell the scent of her now. A little spicy, a little sweet. Whatever perfume she was wearing was going to kill him.

"My bouncers have orders. The men in that bar know me, they know what you don't. I'm a mean fucker, baby. And when I put out the order that they use extreme caution around you, they know what the hell it means."

"Why would you do that?" Breathless. A little excited, maybe. He didn't feel any fear and that was too damn bad. She should fear him more than she did anyone in that bar.

He let himself lean closer, let his nose bury in the soft fragrant silk of her hair. "Because I want to fuck you, Miss Sair," he growled. "I want to fuck you so deep and so hard that neither of us can move for hours later. And I can't have you, baby, because you sure as hell deserve better. So I'll be damned if I'm going to watch one of those sorry bastards in there taste what I know they'd never appreciate.

Go home. Find a nice young man who wants forever and babies, and count yourself lucky that the devil was in a good mood tonight."

A good mood? He was so damn hard, so horny, his cock was like titanium. He could drive spikes into railroad ties with it. And it was so pressed against Sarah's lower back, the only thing separating it from her flesh was their clothes.

Clothes he wanted out of the way.

"Was he?" There was something in her voice that had the hairs standing on the back of his neck. "I don't think it was his good mood." She pulled open the door as he shifted back. "Trust me, Mr. Cooper. There's no such thing where the devil is concerned."

He watched her start the car and drive away. And he couldn't forget the little bit lost, little bit lonely look on her quiet little face. As though she had faced demons, and realized they were stronger than she had ever imagined.

"Fuck!" He propped his hands on his hips, stared after the car, and knew. Hell, he could feel it in his gut. He knew Sarah was going to rock him clear to the soles of his feet.

Before she did, he needed answers. His Sair was too wary, too damned secretive. Striding back into the bar, he made a mental note to have Jake check into exactly who Sarah Fox was.

3

Sarah had learned not to cry a long time ago. She had learned how little tears helped, and she had learned how miserable they made her feel and that no one else really gave a damn anyway.

Ethan Cooper had warned men away from her at the bar. Had word of that warning gone through town? Was that the reason everyone stayed distant?

She went to the grocery store the next afternoon, as she did every day, to buy dinner for that evening. She wandered through the store, chose a few vegetables, a ripe tomato, though she had no idea what she intended to fix. She checked out a slice of watermelon, passed it by. She picked up an apple, placed it in a clear plastic bag, and laid it in her shopping basket.

She felt disconnected as she moved through the store. She didn't want steak or pork. She didn't want another chicken breast. And she had promised herself years ago that she was never eating another TV dinner in her life.

So what did she want?

She wanted to dance. She wanted to be held. She wanted to be touched. And she didn't want a stranger. She didn't want a casual fuck. She wanted something more.

She wanted Ethan Cooper.

She stopped in front of the meat aisle for the second time, frowning down at the variety. They had everything. The problem was, the hunger tearing at her had nothing to do with food and everything to do with something much more instinctive.

"The catfish is fresh."

She tensed at the sound of Cooper's voice behind her.

She tucked in a few stray strands of hair that had escaped the twist at the back of her head and stared down at the chicken.

She picked up a single-wrapped chicken breast, laid it in her basket, and moved on. Okay, an apple, a small stalk of celery, a single green pepper. There was lettuce left in the fridge. God, she so didn't want chicken.

"Are you going to forgive me, Sair?"

"My name is Sarah," she told him quietly. "Or Miss Fox if you prefer."

He breathed out heavily behind her. "No one else calls you Sair. It makes a part of you just mine."

He was close. Close enough that she could feel the heat of him against her back. Close enough that her nipples beaded, her clit grew tight and hard, and her stomach tightened with need.

"You don't want me, remember?"

Damn him. She didn't want to want him. Did he think it was voluntary?

"You won't be served sodas in the bar anymore. I promise." His voice was a quiet, dark rasp. There was a hint of amusement. A hint of something darker, deeper. "And I didn't say I didn't want you."

She lifted her shoulder in a shrug. "I won't be back in your bar, Mr. Cooper."

She moved through the diary aisle. She could probably use another small carton of milk. Sometimes she drank it, sometimes she didn't. She placed it in the basket before selecting a small wedge of cheese she liked with the crackers she kept in the cabinet.

"You're not going to forgive me? Come on, Sair, we're neighbors. You can't hold a grudge against me." There was a tickle of laughter against the top of her head, warming her soul.

Sarah stopped and turned and her nose was nearly buried in his chest. God, he was so close. She lifted her head, stared into his amber-flecked hazel eyes, and felt all the blood rush to her face. And the damp heat of her juices rushing to prepare her vagina, filling it, seeping out to her panties.

"Am I bothering you?" she finally asked him.

His brow arched. "Hell, yeah," he murmured. "You're making me hard as rock. And I'm tired of knowing you're mad at me."

"Very well." She turned away and resumed her journey to the checkout stand. "I won't be angry anymore."

She wasn't angry to begin with. She was hurt. She had been trying desperately to make friends in this little town. Knowing Ethan Cooper had been warning everyone against her made her feel more isolated than ever before.

She had been isolated for most of her life. She didn't want that any longer.

She heard him breathe out roughly behind her again and wanted to turn back to look at him so bad she couldn't stand it. She loved looking at him. She could spend hours doing it.

But she'd decided it was better not to stare. It just made her want.

Cooper watched Sair as she moved away from him. Her trim, delicate figure glided, moved with a sensual unconscious grace that had his balls tightening, his cock throbbing. Hell, if he jacked off much more he was going to risk pulling off his dick.

He stayed quiet as they moved past the beverages. Pulling a six-pack of beer from the cooler at the end, he caught up with her at the checkout, remaining quiet as she spoke to the few mothers in line.

They were wary. It was a small town. Sair was the interloper and it would be years before she was fully accepted, unless someone intervened.

And he had hurt that process. The warning he had put out not to touch had somehow morphed, as it did in little towns, to a message that she was to be pushed away. Hell if he had meant for that to happen. Sometimes, he just forgot what home was like, though.

"Miss Maggie, that baby's growing." He moved behind Sair and stared over her shoulder at the precocious little boy waving his hands at Sair as she turned to amusing the baby rather than trying to push past the reserve of the mother.

Maggie's brown eyes sharpened as he all but laid his chin against Sair's shoulder. Sair was still, silent in front of him.

"Cooper, are you being bad again?" Maggie narrowed her eyes at him.

He had gone to school with Maggie. She was several years older than he was and had several kids now. She had brothers, a husband, and sons. Maggie Fallon was a damn scary woman.

"I'm always bad, Maggie." He flashed her a quick smile, his hand moving to Sair's hip to curve over it as he moved closer and made a face at the baby.

Maggie laughed and little Kyle Fallon gave him a drooling smile. The kid was cute as hell. Sair was as tense as a board.

"Has anyone warned Miss Fox about you yet?" Maggie's gaze

warmed a little as she looked at Sair. "You have to be careful of that rogue behind you. He's a heartbreaker."

"So I've figured out." Sair's voice had just the right amount of husky interest in it, and wary reserve.

He wished he could see her face. Her eyes. Maggie glanced back at him with a smile and wagged her finger at him. "Ethan Cooper, don't go running off the new girls in this town with broken hearts. This town is small enough."

Cooper laughed, and he played. He let his fingers grip Sair's curved hip. His hand pressed against it and he inhaled the fresh scent of her hair, wishing he could let it down.

"If you need any advice where that wild man is concerned, Miss Fox, give me a call." Maggie shook her head at Cooper, amused indulgence filling her eyes. "I've known him since he was born."

"She likes to brag she changed my diapers," Cooper drawled in Sarah's ear, laughing at Maggie. "She was the first girl to get in my pants."

"Ethan Cooper!" Maggie was scandalized, but too amused to do much else but laugh at him. "You're getting worse in your old age."

And Sarah was blushing. He could see her profile, could see the wash of the flush rising in her cheeks.

The cashier was chortling. Mark Dempsey owned the grocery, and worked it often, along with his wife and two children.

But both Mark and Maggie were more relaxed now, their gazes more curious as they watched Sair.

Maggie paid for her purchases and Sair's moved down the conveyor belt where Mark scanned them quickly and rang up her bill.

"Thank you, Mr. Dempsey." She paid him quickly.

Were her hands shaking just a little bit? Cooper wondered.

"You're welcome, Miss Fox." Mark smiled back at her. "You watch out for that one behind you, too. Maggie's right. He's a rogue."

"I'll be sure to do that," she promised.

She must have flashed those pretty, hidden dimples, because Mark's hangdog face softened for just a minute as he gave her change back. And Sarah was walking away, quickly.

The soft dark-blue summer dress, sleeveless again and buttoned to the neck again, swished around her hips and calves as she moved from the store with her purchases.

"She seems like a nice kid." Mark was watching him expectantly. "Neighbor of yours, ain't she?"

"She's a good woman," Cooper nodded sharply. "I don't think she likes me much, though." He laughed.

Mark shook his head on a chuckle. "You need to settle down, Cooper. Ladies know a wild rouser when they meet one. She's a smart one, she seems. Bet she sees right through all that charm of yours."

Cooper arched his brow and smiled. "So she does, Mark. So she does."

Mission accomplished. He could go home and stop feeling so fucking guilty because he had almost made little Sair cry. Shit. Since when had he grown a conscience?

Sarah's next stop was the post office, where Maggie Fallon just happened to be as well. The other woman lived near Sarah, and she had rarely talked to her. But today, she kept her at the post office boxes for nearly twenty minutes, talking. Just talking.

And something inside Sarah had eased. She wasn't certain what it was, and she knew the other woman had loosened up only because of Cooper's teasing. But after Maggie finished talking to her, several other women spoke; the postmaster actually asked her how she was doing, and while she posted Sarah's packages, talked about an upcoming summer festival in the town.

Sarah left the post office with a warm glow. She had lived here for more than two years, and finally, she felt as though there might be a chance she could fit in.

She returned home, put her groceries away, and then moved to the front room as she heard Cooper's truck pull into the drive beside her own. From behind the shelter of her curtains she watched him look toward her house as he got out of his truck, then he was loping to his porch and out of sight.

She should thank him, she thought, biting at her lip. Nothing ventured nothing gained. That was the hospitable thing to do, or so her uncle Martin had always told her.

She wiped her damp palms down the skirt of her dress and left her house, gripping her keys in her hand, and moved across her drive. A six-foot wedge of grass separated her asphalt driveway from her neighbor's.

She stepped up on the porch and moved to the door before knocking with a quick, decisive rap of her knuckles. And she waited. Holding the keys tight in her hand, one sharp point ready if need be. She jerked a little as he opened the door and stared back at her in surprise.

"Miss Sair," he drawled, leaning against the door frame. "What can I do for you?" The amber highlights in his eyes seemed to spark, flare.

"I wanted to thank you." She refused to twitch or stutter. "For what you did at the store."

His expression tightened as he lifted himself from the door frame and stood back. "Come on in."

"But I just wanted . . ."

He reached out, gripped her wrist, and pulled her in before closing the door behind her.

She never once thought to defend herself. She stood in the small foyer, a frown tugging at her brow at the thought. Had she forgotten how dangerous even innocent things could seem? She must have, because she wasn't frightened of the large, dark man looming over her.

"I didn't do anything," he said turning away from her. "Come on out back. I was just putting lunch on the grill. You can share it with me."

"Oh, I wouldn't want to impose." But she did, she really did want to impose.

"Get your butt back here." His voice held a thread of command that had her following him slowly.

He stopped at the fridge in the kitchen, reached in, and pulled out a thick, raw steak before adding it to the platter on the table. There were vegetable kabobs, steaks, and shrimp kabobs.

"Are you expecting company?" There was a lot of food there.

"Nope. Just me." The ever present T-shirt shifted over the hard muscles of his chest, shoulders, and biceps. The action made her mouth water, made her sex swell and come into agonizing contact with the little curved bell that pierced the hood of her clit. "Grab you a beer and come on out. I have to get the grill heated up before I can put on this stuff." He paused as he covered the platter and set it back in the fridge. "Or, the whiskey is in the cabinet." He grinned. "Whichever you prefer."

She chose the beer, though she would have preferred the whiskey, and followed him out to the deck.

The wide wooden deck matched her own. One half was covered, the other open. Cooper moved to the large grill in the uncovered corner and set the flame to it before lowering the lid and turning back to her.

She held the beer in both hands, watching him. Watched as he picked up his beer from the wooden table beside him and took a long drink, staring at her, his gaze heavy-lidded, thick black lashes framing his hazel and amber eyes.

"Are there rules in a small town?" she asked him then, for a lack of anything better to say. "No one wanted to talk to me until you made them."

He grimaced at that. "I checked around. The no-touch policy in my bar got kind of mixed up." He shrugged. "That happens sometimes. People were just a little wary, uncertain of what was going on. In little towns like this, everyone tends to watch newcomers suspiciously for a while, anyway. The twist in the order in the bar making its way around town just snowballed. I'm sorry about that."

"You must have a lot of power in town then." She frowned. She hadn't realized a small town had a power base. Rather like society. It didn't matter how much others liked you; if a prominent figure didn't, you could be ostracized immediately.

Cooper grimaced. "I don't have a lot of power, Sair. I told you, others know what you don't about me. I'm not a nice guy."

"Maggie liked you. And children are incredibly astute. Little Kyle reached up for you several times. And the store owner seemed to like you."

"Doesn't mean anything in a town like this." He sat down on the bench as she stood watching him. "I'm a hometown boy. And I don't take much shit. They would act like they liked me even if they didn't."

His stare was direct, honest. Sarah licked her lips and stared back at him, uncertain what to say. Her body was humming, as it always did around him. Vibrating with need. It didn't make sense. Her nipples were hard and sensitive, her breasts swollen beneath her dress.

"You're wet, aren't you?" His expression suddenly shifted, became sensual, filled with male lust. And if she hadn't been wet before, she would have been in that instant.

Sarah cleared her throat, speechless. "I'm sure a lot of women get wet around you, don't they?"

She surprised him. She watched his lips quirk, his eyes become more intense.

"You're messing with trouble, you know that, don't you, Sair?" His voice deepened, became graveled. Rough. "You're a nice, sweet little thing. And I'm a very, very bad boy. You sure you want to keep watching me with those hot little eyes and tempting me with that pretty body of yours? You should have a nice guy, Sair, not a man that's forgot all the softness in life."

Was he willing to be tempted? Sarah shifted slowly and almost moaned at the feel of the little piercing at her clit rubbing against her.

"Perhaps I want to learn how to be bad," she answered him softly then. "If you're that bad, Cooper, then you could show me *how* to be bad. And I'll remind you of the softer things in life."

Pure, raw lust tore through his system. Cooper stared at her, wondering if he looked as shocked as he felt, looked as damned hungry as he knew he felt.

She stood there, her cheeks a little flushed, gripping that beer bottle with tight, nervous fingers. Her gaze was direct, though. A hint of heat, embarrassment, and something he didn't want to look too closely at, filling her eyes.

As he stared at her, a sudden thought shook him to the core.

"Shit," he muttered. "You're a virgin, aren't you?"

Her lips tilted a bit cynically. "Define virginity. Have I ever been with a man? No, I haven't. But I haven't had a hymen for years, Ethan."

She didn't call him Cooper. Fuck. She was dangerous. Because calling him Ethan struck a soft spot in him he didn't know he had. He liked the sound of it on her lips, the way her eyes softened when she said his name.

He moved toward her then. Slowly, watching her. Her gaze met his, direct, unashamed. A little quiet. A little somber. There were shadows in those pale blue eyes, shadows that made him wonder exactly what lay beneath the surface of this proud little woman.

And there was pride. Immeasurable pride.

"Why?" He moved behind her, bent his head, and brushed his nose against the hair by her ear. He wanted to hear her voice, not be distracted by the need filling her eyes. "Why haven't you been with a man, Sair?"

Her throat moved as she swallowed tightly. "I was very sheltered for a long time, and after that, I had a hard time adjusting." Sadness filled her voice. "And I was working. There was no time." And there was a little lie.

"Don't lie to me." He nipped her ear and felt her jerk. "Never lie to me, Sair. I don't tolerate it well."

She was silent for long moments. "I don't want a one-night stand. I don't want a boy who doesn't know how to touch a woman, or a man who knows only his own pleasure." She turned her head and stared at him. "I'm not looking for love, Ethan. But I want to be held. I want to be pleasured. And I want to know how to pleasure. And I've wanted you since the first day I saw you."

His cock was going to rip past the zipper on his pants, tear right through his clothes, and go for the glory. Hell.

He took her beer and set it with his on the deck railing. Here, beneath the covered porch, the lattice surrounding the enclosed area, there were no eyes to see. Not that he really cared if anyone could see. He wondered if she would care?

Turning her to him, he gripped the back of her neck, watched the pulse hammer in her throat, and stared at the way those pouty lips parted and her tongue stroked over them.

Hell. He was gonna do this. She had said the magic words, though he didn't know if he believed them. She said she didn't want love. She wanted sex. She wanted bad sex.

"Nasty sex," he whispered, lowering his lips until they feathered hers. "Hard sex, Sair. I'm a man. A hard man. And I love sex, baby."

There was the slightest little dip to her lashes and he bet she was creaming her panties. He bet when he touched that bare little pussy, he was going to find his fingers covered in her juices.

"Touch me." Her whispered entreaty tightened his balls. "However you want to, Cooper. Touch me, before I die for it."

"I won't be easy." He wrapped an arm around her hips, bent, and jerked her up to him.

Her eyes widened, innocence sparkled like incandescent lights in her pale blue eyes, and arousal flushed her face. Her lips looked poutier, ready to plunder, to taste, to explore.

Slender hands slid up his forearms as his cock throbbed behind his jeans, pressing against the soft flesh of her covered pussy. He was going to go down on her. As soon as he kissed her. As soon as he stilled the fire raging inside him for the taste of those pretty lips. He was going to lift her skirt, pull her panties aside, and devour her.

"I didn't ask for easy," she spoke against his lips, a stroke of fire, of need.

And he wasn't going to give her easy. There was something in her eyes, in the needy little catch of her voice. The memory of those piercings and the way she drank that whiskey. Sweet little Sair didn't want easy at all. And that was a damned good thing, because Cooper had lost "easy" a long damn time ago.

4

Sarah was swamped with sensation. Lost in it. Her fingers curled in ecstasy against strong, broad shoulders, and her lips parted beneath a kiss that was hot, hungry, and oh so good.

He held her against him effortlessly, her feet dangling from the ground, his heavy erection pressed between her thighs. She lifted her legs as his lips moved over hers, slanted across them, his tongue taking hers. She slid her legs up his—feeling the power beneath them, the bunch of the muscle beneath his jeans—until her knees were gripping his thighs, and one of his hands slid to her ass, cupping it, holding her up.

Oh, that was so good. She lost herself within the dreamy, seductive sensations flowing through her. Flames licked over her flesh, burned in her pussy. She gripped his powerful flanks, eased higher, and lowered herself, a moan tearing past their kiss at the incredible assault of sensation against the piercing rubbing her clit.

Why was it different? Why couldn't she pleasure herself with her own touch? It was the excitement, she decided. The dangerous, pulsing excitement thundering through her bloodstream, swelling in her clit and in her nipples. It was the knowledge that she was in the arms of a very dangerous man. But not a cruel man. She knew the difference. She had lived with the differences for most of her life.

The inherent dark, seductive force of the man holding her drew her. It powered through her.

"Fuck, you're like dynamite," he growled, tearing his lips from her, his head lifting, the amber in his hazel eyes almost like fire now.

It set fire to her senses. He was aroused. Really and truly aroused for her. For *her*.

"Make me explode then," she panted. "I'm certain I have a very short fuse."

Cooper stared down at her, almost shocked. Her pale blue eyes were lit with hunger, with need. Her face flushed with it. Her knees tightened at his thighs as his hand clenched in the curve of her ass.

Hell, he bet she could come over and over again. If Cooper thought he knew anything, then he knew a woman's pleasure. He'd made it his life's work. He'd put a lot of practice and research into the matter. Didn't understand their minds. Had no clue how to decipher their emotions. But he knew how to give them pleasure.

And he was betting his back teeth that he could make this little firecracker come like the fourth of July.

She was innocent, but hotter than hell. He could see it in her, and suddenly the need to know why she was innocent, why she had picked him, was rising in his head.

He'd tackle that problem later. Right now, Sarah was sweet and hot in his arms and he wanted her naked. He wanted her twisting, writhing, begging for release.

"Let's see just what it takes to make Sair come, then." He grinned down at her, watched her eyes darken.

"I want to see what makes Ethan come, too."

She surprised him again.

Her hands smoothed over his shoulders. Her inquisitive little face, filled with hot feminine lust, held him transfixed.

"Want to know what makes me come?" he crooned, lowering his head to touch her lips, watching her eyes flare.

"Yes," she breathed.

"Sometimes, the simplest thing." He nipped at that pouty lower lip. "I came like hell last week. In my attic. Staring down at your pool and watching you touch yourself."

Her eyes widened in shock. "You saw me?" There was the slightest hint of mortification in her voice. Just enough that he knew she was thinking more about her failed attempt to get off than she was about him seeing her.

"I jacked off watching you." He turned to the table that sat beneath the sheltered porch and sat her on it.

"You liked watching me?" There was a hint of shyness, the pleasure building back as he smoothed her dress up her legs.

"I loved watching you. And I'm going to watch you again."

She shook her head. "You touch me."

She was breathing so hard her tight little nipples were in danger of bursting through the front of her dress.

"Oh, I'm going to touch you." Just a little bit. Just enough to get her hotter, to make her wilder. "Then you're going to touch me, Sair. Let's see how hot we can make that pretty little body of yours."

He leaned back, jerked off his T-shirt, and had to clench his teeth. Her hands were there, on the thin mat of hair covering his chest and angling down the center of his body.

Then her lips.

Jesus. This wasn't a woman who wanted all the pleasure for herself.

He lifted his hands to her hair and pulled the clip from all those glorious curls, watching them fall down her back in a swath of silky ringlets. He couldn't wait to feel those fucking curls over his legs as he fucked those full, luscious lips.

"I want to touch you." Her hands moved to his belt and Cooper grimaced at the want, the need in her voice.

Not yet. Fuck, not yet. He wanted her silky and wild first. He wanted her screaming out in need.

And he sure as hell wasn't taking a virgin on a fucking picnic table. He was an asshole, but he hadn't yet sunk there.

"Not yet, baby." He picked her up, ignoring her surprised breath, loving the way her hands clenched his shoulders, her nails digging into his flesh.

He bet she was a wildcat. All claws and silky heat. He couldn't wait.

"Where are we going?"

"My fucking bed, sugar." His voice was tight; hell, his whole body was tight. "I want room to do this right."

Sarah swallowed tightly as he moved into a well-lit bedroom. The bed was huge, dark. Sunlight spilled through the sheer curtains and open blinds on the windows.

"There we go."

He laid her back on the bed, following her, stretching out beside her as he speared his fingers into her hair and held her head still for another of those deep, voracious kisses.

She loved it. Loved his lips on hers, hungry and deep, his tongue licking and stroking, pushing into her mouth and teasing her tongue until she was tasting him, too.

There was no hesitancy in him. Only hunger. Hard, male hunger.

She arched into him as the skirt of her dress slid up her thighs. His hand, big and calloused, stroked her leg, sending flares of white-hot sensations racing through her bloodstream.

When his hand cupped between her thighs, she froze. Stilled. She felt her womb clench, her pussy convulse, and the pleasure. It was terrifying. She had never felt this before. Even in the darkest nights when the need had torn through her, she had never known this sensation.

His lips lifted from hers.

"Like that?"

There was knowledge in his eyes. He didn't move, just held his hand cupped over the curves of her sex.

Sarah fought to breathe. Her eyes were wide, staring back at him, her body poised at an edge she was desperate to fly over and yet terrified to experience.

"When I make you come, I'm going to make you scream my name."

His eyes were narrowed, more amber now than hazel.

"Don't stop." Her hands gripped his wrist as he pulled back.

"Easy, baby. We're not ready to go there yet."

"We are. Really." Sarah was desperate to go there. Her body was begging to go there.

His chuckle was easy, dark.

"Let's get you out of these clothes. I'm not fucking you with that skirt around your hips."

She hadn't anticipated that. "You could pull the shades," she breathed out roughly.

His smile was sexy, dark and exciting. "I like the way you look in

43

the sunlight," he told her. "I want to see it washing over those pretty breasts."

His hands went to the buttons of her dress and Sarah froze. She watched his face as he loosened them. There were dozens, from the high bodice to the hem of the dress. Each one that slipped free filled her with more dread, knowing what he would see.

Would it turn him off? The scars were horrendous. Glaring. She felt her breath still in her lungs as she looked over his shoulder, waiting, fighting back the tears. She'd just wanted to know. She'd thought he'd take her on the deck maybe. Her skirt around her thighs. That she'd at least find release before she had to face this.

Cooper's eyes narrowed as Sarah tightened, tensed, with each tiny button that came loose. By the time he reached her stomach and pushed back the edges of the silky material, revealing her swollen, pretty breasts, she was stiff as a board.

Stiff. Almost frightened.

And he saw why. His fingers feathered over the six, very faint white lines across the tops of her breasts. As though a razor blade had sliced into the delicate skin just deep enough to scar. They weren't zagged or puckered. Almost as though someone had drawn the thin lines over the tops of each curve.

"We'll discuss these later," he told her softly.

She stared over his shoulder, her face pale now. He knew shame when he saw it, knew the fear in a woman's face when she thought something about herself was unattractive.

Watching her, he lowered his head, letting his tongue follow first one faint line, then another.

At the first touch, she flinched. At the second, he felt her forcing herself not to respond. By the time he reached the sixth, her eyes were closed, fists clenched at her side as she fought to hold on to the arousal and the control.

"Do you think those faint little lines are going to get you out of this, Sair?" He reared up on his knees, pulling her up, dragging the dress over her hips before pulling it over her head.

Surprised, she lifted her arms, staring up at him as he pushed her back to the bed.

"Hell. God have mercy," he groaned, sliding from the bed.

He pulled her sandals off her feet, but left the little toe ring she wore. He toed off his boots and shed his jeans so fast it was a wonder he hadn't scraped his dick with the zipper.

Fuck. His hands were shaking.

She was spread out before him like the sexiest little feminine banquet he had ever laid his eyes on. Gold rings pierced her nipples. Little rings that circled the tight, hard buds. Tightening around them.

"Oh, I bet that feels good." He leaned over her, watching her eyes dilate as he lowered his head and licked over first one tight bud then the other.

Sarah jerked, cried out. She felt the sensation clear to her womb, white-hot ribbons of pleasure striking at her, convulsing her lower stomach.

The gold rings that surrounded her nipples had never felt so good. Just the slightest pressure around the hard points. The rasp of his tongue over them. It was the most pleasure she had ever known.

Then, he covered a tip, sucked it into his mouth. Sensation slammed to her womb, arched her, convulsed her stomach. Her eyes went wide, and her fingers, almost of their own volition, rose until her nails were digging into his shoulders.

"There you go, Sair," he breathed a rough breath over her nipple. "Enjoy me, baby. I fully intend to enjoy you."

The rough sexiness of his voice destroyed her. Washed over her. Filled her senses and in the haze she forgot to be self-conscious.

She forgot about the scars. Forgot about the past. All she knew was this. The man. The touch. And finally, the pleasure.

"Oh. Yes." The words escaped her lips, escaped her soul as she felt his fingers touch her between her thighs now.

Her clit was swollen as it had never been before. The little metal ball of the piercing pressed against it, creating an incredible friction.

He wasn't in a hurry. And she wished he was. She wished she could finally touch the ecstasy that always managed to stay just out of reach.

"Please," she whispered as his lips moved to her other nipple, sucked it in, drew on it.

Her skin was so sensitive. Each brush of his flesh against hers was killing her. She needed him.

"Ethan, I hurt," she panted, her head tossing, lost in the pleasure. "Oh God. I need you so bad it hurts."

Cooper almost froze. No one called him Ethan. Not since he was a boy. They called him Cooper. He was Cooper. Even his lovers called him Cooper. Until Sair.

Until today.

His head lifted. Her eyes were dark, her face damp, with perspiration? He lifted his hand, his thumb stroking beneath her eye. Tears.

"Sair?" he whispered.

"Oh God, Ethan, I need to come." She was trembling beneath him. "I can't come. No matter what I do. No matter how hard I try. Please. Please. Make it stop."

"Why haven't you found yourself a man before now, Sair?" He touched the saturated, slick folds of her pussy. She was hot. So incredibly hot. Her flesh swollen, the extent of her need telling him how long she had held back. Years. She was a woman who needed touch, yet she hadn't been touched. She hadn't been held. And he wanted to know why.

46

She stared up at him. "I would have."

"Why didn't you?"

Her lower lip trembled. "I saw you."

Cooper swore his cock swelled thicker, harder. Two years. He had met her the day she looked at the house. And he'd seen her eyes. The shy interest, that little hint of "want to?"

"Why me?"

He moved between her thighs. She was too hot. Too ready. For whatever reason, for him. Hell, his ego was as swollen as his dick now. No woman had ever waited for Cooper.

"Make me feel it," she whispered then, staring up at him, her gaze tortured, her eyes dark. "All of it, Ethan. I want to feel all of you."

She was twisting beneath him, her little nails digging into his biceps now. She was going to blow off his head if he didn't do something now.

He gripped her wrists and slammed them to the bed. Held her there. She arched, moaned.

"Oh yeah, you like that, don't you?"

And he liked it. But he'd be damned if he'd ever seen a sweet little thing like Sarah go for it so easily. The restraint, the wild need clawing between them now.

Hell, how had this happened so fast?

He pushed the head of his cock against the folds of her pussy. Sweet heaven and God have mercy on his soul. Hot. Like silk, like syrup coating the head of his cock.

He blinked sweat out of his eyes. Hell, he himself had never gotten this hot this fast. What the fuck was she doing to him?

He pressed his hips closer, gritted his teeth as he felt the engorged crown of his cock press to the tiny opening of her vagina, felt the piercing at his cock tug with relentless pleasure. She was little.

He wasn't huge, but he wasn't small. A fucking bruiser. Dammit, she needed someone gentle.

The piercing beneath the head of his cock lodged into the tender flesh, stroking her and him, and knotting his balls with pleasure.

Then he watched her breath catch, her nipples darken and harden impossibly as he all but shoved the thick crest just past the entrance to her pussy.

He gritted his teeth, watched her eyes.

"Ethan. More." A breath of sound. A flush of arousal deepening. Her breath catching.

Fuck. She said she'd have a short fuse, he just hadn't believed her.

Leaning over her, he grinned. The best he could do.

"You're not gonna last long are you, baby?"

Her pussy was clenching, tightening, spasming around his cock head. Fuck. How long was he going to last?

She was breathing hard, her eyes dilated until only a thin ring of pale blue color remained.

Oh, he knew what his little Sair needed. Right there, in that instant. Because it was his greatest fucking fantasy. Pushing in hard and deep, first stroke, and feeling his lover come from the excitement of his touch.

Every man's fantasy. His, for damned sure. A pussy so tight it was like a fist knotted around him, flexing and milking, coming and vibrating around him because she wanted him so damned much.

"Sair," he groaned her name. "I don't want to hurt you."

It was the first time in his life he had ever cursed the size of his dick. Which wasn't enormous. She was just so fucking tight.

Her lips parted. "This kind of hurt, I'll survive." She lifted, tightened, and for the first time in Cooper's life, he lost his cool with a woman. Lost his control. He lost everything but that last fragile thread of sanity that helped him pull back on his strength.

But not his dick.

He pushed into her. One hard stroke, pushing past slick, slick tissue, gripping muscle, powering into her until she screamed his name and he felt her coming around him.

Milking him. Flexing around him.

Ah, fuck. He buried in full length and son of a bitch, he was fucking coming. Pouring into her. Spurting hard and heavy without the benefit of latex, and dying with each hard flex and jet of the semen erupting from his cock.

And she was still vibrating around him, arched into him. Her clit grinding into his pelvis, her body shuddering, jerking, her eyes dazed.

Little Sair had just come apart in his arms like no other woman had ever dared. And Cooper had a feeling he might have just lost a little piece of his heart. Not to mention his sanity. Because he knew he'd forgotten the latex, and son of a bitch, he was starting to wonder if he cared.

5

"I didn't use a fucking condom." Ethan fell to his back, but he dragged her to him, draped her over his chest, and forced her to stare at him.

He should have just let her lay against him, because the look on her face was dangerous to a man who had held on to his heart for so long.

Or had he? Hell. He was starting to feel the fucking noose and it felt comfortable.

"I'm protected." A frown flitted across his brow as she lowered her lips to kiss him, and his fingers tangled in her hair to hold her back.

"How do you know I'm safe?" He narrowed his eyes back at her. There came the dimple. A little shy. A whole lot too damned sexy.

"Your friends used to talk when I'd drop off the food while you

50

were recovering," she admitted. "Really, Ethan. You're like a condom fanatic."

He had been.

He let her lower her lips to his. Damned if he could help it.

"I didn't get to go down on you," he growled, pulling at her hair with one hand as the hand around her neck held her to him. "You need to pay for that."

He made her pay, with her mouth. Her lips, her tongue, a kiss so deep he felt it in his balls. Hell! He needed to get away from her. She was fucking dangerous. She was stealing every fantasy he had of a woman, as though she could see inside his head and knew how to give him exactly what he needed.

Her lips were eager, her moans washing over him. Her lithe, incredible little body stroked him from breast to ankle, and he'd be damned if he wasn't harder than he was when he took her minutes before.

"I want to touch you."

He let her pull back. His head dug into the pillows when her lips moved to his jaw, his neck. She may be inexperienced, and hell yes he knew she was. He felt what he had pushed past on that first stroke. She'd been a bit wrong about that hymen. It had been weak, easy to break, but it had been there.

Now, his adventurous little virgin was running her lips over his neck, his chest. Her lips covered the flat discs of his nipples, one at a time, sucked and licked and, fuck him, burned him alive.

Then she was going down. Licking. Kissing. The closer she got to the thick shaft of his cock, the more he felt her distress. Her need. She wanted to go down on him. He could feel it, or hell, maybe he just wanted it that damned bad.

She paused, her breath washing over the head of his cock as she lifted her eyes to him.

"Help me," she breathed, her breathing hard and rough now, the need in her eyes brushing him with heat.

"Oh, baby," he growled, pushing up on the pillows, reclining back. "Just love it with your mouth. A dick is pretty damned easy to please. Suck it, lick it, let it know it's loved, and it will perform all night for you."

That little dimple again. It flashed at her cheek.

"I love it a lot," she breathed, dipped her head and licked over the heavy crown. "A whole lot, Ethan."

God, help him. She made love to his cock. With a little encouragement here and there, and a whole lot of gut-torn moans from him. He was tortured. Paying for his sins in the worse way.

This sweet little virgin was sucking his soul out of the head of his cock and he was loving every second of it.

"Yeah, baby, suck it deep." His hands bunched in the long corkscrew curls of her hair. "Christ. Yeah. Suck it like that." She tucked the head against the roof of her mouth, worked her tongue beneath it, played with the curved ball that pierced the foreskin, as he told her and he almost lost it.

Her hands stroked, caressed. She knew the rudiments, and what she knew, she learned how to work. She loved his cock like chocolate, and he was dying from it. She licked, sucked, moaned around it. She played with the piercing beneath the head the same way he wanted to play with hers. With torturous pleasure. Until he knew, one more touch and he was going to lose it. He was going to fill her mouth when he wanted nothing more than to fill her hot little pussy again.

He lifted her away from him, pushing her back on the bed despite her erotic struggles. She was panting, breathing heavily. And when he jerked her hips forward and laid his lips to her clit, she froze.

She tasted of sweet hot woman, and himself. He wasn't a man

who normally got into the taste of himself on a woman, but with this woman, hell, however he could get his lips on that hard little clit, then he was all for it.

And the taste of them together, damn, it shouldn't be exciting. It shouldn't make his dick harder. But it did. And the feel of her response ripped through his senses.

Sarah bent her knees, unashamedly parting her thighs and allowing Ethan access to her intimate flesh. What he was doing was threatening to destroy her. He was playing with the little ball at the end of the curved metal piercing the hood of her clit, rolling his tongue over it, stroking it against the little bundle of nerves.

Sarah found herself so lost in the pleasure, the spiraling, the incredible hot sensations, that she could do nothing more than writhe and moan beneath him.

It was so good. Better than her dreams.

He was rolling the hard little gold ball against his tongue and stroking her clit at the same time. He sucked both in his mouth, laved around it. Sensations piled inside her. Her heart raced. Blood thundered through her veins. She felt herself—inside and out—twisting with hot licks of such incredible pleasure that she could only cry out against it.

"Easy does it, baby." Calloused hands gripped her hips, held her in place against the bed. "Just let it feel good, Sair. That's my girl." He kissed her. Kissed her clit. Flicked his tongue over it. "So damned pretty. Just let me play a minute and then you can come all over me, baby. Just a minute."

She didn't want to wait a minute. Sarah whimpered out against the pleasure, her hands threading into his hair, pulling at it, trying to drag him closer.

"Come on, Sair," he whispered devilishly. "Tell me what you want."

"I want to come." Her head thrashed on the bed.

"Tell me how to make you come, baby. Come on, tell Cooper how to make you feel good."

"Ethan," she panted, a protest and a cry of need. "Oh God, Ethan, suck my clit. Suck it. Let me come."

He sucked, he lapped, but he only threw her higher, made the pleasure hotter, brighter, the need like jagged forks of electricity racing over her flesh. His tongue played with the little ring and gold ball piercing her clit. He sucked and loved it.

He teased her. Tormented her. Left her sweating, pleading, and when he began to suckle her, firmly, rapidly, his tongue playing over the little gold ball above her clit, she exploded.

She flew. She felt herself melt and went willingly into the rainbow of explosive, torrential heat.

The hard thrust of his cock inside her, the feel of his cock ring stroking her flesh, dragging over it, left her shaking, arching. Crying. And sent another orgasm crashing through her.

"Yes!"

"Fuck, Sair." He dragged her closer as he knelt over her, his hips thrusting.

The pleasure-pain. The stretching burn. The exacting, incredible ecstasy of this. How had she waited? How had she stood back from him for so long, knowing instinctively, to her soul, what being with him would mean?

Her arms wrapped around his neck, her nails bit into his flesh. She lifted and raised, cried his name, and then felt herself unraveling again.

It was too much. The pleasure. It was like dying inside and being reborn. It was like being filled with life.

Above her, inside her, she felt Ethan's release. Deep, hard spurts of his semen filling her and her breath caught at the realization that once again, he hadn't worn a condom. Hadn't one of his friends laughingly said that all his women complained because no matter how protected or safe they were, Ethan always wore latex?

Until her.

Until now.

"Oh God! You just sucked the life out of me." He collapsed beside her and once again dragged her across his chest. "Go to sleep, you little wildcat. I'll feed us later. We'll have to eat before I can giddyap and go again."

His hands were on her back. Stroking her, easing her. He was holding her. Sarah let her lashes drift closed; she let the weariness set it. Just for a minute, she told herself. She would get up in a minute. Because she didn't want to wake up in his arms, screaming in pain.

Sometimes, the nightmares were as brutal as the past itself had been.

"What did you find out?"

Cooper stood on the deck, cell phone in hand, a bottle of beer in the other as he watched the kitchen. Evening was darkening over the house, and Sarah was still sleeping. And Cooper wanted answers.

"You're not gonna believe this shit," Jake, his bartender, stated in surprise. "Man, when I finally tracked that little girl down and cut through all the bullshit, I 'bout flipped my wig."

"Fine, now flip mine," Cooper ordered him.

Jake sighed. Cooper could almost see him running his hand over his bald head as he sat back in the leather chair of the office of the bar.

"Remember that Italian mafia guy? Oh, 'bout eight years ago. Suddenly turned himself over to the Italian authorities, spilled his guts and his evidence on all the families, which caused that split through the crime families?"

"Federico or something like that," Cooper nodded.

"Well, man, get a load of this. What the news services didn't get an earful of is what I found out when I contacted a few friends over there at the embassy. Seems ole Giovanni Federico, alias Gio the Giant, had a pretty little sixteen-year-old daughter who was kidnapped when she slipped out to meet with a rival's son. She was taken, held for Gio's good behavior as they set through Italy killing off some of his strongest allies. Each time good old Gio tried to get back his baby girl, they sent him a video. A video of this tiny little teenager held down, naked from the waist up, a razor blade slicing across her breasts. The old man was going insane. Turned to the authorities. Promised them everything, but they had to get his daughter, like pronto."

Cooper lowered his head and closed his eyes. The scars across Sair's chest. Fuck.

"Okay, so get this. From what my embassy buds say, they rescued the girl quick enough, turned her over to her daddy for a few days, then Daddy was arrested, too. Whole big trial. Threw him in prison, yada yada. We know all that. Well, six months later, little Sarita Federico was killed in a car bombing that took out three more of Old Man Federico's rivals. Or so the reports say. Start digging, and you find out that six months later, Sarah Fox immigrates from Italy by way of our good ally, Australia. Arrives with her uncle, Martin Corelli. Martin takes a security-guard job in Los Angeles, and little Sarah Fox is taking college classes. They move again a year later to Dallas. Sarah Fox goes into computer programming and graphics, and good old Martin is playing security guard again. Until four years ago. Martin dies. I talked to the coroner. He remembers the case, not because the death was anything less than natural, but because the dudes who collected the body were Italian. One grieving little mother dressed in black and a big tall somber young boy who managed only scattered English. They were accompanied, our coroner swears, by the Secret Service, who flashed some pretty impressive ID. The boy with the mother asks if old Corelli had other friends or family. Coroner says no, then asks the boy, How did you know he was here? The boy states, A call from a friend. Nothing more. End of story, everyone goes away. Six months later, you acquire a new neighbor. Miss Sarah Fox."

Cooper could hear the "but." It was there. Tightening in his gut.

"So?" He said carefully, glaring at the boards of the deck now.

"So, we met Corelli," Jake informed him. "Me and you, while we were in Dallas a few years back during leave. We were carousing the bars that week. Remember?"

Cooper had to sit down. Fuck, he remembered. "He just called himself Martin."

"Righto," Jake ground out. "We all drank, had us some laughs, and the dude gets up to leave, says he has to meet his niece and walk her home from nearby. Then when we left and those thugs tried to jump us outside the bar, he was there with that switchblade like hell on fire."

"And said one day he'd take a favor in turn for the help," Cooper sighed. "That one day, if he died, he'd send me the only thing that meant anything to him. And I was to protect it." They'd been drunker than hell, Cooper remembered that. He'd laughed, told Martin he'd protect his firstborn son in exchange. And Martin had told him that what he had was much more important than his firstborn son.

"Well, here's some more good info," Jake snorted. "Corelli was here in Simsburg a few months before he died. I just got some info when I was talking to the Realtor who sold her that little house. Corelli arrived for two nights with his niece Sarah Fox. When the

Realtor asked why they were looking in Simsburg, Miss Fox told her they knew someone in town."

"There was a girl there that night," Cooper mused. "After the fight. She got off the bus on the corner while we were leaning against that bar laughing our asses off."

He remembered it now, as though it were yesterday. Blue eyes in the night, the small figure, her coat hood pulled over her head. Her face had been hidden by the hood, but she'd held keys in her hand. He remembered the glitter of those keys, one sharp point held between her fingers, a laptop bag looped over her neck.

She'd been wary. On guard. But he remembered feeling her gaze go over him.

Son of a bitch.

"Corelli was her guardian. And she came here because of me."

"Actually, Martin was my uncle. And yes, I came here because I couldn't forget you."

His head jerked up at the sound of her voice. How the fuck had she managed to slip into the kitchen without him knowing?

"Shit. Your ass is in the fire now, huh, boss?" Jake groaned. "I'm gone. Good luck."

Cooper flipped the phone closed and stared back at Sarah. Her chin was held high, her dress buttoned a little crookedly. She was carrying her sandals in her hand.

Her expression was stoic. There was fear in her eyes.

He stared at her for long seconds, crossing his arms over his chest before he spoke. "Why didn't you tell me?"

She looked away from him for long seconds, then her eyes came back to him.

"Because I was tired of being someone's responsibility. For once, I wanted to be someone's woman instead," she finally said. "Thank you for today, but I think it's time I leave now."

Cooper blinked as she turned and started through the kitchen. Son of a bitch. Had she thanked him for fucking her? Then decided to leave?

He moved after her, catching her before she had taken more than a half dozen steps and swung her around.

"Oh, it's not that easy, baby," he assured her, his voice rough.

He should be madder than hell. He should be raging. Cooper didn't do responsibility really well. The bar was the biggest weight he wanted on his shoulders, nothing more. At least, until Sarah had knocked him on his ass.

"Why didn't you tell me who you were?" He held on to her even as she tried to pull away.

"Because I wanted you, not your damned promise made to a man while you were drunk, nor did I want you to feel responsible because you flirted with me, made me want you on a night you most likely didn't even remember," she cried out. "I wanted the man I saw that night. The one that was so strong and so playful. A man who didn't hurt his attackers, just wanted them bruised a little. I wanted the man whose bar my uncle and I would slip into and watch once he learned he was dying. I wanted the man I fell in love with once I arrived here and learned he was so much more than I imagined. I wanted you to want me, Ethan. I didn't want you to feel responsible for me."

She jerked back her arm as he stared at her in shock.

"You said you didn't want love," he accused her.

"I said I wasn't looking for love." She threw him a scathing glance. "I'd already found it. I loved you. It was enough."

She shook her head, all those wild curls flowing around her.

"You're free, Ethan." She opened her arms and stepped back. "No harm. No foul. You gave me more than I dreamed you ever would. And you gave it to me, not because of the memory of a debt." There was a flash of pride in her eyes, of feminine pleasure and confidence. It made him hard. Made him want to fuck her again. Right there, in the middle of the kitchen floor.

And he was going to do it.

"We're not finished," he growled, jerking his belt loose, unzipping his jeans. "Not by a long shot."

Her eyes widened, her lips parted.

Just in case she had it on her mind to say no, he covered those pouty lips with his own, jerked her into his arms and lifted her.

"Put your legs around me. Now." He jerked her dress to her hips, kissed her again as she tried to speak and turned, pushing her against the wall as he tore at her panties, ripping them off her hips. He heard her excitement in the moan that filled the kiss, and felt it in the way her hands dug into his hair. Her lips ate at his, her tongue fought against his.

"Hell, yeah. You love this." He pulled her closer, shifted his hips until his cock was pressing into her. "Don't you, Sair? You love my cock."

"I love you," she glared back at him.

"Tell me to fuck you."

A tear slipped from her eye. "Love me, Ethan. Just this once. Love me."

She made his knees weak.

"Damn you," he groaned. He slid the crown of his cock inside her and paused, feeling her, so silky, so hot. "Damn you, Sair."

He pushed into her, easier this time. Slower. He worked his erection into her, feeling all the little caresses, the sucking, milking ripples of her hot little pussy as she took him. So slow. So tight. So much pleasure he felt blinded by it. Felt as though he'd never have enough, could never take her enough to sate his hunger for her.

He buried his face in her hair, felt her legs locking around his back, and he took her slow and easy. Because the pleasure of it was enough to fight for, to die for.

How the hell had she managed to get past his defenses? And she had. Slid right through them and he hadn't even known it. Until he touched her. Until she asked him to show her how to be bad. Then broke through the last of his control when she asked him to love her.

"So sweet. So tight," he groaned against her neck, holding her to him, moving her on him. "God, Sair, what have you done to me?"

His arms tightened around her as he felt her juices gathering, slickening, easing his way even more as his hips began to move faster. Harder. He needed her. Needed more and more until he felt her gripping him tighter, hotter, and heard her cry out his name.

"Ethan!"

Her face buried in his neck, her pussy rippled around him and he lost himself in her. For the third time that day, he poured himself into her. Growling. Groaning. Lost in the pleasure that burned like a supernova through his body, he spilled every ounce into her, and he knew. It wasn't just his body he gave her. It was himself.

6

It was the mother of all fuckups.

Three days later, Cooper paced his attic, stared through the little window, and saw nothing. Fucking jack shit, and it was pissing him the hell off.

Sair had walked out on him. After he pumped inside her until he thought he was going to melt to the kitchen floor, she had all but run from him.

And what the hell had he done? Stood there. Like the fool he was, he just stood in the damned kitchen and watched her go, anger rising inside him as fast and as hard as lust had.

Two years she had lived here. Two fucking years. She had brought him chicken soup while he was healing from knee surgery. Baked him fucking cookies. Talked to his friends and knew things about him she shouldn't have known. And fit him like a glove.

Hell, no woman had ever fit him like Sair did. And no woman had ever affected him as she did. He even missed her.

When was the last time he had ever missed any particular woman? He didn't miss women. He made certain he didn't get close enough to women to miss them. So why the hell was he missing Sarah?

Well, he'd had enough of it, that was for damned sure. He looked at the clock: He had to be at the bar in a few hours. He was dressed and ready to go. He just had to get Sarah ready to go.

As though he hadn't heard the rumors of the dipshits in town hitting on her? She went to the grocery store every afternoon, everyone knew it. No less than three of the bastards had been seen coming on to her. So far, no one had mentioned her flashing that cute little dimple. He'd have been homicidal if they had. That dimple was his, by God.

And he was damned insane.

But that didn't keep him from stomping down to the main level of the house, out the front door, and over to Sair's little house.

He pounded on the door.

His arms crossed over his chest as she opened the door and stared back at him warily.

"What?" She didn't seem hospitable.

Too damned bad.

He pushed his way in between her and the door frame, turning back to glare down at her.

She was wearing another of those damned high-neck dresses. He hated those bastards.

"Get dressed," he ordered her. "We're going out."

"We are?" She closed the door, crossed her own arms over her breasts, and glared right back at him.

And that made him hard. His cock swelled in his jeans to dimensions he swore it had never attained before.

"Where exactly are we going?"

"To the grocery store first," he informed her. "Then to the bar."

God, he was a nutcase.

"And why the grocery store?" Her eyes narrowed back at him.

Cooper bent his head and growled, nose to nose. "Those bastards hitting on you at that fucking store are going to learn who the hell you belong to, starting today. Since when the hell did a grocery store become a singles' fucking meeting place?"

"It always has been actually." Her smile was tight. "You meet all kinds of people there."

"Men!" he snarled.

"If I were looking for a man, then I would have easily found one this week." She shrugged then turned her back and moved through the house. "And I'm busy today. I bought enough groceries yesterday for dinner tonight, so I don't need to go to the store." She looked over her shoulder, those long curls falling down her back. "And I'm not in the mood for you, or your bar."

He stared at her before turning and stomping behind her. She made him stomp, dammit. She was driving him crazy.

"What do you want, Ethan?" She turned on him as they reached the kitchen. "You wanted no strings. Look, no strings." She held her arms out from her, her pale blue eyes reflecting an edge of pain. And oh yeah, there it was, a flash of arousal.

His balls went tight. They knotted up beneath the base of his cock with painful intensity.

"What do I want?" he growled silkily, advancing on her. "First, I want to show all those woman-grabbing yahoos in town that you're mine. Then I want to reinforce that little message while I rub against you on that dance floor at my bar. Once we get finished, I'm going to take you to my office, lay you back on my desk, and eat that hot little pussy like candy and hear you scream my name again. Does that answer your question?"

Her breasts were rising, falling, pushing against her dress with the panting breaths she was taking now.

"You don't want strings," she whispered.

"I fucked you without latex." He grabbed her hips and jerked her ass to him. Hell in a handbasket, he had the least amount of control in the world where she was concerned. "If that's not strings, baby, I don't know what it is."

Her hands gripped his forearms. "But I'm on birth control. There's no risk."

"Have you lost your mind, Sair?" He nipped her ear in retaliation. "I'm the condom fanatic, remember? You think I forget latex at the drop of a hat? You think I've ever trusted another woman enough to spill inside her?" He licked the little burn of the nip. "And I want to do it again. I want to watch while my cock pushes inside your tight pussy. Watch the way I stretch you open. Take you and fill you as you suck me in. Those are strings, damn you."

Sarah felt her knees weakening. She knew she should protest this. She should be screaming, throwing him out, telling him to go to hell.

He hadn't trusted her. He hadn't asked her, but had had her investigated instead. And evidently by someone who knew what the hell he was doing. Because he had found almost everything.

"Physical strings," she whispered, her eyes almost closing as he ground his erection against her rear. "You couldn't just ask me anything about me, could you, Ethan? You had to ask others."

She tried to pull away from him, but he wasn't letting go. And not letting her go, holding her firmly, rubbing his erection against her ass, was killing her.

Three days. She had been without him for three days. How was she supposed to stand this? She thought she could survive. That she would be okay. But she wasn't. She was miserable. She ached. She woke at night needing his arms around her, tormented, hot, crying out for him. And he wasn't there.

She hadn't had enough of him, she assured herself. Just a few more days, and maybe she could have sated the need that tore at her.

"It doesn't go away, baby." She jerked at the sound of his voice, as though he could read her mind. "I've jacked off until my balls are blue and it doesn't help. Nothing's going to help until I have you again."

He turned her around, his hand curved beneath her hair along the back of her neck, holding her in place while his lips covered hers.

She was supposed to fight this? Fight the pleasure that built until it felt like a fire was searing her? Tearing through her mind and melding her to him?

She was supposed to be angry at him, wasn't she? That was what she had told herself for three days. That he hadn't trusted her. Hadn't asked her about her private business but had instead had her investigated.

She should be furious, not holding on to him, her hands digging into his hair, desperate for more of him. She needed his kiss, his touch. When his fingers tore at the buttons of her dress, pulling them from their moorings, opening the material as he tore his lips from hers to rove over the tops of the swollen mounds of her breasts, her breath caught.

Yes. She needed this.

"I missed you, Sair," he groaned, lifting her until he had her on the small center island, pushing between her thighs as he pulled the shoulders of her dress over her arms, along with the straps of her bra.

His lips zeroed in on her nipples, covered them, pulled at the little rings piercing them until she felt shudders of need racing just beneath her flesh. The things he could do to her. The ways he touched her. It was unlike anything she had told herself it could be. It was potent, addictive. It was the height of pleasure.

"Damn. You make me crazy." He pulled back, jerked the edges of her dress together and stared down at her, his gaze sensual, drowsy. "Get dressed."

"I *am* dressed." She stared back at him in confusion.

"Jeans." His hand moved over her ass. "You wear a dress to that bar and I'll end up fucking you before I get you off the dance floor. Go. I'll wait."

Sarah's lips twitched at that command in his tone. "You're bossy, Ethan."

"I'm horny, too, so watch out. Add the two and you could get more of an education in fucking me than you're ready for right now."

Her lips parted and she smiled. He obviously liked her smile because his eyes narrowed, the amber highlights darkened. "I don't know, Ethan," she drawled. "I've always been a very fast learner. Maybe you'll be the one falling behind in the lessons, rather than me."

Oh, he was falling all right, and Cooper knew it. Falling nothing—he had already fallen, hard and fast, for that cute little dimple, those pale blue eyes and long loose curls. Her intriguing smile and her ability to keep him intrigued. Damned if any other woman had ever done that.

"Bet me." He grinned back at her. Because this was sex talk, not love talk. Love talk would come later. As soon as he figured out exactly what it was he was supposed to say in love talk. But he was damned good at improvising.

67

She finally shook her head. "We need to talk before we do any-thing else." She sighed. "You didn't trust me, Ethan."

She stared up at him, that vulnerability, the hurt in her eyes tightening his chest.

"It wasn't a lack of trust, Sair," he promised her, letting his fin-gers run through the soft silk of her curls. "It was the pain in your eyes when I saw those scars. It was the knowledge that someone had hurt you and I wanted to kill them for it. But I didn't want you to see that reaction. I didn't want you to see me if the sons of bitches who did that to you were still alive."

They weren't. Even the young boy who had tricked Sair out of her father's home had died a less than easy death only a few years later. Her father's enemies had died in prison, along with her fa-ther. Anyone who would hurt Sarah was gone from this earth. And that left no one for Cooper to exact vengeance upon.

She dipped her head, moving away from him as she fixed her dress.

"It doesn't change the fact that I may want more from you than you want to give," she told him, turning back to him. "I deceived both of us, I think, to get into your bed."

"So deceive me again, Sair. Just get your ass in a pair of jeans and get back down here." He had to clench his hands and his teeth to keep from grabbing her. "For God's sake, baby, have pity on me here. I'm hard as a rock and starved for that pretty little body of yours. Let's get out of here and do what we have to do."

"Why?" Her hands went on her hips and a frown brewed at her brow. "Why does it matter if we go to the store? Or to the bar? How does it change anything other than your stamp of ownership over my head?"

He nodded decisively. "You're getting the picture there, cupcake. My stamp of ownership. Branding you in a way." He liked the sound of that enough to smile in anticipation. "And that's doing it the easy way. We could do it the hard way. I could just follow you the next time you go to the store and start knocking damned heads together when I catch those bozos sniffing after you. I'd have fun with that, but I bet you wouldn't."

Her eyes narrowed. "You're being very autocratic."

"It's one of my more advanced degrees," he snorted. "Now get dressed. You have five seconds to get your tail upstairs before I start undressing." He lowered his lashes, flicking his gaze over her. "And tomorrow I start batting heads together."

He was serious.

Sarah stared back at him, amazed, perhaps a little outraged, and a whole lot aroused.

"We're going to have to discuss your habit of ordering me around," she told him, backing out of the kitchen.

"Five. Four." He crossed his arms over his chest.

"You're being hideously arrogant."

"Three." He waited a heartbeat. "Two." He lowered his arms, his hands about his belt, as sweet little Sarah turned tail and ran.

And damn him if that wasn't the prettiest little tail.

He grinned at the sound of her running up the stairs. Grinned at the thought of the evening ahead. Then he whistled soundlessly at the thought of the night ahead.

By morning, Sarah and everyone else in this damned town would know exactly whom she belonged to.

They were being followed.

Cooper sat relaxed in his pickup, Sair pulled close to his side as he drove through town. And the little minx laughed at him because he made sure he drove through town, around the town circle, and then to the grocery store on the other side of the small town before he stopped.

"Hey, everyone needs a clear view," he told her with a laugh as he helped her out of the truck, keeping her carefully in front of him as the black sedan drove past, too damned slow.

He hustled her into the store and gave her the list for the bar. It was a list he and Jake had pulled out of their asses to make up an excuse to take her shopping. Items like celery, pepper, salt—bullshit items they had plenty of.

"Let me make sure Jake didn't forget anything." He pulled his cell phone out, hit Jake's number. Counted rings. When Jake answered, he closed the phone in a signal to Jake that there was trouble and smiled to Sair. "He must be busy."

Jake would be getting real busy right about now. He'd be calling every damned bouncer the bar hired, twelve total, and tonight every damned one of them would be on shift. Three would be at that store before Cooper and Sair left.

He was a damned paranoid man. The men who worked for him were just as paranoid. Loners. Soldiers without a war to fight because their bodies refused to do what they had to do now. They were his family. And now, they were Sarah's family.

He wandered through the store with her, his arm over her shoulders, or at her waist. He glared at the men who looked at her, and the few who stopped and talked were treated to a possessive Cooper. Something they had evidently never seen, because he caught the smirks.

Assholes.

He whispered dirty jokes in her ear to watch her blush, and stopped and talked to a few of the women that he knew would make good friends for his Sair. Women who were all safely married, happily married, and would of course tell her how great and wonderful monogamy could be.

He had a plan. Cooper always had a plan. But first, he was going to take care of the damned yahoos out in that dark sedan.

He was taking Sair through checkout when Casey, Iron, and Turk entered the store. Three ex-Rangers, soldiers who looked just as damned mean as they actually were.

"Hey, boss, Jake said don't forget to get change." Turk's voice was a deadly growl as he moved to the register. Dressed in black jeans and a black shirt, unruly black hair falling to his collar, Turk's steely, cold blue eyes glanced at the store owner, Mark, before turning back to Cooper.

"Jake didn't call you," Sarah murmured.

"Jake has a weird sense of humor, sugar," Cooper drawled as he pulled a hundred from his billfold. "Can you give me change, Mark?"

"I can, Cooper." Mark was no man's fool. The few times these three men had run with Cooper, there had always been trouble.

Like the time that damned motorcycle gang had tried to hold up his bar two years ago. Cooper, Turk, Iron, and Casey had walked in and cleared the place without a single broken window. There had been some broken bones, a few concussions, but these four men hadn't been the ones suffering them.

Mark packed the rolls of quarters in a plastic bag and handed them to Cooper. "You take care, Coop." He nodded before smiling at Sarah. "And you too, Sarah. Keep this boy on the straight and narrow."

She wasn't Miss Sarah anymore. She was Sarah, Cooper's woman. Damn, Cooper could almost feel his chest swelling with pride.

"Hey, boss, did you see that new Harley that drove through town earlier?" Casey eased in beside Sarah, Iron was in front of them, and Turk pulled up the rear. "She was a beauty with all that chrome."

Cooper kept up with the conversation, and the sedan. It eased out of the parking lot, windows tinted but he could still glimpse three males inside. The two in the front seat wore dark glasses.

As they reached the truck, Cooper shot Iron a hard look. The other man nodded his head. He'd checked the truck and it was clean.

"Come on, darlin'." He helped Sarah into the seat via the driver's side before moving in beside her.

"You headin' to the bar?" Turk grumbled. His brown eyes were flat and hard, his scarred face resembling a junkyard dog that had won too many fights at too high a price.

"Heading that way, Turk."

Turk nodded. "See you there."

The other three men lifted their hands before loping to their motorcycles. Harleys. Bad-boy motorcycles. Cooper liked his truck.

He started the truck and eased out of the parking lot. Turk and Casey were at the lead, Iron riding behind.

Sarah was too damned quiet. The ride from the store to the bar was hell. Because as he pulled into the parking lot, he knew what the hell had to be done.

She wanted trust. Shit. He didn't like this part.

"Black sedan followed us to the store," he finally said softly.

"I know." She threaded her fingers together and took a hard, deep breath. "I'll have to leave tonight, Ethan." There were tears in her voice. "When I'm gone, they'll be gone as well."

"Like hell." He gripped her neck, pulled her face around until he could stare into her startled eyes. "You're not running, Sair. Not anymore. My town, my bar, my fucking woman. And by God, it stays that way."

Before she could protest, before the first tear could fall, his lips covered hers. The kiss shot fire through his veins, tightened every cell of his body and left him burning for more.

His woman. For the first time in his life, Cooper loved a woman. He'd be damned if anyone was going to take her from him.

7

She thought she would be safe. Uncle Martin had kept track of her father's enemies. They had all died. The lieutenants who would have come after her had been arrested. Or they were gone, buried. Yet, someone had found her, was following her.

And they knew about Ethan.

Her hands were shaking as Ethan—everyone called him Cooper, but to her, he was Ethan—escorted her into the loud, crowded bar.

The Broken Bar was the hangout for every type of carouser, partier, or just plain wannabe-badass. And there were a few real badasses mixed in there, she was certain. The bouncers definitely. There had to be a dozen on duty tonight.

She picked them out instantly, most likely because there were no less than three around her and Ethan at any given time.

She pushed her fingers through her hair as she sat at the bar, tapping her fingers against the slick surface as she watched the large, cavernous room that seemed packed with twisting, drinking, gyrating, half-drunk bodies. A night of fun had never seemed so sinister.

Yes, it had. The last time she had let her fascination for a male draw her from hiding. And now, it was threatening the only man she had ever loved outside of her family.

"One of our finest." Jake pushed a glass of whiskey in front of her. The little shot glass was a joke. She picked it up and tossed it back, grimacing at the pure pleasure of the burn that cascaded through her body.

"Hit me again, Jake." She sat the little glass on the table as she gave the order absently, looking around, trying to make certain she couldn't recognize any of the men she knew were her father's enemies. Or could be.

He sat the shot glass in front of her. She frowned and looked up at him. "How 'bout a double?"

Jake's brows lifted but he poured the shot into a glass, added to it, and handed it to her. He was watching her as though he expected her to just dunk it like she had the one before.

The first shot was for courage. This one she would sip. Drinking too fast only made her sick. She tolerated her liquor really well. What she didn't tolerate well were nerves. And she had plenty of those going on tonight.

She twisted around the bar stool and came face-to-face with Ethan's chest. She looked up the wide expanse to meet his inquisitive look from the glass to her.

"Not to worry," she sighed. "I rarely ever get drunk."

"That wasn't what I was worried about." His hazel and amber eyes were lit with amusement. "I've noticed, though. The only time I've seen you drinking is here, in my bar."

"How would you know?" She looked up at him from the corners of her eyes. "You are very rarely in the house with me, Ethan."

"But I watch you by your pool. If you were going to drink, you'd be on the patio."

Her lips twitched, and she flushed. Because he had seen her masturbating by the pool. And because, damn him, he was right.

She sipped at the whiskey, loving the little bit of a burn that hit the back of her throat and flowed to her stomach. It eased her nerves just enough for her to see the fun that could be had in a crowd. And at home, sometimes, a drink in the evening helped her relax for the night. Though that was rare. She didn't like sleeping at night.

"I'm not used to crowds, that's why I rarely go out," she told him.

"I figured that out. Are you ready to dance with me now?"

Sheer excitement filled her veins. "Seriously?" She looked out at the dance floor. "You'll dance with me?" He'd said he wanted to, but she hadn't been certain he meant it.

"Sair, sweetheart, I'd probably dance *for* you." He sighed, shaking his head. "Come on, you little heart stealer. Dance with me."

He pulled her out on the dance floor and he taught her the country steps, which weren't hard to follow. She laughed as he twirled her around, pulled her against him, and ground his hips against hers with the rousing country beat. Then he let her go, let her wiggle and move, mimicking the other women on the floor before he would grip her, twirl her around, her hair fanning behind her before wrapping around his shoulder, some of the curls clinging to his T-shirt.

He seemed to like that.

Then the beat slowed, became dark and intimate, and he tucked her against his chest, his chin against the top of her head as she closed her eyes and felt him in every beat of her heart.

His hands stroked up her back, over the silky blouse she wore.

76

The one he had unbuttoned to the tops of her breasts and gazed at her. With one hand buried beneath her hair, his lips stroked over her brow, her cheek, her lips.

She whispered a sigh, her lips parting for him, feeling his kiss as she would have felt a caress clear to the depths of her spirit. He touched her that way. Just the thought of him touched her that way.

"You're mine," he whispered into the kiss as her lashes fluttered open. "Remember that, Sair. All mine."

"Always yours, Ethan." She would always belong to him, even if she had to run to protect him. And she would have to run soon. After he fell asleep tonight perhaps. Very soon. Because she couldn't risk allowing him to be hurt.

But for now, she could hold on to him, feel him holding her. Because this was her dream. And this man was her heart.

Cooper pulled her against him, feeling her slight form moving with him as his eyes narrowed on the entrance of the bar. The guy that stepped in was no biker, drinker, or weekend partier.

He wore black jeans, a jacket in the middle of summer, and he was packing heat. Cooper watched as three of his bouncers moved between them and the new visitor. Finally, with a grimace, the stranger left. But Cooper knew his face now. Hell, he had his face. He glanced to Jake, who caught his eye and nodded. They had him on the security camera; all they had to do was run it now. He watched as the assistant bartender took over and Jake headed to the office.

"What are you doing, Ethan?" She lifted her head now, her gaze suddenly too somber, too filled with shadows.

"Dancing with you." He touched her cheek, cupped it. "Protecting you."

She shook her head before pressing her forehead into his chest and he knew she was fighting her tears. He'd seen them glittering in her eyes, felt the shudder that raced down her spine.

"Come on." He caught her hand as the song ended. "I want to show you something."

Sarah let Ethan pull her through the dance floor, back to the bar where they moved into the narrow space Jake called his domain, and to the door at the far wall. There was no way to get back there except through Jake, and the bouncers closest to the bar.

The music became muted as he closed the door and led her through a short hall to a flight of rough wooden stairs.

"Where are we going?" she asked, loving the feel of her hand gripped in his, the warmth of it, the implied connection.

She shouldn't love him so, she thought. She should have held a part of herself back. A part of her heart.

"This is my home away from home." He unlocked the door at the top of the stairs and flipped on the switch. Soft, muted light filled the room.

There was a bed at the far end of the room. A large bed, strewn with pillows.

"And no, I've never had another woman up here." He closed the door and locked it behind him as she moved to the bank of monitors that sat over his office desk.

On one side of the room a tinted window looked out over the dance floor. She realized it was what she believed was a mirror on the wall above the dance floor.

There was a single shaded window by the bed, thick rugs, a table with two chairs, and a lamp hanging over it. Simple. Basic. Yes, Ethan would have come here to work, for the quiet, to brood perhaps. She could easily see him brooding here.

She turned back to him slowly.

He had stripped off his T-shirt and dropped it to the couch that sat against the wall, beside the bed. He toed his boots off, the amber in his gaze deepening as she slid her sandals from her feet and her fingers began to unbutton her shirt. Removing it, she quickly unhooked her bra and dropped it from her shoulders.

She needed him. Needed him until the ache was like talons of hunger tearing at her. She unbuttoned her jeans as he tore at the belt cinching his hips. They moved together, undressed together.

She pushed her panties and jeans down her legs as he did, stepped out of them, and stepped toward him.

"God, I missed you, Sair."

She was in his arms. He lifted her, holding her to him as he kissed her, devoured her lips, and carried her to the bed he had never shared with another woman. The bed that would only know the two of them.

The firm mattress cushioned them as he laid her back. It had been three days. She wasn't content to lay back and just be touched. She wanted to touch.

She rose up, curling her legs under her as he knelt in front of her. Her hands lifted, palms stroking along his chest, down the hard, rippling abs as her lips pressed to his hip.

She needed. Needed to love him. This one night. Enough to last forever.

She gripped the hard length of his cock, smoothed her hands over the shaft as she watched the little pearl of liquid that formed at the slit.

Her tongue touched it, tasted it. And she wanted more. She let her mouth cover the broad crest, her tongue finding the little bar piercing beneath the head, playing with it as she sucked at the crown.

"Hell, Sair." His hands burrowed in her hair, pulling, caressing the strands. "So pretty. So sweet."

She stared up at him, caught and held by his gaze. Oh God. Oh God. He was staring at her in a way she never thought he would. As though, almost as if, maybe, he cared for her?

She whimpered, her mouth filled with him, her hunger for him suddenly ravenous. She had to have him. All of him. Touch him. Learn him. Her fingers stroked the shaft; her palm moved to the tight weight of his balls and she caressed him there as well.

His shoulders looked massive from where she sat. His arms were bunched. The snake tattoo rippled across his bicep, moved, flexed, its red eyes piercing the dim light of the room.

The sight of it brought her a sense of security, not a sense of fear.

"Christ. Yeah. Suck me, Sair. Hell. Your mouth is so fucking sweet. Damn you. Tight and hot and so damned sweet."

He was blunt, explicit, and she loved it. She needed it. Her suckling strokes became deeper as she took him to her throat, moaned, and let her hands pump his shaft.

Evidently she was doing well.

"Hell. I love fucking your mouth," he bit out as the crown of his cock throbbed, seeming to swell thicker against her tongue.

His hands pulled at her hair, just enough. It sent flashes of pleasure racing through her scalp, down her spine.

"Oh yeah, suck it like that," he groaned as she took him deep, her tongue tucking against the piercing and rolling over it. "Damn, Sair. You make me hard enough to fucking cut glass with my dick." He growled the words. They rumbled from his chest, filled her senses.

She wanted to taste him, all of him.

"The hell you're gonna make me blow this fast."

She gripped his hips as he pulled back.

"Ethan, wait."

"Like hell." He pushed her back.

Before she could recover he was over her, kissing her, taking her mouth with deep plunges of his tongue. Licking and tasting her before his lips moved to her breasts.

He sucked her nipples, flicked the little rings then tucked them back around the hard peaks. The pressure around them was heated, agonizing with pleasure.

"I love your body. So sweet and curved. Sexy as hell."

His lips moved down her stomach, kissing, licking. Sarah felt herself dissolving, losing all thoughts of everything but Ethan's touch. His lips, his tongue.

"Ethan! Oh yes. Yes, lick me there. Right there." Her hips arched, her fingers tangled in his hair, holding his head to her as his tongue stroked around her clit. He kissed it, licked around it again. Never truly touching it. Only coming close. So close.

Her legs fell farther apart, need burning inside her. She could feel her juices falling from her, heating her further, preparing her for him. Just for him. She needed him.

"Please. Please. Oh, Ethan. It's so good."

"I love your pussy," he growled. "Sweet, sweet, Sair. Sweet all the hell over."

He sucked her clit into his mouth then and gave her what she needed. Rapture blazed through her. Ecstasy blazed before her eyes in rainbow hues of exploding melting color.

And he didn't wait. He didn't give her time to come down from the high. He rose over her, clasping her face in his hands as his cock pressed into her pussy.

"Look at me, Sair."

She struggled to open her eyes as her legs lifted to clasp his hips.

"Baby," he groaned, touching his forehead to hers, staring down at her as he eased inside her. Slow and easy. "I love you, Sair."

She stilled, blinked. She couldn't have heard him correctly.

"What?" Her voice trembled, hope surged through her.

"I love you, Sair. My sweet little Sair. My heart. I love you."

He pushed in deeper, stealing her breath. Her arms wrapped around his neck as pleasure turned to something brighter, hotter.

"I love you, Ethan Cooper," she cried out, arching as he took more of her. "Oh God, I love you."

He plunged deep. The hard, forceful stroke took her breath, gave her what she needed, a pleasure so rich, so destructive, nothing existed but them. No Sarah. No Ethan. Just *together.*

He pumped inside her, holding her to him, his lips covered hers, his kiss filled her. His groans met her cries, and when ecstasy exploded between them, she felt the sweet, blistering intensity. He filled her as she surrounded him. His release spurted inside her, mixing with hers as it flowed around them.

Sweat-dampened and sated, they collapsed in each other's arms.

"My woman." He pulled her against him, tipped her head up, and almost glared down at her. "You won't leave me, Sair. Do you hear me?"

She had run for so long, did she know anything else?

"Trust me, Sair." His thumb brushed her lips, his voice crooned, seductive, commanding. "Trust me to protect what belongs to me."

Did she have any other choice?

"I love you," she whispered.

"Trust me, Sair."

"I trust you." With her life, but more important, with her heart.

He dragged the comforter over them.

"Damn. Maybe I can fucking sleep now." He sighed. "You've kept me awake, Sair, missing you."

"I missed you, Ethan," she whispered, relaxing against him. "I missed you."

And she hadn't slept.

She slept now. Deep, dreamless. Held in his arms, where he protected her, even from the nightmares.

8

Cooper stared at the bank of monitors over the desk, his arms crossed over his chest, the fingers of one hand stroking at the stubble over his jaw.

He'd forgotten to shave that morning and hadn't realized it until he saw the red abrasions on Sarah's sensitive skin. Now there wasn't going to be time to shave.

He watched the two men who eased up to the bar, their faces deliberately turned away so as not to allow the camera to get a clear shot. There was a third man behind them: a larger man, a ball cap pulled down over his brow.

Interesting.

They were talking to Jake as he poured drinks. Cooper watched as Jake shook his head at the two in front then moved down the bar to serve several other customers.

One of the men looked up at the camera from beneath his lashes and Cooper's eyes narrowed. There was something about that look that he recognized. It wasn't the man, he didn't know the man, but the look itself. A sense of familiarity he couldn't place.

Grimacing, he turned and moved quickly to the bed.

"Sair." He leaned over his sleeping lover, kissed her cheek, felt her arms lift lazily and twine around his neck.

"Hm. Come back to bed," she mumbled, trying to burrow back under the covers.

"Sair, we have trouble, baby."

Her eyes opened immediately. Her arms slid from around his neck and she rolled out of the bed. Her response was too quick, too ingrained. Cooper felt his chest tighten at the knowledge that she had been forced to run too many times in her young life.

Wild, loose ringlets fell around her as she moved through the room, searching for her clothes now.

"What's wrong?" she asked as she hurriedly put on her bra and panties.

She was picking up her jeans as he pulled his T-shirt back on and glanced back to the monitors. At that moment, a red light lit up and a low buzz filled the room.

"What's that?" Sair jerked on her blouse despite the alarm that filled her face.

"That's trouble." Cooper felt his body go on alert. He shoved his socked feet into his boots and strode to the closet at the side of the room.

There, he jerked out the automatic military-issue rifle, snapped the clip in efficiently, and shoved two extra ammo clips into the band of his jeans.

The door behind the bar had just been breached, and Jake or

one of his bouncers hadn't opened it willingly. He moved back to the monitors.

"Do you recognize them?" He pointed to the men moving through the short hall that led to the stairs.

Sair moved to the monitors, pulling on her sandals as she stared at the three men who kept their faces deliberately turned away from the cameras.

She shook her head. "The big guy in the back looks familiar, but I can't see his face for his ball cap."

Cooper heard the fear in her voice, felt it.

"How do we get out of here?" she whispered.

Cooper stared at the three men. Jake was in the lead, his expression furious as he glanced at the hidden cameras as they passed.

But he wasn't giving any signals. Nothing to indicate an attack. Cooper watched his face carefully as he led the men to the stairs. Nothing. Not a flicker of an eyelash, not a tightening of his lips.

"Come here." He gripped her arm and led her across the room. Slapping the side of his hand against the paneling, he stood back as the door eased open to reveal a narrow set of stairs leading down.

Coming up those stairs was Casey, Iron, and Turk. They were heavily armed, expressions set.

He pulled Sarah back as they filed into the room, the same moment a heavy knock sounded at the door.

"Jake didn't say a word, didn't even indicate trouble," Turk growled almost soundlessly. "We didn't know shit till we looked up and he was gone from the bar."

"Hey Coop, I need to talk to you." Jake knocked again as Cooper's eyes narrowed.

"Ethan?" Distressed, frightened, Sarah stared back at him. "We can't leave Jake out there with them." Her hand touched her chest, rubbing against it as though it ached. Cooper felt almost a killing rage.

"Get in here." He pushed her to the small landing behind the paneling.

"No." Gripping his arm, fear brightening her eyes, she tried to tug him in after her. "Not without you. I won't leave you here."

"Dammit, Sair."

"No. I won't protect myself while you stand in front of a bullet for me. I won't do it."

"Sarita."

Sarah froze at the sound of the voice, the name called through the door.

"Have your friend open the door for us, Sarita. I promise, there is no danger. Come, sweetheart. Let Pa-pa see your pretty face."

Her gaze swung to the door as she felt emotions—fear, hope, longing—pouring through her. She shook her head, feeling the tears that built behind her eyes at that voice.

It wasn't Pa-pa. It couldn't be. He was dead. Uncle Martin had cried when he learned the news that Pa-pa was dead.

"No." She shook her head and stared back up at Ethan in terror now. "It's a trick. He's dead. Uncle Martin knew he was dead. It's not him."

"Coop, it's cool, man. They're not armed," Jake called out. "Let's get this shit over with so I can go back to work, okay?"

"You get ready to run!" Ethan shoved his finger at her as he pushed her to the one called Casey. "Casey, if anything happens to her . . ."

"I'm dead meat and turned to sausage." Casey nodded his shaggy head as he gripped her arm and pulled her back to the landing.

Sarah felt her chest erupting with pain, with fear. Her hands gripped Ethan's arm, fear cascading through her as she felt herself shuddering, torn apart from the inside out.

"Sarita, little one. Pa-pa wants only to see his little angel. Would you deny me this?" the voice called from the other side of the door.

Sarah felt the tears that fell from her eyes. It sounded so much like Pa-pa. Her breathing hitched, the pain spearing through her heart like a double-edged sword.

"No. He's dead," she whispered, staring up at her lover, beseeching. "We have to leave, Ethan. Please."

He touched her cheek with his fingertips. "I love you. Stay with Casey and let's see what we have here."

"No." She reached out as he pulled back from her, fighting to follow him as Casey's arm snagged around her waist and pulled her back.

"Don't get him killed, girl," Casey snapped quietly. "Let him do what he has to. Cooper doesn't run. None of us do. We stand and fight, or we're better off dead."

No. No. She couldn't do this. She knew what her father's enemies were like, the cruelties, the absolute lack of mercy. She could feel the scars on her flesh like a fresh brand now, searing her with the memory of how they used a child to force her pa-pa to do as they wanted. Until he had secretly gone to the authorities, turned himself in, and made a deal that destroyed him as well as the other crime families that had struck against him.

Her pa-pa had saved her. But she had suffered for his crimes. A part of her hated what he had been before he died, but another part of her ached for the father she had known. Loving. Strong. So kind.

At least, to those he loved. To those he didn't love, he had been a monster, not unlike those who had kidnapped her.

"Don't distract him, girl," Casey snarled at her ear as he pushed her behind him and Ethan, while Turk and Iron placed themselves at the door.

Ethan moved to the side while Turk and Iron flattened themselves against the wall on each side of the door.

"Ethan. Man. The bar is going to hell without me," Jake called out.

Ethan frowned. Every damned thing Jake was saying was a clear sign that their visitors were unarmed and unthreatening.

He moved to the table, and hit the electronic code to unlock and unbar the door. He stood back, lifting his weapon to his shoulder, bracing it, his finger caressing the trigger.

"Jake?"

"Yeah, Coop?"

"You go back to the bar. If these boys are so nice and friendly, they don't need you anymore, do they?"

Cooper glanced at the monitors and watched as Jake rolled his shoulders.

Jake stood in front of the other three at the landing of the stairs.

"Come on, Cooper," Jake's voice was irritated now. A sure sign he believed whatever crap these yahoos were giving him.

"Bring 'em on in, Jake," Cooper drawled, watching as Turk and Iron got ready.

The door swung open slowly and Jake moved in, ahead of the others. Hands held carefully to their sides, the other three men moved in behind him.

Government. The two in the front were feds, and when Cooper glimpsed the one in the back, he knew who he was dealing with. Giovanni Federico.

"Sarita." Federico pulled off the ball cap, his eyes on Sair as she stood still and silent in the entrance to the escape stairs.

He didn't look as old as Cooper knew he was. Giovanni Federico was fifty years old, but looked ten years younger. His black hair had only a sprinkling of white at the temples. His eyes were like Sair's, a pale blue, his skin swarthy, and he was staring at his daughter the way another man might stare at an angel.

Sarah had to fight the need to run to him. Gio the Giant, he was called. He was her pa-pa. At least, he had been, until she had learned what he was, who he was. Until she had learned he had been just as brutal, as cruel as the men who had kidnapped her.

As Ethan lowered his gun, she moved hesitantly from Casey. Skirting around the crowd now in the front part of the room, she moved slowly to Ethan. She couldn't explain the reasons why, couldn't explain why she needed to hold on to him, but the need was overwhelming. She felt as though the floor were rocking beneath her, as though the world was spinning.

When his arm slid around her and he pulled her close to his side, it felt right. And as she stared back at Gio the Giant, she fought to find in him the man who had rocked her to sleep as a child, who had sung funny songs to her, who taught her to dance and how to play hopscotch.

"Sarita." His face contorted painfully as the arms he had lifted out to her fell to his sides. "I have searched for you since you left Dallas. Two years I looked, after your cousin and aunt learned of Martin's death. To bring you home."

"I am home." She held on to Ethan as though he were a lifeline.

She felt as though her heart were breaking in two. How she had loved her tall, strong pa-pa. Loved him so much that the news of his death, despite her anger at him, had nearly broken her. And now, to learn that that too, was a lie . . .

He breathed in roughly, shoved his hands into the pockets of his slacks in a move that was so very characteristic of him. He stared back at her, his face more lined than it had been, his eyes shadowed.

"Your brother, he is in California searching for you. He thought perhaps you had returned there."

She shook her head. She didn't want to hear about her brother, either. Beauregard, named for an American friend, was his father's son. Not the brother she had imagined him to be.

"Go away," she whispered, feeling Ethan's arms tighten around her.

"Sair," Ethan whispered against her hair. "Let's see what he wants."

She shook her head and cried. "He wants forgiveness. Atonement. Isn't that right, Gio?" She blinked back her tears at the pain that filled his face. "It's the same thing Beau wants as well."

"I want to know my little Sarita, my angel, is safe and happy," Gio said heavily. "Forgiveness or atonement is not what I seek."

"You knew before you came here." She could feel the pain ripping at her, digging merciless claws into her chest. "You checked me out and you followed me, and you sent Beau to California. Why? Shall I tell you why?"

"Sarita," he whispered as a man stricken with grief would have whispered.

"Why, Gio?" She clenched her fists and faced him, years of anger and pain exploding inside her, cascading through her like an avalanche of sorrow and fury. "You sent Beau to California so he wouldn't kill? So he wouldn't do as he swore when I was sixteen and kill any man who dared touch me? Well, I'm no longer sixteen. And I'm no longer Sarita."

"You're still my daughter," he said softly. "The child my heart beats for."

She wanted to sneer, but it hurt. It hurt so bad.

"You killed," she whispered. "Drugs, rape, murder. Ah God." She wiped her face with her hands, shaking, shuddering with the horror of the information she had learned once her father had been arrested. "You, Uncle Martin, Beau, all of you. You were criminals. What Marco did to me when he kidnapped me was gentle compared to your crimes."

"I never harmed a child," Gio bellowed then, his hands pulling from his slacks, raking through his hair. "I never harmed an innocent, nor did I or Beau rape anyone. There were rules. Marco broke those rules when he took you."

"You should have never lied to me," she yelled back furiously. "Why didn't you just tell me you were a murdering mafia lord and that was the reason I wasn't allowed beyond the walls of our estate? My God in heaven, perhaps then I would have understood why they hurt me."

Gio seemed to shudder. Her pa-pa. She saw her pa-pa in this man, no matter how hard she tried not to.

"Beau was not part of that business," he finally said heavily. "It was the reason he was gone so often—he could not stomach the path I could not veer from." He shook his head slowly. "When they took you, I died inside."

"They had me six weeks," she sneered. "Six cuts, Gio. Do you remember them?"

"God, Sarita! I see them every night in my nightmares."

She was only barely aware of Ethan motioning the others out of the room. Even her father's bodyguards left silently, closing the door behind them, leaving her alone with Gio and Ethan.

"Beau was working to legitimize our holdings," he breathed out roughly. "For him, I had agreed to turn the business over to your uncle Lucian. We were negotiating this with Lucian the night you were taken." He shook his head wearily. "I do not excuse my-self, Sarita. Not what I have done, or for what I have been. But you were always my light. My precious child. More to me even than my son. And you know this."

She had been the spoiled princess. The baby. She had been loved by her father, by her brother. Cherished after the death of her mother.

"My name is Sarah," she whispered.

She didn't know what to say, how to feel. She only knew that if Ethan let go of her, she would sink to the floor in pain.

"This one, he calls you 'Sair'?" Her pa-pa nodded to Ethan behind her.

She narrowed her eyes. "Only Ethan calls me 'Sair.' "

"Ah. And only you call him 'Ethan,' when all others call him 'Cooper.' " He nodded. "Yes. It is the way of love, eh?"

She stared back at him silently as he moved and sat down in one of the large chairs that sat close to the wall.

He leaned forward, his tall, broad body almost too large, even for Ethan's furniture. His elbows rested on his knees, his hands were clasped between them as he regarded her.

"Sarah," he sighed her name. "I make no excuses for what I was. And I take full blame for how Marco terrorized you." He shook his head, and when his eyes lifted, she saw the tears in them. "For you, I would have died. Beau searched for you, and I feared he would die in the attempt to rescue you. He was enraged. So I went to the au-thorities. And,"—he spread his hands—"I let you go. You were the only bit of innocence in my life. My sweetest daughter. And I thought I could let you fly as I knew you should, away from the ug-liness of who and what I was." His expression turned fierce. "But I cannot." He rose to his feet, paced, and turned back to her. "You are my child. My daughter. You will give this man children. Blood of my blood." He thumped his chest, crossed his arms over it. "Fight me all you wish. I will move to this town if I must. I will be where you are. I will tell all, you are my daughter, who I love, who I treasure. I will not let you go as you wish." He glared at Ethan, then at her. "And my name is not Gio. My name is Ronald." He lifted his head proudly. "For my great-grandfather. Who was pure. Who was not part of that life you so abhor. I am Ronald Caspari. An immigrant." His voice lowered. "A father."

She stared back at him in shock.

"And you think it's so easy? That I can just forgive?"

He shook his head, his glance moving once again to where Ethan's arms were wrapped around her.

"Not easy," he said softly. "But I hope, perhaps in time, you can find it in yourself to remember the man who loved his Sarita. His precious angel."

That first tear slipped free. Her pa-pa never cried. He was fierce, and he was strong.

"Don't." She shook her head, feeling her eyes well with tears as well. Because she remembered her pa-pa. She remembered, and oh God, how she had missed him.

"Ronald Caspari hasn't committed any crimes, Sair," Ethan whispered.

"Don't excuse him," she cried out.

"I'm not excusing him, baby." He rubbed his chin against her head. "You're allowed the choice, Sair. It's not either-or. And hell, I'm not exactly a saint. We both know that."

"He killed."

"I protected what was perhaps not rightfully, but all the same, mine," her father breathed out roughly. "But unlike Carlos and others, Sarita, I never warred on innocents. I never kidnapped a woman or a child and brought it pain. Neither did I approve such an action. Never could I have. You were my guide, child." He shook his head. "From the day of your birth, you were my guide. Your sweetness and light ensured no child was harmed by my hand."

"Giovanni Federico was known as Gio the Giant. The Gentle Giant," Ethan reminded her.

"Why are you defending him?"

"Because a daughter's need for her father never goes away, Sair," he said. "You'll never stop grieving for him. And you'll tear yourself up inside. Better to pick your battles with him, and make sure he walks the path you choose for him from here on out. He's less of a threat to our peace of mind that way. Besides, someone has to give you away when we get married. I don't think Casey or Turk would look good in a tux."

She swung around. Blinked.

"Did you think I'd let you get away from me?" His smile was pure male confidence and a hint of wickedness. After all, her father was standing there.

"You didn't ask me to marry you," she pouted. "Maybe I wanted all the trimmings?"

He snorted. "Naw. You didn't. Or you wouldn't have picked the shadiest character in town to trip with that sneaky heart of yours. I've fallen, Sair. Right at your feet. I'm not asking for marriage, I'm damn well demanding it." He touched her cheek, cupped it with his palm. "And your father isn't asking for forgiveness, just a chance."

She turned back to her pa-pa, watched as he ran his hands over his face and stared back at her bleakly.

Gio the Giant was dead. Ronald Caspari may not be perfect, but she still remembered the love. Her pa-pa holding her, protecting her, laughing with her.

"Pa-pa," she whispered, shaking, realizing Ethan had slowly let her go.

Her father's lips trembled. She took a step, and then he was there. Crossing the distance to her, his hard arms wrapped around her, lifted her against him, and the scent and sounds of her childhood washed around her.

The father she had so adored. Could she forget his crimes? She couldn't forget. But neither could she forget that he had saved her. Given himself and all he possessed to protect her. He wasn't perfect, but he was still her pa-pa.

Ethan watched, crossed his arms over his chest, and glared at Gio. It was the look of a man determined, imposing his own will. If Sarah's father ever hurt her again, if she was ever harmed again because of him, then Gio the Giant would be dead in fact as well as in fiction. It was a look the other man well understood, and over his daughter's head, he nodded.

"I give to you my daughter," Gio said huskily as Sarah finally moved from his arms. Taking her hand, he laid it in Ethan's. "She is the light to my soul," Gio continued. "My treasure."

Ethan smiled and pulled his woman close again.

"She was mine the minute she moved here and I set eyes on her, Mr. Caspari. I tripped over my own two feet and lost my heart."

"You didn't?" Sarah stared at him, shocked. "You didn't. I would have seen it."

"I covered it damned well." He grinned. "But have no doubt, sweetheart, you were the first girl to make me fall. Head over heels."

Gio Federico stared at the couple. Beau, he wouldn't be pleased, but ah, his son, he was often too arrogant, too certain of life. He had wanted to protect Sarita between them. Having this man, so rough, so obviously a real man, hold his precious sister would grate on his pride.

But, his Sarita was safe. She was loved. And Gio had a feeling any man who attempted to take what Cooper deemed his, would find himself perhaps knocking on the gates of hell. No, Ethan Cooper wasn't a man to cross. But he was definitely the man for Sarita.

She was his child. But she was Cooper's woman. And she was safe.

And, he brightened. Perhaps soon, there would be babies. Ah yes, Gio thought. Grandbabies. Life was perhaps about to get very, very good.

Luring Lucy

by

Lori Foster

To Kay Johnson, a very respected friend who's also a wonderful mother, a giving person who's loads of fun—and a reader besides! Thanks, Kay!

1

Sweltering air, humid and thick, tugged at his hair and blew over his bared skin as he accelerated the car to seventy-five. He'd left the top of his Mustang down, knowing he'd need the exposure to the hot wind and the faded blue sky to counteract his increasingly volatile mood.

The sun was a broiling white ball, reflecting off the hoods and windshields of passing vehicles, making the blacktop waver and swim from the heat. There wasn't a cloud in sight along the endless stretch of I-75, promising nothing but more scorching heat. But the heat of the day was nothing compared to the fire pulsing under his skin, demanding release. Anger. Urgency. *Lust*.

Bram Giles gritted his teeth, and his knuckles turned white as his fingers curled and clenched around the steering wheel. He thought of how the night would end, how he'd make it end, and the turbulent thoughts made his lust expand. No matter what, he wouldn't let her run from him tonight. He'd been too patient too long and now she had some harebrained idea of indulging in a summer fling. *With someone else.*

Bram took the exit from the highway on squealing tires and turned left, heading toward the lake community and the woman who had driven him crazy for more years than any man should suffer. By the time he'd realized what she was up to, when that carnal look in her eyes and the way she'd held her lithe little body had finally registered, she'd already gotten a two-hour head start on him. It had taken Bram another frustration-filled hour to throw together some clothes, rearrange his schedule and his plans, and get on the road.

That one hour had felt like a lifetime.

Was she flirting even now, trying to pick up the first boater who went by? Had she met someone in town on her way to the lake? Maybe she'd even brought someone along with her, guaranteeing her success.

Whoever it was would be swiftly booted out.

Bram's foot pressed harder on the gas, speeding the car along until he hit the narrower gravel road that led to her summer house. She hadn't been to that house in four years, not since she'd caught her husband, David, there with another woman. Bram's stomach tightened with pain.

David was an idiot, now a dead idiot.

Jesus, Bram still missed him; they'd been best friends who were also like brothers.

But more than that, more than anything else in the world, he wanted David's widow. Bram had always wanted her. He had taught himself to live with the clawing desire, to push his needs deep down into his soul so no one else would ever know. But now she was free and obviously over her grief. Now she was ready.

Tonight he would have her.

The winding turns on the old country road forced Bram to slow the Mustang, but it did nothing to slow his thoughts. Sweat trickled down the middle of his chest and stuck his hair to the back of his neck. Was she eyeballing some guy right now? Was she making plans? Handing out come-ons?

Bram wiped the sweat from his brow and cursed. Once he got to the summer house, he'd jump into the crisply cold water of the lake to cool off—*after* he'd set Lucy straight on how things were going to be between them from now on.

She wouldn't like it.

He wasn't giving her a choice.

By the time Bram slipped the Mustang into the sloping drive cut out of the side of the hill behind the house, he almost had himself under control. The road was the highest point on her property, with the land dropping downward toward the lake and the house built in between. The house faced the lake with patio doors and a long, wide deck, while the back butted into the hill, surrounded by mature trees. It was because of the higher vantage point of the road that Bram saw her immediately.

His temper kicked into overdrive at the same time that his lust nearly consumed him.

Lust always rose to the surface when he got near Lucy. As he looked her over from top to toes, Bram cursed softly under his breath. At thirty-nine, Lucy was one sexy-as-sin woman, all lush curves and mature angles. Never before had he seen her put those assets on display.

Today, she was most definitely flaunting her wares. *For another man.*

He drew a deep breath and concentrated on not being a brute, on *not* storming down the hill and terrorizing both Lucy and the guy ogling her by letting his temper loose. It wasn't easy, not with her looking like that.

A sexy little pair of cutoffs, unlike the longer, more staid walking shorts she generally favored at home, hugged her rounded ass like a lover and left a long length of lightly tanned thighs exposed to the casual viewer. Her silky dark hair hung loose to her shoulders, playfully teased by a soft hot breeze, and her bare feet nestled in the thick summer grass.

Worse than that—or better, depending on your point of view—she had on a cream-colored halter top that left her back bare and had the young worker she spoke with fidgeting with lecherous interest. The worker kept looking at her chest, and Bram had the horrible suspicion that her nipples could be seen through the soft material.

A haze of red clouded Bram's vision and he slammed his car door hard, deliberately alerting them to his presence. Both Lucy and the worker, unaware of him until that moment, turned to look up the hill. Lucy shaded her eyes with a slim hand, but the worker took two steps back, obviously seeing the fury on Bram's face despite the mirrored sunglasses still covering his eyes.

Good.

If the guy had any sense at all he'd have already abandoned the mower and headed for his service truck.

Lucy started up the hill, her brow pulled into a worried frown. Bram saw that her nipples were, in fact, puckered against the material and quite noticeable. Every muscle in his body tensed in reaction.

"Bram? What's wrong?" Then with a touch of panic: "Did something happen to the kids? Are they all right?"

Her anxiety smote him hard. Damn, he hadn't meant to scare

her; she was a mother first and foremost—which was one of the most appealing things about her. Ignoring the nervous worker as he headed straight toward Lucy, Bram rumbled, "The kids are fine, Lucy. They're at Marcy's."

Her gaze skipped over him, from his athletic shoes up his bare legs to his wrinkled shorts to his sweat-dampened T-shirt with the sleeves cut off. "But I thought you were taking them camping."

Bram had thought that was the plan, too. As an honorary uncle to David and Lucy's two teenage children and as David's best friend, he'd filled the bill of doting uncle rather nicely. The kids loved him, and he loved them—just like they were his own. They'd willingly agreed to accept Marcy as the provider for the next week when he'd told them something vitally important had come up. At fourteen and sixteen, they didn't need a babysitter, but Lucy insisted that an adult be available in case of an emergency.

Bram took his responsibilities to the kids seriously and had made certain they were settled securely before he'd been able to leave.

He hadn't told Karyn or Kent why he had to renege on their camping trip, but he could tell by the look on Marcy's face that she understood. She was Lucy's best friend, the only one who hadn't gossiped about her during the divorce and the horrible scenes that David had caused. Oh yeah, Marcy knew that Bram wanted Lucy. The woman wasn't blind.

Not that Bram minded. Soon everyone in Lucy's neighborhood and his own would know that he was staking a claim, and to hell with any gossip that might ensue.

Lucy glanced nervously at the worker as Bram descended on them. She was confused by his appearance and probably disheartened to have her illicit tryst interrupted. The little darling had been on the make, and she'd apparently already picked out a conquest.

Bram wanted to take the younger man apart but couldn't really blame him for his interest. He knew any male in his midtwenties, which this guy looked to be, was likely to have been interested. He couldn't go around destroying every guy who looked at her, especially if she started issuing invitations. What he had to do was give Lucy a new target for her erotic curiosity. *Himself.*

Bram didn't slow in his pace and stalked right up to Lucy until he stood mere inches in front of her. Her long dark lashes left feathery shadows on her smooth sun-kissed cheeks, and her full mouth was parted slightly. Her eyes, so clear and bright a blue they put the sky to shame, watched him warily.

Bram could detect the subtle salty scent of her warmed skin and hair. A very light sheen of perspiration glowed on her upper chest and in the cleavage she had clearly on display. Her honey-colored shoulders glowed, too, as did her supple thighs.

Bram felt his own flesh heating with sweat, and it had a lot more to do with the proximity of his woman than it did with the unrelenting sun.

"Bram?" Her voice emerged as a breathless whisper, uncertain, a tiny bit frightened. And, if he didn't miss his guess, tinged with sudden awareness of him as a man. "Why are you here? What's going on?"

Showing his teeth in what Bram hoped looked more like a grin than a warning, he growled, "Because I missed you, of course." Then taking her totally by surprise he caught her arms above her elbows, lifted her to her toes—and kissed her the way he'd been wanting to kiss her for a very long time.

Her parted lips gave him the advantage, letting his tongue slip in deep to taste the sweet hot recesses of her mouth and move lazily along her own tongue. Lust boiled inside him, savage and hungry—and it was just a kiss.

Bram could only imagine how intense it would feel when it was his cock sliding into her tender body, when her legs wrapped tight around his waist and he could fill his hands with her breasts, her luscious ass. He nearly groaned with the thought, imagining her hot and wet, thinking how tight she'd be after four long years of abstinence. . . . His testicles tightened and he did groan, low and raw.

Lucy was obviously stunned by his primal display, but the worker got the message loud and clear—just as Bram had intended.

Lucy held her breath, amazed and embarrassed. She felt caught in a whirlwind, naked and on display, and she didn't understand.

Bram was a friend, practically a member of the family. He'd never touched her sexually before, but wow—he was touching her now!

Ignoring Bram's kiss was out of the question. It wasn't the first time he'd ever kissed her, but the others had all been brotherly pecks and in laughing friendship. Never like this. Never so . . . carnal.

This was a kiss of possession, a kiss of incredible passion. She'd never experienced anything like it, even through fifteen years of marriage, and her heart did two wild flips before settling into a frantic rhythm of panic, excitement, and, amazingly enough, response.

Lucy flattened one hand on Bram's chest, wanting to push him away but using it for balance instead. The damp cotton of his shirt did nothing to shield his hot masculine flesh. He felt blistering hot and wonderfully solid against her palm. She realized he was coiled tightly, his muscles iron-hard and straining, his heartbeat thumping in a fast gallop that mirrored her own.

The young worker whom she'd specifically hired because he'd flirted with her cleared his throat loudly. Bram ignored him, which left her no option but to do the same.

All too aware of the heat of Bram's mouth, his delicious taste, and the overwhelming strength in his muscled body, Lucy tried to protest. All that emerged was a small sound, barely audible, a mere whimper that could have been interpreted any number of ways.

Abruptly Bram released her. Her lips felt swollen and wet, her body both tight and too soft. She would have fallen down the hill and tumbled into the lake if Bram hadn't reached back out for her, throwing one bare, heavily muscled arm around her shoulders and literally anchoring her to his side. Caught in the cage of his body, Lucy felt small and defenseless, and strangely enough, that feeling stirred others, rousing emotions she hadn't dealt with in far too long. Female to male, soft to hard.

The idea of flirting with a stranger had titillated her senses. Bram's kiss had gone far beyond that. She felt as if she'd been torched.

Her brain may have turned to mush, but her body was working on full alert.

Lucy shook her head, attempting to regain control so she could figure out just what it was Bram was doing. Why had he kissed her? Did he think to somehow warn off the worker by intimating a nonexistent involvement? To protect her virtue?

Ha. Bram couldn't know that she wanted the indiscriminate fling. She wanted to *feel* again, to be alive as a woman, as a sexual being— and then she'd sell the summer house and get over the past, burying all the hurt once and for all.

The worker looked at her nervously, as if asking for instructions. The difference between Bram and the young man she'd hired was like the difference between an impressive oak and a new sapling. The younger man was rangy with muscles, lean and toned. But Bram was solid and thick with layered muscle, large and in his prime. Over-whelming. He exuded sheer masculinity and iron will.

Lucy wanted to fan her face, still reeling from that kiss. She used to wonder what it'd be like to be kissed by the infamous Bram

Giles. Shortly into her marriage, when David had lost interest with teasing and nuzzling and foreplay, she'd thought of all she knew of Bram, how the women sang his praises and his own testament—by word and deed—to loving sex and females. She'd always thought that sex with Bram would be something almost too delicious to bear.

Now she knew what it was like to have his mouth, and she doubted she'd ever sleep peacefully again. His kiss alone had been more sexual than anything she'd experienced in half a decade.

What did that kiss mean?

Bram turned his head toward her, but with his reflective sunglasses on she couldn't even begin to read his expression. A little embarrassed, she hoped he didn't see her reaction, that he wouldn't know his tactic to warn off other men in a half-baked plan to protect her had actually turned her on. He was so cavalier about sex and intimacy, accepting it as a natural, healthy part of his life. After her marriage, he probably assumed she was, too.

He'd have been far from the mark on that one.

Lucy held her breath until Bram again looked away. With his free hand, Bram dug into his pocket, pulled out two twenty-dollar bills, and handed them to the young stud she'd hired to tend her lawn—with hopes for more.

"Get lost," Bram ordered in a low rasp, and the worker, after snatching up the money, fled.

"Bram," she protested, looking around at the yard with only half the work done, "he hadn't finished."

"He was finished, all right." She couldn't see his eyes, but she read his fierce expression all the same.

Lucy lost her temper. Oh, he'd thrown her with that kiss, but she was squarely on her feet now. And he'd just chased off her most promising prospect.

If Bram had some macho notion of looking after her, keeping her *pure,* she'd just have to help him rethink it. For this one week, for one time in her life, she didn't want to be pure. She wanted— *needed*—to feel the burning satisfaction of lust one more time.

"Are you nuts?" Lucy demanded in a warning growl. "Just what the hell do you think you're doing, Bram?"

Bram stared out over the diamond surface of the lake. It shone with twinkling sunlight and the occasional ripples from a fish. During the week, the tourism was thankfully low, leaving the area quiet and serene for those who owned lakefront property. On the weekends, though, it got downright rowdy, boats and water-skiers and Jet Skis everywhere.

For now, Bram thought, watching the worker drive away in a cloud of spewing gravel and dust, he had Lucy all to himself. She could rant and rave as much as she wanted, but there would be no one to hear.

Without bothering to explain his intentions, Bram scooped her up into his arms and headed for the house. His body relished the feel of her, her gentle weight. Damn, it felt good to finally hold her, to have her in his arms where she belonged.

Lucy gasped so hard she choked, and when she was finally able to pull in a wheezing breath he was already on the steps leading to the deck. She smacked him hard on the side of the head. *"What . . . is . . . the . . . matter . . . with . . . you?"*

He kissed her again. He wanted to keep kissing her, every-where, all over her delectable body, but he knew they'd both end up rolling down the hill if he didn't give appropriate attention to where he stepped. "I have something to explain to you, woman, and it's best done in private just in case there's anyone fishing on the lake who might hear you yelling."

"Why," she asked loudly, "would I *yell?*"

"You're yelling now," he pointed out, thinking he sounded most reasonable.

She started to club him again, so Bram squeezed her tighter. Lucy generally wasn't a violent woman. Of course, she usually wasn't on the make, either. "None of that," Bram told her, trying to contain his satisfaction. "I can't very well explain if you knock me silly."

"You can explain no matter what, starting right now!"

The bare flesh of her soft thighs draped over his hard forearm was a torturous temptation for Bram. He wanted to feel the silky skin of her inner thighs on his jaw, his mouth, his hips as he drove into her.

Her breasts, more bared than not, felt so plump and full against his chest. He thought about pressing his face into her cleavage, tasting her pointed nipples through the cloth until she squirmed.

And her mouth—*hell yes, her mouth*. Set in outraged, mulish lines, it made it hard to concentrate on what he was doing.

The second he stepped across the sprawling deck and through the tinted patio doors, Lucy wiggled free. Bram let her go, but not far. Her feet were barely touching the hardwood floors and she was still against his body, where she belonged, when he said bluntly, "I want you."

Lucy pulled back. Her clear blue eyes were wide, her lips parted. She went alternately pale, then flushed.

The need to kiss her again was a clawing ache.

Bram touched her cheek, needing the contact, but she flinched away. "I want you, Lucy," he said again, harder this time to make sure there was no mistake, no misunderstanding. "I've wanted you for a helluva long time."

She shook her head, either denying him or not believing him.

It didn't matter which to Bram, because neither one was acceptable. He fully intended to have his way. "Yes. And I'll be damned if I'll sit back now and watch you indulge in some sort of prurient idiocy."

Her face went blank with shock, then burned with mortification. "Dear God," she rasped, sounding appalled, "what . . . what are you talking about?"

Bram straightened to his full height. At six feet, four inches tall, he stood a good foot above Lucy. She didn't look the least intimidated.

Bram frowned. "Don't bother to deny it, Lucy. You came here to get laid."

Guilt flashed over her features before she sputtered, "That's utter nonsense."

Leaning down close to her, Bram met her nose to nose. "Oh no you don't, sweetheart. In general, I know women too well to be fooled, and specifically, I know you as well as I know myself. The second you told me you were coming to the lake, I knew what you were up to."

She didn't want to believe him. "You can't possibly—"

"The hell I can't. This is where David cheated on you; this is where you want to get even."

Crossing her slender arms around herself, Lucy turned away. "David is dead. I can't *get even*."

"In your mind, you can." Bram stepped up to her back and slipped his own arms over hers. He wanted to comfort her, console her. He wanted her digging her nails into his back as he gave her a mind-blowing orgasm. Hands, mouth, penis, he didn't care how he accomplished it; he just wanted it to happen.

"He ruined your marriage by fooling around here, in the family vacation home. A place where you brought the kids, a place you used to love."

In a small voice, she said, "I still love it."

"You haven't been here since, not in four long years. But now you're here, looking incredibly sexy—"

"What?" She tried to twist to see him, but he held her still.

"—and eyeballing a guy who, if I don't miss my guess, is close to the age of that girl you caught here in bed with David. That sounds like getting even to me."

She gave a self-conscious laugh. "Funny. To me, it sounds like a woman who's desperately horny."

Shaking with the possibility of that, Bram gentled his hold, stroking her arms, bringing his groin in closer to her lush ass. Though he had a damn good guess, he still asked, "How long has it been for you, baby?"

She stiffened, but Bram secured his hold, refusing to let her sidle away.

"Don't be embarrassed with me, Lucy," he urged. "We've known each other too long for that. We're friends." And he wanted them to be lovers. He wanted all of her, every way that he could take her.

"If you're asking how long I've been without a man," she replied stiffly, "it's really none of your business."

Bram rocked her. "I'm guessing it's been over four years. You and David were a little on the rocks even before he blew it." He pressed his mouth to her temple in a reassuring kiss. "Am I right?"

He felt her tremble, heard the shuddering breath she drew in. "Bram, don't."

He ruthlessly ignored the pleading in her tone. It was his damned sympathy, his misplaced understanding, that had led her here today with plans to crawl under another man. He wouldn't make the same mistake again. "Four years, Lucy. A short lifetime to go without letting another man get close."

She yanked herself away from his hold and whirled to face him. "What was I supposed to do, Bram? Pick up a guy in the grocery store? At the school? Being a mother to two kids, the president of the PTA, and already the object of scandal made it just a little bit tough to go looking for sex, didn't it?"

For about the hundredth time Bram wished he'd beaten the hell out of David before he died. "No one has ever blamed you, Lucy."

"Bull!"

"David was responsible for his own actions." Sadness welled inside him, but he shook it off. "He was the only one responsible for his death."

"I guess you never heard the neighbors whispering. They think I'm coldhearted, that during one of David's crying jags I should have taken him back."

Bram shook his head. "He was a partier. And it had come close to happening before that." David had slowly grown out of his marriage and had begun flirting, testing the waters. He'd been on the prowl long before he'd gotten lucky. *Or unlucky,* as Bram saw it, thinking of all he'd lost.

"I know," Lucy whispered. "He ogled women everywhere we went." She cast Bram a narrow-eyed glance. "And he envied you."

Bram gently shook her. He couldn't, wouldn't, let her draw a comparison or blame him in any way. She had no idea of the lengths a man would go when the woman he wanted was married to someone else.

"A man who cheats is a cheater," Bram told her, determined to at least ease any ridiculous guilt she might feel. "If it happened once, there's no guarantee it wouldn't have happened again. You can't blame yourself for not liking the odds."

And, Bram thought savagely, a man who cheated on Lucy didn't deserve a second chance. He'd loved David as a friend, but he'd known all along that David wouldn't make her happy. Too many times, David had told him that he resented the restrictions of marriage.

And time and again, Bram had told him what a lucky bastard he was.

Tiredly, as if she'd rehashed the story too many times, Lucy said, "I kicked him out, he went on a two-year drunken spree, and he died in a damn car wreck because of it. *I blame myself.*"

Bram wanted to shake her again. "Lucy," he said, chastising. "You're too smart for that, honey. And too realistic to think you had control over David. He chose his own way, then regretted it. No one made him cheat; no one made him ignore you or the kids. And no one made him drink too much or drive too fast."

He squeezed her shoulders and said quietly, "I know the past few years have been ugly."

Her blue eyes lifted to his face. "You made it easier. You've been such a help, with the kids, with everything."

Bram shrugged. "The kids are important to me, you know that. I love being with them."

"And they love being with you."

That hurt, too, because he wished they were his own, not David's. Bram loved them like his own. He shook his head. "It's time for you to get on with your life, Lucy."

She ran a hand through her hair, and her bangs ruffled back into place, a little mussed, a lot sexy. Indicating the summer house, which she'd had freshly cleaned and aired, she said, "That's what I was planning to do."

Bram realized that a hard-on was totally inappropriate to the moment, but he'd long since lost his control around Lucy Vaughn. And now, knowing it was only a matter of time until he could get inside her, his body rioted with need.

He held her gaze and whispered, "Good. Now you can plan on me taking part, too."

2

The air-conditioning kicked on, activated by the open patio doors. He hadn't felt the heat building inside the house, but then, he was so hot himself, it'd take a lot for the external air to catch up to his body temperature. Lucy made a face and stepped back out to the deck.

Watching her, Bram took two deep breaths, concentrated on relaxing his knotted muscles, then followed her out. She stood at the rail, her hands clasped on it at either side of her waist, staring at the lake. The sunshine made tendrils of her dark hair look almost blue; around her temples, her hair was damp, clinging to her skin. The frayed hem of her shorts teased just below the rounded cheeks of her sweet behind, making his fingers twitch with the need to touch her. He'd always thought Lucy had a world-class ass, not skinny and narrow, like so many of the women he knew, but full and soft. He could spend hours just cuddling that bottom, kissing and stroking.

Through the years and two pregnancies, she'd picked up weight in her bottom and in her legs. He'd heard her laughingly complain about it and always reassured her that she had nothing to worry about. Lucy had never known how serious he was.

To him, she was so sexy it hurt just to look at her.

She was rightfully confused now, Bram knew, but he didn't know how to make things clearer to her except to be brutally honest and up-front.

He slid the glass door closed.

"You were his friend," she said, not looking at him but knowing he'd followed her out. "His best friend."

Bram replied quietly, "I loved David like a brother. That doesn't make what he did right."

"He told me once that . . ." Her voice broke and she hesitated, then cleared her throat. "He told me you felt sorry for him."

Bram went to her side and leaned back on the railing. He could see her face but made a point of not looking directly at her. Though he knew David had probably slanted that sentiment, making it sound like he blamed Lucy, Bram admitted, "I did."

She jerked as if he'd struck her, then gave a humorless laugh. "Well, you weren't alone. Everyone felt sorry for him. But what about me? I was the one who caught him in bed with that woman. Do you have any idea how that made me feel?"

"Yes." Bram knew damn good and well exactly how she'd felt. He'd watched her closely every time he'd seen her after that, and he'd read the strain, the embarrassment and hurt, on her delicate features. It had made him sick with the need to retaliate in her defense. But he hadn't. He'd done his damnedest to stay impartial in case the marriage had succeeded. He'd loved them both too much to get in their way.

But the marriage had crumbled anyway. By the time David had realized all he was throwing away, there'd been no helping him. Thank God the car crash that had taken him hadn't involved anyone else.

Bram had grieved and suffered guilt and helped Lucy and the kids in every way he could.

And now it was finally his turn.

"You felt defeated," Bram told her. "You were betrayed and lied to, and it hurt. You gave up on your marriage and you threw him out. That took guts, Lucy. And I was so damn proud of you."

When she looked at him, not understanding, Bram added, "I felt sorry for David because the dumb son of a bitch had given up the best thing he was likely ever to find in this world, all for a quick fuck with a woman not worth the effort."

Lucy trembled, her eyes direct on his face. "You knew her?"

Softly, intently, he said, "I knew she wasn't you."

She turned away again and paced the length of the patio, stopping at a new perch a good distance away from him. Bram smiled. He had her on the run, but here, at the isolated summer house, she could only go so far. And never out of his reach.

"What are you really doing here, Bram?"

His heart raced as he stared at her slender back, bared by the halter top. His muscles tightened in anticipation and his cock felt full to bursting. "I'm here," he murmured quietly, honestly, "because you want sex, and I'm damn well going to be the only man to give it to you."

He saw her shoulders stiffen the tiniest bit, her back expand as she drew in a sharp breath. She didn't face him when she asked, "Why?"

"Why what?"

"Why would you want to . . ." Lucy gestured with her right hand, but there were no words to accompany her thoughts.

"Why would I want to make love to you?" He stepped toward her, slowly, letting her feel his approach, letting her awareness of him grow to a razor-sharp edge. Sweat trickled down his temples from the suffocating heat. His heart pounded, sounding loud in his ears.

He came close enough that the heat of his body mingled with the heat of the sun to envelop her, to wrap her up in his scent. "Why do I want you naked and under me?" he growled. "Why do I want to be the man to give you what you haven't had in four impossibly long years?"

"Yes." Her hands curled into fists, tighter and tighter. She jerked around toward him and shouted, "Yes and *yes!*"

The look on her face was haunted. Hungry.

"Lucy—" He couldn't tell her yet what was in his heart. He had to get her past the emotional restrictions of being with a man who had been her husband's best friend. He knew Lucy; she'd automatically rebel against the idea, finding it too intimate, too complicated. She'd rather have an indiscriminate fling with a stranger than risk the emotional complications of making love with a man she'd known for a very long time.

"Why, Bram? You can have any woman you want. You *have* every woman you want."

"I haven't had you, so that's obviously not true."

Her chest heaved, but she ignored his interruption. "They're all young and sexy with flat stomachs and enormous boobs and legs to their chins. They're not tired thirty-nine-year-old divorced mothers—"

"Officially, you're not divorced," he pointed out, just to stall her tirade. Voices carried on the lake, and though Bram doubted there was anyone around to hear, he didn't want Lucy to be embarrassed later. "David died before the divorce was final, remember."

"*Widowed,* then! They're not like me."

"Thank God," he said with heartfelt sincerity. The dissimilarities from the women he usually dated were what made Lucy so special.

"The women you gravitate to are twenty-year-olds who fawn all over you and screw you all night and every day—"

Bram laughed. He didn't mean to, but the humor struck him and he just couldn't hold it back. She sounded almost jealous—which thrilled him. And she looked appalled that anyone would want sex that much, which made his chest swell with tenderness.

But he'd show her. Before the week was out, Lucy would learn to love sex as much as he did.

"I'm forty-one, Lucy. Round-the-clock sex is for the young studs, not for me." And with a grin: "Though once at night and a coupla times during the day with you would be a pretty nice balance."

Apparently grinning was the wrong thing to do.

Big tears clouded her eyes and she started to stalk away. Contrite, Bram pulled off his sunglasses and followed her. He almost got squashed in the sliding door when she went to shove it shut this time—hoping, he knew, to close him out.

He figured he'd been closed out too long already.

"Are we going to keep marching in and out?" he asked, trying to tease her into a better mood. He didn't want this to be a battle. He wanted to gently seduce her as she deserved. At least, he hoped to start it that way. Ending it with a hard ride would suit him just fine.

Lucy headed down the short hallway of the one-floor house for the bedroom. "I'm going to go to the lake. You're going to leave."

He followed her straight into the room. "Not on your life, babe. Not with you still planning to—"

"Get out, Bram." Her voice shook audibly and she looked none too certain of her position. She pointed to the door, trying to be forceful. Bram merely crossed his arms over his chest and leaned back against the wall.

"Why?" he asked. "So you can call that young worker back?"

Her chin lifted with defiance. "Maybe."

Jealousy stabbed at him, but he resisted it. She was vulnerable now, doing things she'd never done before. Turning forty did strange things to women, so he could just imagine where her head was with her birthday not too far around the corner. Before the week was over, Lucy wouldn't have a single doubt that she was an incredibly desirable, sexy woman. He'd prove it to her in a hundred different ways.

Damn, he was looking forward to it.

"Is he your type, hon? Midtwenties? Too dumb to really know how to pleasure a woman?"

She looked briefly shocked at his bluntness. "Maybe he would surprise me."

His smile hurt, but Bram managed it. "I don't think so." He tilted his head. "Where'd you find him anyway?"

"Not that it's any of your business, but I met him in town when I stopped to pick up some groceries. He agreed to . . . work on the lawn."

"Oh, he'd have worked all right. But it wasn't the lawn he had on his mind and you know it."

"Is that so?" She looked pleased with the idea, making Bram almost smile again.

"Any red-blooded male with good-enough vision to see is going to want you, Lucy. You're a hottie."

She scowled at him. "That's a weak line for a man with your reputation, Bram."

"Always go with the truth, I say." Deliberately he looked her over from her head to her curled toes; then whistled low. "I can't believe you're unaware of the way you turn heads." *Mine especially,* he wanted to add but didn't.

"I'm not the least surprised, though," Bram told her, seeing that she was hungry for the compliments she should have been getting all along, "that the first guy you smiled at jumped at the chance to try his luck. Hell, at that age males are more testosterone than anything else and a sexy woman is an impossible temptation."

Lucy looked both complimented and annoyed.

"But he doesn't know you the way I do, Lucy," Bram told her, dropping his tone and watching her closely. "He doesn't know what you've been through and what you're after, what you deserve. He'd grope you real quick, have your shorts off in a flash, and two minutes later he'd be walking away, anxious to go brag to his buddies about the eager woman on the hill."

"Shut up, Bram."

"Is that what you want? A reputation with all the guys who're looking for a good time but no commitment?"

Her face was closed, but she shrugged. "It doesn't matter. I'm selling the place anyway."

That surprised Bram and made him wonder if her decision was financial or emotional. Either way, he didn't like it. "Reputations have a strange way of following a person."

She crossed her arms. "I notice a reputation hasn't done you any harm."

"No? Then why are you arguing with me so much now? Why don't we just get our clothes off and I can start helping you enjoy the week?"

Her gaze inadvertently skimmed his body, catching on his groin before she forced her attention back to his face. Her cheeks warmed with color; her eyes darkened. *She wasn't embarrassed.*

"I have no idea," she said a little breathlessly, "what's gotten into you, Bram. Are you trying to shock me?"

"I'm trying to be honest." Bram narrowed his eyes, all humor evaporated. "If you want to get laid, babe, fine. Come and get it. But it'll be with me and only with me."

She licked her lips and her eyes searched his. "I'm too old to play games, Bram."

"I can teach you new games." He stared at her mouth, fascinated with the way she kept chewing her bottom lip, which told him she was nervous. "They're best played in the buff."

Her chin lifted. "I'm also too smart to think you need to chase after me just to have sex, not when you have a string of women at home sitting by the phone. What are you really up to?"

She didn't believe him? Bram shrugged, catching and holding her gaze. "I don't want any other woman. I want you. Naked. Under me or over me, or whatever way you'd like. But I want inside you real bad and I want you to be holding me tight and I damn well want to hear you come."

Her composure wavered, her mouth opening in a small *o* for just a second. Then she regathered her wits. One of the sexiest things about Lucy was her backbone. She had gotten through a lot of strife in her life, and she'd not only landed on her feet, she'd raised two terrific kids besides.

As if for battle, she stood with her thighs locked, her feet braced apart. And she sounded deliberately suspicious. "Since when, Bram? Let me see, wasn't it just a few weeks ago that you were boffing Dede what's-her-name from your gym? Kent came home all bug-eyed with adolescent lust and overflowing with awe for his 'Uncle Bram's' prowess. I got to hear the blow-by-blow dimensions of the woman's body in a leotard. According to Kent, you personally showed her how to use every single piece of gym equipment."

Bram lifted one brow. So Kent had tattled, huh? He'd box that rascal's ears when next he saw him. Then another thought occurred and Bram half-wondered if his touted—and surely exaggerated— exploits had anything to do with Lucy's sudden determination to get frisky. Maybe he had inspired her.

"It was nothing."

She scoffed, adding with disdain, "And here I'd stupidly thought that, as the owner of the gym, you left chores like personal instruction to your employees."

"I never slept with Dede."

"Yeah, right. And I've never touched up the gray in my hair."

Bram bit back a smile. Lucy had started getting silver streaks in her gorgeous inky hair when she was only thirty-five. Now, at thirty-nine, they had all been covered over. Forcing himself to be as somber as the accusation warranted, he said, "Don't get confused here, babe. I'm not David. I've never lied to you and I never will."

That threw her for a moment, and then she rallied once again. "So now you're claiming to be a monk?"

"Far from that." Bram weighed his next words carefully. "I have no doubt that through fifteen years of marriage David caved in to the temptation to talk about me now and then?"

Bram waited, wanting to know how much she knew of him, dying to figure out if her curiosity had ever been as extreme as his own. He hoped she'd asked about him. He prayed that she'd fantasized a time or two, because God and his own conscience knew he'd dreamed about her far too often.

Lucy shrugged. "Yeah, so?"

Satisfaction settled into his bones. "So you already know I'm

about as far from a monk as a man can get. I like women. I love sex."
He leaned toward her and reiterated, "But I didn't sleep with Dede."

"You're telling me Kent made it all up?"

"Of course not. I can't imagine Kent outright lying to you like that. But he probably only told you what he saw, which was a little flirting. And the truth is, I considered sleeping with her. You wanna know why?"

"Let me guess? A double-D bra size?"

She was such a prickly little cat today, Bram noted with amusement. Never before had they been at odds. From the time she and David had started to date, they'd all three gotten along. Lucy had often treated him like a brother, so he'd done the honorable thing and kept his wicked thoughts to himself. He'd loved David, and by association he'd learned to love Lucy. There was nothing wrong with that.

It was the lust, and more, that had made him feel guilty.

But he was done with guilt. He hadn't played a hand in their marital problems, and no one, before his current confession to Lucy, knew that he'd been obsessed with her. Lucy wasn't guilty of wrongdoing, and neither was he.

From here on out, he was going after what he wanted. And that meant he was going after Lucy.

Pushing himself away from the wall, Bram closed the distance between them. Lifting his right hand, he stroked her silky dark hair. It was baby fine and arrow straight and he loved it. "Her hair is almost as sleek as yours."

Lucy caught her breath.

"And her eyes—" He looked at Lucy's face, then tilted up her chin so she had to meet his gaze. "She has blue eyes, Lucy, that when I tried real hard reminded me of you."

Lucy shook under his intense regard. "So," she whispered, "the double Ds had nothing to do with it, huh?"

Bram took a step away from her. If he hadn't, he'd have kissed her again, and with the bed right behind her, things might have gotten out of hand. She was already prepared to bolt, so pushing her wasn't a good idea. "Let me be clear about something here, Lucy. When I get alone in my bed at night and decide I can't take it anymore, it's not Dede's body I think about." He stared at her hard, saw the way her pupils dilated, and admitted gruffly, "It's yours."

Lucy looked frozen and enthralled. "Good God. You're not telling me that you . . . ?"

"Yeah, so what?" Bram figured he was far too old to be embarrassed over his body and the things he felt, the needs he dealt with. "We've already established that I'm not a monk. And at the moment, no other woman is appealing to me. I want *you,* Lucy. I've been wanting you since before David died." He didn't have to tell her yet that he'd always wanted her. That might be a bit too much.

For the first time since he'd arrived, she appeared to be softening. Wryly Bram wondered if she felt sorry for him because he'd admitted to flying solo. The amusing thought brought with it another, and his pulse raced.

Softly he asked, "What about you?"

Wariness returned to her gaze. "What about me?"

"It's been a long time since you filed for divorce. You haven't dated one single time since then." It sometimes made Bram break out in a sweat thinking about a woman like Lucy, a woman so alive and so filled with love, going to her bed all alone every night.

"Don't you get lonely, Lucy? Doesn't your body burn sometimes, wanting the touch of a man? Wanting relief? To the point where you just can't take it anymore?"

In a tone that matched his own, she whispered, "That's why I'm here." She looked away from him, then back again. "What you said, being alone . . . that's not the same as being with someone."

His heart thundered. "No, it's not. It's a damn poor substitute."

"Things . . . things were bad between David and me for a while before he cheated. But even then, even when I knew I was losing him, it was nice to have a man close sometimes, a warm body in the bed with me at night." She swallowed and in an attempt to explain, she said, "There's a certain type of comfort in just knowing you're not alone, in feeling the body heat, hearing someone else breathe."

Bram's lungs constricted with fresh pain. Through the years of her marriage, it had been a unique form of hell knowing that David made love to her and Bram would never be allowed to. Now he had a chance and he'd be damned forever before he lost it.

He caught her chin on the edge of his fist. "I want to be the man who touches you now."

She immediately shook her head. "Bram, I can't compare with all those young, beautiful women you date."

"Christ." How could she not know, not understand? David had been a bigger ass than he'd suspected. "You don't have to compare with anyone. You're in an entirely different league."

"The minor league?" she teased, but Bram saw her uncertainty, the misconceptions she had about herself as a woman.

Desperately he tangled his fingers in her hair and drew her up against his chest. "I want you for who you are, Lucy. I've always respected your intelligence and your loyalty. I adore your sense of humor and your sense of responsibility."

"Bram." They'd hugged often over the years, and the way she hugged him now was familiar and sisterly. He hated it. "It's not a woman's sense of humor a man sees when she's naked."

He shuddered with the thought. "Seeing you naked," he growled near her ear, "would likely make me come in my pants."

She laughed. "Bram."

Bram took her hand and carried it to his distended fly. His breath hissed sharply when her warm palm pressed against him.

"Ever since I realized what you intended to do," he gasped, "I've been hard. Thinking about you wanting another man enrages me, and still I'm hard. Knowing you would plan this week rather than come to me makes me want to howl—*and still I'm hard.* Sex with other women is a hollow thing, babe, even worse than jacking off, because I want *you.*"

"How . . ." Her fingers didn't leave him and, in fact, curled around him tentatively instead. She was getting used to the idea, Bram decided, and he wanted to roar with his triumph. "How did you know what I was going to do?"

Bram hesitated. The closeness of talking with her like this, touching her like this, had always been no more than a dream. The reality was so much sweeter, so much sharper, that Bram didn't want to run the risk of destroying it. But he had promised her that he wouldn't lie to her, and so he wouldn't.

He kissed the top of her head and said, "Unless you want me to take you now—and I don't think you're quite ready for that yet—we'd better stop what we're doing."

He heard her swallow. "I'm not. Ready, that is." She looked up at him. Her fingers were still curled securely around him through the jean material of his shorts, and he felt them tighten the tiniest bit. "You're . . ." She stopped, took two deep breaths. "Well, you're *huge.*"

Women had been commenting on the size of his prick since he was eighteen, and he'd always wallowed in the praise. Now all that mattered was that Lucy was intrigued. If his size helped to interest her, then Bram was doubly thankful for what he'd been given.

His hands gently stroking her shoulders, he said, "I would never hurt you, Lucy."

Her breath came in small pants now. Small *excited* pants. "I don't know about that. I mean, it's been a while for me. A long while—you were right about that." Idly she slid her palm up and down his length, measuring his dimensions again, making Bram lock his jaw with the pleasure of it.

Feeling nearly hollow with desire, Bram growled, "I'd be careful with you, baby. We'd go real slow and I'd make you so wet first, so hungry for it, sliding in will only be pleasure. I swear."

Lucy shuddered, and her hand stroked him one more time, nearly devastating him, before she pulled away. Her eyes were huge, filled with conditional trust. She would try, he realized, but she wasn't making any promises.

For a long moment, Bram simply concentrated on breathing, on not losing control. He could hardly win her over with devastating sex if he came in his shorts from a simple fondling.

When he felt able, he took her hand and led her from the bedroom. "Here's what we'll do." His voice was abrasive and deep, unsteady. "A swim—because I badly need a dousing of ice water—then a fast boat ride just to distract us. While we're on the lake, I'll explain things to you. We can . . . talk." He pulled her out onto the deck again. The heat and the sun hit them like a wave, sealing in the lust, the hot craving. Still somewhat shaky with need, Bram asked, "Do you need your shoes?"

Lucy, too, was trembling despite the steamy summer afternoon. "No." She looked up at him, her eyes slightly heavy with desire, and Bram had to lock his knees to keep from carrying her back inside. "I want to be totally free this weekend. No shoes, no bra. No laundry or phones or nosy neighbors or gossip."

Her statement sounded like a sensual promise to Bram's sensitized nerve endings. Or maybe he was just so damned horny, anything she said would have exacerbated his lust.

He nodded in agreement and they left the patio to follow the stone path down the hill to the lake. Bees buzzed around their feet, going from one clover blossom to another. Bram watched closely where they stepped, not wanting Lucy to get stung. Somewhere far off a cicada split the air with its noisy call. A black bird took flight.

"Do you have the keys?"

Her voice hushed with lingering uncertainty, Lucy said, "They're still in the boat. Life preservers are in the boathouse."

"You've been out in her already?" She should have only been at the cabin a few hours without him. Bram had cleared his calendar and quickly packed once it had dawned on him what she was up to. But she'd had time to scout out the area for other vacationers, if she'd done so right away.

"No, just started it up to make sure everything was in running order."

Bram stopped at the irregular shoreline before walking onto the long wooden dock where the boat was tied. She'd brought it out of the boathouse and removed the tarp cover.

Greenish lake water lapped at the rock retaining wall along the shore with a gentle splash. Sunlight glittered and sparkled, making it necessary for Bram to replace his sunglasses. The air was thick, the sky so vivid a blue it was nearly blinding.

Before he'd gotten run off, the worker had cut the grass, but he hadn't yet trimmed. Everything smelled fresh and new, scents intensified by the damp air and baking sun, filled with possibilities. Bram kissed Lucy gently on the mouth. "When we get back, I'll finish the yard work. Did you pack anything to grill?"

"I figured I'd eat sandwiches. Grilling seemed like too much trouble."

Bram made a mental note to stop by the one and only grocery store located on the lake. He'd talk with Lucy, feed her, and tonight he'd show her part of what her body could expect to feel with him. Before he was done, she'd crave what he could give her. She'd crave him.

"I'll take care of it. I'm a good cook." ·

She snorted and headed past him to step off the wooden dock and into the boat. "You're good at everything you do and you know it."

Bram watched her settle herself onto the white leather seats. Knowing he was damn near a goner, he took a quick walk off the end of the dock and into the icy water. His shirt floated up, leaving his abdomen bare; his athletic shoes felt heavy on his feet. The water closed around his head, stinging his heated skin but doing very little to cool his lust.

He doubted a massage with an ice cube would cool him down right now, not when he was so close to having what he most wanted.

Lucy was turned around watching for him when he resurfaced. He slicked his hair back and smiled at her, then slapped some water her way. With her own smile, she ducked back into the boat.

Taking long strokes, Bram swam to the ladder leading into the boathouse and commandeered two life vests. It was cooler inside the boathouse, and dark. Cobwebs hung from every corner, testifying to how long it had been since anyone had disturbed the boat. Exiting the door leading to the dock instead of the water this time, Bram walked around the dock to the sleek inboard. His shoes sloshed with every step, and his shirt stuck to his torso. Lucy wasn't looking at him. He tossed the preservers into the back before joining her up front. She was in the passenger's seat, so he assumed she wanted him to drive.

David had bought the expensive boat not long before Lucy had walked in on him with another woman. As far as Bram knew, this was the first time Lucy had been in the boat since.

Bram deliberately let water drip from him onto her as he adjusted himself behind the wheel. She had slipped on dark sunglasses and a floppy white hat that shielded her face from the sun—and from his view. She had her long legs stretched out before her, her feet propped on the dash.

Refusing to be ignored, Bram trailed one wet fingertip up the length of her leg, from her ankle to the outside of her thigh. She shivered, and a small smile teased the corners of her mouth.

Tonight, he thought, appreciating her body, imagining her naked, she would do more than smile. Tonight she'd be screaming his name.

3

Lucy eyed Bram through her dark sunglasses and the whip of her hair blowing into her face. She had to hold her hat on with one hand because he drove the boat so fast, but it felt good, the rush of the wind and the sound of the wake behind the boat. There were only a few other boaters out, and so the ride was relatively smooth, with only a few choppy waves here and there.

As usual, she was all too aware of Bram, but now it was different. She'd always seen him as a sexual being, a man who beckoned women with his looks, his masculinity, and his smile and charm. But now she knew firsthand how devastatingly clever his mouth was, how he could kiss a woman into a stupor, and how blunt he was about his sexuality. He had no shame, no modesty.

She had a feeling Bram wouldn't know a thing about insecurity or shyness in the bedroom. His only concern would be giving and receiving pleasure.

Her body tightened with the reality of that, her nipples puckering, her stomach flip-flopping. Oh God, he was incredible, more so than she'd ever even realized.

Owning a small, exclusive gym made it possible for Bram to stay in the best possible shape. Working out was a part of his daily routine, and it showed. He didn't have a single ounce of fat on him anywhere, and his power, his strength, was evident in every line of his tall body.

But who was she kidding? The man had always looked that way, even before he'd bought the gym. Back when she'd first met David, she'd been distracted by Bram's body, and he hadn't been much more than a teenager then, because she and David had married when she was twenty.

Perfection was the only word to describe Bram. And disturbingly enough, the older he got, the better he seemed to look.

At forty-one, he had a wide, hard chest with clearly defined muscles that could make a female of any age hungry. His streaked blond hair, always in a somewhat shaggy, unkempt style, was shades lighter than the dark brown hair on his body. Through Bram's wet, tattered T-shirt she could see the muscles moving and shifting on his chest as he turned the steering wheel on the boat, slicing through a bigger wave. She could also see the sprinkling of hair that spread out over his upper chest and then narrowed to a silky line down his abdomen. Lucy realized she was undressing him mentally and tried to pull herself back.

David's chest had been hairy, too, but he hadn't looked like Bram.

Guilt slammed into her and she looked away, determined to keep her thoughts on something other than Bram's magnificent body.

But as if he'd read her mind, he slowed the boat and pulled his wet shirt off over his head, giving her an earth-shattering view of the object of her distraction. He was tanned darker than she, with shoulders twice as wide and narrow hips barely covered by loose-waisted faded jean cutoffs. Soaked, the waistband of the jean shorts curled out away from his body. Lucy could just see the edge of a pair of dark snug boxers.

It was difficult to breathe with so much hunger swirling inside her.

Lucy watched as Bram lowered one large rough hand to his ridged abdomen and lazily scratched. With the other hand, he steered the boat.

Her tongue stuck to the roof of her mouth.

She wanted to touch his abdomen, too. She wanted to hear that enticing rasp in his voice that told her he was aroused. She wanted to tease his navel with her tongue, do things to him that she'd never been able to do with any other man—including her husband.

Lucy closed her eyes against those thoughts. Imagining letting go with a total stranger whom she'd never have to face again was entirely different from thinking of doing wild, wanton things with Bram. She knew him and knew that he thought of her as a lady. How could she confide in him her darkest secrets, her most forbidden fantasies?

"Now," he said, his voice loud over the rumbling purr of the engine, "are you ready for me to explain?"

She was ready to jump overboard.

Maybe the cold water would help her, though looking at Bram's fly, she saw that it hadn't cooled his ardor one bit. There was a very visible ridge in his shorts, a large, solid ridge that couldn't be mistaken for anything other than what it was.

That thrilled her, even as it confused her. She could hardly warrant that Bram wanted her. But looking at him there wouldn't do a damn thing toward getting her calmed. All the stories she'd heard about him were real; he was very well endowed and supposedly knew how to use what he had. A slow explosion of heat nearly took her breath away.

She didn't know if she could really handle all of him, but she very much wanted to find out. Her body clenched with the need to find out.

"Explain what?" she asked stupidly, her mind still on his big hand and his bared flesh and the clear delineation of his maleness beneath his fly. He said he'd been hard for a while. Well, he was hard still. Her heart could barely keep up with her racing pulse.

Glancing at her quickly, Bram reached out and tucked a tendril of her flying hair behind her ear. "I can hear the excitement in your voice, Lucy." He stroked her cheek and over her bottom lip. "Now—and then."

She couldn't deny the now. She didn't *want* to deny it. Bram was here, and even if she couldn't be totally free with him like she could have been with a stranger, neither could she resist him.

But earlier, when she'd given him permission to take the kids camping and explained that she'd be away for a week, Lucy knew she'd been very discreet. She hadn't admitted a word of her real intent to a single soul. She took her status as mother seriously and would never, by word or deed, deliberately make her children uncomfortable.

Planning a brief fling with a stranger was bound to fit into the "uncomfortable" bracket.

Yet she was so lonely, her body so hungry. She was sick and tired of going to sleep with the need to touch and be touched making her crazy. The only thing she'd been able to come up with was a one-nighter to assuage the fever. She was human; didn't she deserve some gratification, even if it was only sexual?

Bram slowed the boat, steering it easily along the shoreline, staying just far enough out to avoid submerged logs and large rocks that could damage the bottom of the boat. Hanging branches from tall trees dipped into the water's edge, shielding snakes and frogs and turtles. Bright orange tiger lilies, black-eyed Susans, and Queen Anne's lace grew in profuse, wild tangles, enticing hummingbirds to flit about.

Farther out on the lake, a bass jumped, drawn by the hot sunshine.

Using just that one rough fingertip, Bram continued to stroke her face. Lucy shivered. His touch was almost casual, as if he'd decided he had the right to touch her and no one was going to stop him.

"I saw your purpose in the way you spoke, the way you held your body. There was anticipation in every muscle, and a glow in your eyes."

Lucy scoffed at such a notion. "Poetic nonsense, Bram. If sexual intent was that easy to read in a person, I'd have known that David was going to cheat."

Bram withdrew, and for several moments he was silent. "Maybe," he finally said, "I just know you better than you knew David. Maybe I'm more observant where you're concerned."

Lucy stiffened, hearing his words as an insult. David had told her many times that she neglected him. She hoped Bram wasn't saying the same. "How so?"

"I watched you marry David." His voice was so low she could barely hear him. His blond hair, still damp, blew straight back from his forehead. The sun glinted off his mirrored glasses. He hadn't shaved that morning, and a light shadowing of whiskers darkened his lean jawline and upper lip.

He had the most sensual mouth Lucy had ever seen. Beautiful white teeth, a strong chin, high cheekbones. But it was the innate sensuality in his eyes, in his every gesture, that usually had women taking a second and third look.

Right now, there was an expression on Bram's handsome face that made her stomach curl with some unnamed emotion.

"I knew what you felt then, too," he said. "During the wedding, and after. I've always been able to read you." He smiled slightly, turning her muscles to soup, and added, "When you were pregnant, I thought you were the most beautiful woman I'd ever seen."

Lucy remembered his fascination with her then, the questions he'd asked, the awe in his expression the first time she'd convinced him to feel the baby kick. She also remembered how he'd avoided her whenever he could. He hadn't come around nearly as often during her two pregnancies. Not until the end of her second pregnancy, when he'd realized that David couldn't keep up with his work at the office and help her around the house, too. Then suddenly Bram was there, proving himself a true friend by keeping the grass cut, carrying laundry up and down the steps for her. He always came when David got home, and together they'd get the extra chores done. Lucy never saw Bram except when David was there.

Something about that memory nagged at her, but she put the thought from her mind.

"When I was pregnant," she half-teased, but knew it was true, "I was fat."

A grin flickered over his mouth. "Lush."

"What?"

"You weren't fat, babe, you were lush." They neared the boat docks where vacationers could purchase bait, basic groceries, and other necessities. "I remember thinking you got sexier the further you went along in your pregnancy. Your breasts were incredible, and your eyes were so pretty. And after Kent was born and you nursed him . . . it used to choke me up."

Lucy leaned around to see his face, stunned at what he'd said. "It didn't."

"Hell yes, it did."

He sounded so sincere, her heart twisted. Without thinking, she touched him. His thigh was hard and hot and roughened with hair. She felt the muscles flex, go rigid. "Why, Bram?"

He expertly steered the boat into the dock where a worker grabbed the lead line and secured it to a grommet. Bram just sat there, his hands resting loosely on the steering wheel, his gaze straight ahead. Around them, people on a pontoon chatted and laughed. Another man sat on the side of his speedboat, reeling in a ski line.

Bram went so long without answering her, Lucy began to think he hadn't heard her at all.

Then his hand covered hers on his thigh and he pulled off his sunglasses. His golden brown eyes blazed with intensity, with emotion. *And with desire.*

He lifted her hand and kissed her palm, the pads of her fingers. "I got choked up," he explained against the sensitive skin of her inner wrist, "because I knew I'd never have what you had. And I thought it was all pretty damn special."

Lucy blinked hard. She cared about Bram, she always had. Now, more than ever, she understood why. He wasn't just a sexier-than-sin, macho ladies' man. He was also a sensitive man, caring about the kids' needs and attentive to them all as a family. For the first time she realized how he might have felt like an outsider.

She stood, smiling slightly, and, using her free hand, ran her fingers through his fair hair. It was tangled from the hot wind, thick and soft. "Of course you could have those things, Bram. You just have to stop tomcatting around and settle on a single woman."

She meant her tone to be teasing, but instead it sounded gruff. Touching him, even casually now that he'd made his desire known, unsettled her.

Bram hesitated, his lips pressed to her wrist, then he shook his head. "I'm not looking for a new woman these days, Lucy. Right now, all I want is you. And tonight I mean to show you just how much."

The sensual threat nearly made her gasp with anticipation. Her knees trembled, and desperately she locked her legs to stay upright. Lucy watched him leap from the boat, then offer her his hand. She didn't know if she could touch him after he'd said such a thing. She was beginning to realize that this wasn't just a lark for Bram. He wasn't just teasing to make her forget about a fling. He wasn't merely flirting to ease her transition at turning forty. He wasn't just in search of a quick and easy sexual adventure.

He really did want her. Bram Giles, lover in hot demand, bachelor in every sense of the word, wanted her. Not just as a conquest, not just because she was handy and desperate. He wanted *her,* as an individual woman. As a woman he found sexually attractive.

"Give me your hand, Lucy."

She looked at him, saw the implacable command in his eyes, the erotic promise. She felt helpless against him and couldn't resist. She reached out to him. *A sexual fling with Bram Giles.*

Talk about shooting for the moon!

They'd taken no more than five steps up the cement walkway when two women, scantily covered in string bikinis, left the shop and started down the walk toward them. The women looked to be in their late twenties, perfectly toned and perfectly tanned, their hair Barbie doll long and just as blond. One of them carried a six-pack of beer, the other a brown paper bag filled with a variety of chips.

They stopped talking when they saw Bram. Even their body language changed, from casual movement to seductive fluidity. They no longer walked, they swayed.

Trying to be inconspicuous, Lucy released Bram's hand. She knew what was about to happen, what always happened when women caught sight of Bram. They'd flirt and simper and strike up a conversation. She didn't want to be in the middle of it when it happened. At nearly forty, she was feeling every single year of her age and didn't care to stand side by side with model look-alikes.

The problem was, though she released him, Bram held on. And he ignored the women, managing to nod politely while not quite looking at them. He dragged Lucy along reluctantly in his wake, and despite herself she snickered when the women frowned at her. "Now you've confused them."

Bram lifted a brow at her. "Hmm? What was that?"

Stunned, Lucy realized he really hadn't paid any attention to the women. She indicated them with a toss of her head. "You missed your newest fan club."

Bram glanced over his shoulder toward the women, then smiled. "Sorry. I was thinking about something else."

"Really?" She found it a little incredible that he had missed the women's attention altogether.

Bram gave her a crooked smile. "Tonight. I was thinking about tonight and how long I've waited and how damn good I know it's going to be."

Lucy only had time to gasp before they stepped into the small grocery shop and icy cold air blasted them from a struggling window air conditioner. Bram tugged her toward the back aisle where the meat was kept. She moved along like a zombie, caught in a sensual trance.

"Bram." She wrapped her arms around herself, trying to contain her heat. "You really were thinking about me?"

As he examined a package of steaks, Bram said idly, "Yeah. You. Naked." He glanced at her. "I'm obsessed."

Heat flooded over her, counteracting the too-cold artificial air. Lucy quickly looked around, but no one was listening. There were only two other people in the store besides the salesclerk, and they were in the farthest corner contemplating a variety of fishing lures.

"Bram," she chastised, unwilling to even consider what he might think if he saw her totally unclothed. She was almost forty. She'd had two kids. And she had no spare time to invest in working out, as he did.

Bram drew his attention away from the steaks, took in her flustered expression, and grinned. His large hand curled around the nape of her neck, and he drew her close. Against her lips he murmured, "I can't wait to see all of you, honey. I expect it'll take me a good long time to look my fill, so you might as well start preparing for it."

Lucy was going to tell him to hush, but he kissed her. Not a killer kiss like earlier, just a nice, soft pressing of his mouth, so warm, so gentle. She leaned into his chest and returned the kiss, wanting so much more.

Bram stroked her cheek and smiled at her. "Damn, I shouldn't start this here."

"No, you shouldn't," she managed to say with less than realistic conviction.

"The cold made your nipples hard," he informed her in a whisper, and bold as you please, he dragged one knuckle over her left breast, teasing the taut tip.

Lucy's breath caught, the touch was so electric. She felt the sweet, aching pull of desire everywhere, but especially between her thighs. She started to turn away, and Bram caught her shoulder. "No, don't abandon me. I've got a boner and it's just a little noticeable."

She glanced down and then quickly closed her eyes. *Little* was not an apt part of the description.

Bram grinned at her. "I'll stay behind you."

Lucy started to nod, not seeing any other recourse, but he just had to go and breathe real close to her ear, "It's a favorite position of mine anyway."

She turned and stalked away, figuring he could either follow her or not. If she'd stood there one second longer, the look on her face would have given her away and everyone in the store and outside would have known what she had on her mind.

When she reached the counter, Bram's warm breath touched her nape, assuring her he had indeed followed. When she got him home . . .

She drew up short on that thought, uncertain exactly how to proceed. And equally uncertain as to what he'd expect.

Bram reached around her, putting not only the steaks on the countertop but two large baking potatoes and two ears of corn as well. Where he'd snagged them she didn't know, and she wasn't about to ask him. It'd be just her luck that her voice wouldn't work and she'd squeak like a ninny.

Then she *did* squeak, when Bram leaned into her and she felt the full hard length of him against her bottom. He pointed to a T-shirt hanging on the wall and said, "An extra large, please."

The shirt read: WET AND WILD and included a logo from a popular brand of skis. It was also long enough to cover his fly. Lucy sighed in relief. Out of sight, *not quite out of mind,* but at least she ought to be able to stop staring.

The two women they'd passed on the way in were sitting on the edge of the dock when they walked back out. Lucy knew they were waiting and almost resented them, but when she glanced at Bram she couldn't blame them. She'd have waited for another peek, too.

"A few years ago," Bram whispered to her, keeping her close with one arm around her shoulders while he held the bag with his free hand, "I knew a woman who looked just like the one on the right."

Startled, Lucy asked, "Is that maybe her?"

"No, but the similarity is uncanny."

Feeling a tad snippy, Lucy said, "She was rather memorable, I gather?"

"Yeah, she was." Bram led her around another couple coming up the walk, then again steered them toward the boat. "She'd been coming to the gym for about a month before I said anything to her. As soon as I did speak to her, she told me she and her boyfriend had just broken up and she invited me over."

"And of course you just had to go."

Bram shrugged. "You and the kids had just taken off for vacation. I didn't have anything more exciting to do, so yes, I went."

They had reached the dock, and both of the women turned, smiling at Bram. They didn't seem the least put off that he was with another woman, Lucy noted, and she wanted to push them both into the water for discounting her so completely.

Instead she smiled and said, "Hi."

They ignored her.

Bram ignored them.

It was small consolation to watch their faces fall as Bram gave Lucy all his attention. Exhibiting true gentlemanly tendencies, he helped her into the boat, then handed her the bag. Before he stepped in himself he untied the rope from the grommet. One of the women asked, "Want me to give you a push?"

Distracted, Bram glanced at her as he sat behind the wheel and said, "No thanks. I've got it." Using one long arm, he pushed the boat out and away from the dock, then started the engine and put it in reverse.

Lucy waited until they were well away from the gas docks to say, "OK, so what was so memorable about her?"

Bram glanced at Lucy. "I'll tell you when we reach the house."

"Tell me now."

"Can't." He shoved at the throttle and the boat leaped forward, the engine roaring. "It's tough to talk over the engine," he yelled.

Lucy turned away from him. She hadn't really wanted to know anyway. Thinking of Bram making love to a woman with a perfect body would only disturb her. She wanted to think about him having sex with her instead.

Unable to resist, she turned to watch him as he steered the boat, cutting through the waves with barely a bounce. Tonight, she thought, she'd get to find out what all the talk was about.

She only hoped Bram wouldn't leave disappointed.

"Are you getting hungry?" Bram asked her, watching her face as they carried the few groceries in to the L-shaped dining and kitchen area.

He saw Lucy's shoulders stiffen just a bit, and she said, "I can eat whenever you're ready."

"But you're not overly hungry now?" Bram kept one eye on her while he put the corn and steaks in the refrigerator. She was aroused, bless her heart, not interested in food, but unwilling to be aggressive enough to initiate things. He'd get her over her shyness soon enough.

Lucy kept busy folding and refolding the grocery bag before finally putting it away in a drawer. She had her back to him, but he didn't need to see her face to know what she was feeling. He felt it too, in spades.

"No," she said, "I'm not very hungry."

"Good." Bram closed the refrigerator and approached her before she could turn. He caged her in by flattening his hands on the counter at either side of her hips. He pressed into her bottom and nuzzled her neck. "That woman I told you was somewhat memorable?"

"Yeah, so? What about her?"

Her disgruntled tone tickled him, and he smiled against the nape of her neck, then whispered, "She wanted me to spank her."

Lucy drew tight, her head lifted to attention. *"What?"*

She sounded just like a schoolmarm, scandalized but at the same time entranced. Bram continued to nuzzle against her. "Yeah, she was a little kinky. Sort of took me by surprise, bringing it up so fast and all. I mean, it'd been our first time together."

"Did you . . . that is . . ." She shifted, and her fingers moved nervously on the countertop in front of her.

"Did I oblige her?"

Lucy nodded.

"I always oblige," he rumbled softly. "When I'm with a woman, I want her to be happy. And I insist she leave satisfied. If a red bottom will do that for her, hey, I can handle it." Keeping the laughter out of his tone was difficult. Lucy was downright rigid with indignation.

Very lightly, he bit her neck, right where her pulse was suddenly rioting. "What about you, sweetheart? You have any kinky fantasies?"

"I don't want to be spanked, if that's what you're asking!"

147

Bram laughed. "I wasn't that into it myself." He couldn't stop kissing her, touching her. "And I'd never ask you to do anything that made you uncomfortable, so I don't want you worrying about that, all right? But most people have something they like to fantasize about, something a little wicked that turns them on."

"Do you?"

"Absolutely." And most of his fantasies centered around her. "I just want you to know you can tell me anything, ask me anything. Okay?"

Again she shifted, those nervous little movements that told him so much. He wanted to squeeze her close, crush her to his heart. Instead he waited.

"Did you date that woman much?"

"A date implies time out somewhere, so no. I had sex with her off and on for about a month." Bram trailed the fingertips of his right hand up her arm to her bare shoulder. He saw goose bumps rise in his path. "Sex is a hollow thing when it's between strangers. For a while, when you're young and stupid, that can seem exciting. It can seem like enough. But the older I get, the more I want . . . more."

Idly, Lucy turned her head to rub her cheek against the back of his hand where it rested on her shoulder. The gesture was tender, loving, and his heart twisted.

"Between David and me," she whispered, "things got really . . . stale. I guess we'd known each other too long, gotten too comfortable. Doing anything risqué or different seemed silly. Whenever I tried spicing things up, I ended up feeling foolish."

Struggling not to curse, Bram said only, "David was the fool."

She shook her head. "I don't know. Everything that went wrong wasn't his fault. I'm to blame, too. I guess we'd just known each other too long to change things from mundane to erotic." She gave a self-conscious laugh and added, "The last few years, before I filed for divorce, David had totally lost interest. Sex was something that happened more out of boredom for him than out of love or lust. He didn't want to cuddle, or hold me, or kiss me. He'd say, *'Are we screwing tonight or what?'* And I . . . I just couldn't."

Talking about her with David was killing Bram on several levels. He hated the thought of her with another man, even her husband, and beyond that, he hated knowing how frustrated she must have been, emotionally and especially physically. She was the very essence of feminine sexuality, but all her innate responses had been stifled rather than encouraged.

By word and movement and look, Lucy was a very sensual woman. She deserved to have all her needs met, in any and every way. He wanted to ignite her basic nature, enflame her body. He wanted everything she had to give a man.

"I think," he breathed into her ear, "that we should work on stage one of this week."

On alert, she asked, "Stage one?"

"Yeah." His heart pounded and his temperature rose. "That's the part where I get to take your shirt off you and kiss your pretty breasts and maybe make you half as nuts as I am."

"Right . . . right now?"

"Hell yes. I don't think I can wait much longer." Bram coasted his fingertips back down her arm, over her abdomen, and lower, to fondle her belly. She was soft, giving, and he wanted to tease her, to drag out the fun. Bram angled his fingers upward and just barely touched the underside of her left breast. "I want to move slowly, for both of us. I've wanted you too long to be able to do everything I want to do to you if I get you completely naked. And you're still a little hesitant about things, aren't you?"

"It feels . . . weird, being with you." She rushed to clarify that, in case he'd misunderstood. "I mean, we've been practically related for a long time."

Bram cupped her breast in his palm and felt her heartbeat quicken. Her nipple was elongated, puckered tight, showing her arousal. "Does this feel familial?" he asked, groaning just a bit with the voluptuousness of the moment. "Christ, Lucy, I've wanted to do this forever."

"Bram . . ." Her head tipped back to his shoulder and she shuddered delicately.

Bram caught her nipple and tugged the tiniest bit, rolling the swollen tip, plucking at it.

"Oh, God." Her back arched, her legs stiffened.

She panted, thrilling Bram with the measure of her response. Softly, wonderingly, he whispered, "You need this almost as much as I do, don't you, baby?" Using his left hand, he again stroked her belly, then lower. The heat of her through her shorts scorched him. The soft, worn denim did nothing to disguise her sex. Bram could feel the swollen, delicate folds and the soft tender flesh between.

He slowed, moving deliberately, carefully. He searched her through the denim while he continued to torment and ply her nipple.

"I want to feel your naked flesh," he groaned, "but I'm so goddamned close to the edge, one touch of you and I'd explode myself."

While he watched, fascinated and intensely proud, Lucy's body flushed with the first wave of a building climax. Her legs trembled and parted more, and Bram accepted her invitation, spurred on by her gasping breaths, the heaving of her chest. "Move with my fingers, sweetheart," he instructed, and when she did, when her hips lifted into his touch, he growled, "That's it."

She reached back and her nails dug into his naked thighs. Bram hissed out his pleasure, knowing she was close and it had been so easy. He released her breast to delve into her halter, shoving it down as he did so. It caught and held beneath the weight of her heavy breasts. Looking over her shoulder, Bram could see her large, darkly flushed nipples, pulled tight with desire.

His vision blurred with heat, his cock flexing in reaction to the sight of her. He had to grit his teeth to hold himself in check, to keep from sitting her on the counter and removing her shorts. He wanted to feel her wetness, wanted to taste her, to know every part of her.

With a harsh groan, he opened his mouth on her throat at the same time that his rough fingertips found and captured the naked, sensitized tips of her breasts. From one to the other, he teased them, pinching just hard enough to take her to the edge, then rolling them softly, gently, soothing her so that the next rough touch would be that much more acute. And all the while his hand between her legs kept up a pressing rhythm, pushing her and pushing her until suddenly she cried out, and the sound was one of the most beautiful he'd ever heard.

His balls tightened in response to the quickening of her flesh and he had to struggle not to come with her. It was a close thing. Though he hadn't made that kind of faux pas since he was a kid, now it was nearly impossible to contain the tide of emotion and sexual sensation brought on by her orgasm.

Lucy held herself back, biting her lip, keeping herself as still as possible while the climax rolled through her. Bram knew it, but for now it was okay; for now he'd let her get away with it. After all, they were in a kitchen and this was their first sexual experience together.

Later, when he had her naked in bed, he'd get her to let loose completely. He wouldn't allow any timidity then.

Lucy gulped for air, slumping against him. Her hands dropped away from his thighs, leaving behind small, stinging half-moons from her nails. Bram continued to lightly stroke her, knowing that she was now ultrasensitive and anything more than the most delicate touch would be too much. But letting her go completely was impossible.

"You're so wet," he whispered, and his voice shook as much as his hands. "I can feel how wet you are even through your shorts."

"Bram."

"Hmmm?" She sounded mortified and amazed, and it amused him. He nuzzled her throat, kissing, tasting her skin. He wanted to drown himself in her.

Her swallow was audible, a sign of nervousness. "I . . . I think I'm a little embarrassed."

"I think you're amazing." He kissed her ear. "And sexy." He hugged her tight, rocking her. "And I want more. A whole lot more." Then: "Why are you embarrassed?"

Very slowly, she straightened up and removed her weight from him; her legs were shaky, but he didn't force the issue. He just stood behind her, there for support if she wanted it.

With trembling hands, she pulled her halter back into place. Bram wanted to protest; he loved looking at her breasts and he wanted her to face him, to let him get his fill of looking. He wanted to see her nipples and kiss them and suck them. He wanted to hear her moan as he drew off her, licking and tasting until she couldn't bear it and neither could he.

For years now he'd imagined what she'd look like, whether her nipples were mauve or pink or brown. Were they large or small? Seeing her breasts had been a fragment of a fantasy, pushing him closer and closer to his ultimate goal.

Lucy shook her head. "I'm standing here," she whispered, "in the middle of the kitchen of all places and half-naked and there you are, fully dressed and—"

Bram smiled at her back. "I can drop my shorts if you want."

She didn't refuse him. Instead she warily turned to face him, and her gaze was all over him, but especially on his crotch. He throbbed beneath her intense scrutiny. She might as well have touched him, her look was so carnal, making him swell even more until he hurt with the need for release.

With a deep breath, she said, "Would you? Really? I mean, it wouldn't embarrass you?"

Bram reached for the snap at his waistband, and she caught his hands. Laughing a little in excitement and disbelief, she said, "I think I need to sit down for this."

Heated excitement coursed through Bram. He could barely draw a deep breath, but he mustered up the strength to catch her hand and drag her from the kitchen.

When he headed for the front room, she balked. "Bram? Aren't we going to the bedroom?"

"Not yet." His voice was a rasp, barely discernible, raw with need. "Let's get through stage two first, and if we both survive that we'll eventually make it to the bedroom before the day is through."

Her own voice low with need, Lucy said, "Stage two?"

Bram reached the leather couch that faced the sliding patio doors and pulled Lucy down into the plush cream-colored cushions with him. He kissed her hungrily, devouring her, and to his immense pleasure, she kissed him back. It wasn't easy, but Bram managed to lift his mouth away from hers. "This," he growled, "is where you make me come. And God knows, honey, I need it."

He needed it so badly, in fact, that his body was already pulsing with the expectation of release, like the first stages of orgasm.

Lucy stared down at his lap, her beautiful blue eyes slumberous, her lips slightly parted and swollen. And with a type of incredible feminine torture, she licked her lips.

Bram groaned. He pulled open the snap to his shorts, now dried stiff from his dip in the lake. Carefully, because he was as hard as he could possibly be, he eased down his zipper and guided her small hand inside. His breath caught and held in his chest, making him dizzy.

"Oh my."

There was so much heightened pleasure in her words, such gentle sensuality in the way her soft hand curled around him, that Bram knew he was a goner right there and then.

4

Lucy was awed by the size of him. She'd heard stories, of course, but had discounted them as typical male exaggeration. Even after feeling him through his jeans shorts earlier, she hadn't been prepared for the actuality.

Her hand barely circled him, her fingers not quite touching together. Sharp awareness blossomed in her belly, spreading outward until she wasn't sure she could breathe. As a mature woman, she knew size didn't matter. But maturity had nothing to do with fantasies and eroticism. His erect flesh was so hot, throbbing with a life of its own.

Using her thumb, she tested the velvety texture from his hair-roughened testicles, now drawn tight, up to the smooth, broad tip and heard him curse very low.

"Bram?"

His head was pressed back against the couch, his eyes squeezed shut, his jaw locked. He looked like a man in pain or incredible pleasure. The muscles in his arms rippled and bunched as his hands curled into hard fists at his sides. "Squeeze me," he muttered through his teeth. *"Hard."*

Fascinated by him, by his totally open response to her touch, she did as he insisted. Never had David looked this turned on, this turbulent. Yet Bram didn't seem to care that he was partially exposed to her, sprawled out on a couch, at her mercy. He literally writhed from her attentions.

When her fingers gripped him tighter, he groaned low, then gave a rough laugh. "Christ, having your hand on me is a dream I never thought would come true."

He gasped brokenly as she slowly stroked down his length, then back up again. He caught her wrist. Molten hot and fiercely direct, his eyes opened and captured hers.

"Like this, baby," he instructed, guiding her hand to the base of his shaft, then all the way back to the very tip until her thumb brushed over the end and he froze from the pleasure of it.

Lucy watched his face, as enthralled with his expressions as she was with his nudity and his instruction. She'd fumbled around with David for years, trying to learn what pleased him, embarrassed when she hadn't succeeded. For Bram, it seemed no matter what she did, he enjoyed it. And he was more than willing to teach her, without hesitation, without reserve. His sheer lack of inhibition was a turn-on.

Though the flexing erection she held was fascinating, she couldn't take her gaze off his face.

"What is it?" he asked, his eyes sensually heavy, his high cheekbones slashed with aroused color. "Tell me, Lucy. Anything you want."

She licked her lips, working up her nerve. But the whole point of coming to the summer house had been to indulge her every fantasy, to rid herself of the social inhibitions caused by being with people she associated with on a daily basis. She would not turn coward now.

She cleared her throat. "Will you . . . will you take off your shirt so I can look at you?"

Without a word he grabbed the hem of the T-shirt in his fists and yanked it over his head. The shirt got tossed to the other side of the couch, then Bram spread his arms out along the back of the couch and affected a relaxed pose. His small brown nipples were erect points visible through his sweat-dampened chest hair. His arms were long, roped with muscle, and tufts of lighter, softer hair shone in his armpits. With his lids lowered and his body rigid, he offered himself up to her.

Lucy didn't want to let go of his erection, so she shifted slightly until she could comfortably hold him in her right hand, and with her left she explored his chest. Having Bram watch her, seeing the pleasure in his eyes, made the whole experience more erotic.

"I want to kiss you again."

Bram smiled. "Any time, any place."

Lucy hooked her left arm around his neck and took his mouth. He didn't control the kiss, but he did gently guide her, tipping his head slightly so that their mouths completely meshed, urging her tongue into his mouth by teasing it with his own. He nibbled on her bottom lip until she did the same to him, then he gave a rough sound of pleasure, like a jungle cat purring.

Incredibly, his penis grew harder, longer, in her fist.

Having access to Bram's body was a sensual feast. His skin felt like heated silk, taut over muscles and bones and sinew. She opened her mouth on his throat and relished the taste of him, the saltiness of his skin. Burrowing lower, she kissed his chest and nuzzled her nose through the soft chest hair, drinking in his scent. When she found his small nipples she licked, and felt his reaction in the flex of his body and the way he gasped.

Lifting her head, Lucy asked, "You like that?"

Bram stroked her hair. "Lucy," he said tenderly, smiling. "You have my cock in your hand, your mouth on my body. Of course I like it."

She felt color rush to her cheeks, but she ignored it. "I meant this"—she licked his nipple again—"specifically."

His nostrils flared. "Any place you want to put that sweet little tongue is fine by me, but yeah, I suppose it feels close to the same for me as it does for you."

And before she could recover from that discovery, he asked, "Why don't you lose your top, too?" His gaze darkened. "Then I can return the favor."

Lucy froze at just the thought. She didn't want him looking at her thirty-nine-year-old body with all the flaws that came with age and pregnancy and nursing. He would compare her to the other women he'd been with, and she couldn't bear that.

Refusing to lose control of the situation, she summoned up a teasing note and said, "Oh no you don't. You told me we'd do stage two, and me being topless isn't part of it."

"You being topless should be part of everything." He caught the hand she had wrapped around his penis and started her stroking again. His voice dropped an octave, husky and warm. "Cooking breakfast, doing laundry . . . pleasuring me. Everything could be enhanced if I could see your breasts."

Lucy laughed at him. "Not yet. Let me concentrate on what I'm doing."

With his unshakable gaze locked on hers, he asked, "Do you want to see me come?"

Intrigued by the prospect, Lucy looked at his erection and saw a drop of fluid beading on the tip. "Yes." She felt her own body growing damp again in gathering excitement. "I've never . . . you know. Watched that before."

"But you're curious?" He gasped as she again smoothed her thumb over the tip, spreading the drop of semen around and around. His legs shifted, his heels pressing into the hardwood floor.

Leaning down, Lucy kissed his lower chest. She took little nibbling pecks down his lightly furred abdomen. "Yes. Very curious." His incredible scent was stronger this close to his sex, and it drew her. His chest heaved and his back arched slightly. "I wanted to do things this week," she admitted, "that I've never done before. I wanted to be as wild, as improper and earthy, as any young liberated woman might be."

"Yeah."

Lucy might have smiled at Bram's nearly incoherent agreement— or was it encouragement? She wasn't sure. But she didn't smile because she, too, was caught up in the carnality of it.

Her inky black hair was spread out over his hard belly, and his erection throbbed and pulsed and Lucy knew that this, at least, was one thing she could do, one desire she could satisfy. Squeezing him a little tighter in warning, she kissed just above where her fingers held him, awed by the velvety texture of his shaft, feeling his pulse beat riot against her lips. She circled the head of his penis with small damp kisses, letting her hair tickle him as she did so. He smelled nice, felt nice, and she flattened her tongue over the head of his penis and tasted him.

Bram nearly shot off the couch.

Suddenly his hands were in her hair, holding her, guiding her back while he murmured words of pleasure, words of need and pleading. Lucy licked him again, and again, until Bram was making incoherent sounds of pleasure, his body vibrating, the air charged around them. She opened her mouth and let him in.

He was so large, it wasn't easy, and it turned her on so much, made her so excited and wild to taste him, to know that he was ready to explode. She couldn't take him very deep, just the head. So she concentrated on working on what she could get into her mouth, using her hands to tease the rest of him.

Bram's fingers tightened suddenly in her hair and he groaned roughly. *"Lucy . . ."*

Her tongue swirled, softly, gently, and then she sucked.

Again, his reaction was immediate. "Stop, Lucy. I can't hold back. Baby, *stop.*"

Instead she struggled to hold on to him, to take as much of him as she could, and as if accepting her decision, Bram stroked her nape, curled his fingers around her head—and he came with a shout that echoed through the summer house.

His hips lifted again and again, his big body trembled and shuddered, and finally after a long time he quieted, only his strenuous breaths reverberating in the air. Lucy lazily licked him, pleased with herself and smiling at the way his body continued to flinch with pleasure.

Bram curled himself around her, hauled her up to his lap, and pressed his face into her shoulder. His arms, his whole body, were still shaking.

Stage two, Lucy thought with a smile, *successfully completed.*

Bram watched Lucy as she sliced into her steak. They were both nearly done eating, and while the food tasted good, looking at Lucy was better. There'd been a comfortable silence between them since that incredible episode on the couch, but a secret little smile kept playing around her sexy mouth. She liked it that she'd made him lose control.

Hell, he liked it, too.

Now he wanted more. He wanted her naked. He wanted her to offer herself to him in the same way he'd given her free reign of his body.

He still could barely believe what she'd done. It wasn't the first blow job he'd ever gotten, but it was by far the most emotionally devastating. Having Lucy's mouth on him guaranteed to reside at the top of his list of most erotic and satisfying encounters ever.

"Worked up an appetite, didn't you?"

With her mouth full, she looked at him and promptly choked. Bram reached across the table and patted her on the back until the wheezing turned into laughter. She looked so damn proud of herself that he couldn't stop smiling, either.

A rose blush colored her cheeks, enhanced by the early-evening sunlight filtering through the trees to the deck. This time of day, the deck was more shaded than otherwise, making it comfortable to eat outside. An occasional boater went past, laughter from the vacationers drifting up the hillside, mingling with the chirping birds and the droning insects.

At first, Bram hadn't wanted to leave the couch. With his legs like rubber and his heart still pounding, he wasn't sure he was even able to leave the couch. And he'd been more than willing to move right into stage three—once he'd regained his strength.

But she'd slipped away from his hold, giving him no alternative but to follow her.

The yard work was now done and he'd brought down his few bags from the car, unpacking them into the same dresser Lucy had used. Whether or not she'd noticed the significance of that, Bram wasn't sure. But she hadn't said anything about it, so neither had he.

While she put fresh linens on the bed, he'd gone for another swim. At the moment, he felt lazy and relaxed and warm with satisfaction.

Lust was just below the surface, waiting for a look, a smile, from her that told him she was ready to go on to the next step. And even if she didn't make a gesture, in a few more hours the sun would set, and he'd already told her what he planned.

They had the whole night ahead of them.

Before dinner, they'd taken turns showering, and now Lucy wore a soft pale green cotton sundress. She'd also combed her hair at some point, and it hung in a silky fall to her shoulders. He loved her hair and didn't give a rat's ass if she colored her silver streaks or not. Either way, her hair still felt the same, and it was still a part of Lucy.

He'd agreed to grill the steaks while Lucy prepared the potatoes, after she'd informed him that she was, at last, famished. It was damn tough not to touch her, not to be as familiar as he now felt he could be. But even though Lucy kept smiling and looking secretly happy, she had DO NOT TOUCH signs plastered all over herself, warning him from pushing too fast.

Lucy glanced up and shook her head at him. "Stop that."

He smiled. He'd been smiling nonstop since she'd had her orgasm in the kitchen. He couldn't recall ever being so happy before.

He took a leisurely drink of his soda before asking, "What?"

"Staring at me. You're making me feel . . ." She hesitated, licked her lips, then shrugged. "Nervous."

"You were going to say 'naked,' weren't you?" He loved teasing her. He loved loving her. "I make you feel naked, when I watch you. Isn't that right?"

Primly she replied, "I don't want to put any ideas into your head." A bird flew close, then landed on the railing to watch them. Lucy tossed a piece of bread to it, and the blue jay snatched it up and again took flight.

Laughing out loud, Bram told her, "Too late, sweetheart. I've had ideas about you for a long, long time!"

"You did not." It was too absurd to be true.

"Did, too. You're beautiful and I can't help myself."

Carefully, with emphasized precision, she laid her fork beside her plate. "Do you mean that, Bram?"

"Cross my heart. You, sweetheart, replaced all my adolescent fantasies, which I gotta tell you were pretty goddamned vivid."

"Even while David and I were married?"

Realizing the seriousness of her tone, Bram, too, pushed aside his food. He felt mellow and semisated after his release and was more than willing to do some of the talking he knew needed to be done. "You're gorgeous, Lucy. Sexy. Smart and caring. Of course I had ideas about you. I'm just a man, susceptible to the same lusty thoughts as any other guy. I tried real hard not to let them show, though."

She seemed to be considering that, then said, "I'm almost forty."

"I know." He shrugged one shoulder. "I'm already forty-one. So?"

"I'm not a gorgeous forty. I'm . . . lumpy."

Bobbing his eyebrows at her breasts, he said, "Nice lumps."

"That's not what I meant."

Bram sighed. "You're talking normal wear and tear, honey. Trust me, I like your body just fine. More than fine. Hell, I *lust* for your body in a big way. Any man who looks at you would feel the same."

Lucy shook her head. "I used to be attractive, I know. It's what drew David in the first place. But now . . . I'm tired-looking and my waistline is shot and I'm . . . average at best."

Bram left his seat across the patio table to settle at her side. He reached for her hands and ignored her reserved attempts to pull away. "Do you know what I feel when I look at you?"

Blue eyes crystal clear and wide with curiosity, she shook her head.

Bram kissed her quickly, softly. "Whenever you're around me, my stomach gets all jumpy, just like it used to when I was fifteen and getting laid seemed about the most important goal in the world. A girl would give me that certain look and I'd get the inside jitters just thinking about what I was going to do. *You* give me the jitters still."

He touched his open palm over her head, delighting in the feel of her baby fine hair heated by the sun and teased by the hot breeze. "You toss back your hair and I feel it like a punch in the gut. You laugh and I get hard. When it's cold outside and your nipples get puckered, I shake like a nervous virgin."

She laughed at him, shyly.

"And babe, there's no two ways about it. You have always had a world-class ass. When you walk down the street, it doesn't matter if you're wearing a skirt or jeans or baggy slacks, male heads turn."

Her mouth struggled with a smile and lost. "Bram," she said in admonishment.

"Lucy," he teased right back. "You might not think you're beautiful, but my gonads strongly disagree."

Lucy stared at their clasped hands rather than at his face. "I look a lot different without my clothes than I do with them on. Clothes hide a lot of flaws, you know."

He curled his hand around the nape of her neck. "When I have you laid out naked before me, you can bet it won't be flaws I'm looking at."

The smile changed to an outright laugh. "Maybe. But you'll see them all the same."

"Lucy, no man in his right mind expects a woman to be perfect, because men aren't perfect, either."

She thrilled him when she said, "You are."

Bram bit back a grin of sheer joy and remarked teasingly, "Want me to get naked and you can check to see for sure? It'd probably take a real close examination, but I'm sure you could locate a few imperfections."

"Yes. I'd like that."

"Dirty pool, Lucy!" He could feel her words stirring him, making his muscles tighten anew. "And I'll tell you right now, if you give me another boner you're going to have to take care of it."

She trailed one fingertip over his jaw. "I wouldn't mind."

He groaned at the husky way she said it. "Now stop that, woman. The next time we get something going—which, if you have any mercy at all will be real soon—it'll be the full mile, and we'll both be naked."

Lucy looked out over the lake, at the way the slowly setting sun turned the water different colors. She said abruptly, "I thought about getting a boob job."

Startled, Bram stared at her. "Good God! Whatever for?"

She looked down at her chest with a wry expression. "Pregnancy and nursing is hard on a woman."

Bram cupped both breasts in his hands. Leaning down to see her face, not letting her shy away from him, he said, "You're soft and sexy, just the way a woman should be. You sure as hell don't need anything plastic added."

"I'm not . . . pert, anymore."

Holding her gaze, Bram reached around her and with casual ease lowered the straps of her sundress. Moving slowly so that she could protest if she chose to, he let the material drop to her elbows, then pulled it away from her breasts and down to her waist.

Dappled sunshine danced across her pale skin, moved by the slight breeze rustling through the tree leaves and stirring the humid air. Sitting there, stiff and uncertain, her backbone straight, Lucy was the most breathtaking sight he'd ever encountered. Bram couldn't take his eyes off her.

"Oh, babe. Anything you don't have you don't need. I swear."

Her breasts rested softly against her body, still full but, as she'd said, no longer so firm. There were a few faint lines, stretch marks from when she had filled with milk to nurse the kids. Bram traced one faded line with his pinkie fingertip, all the way to her nipple. Her nipples had been plump and soft, but now they beaded, drawing into points.

Bram swallowed hard, nearly strangling on emotion, and lowered his head to close his mouth very softly around her. Her nipple was sweet, and he stroked her with his tongue, tugged gently with his lips.

Lucy caught her breath. Her hands settled in his hair, petting him, pulling him closer as her head tipped back. With a low moan she said, "Bram, that feels so good."

"Mmm. I'm enjoying it just as much."

Lucy shook her head, breathless, heated. "No way."

Bram looked at her wet nipple, then blew gently on it and watched her shiver. She was so responsive. Touching her was an incredible pleasure. "When you were kissing me on the couch," he said, "did you enjoy it?"

Her breasts shimmered with her uneven breaths. "Oh yes."

"Because it made you feel good, too?"

She blushed a little but admitted, "Just seeing you like that . . . It made me hot to see you getting so hot." She swallowed hard. "It was incredible."

"Yes." Her words burned into him. "Exciting you excites me. And you are excited, aren't you, Lucy?"

She nodded.

"And wet?"

Lucy squirmed just a little, then shrugged.

"Don't ever lie to me, sweetheart. I know you're wet." He stroked her nipple, squeezed a tiny bit. "Admit it to me."

Her lips parted. *"Yes."*

"You want my fingers on you again? In you this time? Nice and tight?" When she nodded, he ordered abruptly, shaking with his own lust, "Straddle the bench."

He helped her, lifting her right leg up and over so it rested on the other side of the bench. Teasing her and himself, Bram lightly dragged both hands up her legs, from her knees to her groin. The skirt of her sundress rose with the movement of his hands. Bram watched her breasts as he slowly, so very slowly, brought his fingers to the juncture of her thighs, to the wet, swollen lips he could feel even through her underwear.

She jerked, her eyes nearly closing.

Bram pressed a warm kiss to her open mouth. "Your panties are soaked," he whispered.

She reached for him, but he caught her arms and brought them behind her back. "Brace your hands behind you, babe. C'mon, trust me."

Tentatively she did as he asked. The position thrust her breasts out and made her legs sprawl more widely. Bram wanted to get the damn dress all the way off her, but her expression was a mix of anticipation, excitement, uncertainty.

He slipped his fingers beneath the leg band of her panties and encountered slick flesh, swollen and ripe. His voice a rasp, he said,

"I want to see how tight you are." And he pushed his middle finger into her all the way, not thrusting hard, but not slowing down until he was as deep as he could be. Her inner muscles clamped down hard on him; Lucy's hips lifted on a gasp.

"Shhh. Easy now." She was snug on his finger and Bram broke out in a fresh sweat just thinking of how she'd feel on his thick cock, how she'd squeeze him, how damn tight she'd hold him.

He couldn't stand it. "Lucy, honey." He removed his hand and lowered her skirt. Her eyes shot open, alarmed, but Bram stood and lifted her. "I can't wait. I need you now. Tell me," he insisted, holding her to his chest with trembling arms. *"Tell me you're ready."*

"Yes."

Bram nearly went through the patio doors, he was in such a rush. His earlier release might not have happened, his control was so shaky.

And then he was finally in the bedroom. He dropped onto the bed with Lucy and her hands started exploring him and Bram decided it didn't matter. It would be okay.

It had to be okay—because he couldn't bear to be without her anymore.

Lucy felt the tight grip of Bram's fingers around her wrists and then she was on her back with him over her. He kissed her naked breasts, her midriff. His mouth was open, biting gently, consuming. "Let me see you, Lucy, all of you," he groaned.

At that moment, modesty had no place. She felt only a slight prickling of unease as she lay docile, allowing him to reach beneath her dress and tug off her panties. Bram came up to his knees, kneeling between her legs, and lifted the damp fabric to his face, rubbing her panties over his cheek, inhaling her scent, while he stared down at her body. His voice was so low and deep it wasn't recognizable.

"I can't believe this," he growled. "I have you beneath me, on a bed, hot and wet, and it's reality, not just fodder for dreams."

"Bram." She'd never been wanted like this, not even when she and David had been young and overflowing with sexual energy.

"Lift your hips."

She did, and the dress was whisked upward. They each struggled until it was over her head and thrown across the room with her underwear.

Bram froze, his eyes hot on her body, his hands hovering just over her thighs. He swallowed hard, his nostrils flaring. *"Christ."*

Very gently, almost with awe, he pressed her legs open. She'd never been exposed in such a way, literally put on display, but it was wonderful and she didn't worry about how soft or fleshy her thighs had become or that her stomach was no longer concave. The look on Bram's face more than reassured her.

His hands drifted over her pelvic bones, his fingers spread until they were tangling in her public hair. His lips parted on a deep breath. Using his thumbs, he spread her open, and she groaned, then cried out as he bent and covered her with his mouth.

Voracious, ruthless, he tasted her, delved and lapped and tormented with his tongue, taunted with his teeth. Lucy screamed as he drew her clitoris into his mouth and suckled. She couldn't hold still, couldn't hold back the orgasm that raged through her.

The pleasure was so intense, so startling, she nearly passed out from the throbbing waves of sensation.

When she finally got her heavy eyes to open again, Bram was standing beside the bed, breathtakingly naked and rolling on a condom. His body was sculpted of hard muscle and thick bones, his legs braced apart, his wide shoulders gleaming with sweat. There was a tightness to his expression, a stormy glitter to his eyes, that told her his control was a thing of the past.

Lucy moaned, seeing his long fingers roll the rubber up the length of his rigid erection. It was long and thick and throbbing, and something insidious expanded inside her; she didn't know if it was anticipation or fear. Staring at him, she said, "I don't know about this, Bram."

Evidently done with wooing her, he didn't give her a chance for second thoughts. He lifted her under her arms and straightened her out on the bed, moving her limp, nearly lifeless body just like he would a doll. Almost the second he laid her flat, he had two fingers pushed deep inside her, stroking. Her sensitized tissues jolted at the invasion, causing her body to shudder and flinch.

"Don't fight me, Lucy. Relax. You can take me." He ground out the words from between his teeth, sweat dotting his forehead, his temples. "It'll be so goddamned tight I'm liable to die, but I won't hurt you."

She had no reply to that and couldn't have spoken anyway, because Bram kissed her. His body covered hers and his mouth stole her breath and then she felt him at her opening and the burning pressure began.

Wriggling, she tried to adjust to his entrance. Bram caught her legs under her knees and lifted, opening her wide, alarming her to the point that she stiffened.

"No, Lucy. Relax, baby. Don't tense up on me." He panted out the words, every muscle on his body straining. And still he pressed on, coming into her by agonizingly slow degrees, continually driving forward, deeper and deeper. True to his word, for her there was no real pain, only the acute pleasure of being filled once again by a man.

But it was even more than that, because he wasn't just any man. He was Bram, so very special, so male, so overwhelming in every way.

He paused, his eyes squeezed shut. Lucy tentatively stroked his chest and neck, down to his nipples, where she flicked and teased them. His back arched and he pushed deeper still, causing her to gasp.

"That's enough, Bram." Her heart pounded so hard it rocked the mattress. If Bram heard her, he showed no sign of it. He didn't move, but he didn't pull out, either.

Lucy couldn't get a deep-enough breath. He really was too huge, she thought, almost panicked. "Bram . . ."

"Just a little more, baby." He opened his eyes and locked his heated gaze with her wary one. "A little more."

Gently, inexorably, he pressed. Their strenuous breathing filled the otherwise silent room. His chest heaved, his arms trembled. Dark color slashed his high cheekbones and his mouth looked hard and sensual. In a rumble, he urged, "Take all of me, Lucy. Tell me you want all of me."

She wanted to say yes, but she didn't think she could. Fantasizing about a man so large didn't even begin to touch on the reality. She tried to relax, tried to accept him, but she felt impaled, ready to break.

Moving her legs over his shoulders, Bram came down to one elbow, balancing himself. With his other hand, he smoothed her hair away from her face. He looked at her mouth and kissed her while he trailed his fingers to her breast and began tormenting her nipple with rough fingertips. Her muscles clamped around him in reaction, making them both moan.

She didn't think she could take any more, but he proved her wrong. Her body was burning, on fire, her breasts throbbing, her nipples painfully tight. And Bram kissed her gently as he reached between their bodies and stroked her swollen sex where she held him. Lucy caught her breath.

"That's it," he murmured, continuing to tease sensitive tissues before readjusting his hand and smoothing his thumb over her turgid clitoris. She jerked hard, crying out.

"No, Bram." Her voice was a whimper, a plea. She was too sensitive, and it felt like too much.

He continued the light touch, growling, *"Yes,"* and there was no way she could stop him. All she could do was accept him and try not to scream as sensation once again built within her.

The pleasure was too sharp, too much, making her squirm and inadvertently helping him to sink into her. Every place on her body was affected by him, her nipples rasped by his chest hair, her mouth caught under his, his erection more than filling her, his thumb driving her insane, and then, to her amazement, Lucy began to climax again. It wasn't your average, run-of-the-mill orgasm. Her body burned with feelings, her muscles all clenching hard so that she ached at the same time the pleasure overcame her.

Bram took swift advantage, pushing himself the rest of the way in so that she screamed after all, but with incredible enjoyment, not pain. He drove into her, his movement rhythmic, slick, deep and deeper. He threw his head back and arched hard into her as he groaned and Lucy managed to get her eyes open enough to watch him. It was wonderful. It was beautiful.

All because it was Bram.

The week went by in a blur. They made love in the lake, late at night, torturing each other with the necessity for quiet. Bram didn't make it easy on her. He seemed to take delight in making her scream, in driving her past the brink of a mere climax.

They made love on the deck in the hot sunshine, hurriedly because of the risk of being caught, which added to the thrill. Though at first she'd honestly believed he was too large, Bram showed her how to accept him in a dozen different ways—in the bed and on the kitchen counter. And on the couch.

He filled her up, indulging her every need, pampering her

every desire. He seemed to know her fantasies without her having to ask. And he never hesitated to share his own.

He convinced her to spend one entire day naked, and they never left the cabin. They barely left the bed. She felt drowned in sensual pleasure, but in emotion, too. It had been a lush, indulgent, sultry week.

Lucy felt a little sick with foreboding when the last day of the vacation rolled around.

Bram was sprawled on the deck in the sun, dozing after having just made love to her. He wore only a pair of dark cotton shorts and looked so beautiful, tears blurred her eyes. She'd slipped away from him, promising to return with drinks.

Holding one glass over his chest so that the icy sweat of the glass dripped on him, Lucy decided to face her demons. Bram jerked awake with a curse, saw her, and laughed. He took the glass, but his gaze was wicked as he said, "Paybacks are hell, sweetheart. You can't imagine the things I can do with an ice cube."

No, she thought, but she wanted to find out. "This is the last day of the vacation. When will you pay me back?"

Bram went still, causing her heart to do the same. Then he shrugged, deliberately nonchalant, though his eyes burned with intensity. "If I tell you," he asked quietly, "how can I take you by surprise?"

Lucy pulled up a patio chair beside him. Looking at her glass rather than at him, she said, "I think I've decided not to sell the summer house after all."

Bram watched her closely. "Oh?"

She wished he'd say more than that. He could have been a little more helpful with the situation, maybe given some clue to his thoughts. He was so damned open about everything else. "I . . . I thought, seeing as how we got along so well here—"

"Got along how?"

She couldn't read his expression, and it made her nervous. Lifting her chin, she said, "I didn't know sex like this even existed."

"And you want more?"

Her heart pounded hard, making it difficult to think. "Yes."

"We're in agreement on one thing, anyway."

"I'm serious here, Bram!" Deciding to just blurt it out and get it over with, Lucy said, "If I keep the house, we can make it a special getaway. No one back home would ever have to know what we're doing."

Bram came out of his lounge chair so fast it nearly tipped over. She could read his expression just fine and dandy now—and wished that she couldn't. He was furious.

"So you want to carry on some illicit little affair, is that it?"

Slowly Lucy stood. "Bram . . . You know how much gossip I had to put up with. All of our friends—"

"David's friends. They were never yours to begin with or they'd have understood."

That was an unvarnished truth. Her true friends, like Marcy, had stood behind her all the way. She cleared her throat. "The kids were hurt by all of it."

Bram's muscles bunched, from his shoulders down to his fists. "I had nothing to do with that, Lucy, and you know it."

"I know," she rushed to assure him, "but I don't want to even guess at what the neighbors will start saying if they see us together now."

"Fuck the neighbors."

She reeled back, appalled by his anger.

Bram stalked her. "What I want doesn't matter? Is that what you're telling me?"

Half afraid to ask, Lucy said, "What is it you want?"

"You. The kids. Happy ever after. The whole shebang. *Every-*

thing." He caught her face to still her retreat. "I want to marry you. I want us to be a family. I want the right to touch you every damn night and all through the day, not just when we can slip away."

"Bram." Her heart thundered, with emotion not fear. "I . . . I can't. Try to understand."

He let her go so fast, she nearly stumbled. Rubbing his hand over his face, he turned toward the lake. With his voice sounding cold and remote, he said, "You can, Lucy. But you won't."

She wanted to touch him, yet didn't dare. She was afraid he'd push her away. "Bram, why can't we just have this? Why can't we just—"

He didn't look at her. "Because I don't feel like another illicit affair. It's all or nothing, Lucy. You decide."

Appalled, tears prickling her eyes, she whispered, "What does that mean?"

"It means I can't be a casual friend. Not anymore. I can't sit back and pretend I don't love you."

He waited, but she had no idea what to say to that. Bram loved her? Then her own anger ignited and she heard herself shout, "Since when?"

Bram looked at her over his shoulder. His hair was gilded by the sun, and his back looked like polished bronze. She felt snared in his gaze as he muttered very quietly, "I've loved you ever since I've known you."

Lucy's mouth fell open. "But—"

"But you were married to someone else?" He turned and leaned on the railing, his arms crossed over his chest, his eyes hard. "It's a fact I choked on every goddamned day. When you carried the kids was the worst. You were pregnant by David, and I couldn't bear it."

"He . . . he was your friend."

"Until the day he died. I'd never have done anything to hurt either of you. But that sure as hell didn't change the way I felt."

Lucy stumbled back into a seat, dropping hard. "But . . . you sleep with young, beautiful women. You're a . . . a stud."

"Yeah? *Big deal.* I'm a forty-one-year-old man who wants more in his life than a string of one-night stands with women looking for a father figure or a guy who's settled enough that he can buy them a good time. They see me as responsible, mature, when they're anything but. The sex is great, but is that supposed to make my life worthwhile?"

"I don't know." At the moment she didn't feel like she knew anything. Everything had changed so suddenly she couldn't get her bearings.

"Well, let me tell you," he shouted, "it doesn't."

Lucy flinched, and Bram instantly lowered his tone, drawing a deep breath in an effort to calm down.

"Being with you, that's what matters." Bram knelt down in front of her and caught her hands. "This week has been the best of my life. Not just the sex, though God knows you send me through the roof. But it's you, sweetheart. Talking with you, laughing with you. Loving you."

Hearing him say it again made tears roll down her cheeks. She sniffed and then smiled because she couldn't *not* smile. Bram loved her, and according to him, his feelings weren't new.

He smoothed her cheeks, brushed her mouth with his thumb. "You can't begin to imagine all the times I've fantasized about you, about having a moment like this, being able to tell you how I feel. You're my life, Lucy. You're all I want, not some young female just out for kicks."

Lucy touched his mouth, almost laughing now. He made a

"young female just out for kicks" sound like a bad thing, when most men would have done anything to be in his position.

He kissed her fingers. "I want a woman who matches me in maturity, who's intelligent and settled and honorable—and still so sexy that even when she's sitting here crying and telling me she might walk away, I still get hard."

Lucy threw her arms around him, chuckling and sniffling at the same time.

Bram held her, his big hands moving up and down her back. His touch was so gentle, so uncertain, it broke her heart.

And then he asked, so quietly she could barely hear, "Do you love me, Lucy?"

"I always have." That was one truth she could easily admit to.

"No, not like a friend." He pushed her back and held her there, his gaze boring into hers, into her soul. "Did you ever fantasize about me while you were married?"

Such a thing seemed sinful, by thought if not by deed; she couldn't get the words to come.

"Lucy?" His voice was hard, bordering on impatient. "Admit it—you did dream about me, didn't you? I can't be that wrong."

"I . . . I was married to David," she hedged, feeling breathless and guilty and confused, "and even though things weren't great, we—"

Bram shook her. "Damn you, tell me the truth! Tell me you dreamed about me."

"Bram . . ."

"Tell me you wanted me even then!"

"Yes!" Lucy saw his vulnerability, his fear, and everything else ceased to matter. Gently, love consuming her, she cupped his face in her hands. "Yes, Bram. In the beginning of my marriage, I only noticed you as an extremely attractive man. I was so curious, but your girlfriends were always around, always bragging, so I knew, without having to ask much, that you were a good lover. And of course that made me . . . wonder."

Bram turned his head and kissed her palm. His eyes were closed in relief, some of the tension leaving his shoulders.

"When things started to go wrong between David and me," she continued, willing to tell him everything now that she knew he needed to hear it, "I . . . I pretended sometimes that he was you."

Bram jerked around to stare at her. Lucy kissed him, giving him the words without making him ask. "That wasn't any good, because David had stopped caring about what I wanted or needed and sex was . . . Well, I still loved him as a father to my children, as a man I'd known for so long, but I didn't desire him anymore. And pretending didn't help. I knew, intuitively, that being with you would be incredible."

She drew a shuddering breath, guilt melting away with the heat of the summer day and the warmth in Bram's gaze. "So yes," she said, smiling just a little, "when I was in bed at night, alone and lonely, I thought of you." Lucy laughed, then wiped her teary eyes. "You're even better in reality than in my dreams."

Bram stood, caught her arms, and pulled her up, too. "I love you." He kissed her, long and hard. "I love the kids. Let's be a family, Lucy."

Lucy toyed with the hair on his chest. She felt like she was floating, then realized Bram had lifted her completely off her feet. "I love you, too. I think I've been in love with you for a long time, but I just never imagined . . ."

"Your self-esteem was low," he explained gently, rocking her back and forth. "It was a nasty separation and you took it to heart." Then he grinned. "Marcy knew all along how I felt. When I told her I had something to do this week, she knew that I was coming after you. And given how quick she agreed to fill in for me, I'd say she approves."

"Others won't be so generous," Lucy warned. "They'll say that we were fooling around all along, even when I was married. They'll make up stories that you had something to do with the separation—"

Bram released her and turned away. "And you don't want to take the risk of more scandal, is that it?"

Lucy caught him before he'd taken a complete step and hugged him from behind. "No, I just want you to be prepared, that's all."

Bram twisted around to her, his eyes darkened to near black. "Then you'll marry me?"

She smiled and threw herself into his arms. "On one condition."

Bram squeezed her so tight she could barely breathe. "Name it."

"Promise we'll come back here at least once a year, just the two of us."

Bram held her face and kissed her hungrily. Lucy took that kiss as wholehearted agreement. Seconds later Bram lifted her over his shoulder and started for the house.

Lucy squealed from her upside-down position, "Bram! What are you doing?"

"Getting some ice."

"Ice?" She started to giggle until Bram smacked her on the bottom.

"Damn right, woman. I told you I'd get even." He kissed her hip and brought her around to hold her gently in his arms. "And I always keep my word."

Lucy started to feel weepy again, she was so full-to-bursting with love.

Then Bram opened the freezer and pulled out the ice tray, and she took off running, laughing, loving—having the time of her life.

The Edge of Sin

by

Cheyenne McCray

A huge round of thanks to Officer T. J. Leonard, patrolman with the Boston Transit Police Department. Much appreciation also goes to Texas Police Officer Jerry Patterson Jr.

As Willow would say, *"I'm a big girl and any and all mistakes are my own."*

1

His life was based on lies.

Zane Steele rubbed a hand over his jaw, his gut tightening as he studied the blond sitting on a park bench in the Common.

Sunlight winked through the trees and caressed the woman's lightly tanned arms and legs. A light summer wind lifted her sun-streaked hair from her shoulders.

Boston might be a little on the humid side this morning, but his throat was completely dry as he watched her eat an ice cream cone, her tongue darting out delicately as she licked the ice cream. He hardened as he imagined exactly where he'd like those lips and that tongue to be.

Zane hitched his shoulder up against a tree and found himself unable to take his gaze from her. He shouldn't even be thinking of introducing himself.

This wasn't a one-night stand kind of woman. This was a woman a man would want to come home to at the end of a long day and warm his bed every night. And for Zane, pursuing any kind of relationship while living a life of secrecy in order to protect everyone he knew, was downright insane. But that didn't stop him from staring.

As far as he knew, most Recovery Enforcement Division, RED, agents who had relationships with civilians didn't have the same qualms about keeping their real occupation secret from the ones they loved.

He wasn't one of those agents. He couldn't have a relationship based on not being able to share everything with the woman he loved.

Zane pushed away thoughts of commitments and studied the woman slowly licking her way around the ice cream cone. She wore a skirt that landed just above her knees before she'd sat down. When she'd made herself comfortable, the skirt hiked up her thighs just enough to tease. His heart almost stopped when she'd crossed her legs and her skirt inched up higher.

Dear God, those long legs were made for wrapping around his hips as he sank into her as deep as she could take him. Moans and whimpers would come from that pretty mouth that would beg him to fuck her harder as they rocked together. Her breasts would be perfect handfuls with beautiful nipples that he would suck and nip.

He'd bet she made a lot of noise in bed. She'd call his name as he brought her to orgasm after orgasm. She'd beg him to stop.

He wouldn't stop. He'd just take her again. And again.

The sound of shoes pounding along the path had Zane looking over his shoulder. Out of habit, he moved his hand closer to his Glock.

It was a male jogger. He passed by and the woman smiled. The jogger acknowledged her with a nod and a wink.

The surge of jealousy that slammed into Zane almost knocked him on his ass.

What the hell?

Goddamn, but she made him want her in ways he'd never wanted a woman before. He wanted to claim her. He wanted to make her his in every way. Not just for one night. He wanted to come home to her, wanted to hold her when she slept, and he wanted to wake up to her in the morning. And he hadn't even touched her yet.

In the past, he'd refused to take any relationship beyond the mutual understanding that it wouldn't go beyond sex and friendship—pretty much in that order. The woman could never question him on any aspect of his life. If she came to his bed, it was just for fun. Pure animalistic, unadulterated, hard-core fun.

Zane's throat worked again as he watched the woman in pink slowly run her tongue up the cone as she licked it where it had started to drip.

Shit. With this one, he wanted more.

But he didn't want to bring anyone into his life whom he would have to lie to every single day for God knew how long. Maybe forever.

The only family member who knew the truth was his younger sister, Lexi, who lived the same life and also worked for the clandestine government agency, RED. It was an offshoot of the NSA and technically didn't exist. Not even their big Irish family knew what Lexi and Zane really did, what there careers were.

Only RED's director; the deputy director; a federal judge; a federal prosecutor; the head of the NSA; Senator Jeannette Shelton; and the President knew. Not even the Vice President or the President's cabinet members were aware RED existed.

RED had four divisions and Zane worked Narcotics and Weapons Trafficking.

At least when he was in the Secret Service it didn't matter who knew and they just had to understand that he couldn't talk about work. Same for Lexi when she was Army Special Ops.

Zane shifted against the tree, feeling the rough bark through the overshirt that hid his Glock. He shouldn't be watching the woman like this. He shouldn't be *wanting* her like this.

But he couldn't fight back the images of pushing her hair from her heart-shaped face and tasting the perfect fullness of her lips. Of cupping her breasts while sucking her nipples. Of tasting the sweetness between her thighs then the caress of her long sun-streaked hair over his skin as those beautiful lips slipped over his cock.

Christ.

He dragged his hand over his jaw again. His informant would be here in the next half hour and he needed to concentrate on his current case. Not on some woman he didn't even know.

Willow Randolph did her best not to look directly at the man who was focused on her so intently.

Law enforcement. He had it written all over him. It was the authority that radiated from him even though he was thirty, maybe forty, feet away. It was almost tangible. She felt like she could reach out and wrap herself in all his power.

From beneath her lashes she saw his throat work as she licked her ice cream and sucked some through her lips. His expression was pained and she did her best not to smile at the nice-sized bulge in his jeans.

Dangerous, that's what he was. The kind of man who'd be hazardous to a woman's heart.

He had "Bad Boy" written all over him.

She'd bet a month's salary from her job at Macy's—well maybe a week's—that he was something other than a police officer, but still in some branch of law enforcement. Definitely not a desk jockey.

His hands looked strong enough to snap a man's neck yet she imagined that those same hands would be gentle on a woman's skin.

Willow could almost feel his fingers glide over her body. That simple thought hardened her nipples beneath her pink blouse and sent a heated shard of desire straight to that place between her thighs.

He was a stranger, but she had the incredible urge to run her hands over his muscular chest before she slipped her fingers into his black hair. His carved biceps and strong forearms would hold her tight as he slid deep inside her.

She almost moaned as she licked her ice cream. She could picture herself wrapping her arms around his neck, and bringing him down for a kiss as she pressed her body close to his. He had a quarterback's build from his broad shoulders to his lean hips, so he would feel hard and strong against her softness.

Willow licked the cone again and imagined it was his erection. Strong as steel but soft under her fingers and in her mouth.

Maybe it had just been too long since she'd had sex, because the way he made her feel just standing there watching her and the way she was fantasizing about him was insane.

She crunched on her cone while he watched, then she slowly and deliberately sucked each of her fingers clean.

Let him go home and wish he had at least come up to her and introduced himself. Let him wonder what it would be like to be with her and wish he'd had more guts.

Coward.

No, there was nothing in the least bit cowardly about this man. He didn't make decisions without weighing his options.

The man pushed away from the tree he'd been leaning against.

Willow couldn't help it. She raised her eyes and met his. Green. His eyes were such a beautiful shade of green.

The pounding of her heart seemed to rise from her chest to her throat. Swallowing at this moment wasn't an option. She couldn't have torn her gaze from his for the life of her.

Heat traveled through her as he made a more blatant assessment. His gaze started traveling over her from her ankles to her nearly bare thighs, up her belly, and rested on her breasts. Her nipples grew so hard that he had to see the effect he had on her.

Two could play this game.

A breeze teased her hair as she parted her lips. She tasted the sweetness of ice cream on her lower lip as she ran her tongue along it. But it wasn't the ice cream that she was trying to taste. It was the image of herself on her knees in front of him, taking him deep into her mouth that was firmly in her mind.

How would *he* taste?

She let her gaze freely roam over his powerful form. Such incredible thighs and muscular build. Just to push him closer to the edge, she let her gaze rest on his excellent package before she met his eyes again.

Willow curved her lips into a wicked smile as she braced her hands to either side of her hips on the park bench.

I dare you, she told him with her expression.

He dared.

2

Zane couldn't have stopped himself if he tried. When the woman gave him that challenging little smile that was all it took.

He never backed down from a challenge.

She looked surprised then almost amused as he walked toward her. When he reached her she looked up at him and smiled again.

"You've been driving me out of my mind," was the first thing that came out of his mouth.

Her smile turned into a grin. "I know."

Zane wanted to smile in return but instead he sat a couple of feet away from her on the park bench. He rested his forearms on his thighs and leaned forward, studying her.

Goddamn but she was even prettier up close. The breeze carried her scent to him and reminded him of the ocean and sunny days as his gaze rested on the curve of those perfect lips. He met her eyes that were such a pretty sea blue it would be like getting on a boat and getting lost for days on the brilliant Caribbean Sea.

"Zane Steele." He used his real name and not one of his undercover ones as he reached his hand out to her. He only used his real name when it came to personal things.

Everything about this woman would be personal.

"Willow Randolph." She took his hand and her warm touch had more than his gut tightening. His jeans were going to strangle him if he got any bigger.

It seemed they were both reluctant to part as they slid their hands away from each other. Her touch tickled his palm in a way that made him think of those fingers all over his body.

"Randolph . . ." Even as he reveled in Willow's touch, a combination of anger and pain burned his skin at the memory of another Randolph. "My sister, Lexi, just lost a friend, Stacy Randolph." On an undercover op with RED, he added silently. No one outside RED knew she'd died a hero and not a victim, because no one knew she had been a special agent with RED.

Willow's smile faded a little. "Stacy was my cousin. She was one of my best friends." Willow sighed as sadness crossed her features. "I'm staying with my aunt and uncle for a while so that they're not alone now that Stacy's gone. She was their only child."

They were both silent for a moment but they never broke eye contact. Those sea blue eyes would be easy to get lost in.

"Your accent isn't New England," he finally said. "I'd guess Upper New York."

"You're good." She smiled and her eyes had an edge of amusement to them again. "But then a cop is trained to notice everything."

A small shock jolted him. He tried to keep his expression from showing he was startled that she'd come close to nailing him. "What makes you think I'm a cop?"

"Not really a police officer." She cocked her head as she studied him. "But definitely law enforcement."

Shit. If he was this easy to read how the hell had he made it through so many undercover ops?

"Secret Service," he said. He had been SS and everyone thought he still was. "You pegged me. Now I want to know how."

"Ah. Secret Service." She crossed her legs at her ankles. "Taking some time off?"

"Something like that." Funny she hadn't answered his question. He glanced at his watch. His informant should be here soon and he shouldn't be sitting here having this conversation.

"Are you going to ask me to dinner?" Willow had a clearly curious expression. Not like a woman who expected a man to ask her out, but a woman who was observant enough to know when a man was attracted to her.

Zane put his hands on his knees and straightened. "I'm not so sure you'd want to go out with me."

Willow now looked intrigued. "Why not?"

He sighed and glanced down at the grass at their feet before looking at her again. "I'm not into relationships."

She shrugged. "Who says I am?"

"It's written all over you, honey." Zane put one arm on the back of the park bench. "You don't do one-night stands. You expect to see a man at least a few times before you make up your mind whether or not you want to date him anymore."

"You are observant, Zane." The way she said his name brought to mind thoughts of her saying his name over and over again as he took her. "But in other words you're afraid," she added.

"I've never been afraid of anything, Willow." He got up off the bench seat. Better get the hell out of here.

She tilted her head and met his gaze. "This time you are."

Willow had challenged him again. Damn. Even though he never backed down, in this case it would be the smart thing to do. Real smart.

No one had accused him of being smart all of the time.

Zane glanced at his watch. Henry should be walking down the path any moment. "It's closing in on noon." He looked up at her. "How about I meet you for lunch at the Irish pub on Province at one?"

Ah, hell. What did he go and do that for?

Willow gave him her beautiful dimpled smile, which did damned funny things to his gut. "This is my lunch break and I have to get back to work. Let's say dinner at that contemporary American restaurant and lounge at Stanhope and Clarendon. I'll meet you there."

He stared down at her for a long moment, taking in her unpretentious beauty and the kind of confidence that came from a woman who was comfortable with herself and her choices. Willow was dangerous to him in more ways than he could count.

Zane found himself giving a slow nod. "Seven?"

"Perfect." Willow stood and her skirt slid back to just above her knees. What a shame. Those thighs were meant to be seen. "I'll meet you in the waiting area."

Their eyes met and held again. "I'll be there," he said.

"I know you will." She turned away and headed toward the downtown area.

He shook his head. *You're in deep shit now, Steele.*

In a corner of Macy's cosmetic department, Willow hummed silently as she taught her client how to apply a new look with some of their latest products. The cosmetics company she worked for was one of the best.

"It's all in the brush." Willow took a sterile mascara wand from a package in a pocket of her black smock and after dipping it into a tube of black mascara, handed it to Mrs. James. Willow would toss the wand once the woman used it. "This side lengthens while this end of the brush thickens and separates."

"What an interesting concept . . ."

Willow's thoughts wandered, Mrs. James's words turning into white noise as she thought about Zane.

Zane Steele.

Being close to him had left her feeling charged and needy all at the same time. He'd smelled so good that she could almost taste him. Earthy, male. And his deep voice had sent delicious shivers down her spine when he'd said her name.

"You're up to something." Linda passed by in a wake of their brand of perfume that smelled of freesia and magnolia blooms. "I can see it in your eyes."

Eyes. Oh, Mrs. James.

"I'll tell you about it later," Willow said to Linda as she took the mascara wand from Mrs. James and threw it into a wastebasket. "It's the finishing touch on really bringing out your eyes," she said to the woman who was probably in her fifties but now was appearing more like she was in her early forties, thanks to the cosmetics.

Next, Willow showed Mrs. James how to apply her blush and then her lipstick.

She couldn't help her thoughts turning back to Zane and picturing his powerful build and the way he made her feel just by being close to her.

Oh, yeah. That man was Danger with a capital D.

"Willow?" Mrs. James's voice brought Willow out of her daydream. Which had to be at least her tenth daydream since returning to work.

The woman batted her eyelashes as she studied herself in the huge lighted mirror. "I love it." Mrs. James smiled at her reflection and looked even prettier. "I can't believe it. What a transformation."

"Beautiful," Willow could say with complete honesty. The gradual change in Mrs. James's appearance was like watching a bud bloom into a full-fledged rose. "What interests you the most out of everything?"

Mrs. James didn't even pause. "All of it."

Cool.

"I'll get your product for you and then ring you up." Willow left Mrs. James admiring her own reflection, obvious delight in her gaze.

Willow couldn't resist taking a crumpled piece of paper out of her pocket and taking a shot into the wastebasket by the stockroom door. "She jumps, she shoots, she *scores*." The paper ball landed dead center in the wastebasket.

"That's a three-pointer if I ever saw one," said the chic, completely fashionable Linda just before she entered the doorway of the stockroom ahead of Willow.

"Nothing but net, baby," Willow said.

"Terrific job on that lady." Linda reached for a box off a shelf that contained liquid foundation while Willow pulled out her products for Mrs. James. "Now tell me what the smiling, humming, and daydreaming are all about."

"I met a man today." Willow smiled and then winked as she added, "A *real* man."

"Hmmm . . ." Linda's stylish chin-length black hair swung forward as she searched for a particular shade of blush in a long row of boxes containing blush compacts. "Does he have any brothers?"

"I'll find out." Willow grabbed the last shade of eye shadow she needed. "Tonight."

Linda drew out a box containing blush then turned to Willow and raised her perfectly arched eyebrows. "You never go on dates."

"That's because I hadn't found the right man." Willow backed out of the stockroom, checking over her shoulder first to make sure she didn't run into anyone. "I think I need to do a little more investigating."

Linda smirked and still managed to look beautiful. "Uh-huh. You just found a guy you'd like to sleep with."

The grin that flashed across Willow's face was something she couldn't help. "If you saw him, believe me, you wouldn't be calling him a 'guy.'"

"What does this *man* do?" Linda asked as she stepped away from the shelf.

Willow laughed. "Would you believe he's in the Secret Service?"

"No way."

"Yup." Willow juggled the armload of products for Mrs. James. "Spotted Zane as law enforcement the moment I saw him in the Common."

"Secret Service Agent Zane, huh?" Linda cocked her head. "Sure he's not full of—"

"Absolutely."

"Complete report expected tomorrow afternoon." Linda swept past Willow. "You're not allowed to spare any details, so have a great time. And I'll live vicariously through you."

As if Linda had any shortage of guys.

But not a real man.

"Knock him dead, Willow." Linda's voice carried over her shoulder as she headed to the cash register with her hands full of products.

Willow smiled.

That's exactly what she intended to do with Zane tonight.

Knock him dead.

Or maybe . . . just knock him into bed.

3

"Zane." Lexi rapped on the door frame to his office at RED HQ and he looked up from the intel that he'd been staring at but hadn't really been seeing. "Jeez, where are you?" She folded her arms and leaned her back against the door frame. "I knocked twice. Not like you to zone out like that."

"Work." Yeah, like he was going to tell his younger sister about the woman who just wouldn't get out of his head. "What brings you from the fifth to the second?"

Lexi worked in Human Trafficking and Sex Crimes on the fifth floor of RED's five-story building on Portland Street in Boston. Fourth floor was Terrorist Activity and Organized Crime; third floor Technology Theft; and the second, Zane's floor, Narcotics and Weapons Trafficking. The first floor was admin, but also served as their front, posing as an interpreter firm.

"I need to see Georgina." Lexi glanced over her shoulder to the Command Center, which was a lot like the CCs on every floor. "She hasn't been at home when I've stopped by her apartment the last couple of days, and I can't get a hold of her on her personal cell."

"I sent Rizzo undercover." Zane closed the manila folder he'd supposedly been looking at. "There's an arms deal going down that we got wind of and she's the right agent for this job."

"If she comes in, tell her I need to talk to her." Lexi gave a mischievous grin. "It's *really* important."

"Probably has to do with your partner." Zane gave a wry look. "You and Donovan spend plenty of time *working* together."

If his former Army Special Ops sister ever blushed now would be the time. "Nick Donovan and I are Team Supervisors who happen to be paired up."

"Uh-huh." Zane leaned forward, his forearms on his desk. Before Lexi could get in another word, he said in a subdued tone, "I met Stacy Randolph's cousin today."

Lexi's features tightened and any trace of teasing was gone. It had only been a few months since Agent Randolph had been raped and murdered. Lexi had taken Randolph's death hard since she'd been the one to send Randolph on the undercover assignment that had led to her murder.

"Her cousin Willow." Lexi gave a slow nod. "I heard about her from Georgina. Nice of her to stay with Stacy's parents."

Zane couldn't say anything because the next words he'd have said might have been, "She's so damned beautiful and fascinating that I can't get her out of my mind." But he managed to keep his mouth shut.

"Don't forget Mammy's making bangers and mash on Sunday." Then she gave him a teasing smile before she added, "When you go out with Willow, ask her if she'd like to come."

His jaw almost dropped. "What—"

"I'm your sister." Lexi started to turn away. "From a mile away I could see that you've got a thing for her."

Well, hell. If two women could read him so easily in one day he might as well turn in his credentials.

For at least the hundredth time, Zane wondered why in the hell he was here at the restaurant bar waiting for Willow.

And for at least the hundredth time, he thought of how beautiful and intriguing she'd been.

He took another swallow of his mug of Guinness on tap. His gaze never left the doorway as he leaned against the bar and waited for her to walk through. He'd come a half hour early, needing a beer before he saw her again.

There was something about that woman that drew him. Maybe she wouldn't be the same intelligent, insightful woman who had captured his attention. Maybe she wouldn't be as beautiful—

He just about dropped his beer.

A supermodel stepped through the doorway of the restaurant. Willow.

Zane barely registered the fact that he'd left a twenty in his empty beer mug as he slowly walked toward Willow. She was beautiful to begin with but now he knew the true meaning of the word "stunning."

She had the same unpretentious smile, the same casual confidence as when he'd met her. But now she looked like she could be on the cover of some chick magazine. Hell, the cover of the next *Sports Illustrated* swimsuit issue.

Willow wore a little black dress that he didn't notice so much as the amount of cleavage and thigh it exposed. The same smooth golden skin, the same sun-streaked hair, the same long legs. It was more the sexy wave of her hair and the way her sea blue eyes looked bigger, her lips even more delicious.

Shit.

He'd known he was in trouble before, but now he didn't have a doubt that he was in deeper than he could swim.

Zane hit some guy's shoulder with his own but he didn't bother to mumble an apology to the guy because he was too damned focused on Willow.

When he reached her, she continued to smile at him as she tipped her head. At six-two, Zane only had about three inches on her, less tonight since she was wearing high heels. She was as tall and willowy as her name. Somehow he hadn't noticed that before, and he was trained to notice everything.

Christ, he was slipping all over the place when it came to this woman.

"I reserved a table for us," he managed to get out as he stared at her and drank in her scent that again made him think of sunny days and an ocean breeze.

"Good." She slid her hand into his, interlocking their fingers. "I'm starving."

Zane tried to ignore the out-of-control sensations pinging through his body at the feel of her fingers locked with his. "I thought supermodels didn't eat."

Willow laughed. An honest, friendly laugh that did more funny things to his gut. "Grad student and part-time cosmetologist," she said as they reached the hostess who was waiting with a pair of menus. "Most definitely not supermodel."

"Could have fooled me," Zane said as they followed the hostess to a corner table.

The way Zane had looked at her sent a shiver of delight down Willow's spine. She could read so much from his eyes. Definitely desire, but also a genuine interest in who she was and not just in her appearance.

Talk about appearances. Good lord, he was gorgeous. Just like she'd remembered from his broad shoulders and chest to his carved biceps and strong forearms. Those were arms made to hold her tight as he drove deep.

The hostess guided them through the main dining area of the redbrick-walled restaurant that was elegant yet contemporary.

Willow squeezed Zane's hand tighter and he rewarded her with the sexiest smile that made her sigh. Even the smells of lobster, steak, and other delicious meals didn't appeal to her as much as Zane did.

He wore a dark green shirt with an overshirt, probably to cover his weapon. But he had another weapon he couldn't disguise behind his jeans. And it had looked primed and ready for what she wanted tonight.

Zane's short black hair had the slightest wave to it that made her want to run her fingers through it. Yeah, she'd do that.

The hostess showed them to the perfect table for two in front of a tall rectangular window. The atmosphere in their part of the restaurant was romantic and only added fuel to the incredible fire burning within her.

He looked like he hated to release her hand as much as she didn't want to let his go, but he did and pulled out her high-backed cushioned chair for her.

"And you're a gentleman, too," she said as he seated himself.

The hostess left the menus and said something about wine but neither of them paid attention to her.

Zane focused his gaze on her. "Honey, if you knew what's going through my head right now, you wouldn't think I'm anything close to being a gentleman."

Willow picked up her menu and gave him her best naughty grin. "Then you and I must be thinking the same thing."

At first Zane looked taken aback but then he had a teasing glint in his eyes. "That I have great breasts and the most gorgeous legs you've ever seen?"

She laughed. "I know what you're really imagining." She leaned close to him. "Instead of being in this restaurant you'd rather be in bed. With me."

He cleared his throat. "If I could make it that far."

Willow looked at her menu before looking over the top of it at him. "Let's see if we can make it through dinner."

Zane picked up his own menu. He cleared his throat again. "Not sure I'll live that long."

"You know what?" Willow settled her hand on his knee and slowly moved her fingers up his thigh and kept her tone low. "They have two very private, very elegant, very clean restrooms here. With locks on the doors."

Zane raised his eyes from his menu, a hungry, primal, and pained expression on his face as she inched her fingers upward to what she really wanted to touch.

"When the server comes, you order our appetizer and wine and I'll get up and go to the ladies' room." She skimmed her fingers over his long, thick erection. "You follow me as soon as you finish ordering."

Zane glanced around them before looking back at her. "Uh, Willow—"

She gave him another wicked smile. "I dare you."

4

Not a second after Willow flashed that naughtier-than-hell grin the server came to the table. For a moment Zane forgot the server as he watched Willow get up and slowly walk toward the ladies' room.

That tiny little dress barely covered her breasts and ass. His mouth watered at the thought of those long legs wrapped around his hips as he thrust deep—

"Sir?" The waiter's voice was barely enough to bring Zane out of his fantasies. Damn. He'd been doing that all day and it probably wasn't going to stop until he had her. "Wine? Appetizer?" the server asked.

"Uh, yeah." A sudden rush come over Zane as images of being inside Willow kept repeating over and over again in his mind. He tried not to look in the direction Willow had disappeared as he picked the first thing his gaze landed on. "Oysters. Wine, you choose."

"Yes, sir." The server gave a slight bow. "I'll bring your wine to you shortly."

"No rush." Zane rose and strode toward the restrooms as soon as the server turned his back.

His cock was throbbing, raging with need. Half of him knew this was crazy, that he was out of his ever-lovin' mind. But his other half said "get lost" to the first half.

Zane's heart rate had jacked and his body burned like fire. Willow better not have been teasing him because he'd die if he couldn't take her soon.

It seemed forever before he reached the women's restroom and he jerked the door open. The moment he stepped through, Willow was on him. She wrapped her arms around his neck and brought him to her for a rough, hard kiss.

He barely remembered to shut the door behind him and press the lock before he grabbed her by her ass and she wrapped her long legs around his hips.

She wasn't wearing any underwear.

A growl rose up in Zane's throat as he swung around so that her back was against the door. She moaned into his mouth before she drew away and pulled down the front of her dress, freeing her breasts.

Hungry for all of her, Zane licked and sucked her nipples. It was so easy to tell she was trying to hold in her moans and cries as she squirmed and rocked her hips against his.

"I've got to be inside you." He raised his head and kissed her before he said against her lips, "I need to fuck you. I can't wait any longer."

"Yes," she clamped her legs around his hips and gripped his shoulders. "I've been wanting you all day."

Someone tried the door handle and it jiggled, but Zane didn't give a crap about anything other than finally being where he belonged.

As Willow held on, he unfastened his jeans. It was only a slight relief to finally have his cock free because his erection only seemed to grow bigger and thicker and throb even harder. He jerked a condom out of his pocket and had that sucker on in two seconds flat.

He kissed Willow to swallow her cries as he thrust deep and buried himself in heaven.

It had been an insane idea but Willow thrived on impulse and instinct.

Zane drove his erection into her and thank God he kissed her so hard because she couldn't help the scream of pleasure and pain at the unexpected thickness and length of his cock. She could almost swear he touched her belly button with every thrust.

He didn't ease up as he moved his mouth from hers. She tried to hold back her gasps and cries as he moved his mouth to her ear. "I wanted to take it slow and easy with you our first time, honey. But now I can't have you fast enough."

"Don't even ask me to think." She kissed him and her breathing was rough, her words hard to get out. "The only thing that matters is how good you feel." She bit back another cry. "Zane. Oh, God, I'm about to lose it."

The door handle jiggled again and that sound, knowing that people were on the other side of that door as Zane fucked her, threw her over the top.

This time she dove for his mouth and let him take her cries as the most powerful, most incredible orgasm of her life tore through her. Her body shook and trembled and it felt so good as Zane didn't stop and drew out her orgasm. Her core contracted around his cock and every throb caused her body to jerk and her mind to hum.

She'd bet Zane held in a shout of his own when he came and he came hard. He threw back his head, his jaws clamped shut, his face dark as he fought for control.

He was so big that she felt every pulse and throb of his orgasm.

Willow collapsed against Zane, her arms around his neck. She felt weightless and light-headed, and she wondered how she was going to be able to walk out of there.

There was a jiggle then a knock at the door. "Hello?"

"Just a minute," Willow said. "I'm having a little problem from something I ate."

"Oh." The woman's voice sounded like she was definitely having second thoughts about using the restroom. "Okay. Hope you're all right."

Willow sniggered as she pressed her face against Zane's shirt. "Actually I haven't had a chance to swallow what else I'm hungry for."

Zane groaned and she felt him thicken and lengthen inside her. "We'd better get out of here before I fuck you again." She drew away and looked at him with a sly smile. He clamped his hand over her mouth, a dangerous glint to his eyes. "Don't you *dare*."

She could barely hold back a laugh as he slid out of her and set her on her feet. She almost fell because her knees were so weak and her heels too high. When Zane steadied her, he tossed the condom and arranged himself as she tugged her dress back into place and tried to make her hair look like she hadn't just been taken up against a door.

When they'd washed up and were ready, as ready as they could be, Zane said, "There might be a whole line of women out there."

Willow reached up and kissed him. "Don't worry. I've got that covered."

———

Zane snorted while he stood in the bathroom as Willow left and closed the door behind her, saying things that would drive away any crowd. "Smells just awful . . . plugged up . . . need to get management."

He shook his head then waited a few heartbeats before opening the door and thanking God that no one was in the hallway. Apparently Willow had done a good job of scaring away the mob.

His body still hummed and burned with heat as he headed to the table. The fact that he'd just taken Willow up against the door in a restaurant's restroom just about blew his mind. He hadn't done anything as daring as that since his young, wild days. Even then what he and Willow had done made everything in his past seem tame.

Zane approached the table and watched Willow as she spoke with the server. She approved the wine before the server poured two glasses and then he left the bottle on the table as Zane sat.

Christ, Willow was beautiful. He couldn't help smiling at how her hair was a little ruffled in the back. The just-got-fucked look only added to her stunning beauty.

"You chose well." She smiled while he pulled up his seat, candlelight from the holder in the center of the table flickering over her features. She circled the rim of her wineglass with a finger. "A 2004 Vincent Girardin Chardonnay."

Yeah. The waiter probably picked the most expensive wine in the store, but Zane didn't give a shit. All that mattered was the beautiful woman he couldn't take his eyes from.

He raised his glass as did she, but she got to the toast before he did. "Here's to fabulous restroom sex in one of the finest restaurants in all of Boston."

God, this woman made him want to laugh and smile and grin—things he rarely did, especially in his line of work.

They sipped and he raised his glass again. "My turn." She brought her glass close to his as he said, "Here's to meeting in the Common one of the most beautiful, genuine women in the world."

Willow flashed her dimpled smile and he knew he was getting deeper and deeper with every moment they spent together. The thing was, he couldn't imagine not seeing Willow again, not being around her whenever he could.

He set his wineglass on the table and rubbed his temples. *Shit. What happened to no relationships, Steele?*

"You're scared again, Zane." Willow spoke in her easy, direct tone. He looked at her and she had her arms folded on the table in front of her as she leaned forward, her expression clear and thoughtful. "You're worrying you'll end up caring for someone."

5

The server appeared with their oyster appetizer and settled it on the table, saving Zane from having to respond to Willow. The woman was too observant for her own good.

He couldn't take his eyes from her as she handed the server her menu. She was so damned beautiful. But what mattered to him more was her unpretentiousness and even her directness when she asked questions he didn't want to answer.

Vaguely he heard Willow tell the server, "I'll have the salmon, with the creamed spinach and the sautéed mushrooms as sides."

Zane sucked in his breath and took a quick glance at his own menu and just chose whatever struck him first. "Surf and turf, the filet medium rare." He returned his menu to the server. "Mashed potatoes and asparagus."

When the server left, Zane continued to study the beautiful

woman across the table from him. Christ, he couldn't keep staring at her. Even though his body still felt flushed with his orgasm, and his cock had hardened again, feeling strangled beneath his jeans, he had to say something.

"You know what I do for a living." *Liar.* "What about you?"

"I have my Mister Ed and I'm working for my Doctor Ed." She smiled and he raised his brows. "That just means I have my masters and I'm working on my doctorate in Education."

She continued and added, "I'm fifth year ABD at NYU. All But Dissertation. I'm working on my dissertation while I'm in Boston, and then I'll go back to New York University to present it before a committee."

"Dr. Randolph." Zane offered her the plate of oysters on the half-shell. She took a couple and put them onto her plate. "Has a nice ring to it."

He took a few oysters himself as she replied, "So does Special Agent Steele."

"You said you were on your way to work when I met you at the park." *And I was about to hook up with an informant regarding an arms deal.*

Willow shrugged. "For the time being, most afternoons I work at Macy's in the cosmetics department. Once I have my doctorate, I'll start looking for a position somewhere on the Eastern Seaboard."

Zane didn't have a clue about cosmetics and wasn't sure he wanted to. "Any place in particular that you'd like to end up in?"

"I really love Boston. I always have." That dimple again. "Before Dad left, we'd travel to Boston from Buffalo so that he could visit his brother, my uncle."

For the first time since Zane met her, a troubled expression crossed Willow's features. "Dad . . . a couple of years ago he ran off with a 'cute little thing' who's younger than me."

The troubled expression disappeared like a shadow replaced by sunshine when she changed the topic. "I have two bickering sisters, considerably younger and they still live in Buffalo with Mom."

"They're in college?"

She shook her head. "Twins in their senior year in high school. Wendy and Sarah are ten years younger than me." She rested her forearms on the table and gave him that compelling, insightful look. "I'll bet you're the oldest brother, whatever your family size."

"How do you do it?" Zane met her sea-blue gaze. "Read people."

"I see it in your eyes." Willow tilted her head to the side. "You worry about them and anyone else you love and care for."

He cleared his throat. He didn't like the direction this conversation had headed. "I have a very large Irish Catholic family."

"Ha! I knew it," Willow said with a grin. "How many brothers and sisters?"

"Four brothers, two sisters." Zane couldn't help smiling in response. Her grin was so damned infectious. "Mammy and Dad have been married for almost forty years."

Two servers arrived with two large trays of their dinner and loaded the table with all of the dishes they'd chosen. Willow took a couple of sips of wine until the servers finished and left.

"Hmmm . . ." Willow spooned creamed spinach onto her plate next to her salmon. "Bet everyone in your family lives around here and you get together regularly."

"Every Sunday the whole mob usually shows up at our parents' home. With the exception of Ryan who's in the Marines." *Or when either Lexi or I are undercover,* he added to himself. Zane cut a piece of his filet. Before he knew the words were coming out of his mouth, he said, "Would you like to come to lunch with my family this Sunday?"

You are one screwed-up SOB, Steele. What happened to no relationships? You're moving way too fast, buddy.

Willow's brilliant smile did such strange things to his gut that made him crave one smile after another from her. "Great. I have Sunday off."

Zane started cutting his filet. "Mammy is going to love you."

"Cool." Willow took another sip of wine. "Can't wait to meet all of them. Bet your mother fixes great Irish dishes, too."

"She bakes one hell of a shepherd's pie." He shook his head at the same time. "But honey, as far as betting goes, I'm not betting with you on anything again."

Willow slipped her hand into Zane's and smiled up at him as they walked outside into the summer evening.

The way he looked at her—entranced, yet the fear of relationships was constantly in his eyes.

A mystery, yes, but she'd bet it had something to do with his job. He didn't have the look of a man who'd been burned—because he'd never let himself get that far in a relationship. He ran before it got too serious.

She might just have to change that.

"Where are you parked?" His smooth deep voice flowed over her and it gave her delightful shivers.

"I took a cab."

"From West Roxbury?"

"I hate driving in Boston." She ran her hand from just below her breasts to her hip in a slow movement and watched his eyes follow her hand. "And I wasn't crazy about riding the T dressed like this."

Zane had that hungry look in his gaze again. "You'd better *not ever* ride the T dressed like that."

Willow leaned against his shoulder as they walked and he squeezed her hand tighter. "Oh, yeah?"

"Yeah." His voice sounded concerned and possessive all at once and she wondered if he realized it. "I'll take you back to your aunt and uncle's."

"I have a better idea." She tilted her head to look up at him. "Why don't you show me your place and we'll finish what we started?"

She wondered if he realized he was squeezing her hand so hard or that she was holding her breath for his answer. "It's a mess."

Willow drew him to a stop at the corner near the parking garage. She looked at him, meeting his gaze, wishing she could see his green eyes better. "I'm not interested in what your place looks like. I'm interested in you."

In the dim light coming from a nearby lamppost she saw his throat work. Then he caught her completely off guard by releasing her hand and holding her face in his palms. And he kissed her.

Not a wild, hard kiss like his powerful kisses in the restaurant, but gentle and demanding all at once. The moans rising up in her throat came out like a soft purr as she moved her hands to his hard chest and explored his muscular pecs, shoulders, and biceps as his tongue moved with hers and they tasted one another.

His flavor was masculine and delicious, and included a hint of the wine they'd been drinking. And lord, his scent. So male, with a touch of a musk-scented aftershave.

Zane lightly bit her lower lip then kissed her harder, even more demandingly, as he moved his hands to her waist and drew her close and tight against his erection. Willow sighed into his mouth and brought her arms around his neck. She slipped her fingers into his black hair and ruffled it just like she'd been wanting to all night.

The heavy rise and fall of his chest brushed her breasts, and her nipples were so tight they ached. He kissed her long and hard until she started to feel dizzy.

"Yeah." Zane broke their kiss and stared down at her before he took a step back and captured her hand in his again. He sounded out of breath when he spoke. "My place. Before I take you right here on the street."

"The street, huh?" She ran her free hand over his chest and felt the rapid beating of his heart. She continued to trail her fingers down to his cock and he hissed when she cupped his balls. "That's not such a bad idea," she said, knowing mischief was in her eyes, her expression.

Zane immediately clamped his hand over her mouth and his tone was almost dangerous. "You'd better not dare me again, honey, because I might just take you up on it."

6

With Willow sitting on the other side of the console, fire coursed through Zane's body as he drove his Chevy Silverado to his home in Quincy. Images of taking Willow in every way possible continually rolled through his mind and he had to grind his teeth to keep his focus on the road.

He glanced at Willow. "You don't strike me as the type of woman who meets a man in the Common and goes to bed with him the same night."

Her dimple was easy to see in the glow of the dashboard lights as she smiled. "Like my friend Linda says, I don't even date, much less have sex with strange men."

Zane had to force himself to keep his eyes on the road before he glanced at her again. "Why me?"

"The moment I noticed you watching me, I felt a connection."

Willow raised her slender arms and drew her blond-streaked hair over her shoulders before she lowered her hands to her lap. She looked at him with frank honesty in her eyes. "A connection that I've never felt with anyone."

He tried to swallow but his throat was too dry as he looked back to the road. "I told you I don't do relationships."

"Why?" she asked with clear curiosity in her voice. "What are you afraid of?"

Zane couldn't believe he was having this conversation with any woman. Yet with Willow he felt comfortable for the first time in telling the truth.

He looked at her and then the road again. "My job is dangerous and the people I care for could be in just as much danger if they knew the truth."

"You're not actually Secret Service." She said it with such ease and lack of judgment. "You're with whatever agency Stacy was in."

Zane almost stomped on the brake from the shock that tore through him. He cut his gaze to her. "What did Stacy tell you?"

"Nothing." Willow shrugged. "I just knew she wasn't an interpreter no matter that she could speak five languages. I had no doubt she was in some secret branch of law enforcement."

He focused on the road long enough to make sure he was in the right lane and not about to tumble his truck thanks to the shock.

Willow clasped her hands around her knee. "It was in the way she always sat facing a doorway when we would go out to lunch, the way she observed everything and everyone around us without actually looking like she was doing it."

Shit.

"Stacy had a kind of tenseness about her on some days but other days she would be relaxed and it was obvious she was truly enjoying herself," Willow said. "That was mostly at her home. She didn't like to go out of the house much when she wasn't at work."

Zane didn't say anything. He didn't know what to say that wouldn't just compound the lies he already lived.

Willow stared out the window at the dark scenery streaking by. "I asked her about it once and she almost choked on a bite of chocolate cake. She denied it of course, but I could see the truth in her eyes, along with a touch of fear—for me because I'd guessed."

When he glanced back from the road, Willow was studying him again. For the first time he saw true pain in her gaze. "Tell me Stacy didn't die randomly. That she wasn't just in the wrong place at the wrong time. I won't ask anything else and I won't say a word to anyone. I just need to know."

What could he say? Zane only knew he couldn't lie about Stacy to Willow.

He waited a couple of heartbeats as he gripped the steering wheel. Finally he met Willow's eyes and managed to get out the words. "Special Agent Stacy Randolph died a hero."

"Thank you." Willow whispered the words as she looked at her hands in her lap.

Zane cleared his throat. "My—one of the agents found the sonofabitch who did it and made sure he got what he deserved and then some."

"Good." Willow nodded and his heart almost crumbled for her when she wiped a tear away that had streaked down her face. She kept her gaze on her lap. "I knew the agency would take care of whoever killed my cousin."

"If everyone was so damned observant as you," Zane said as he glanced at Willow, "we'd be in deep shit."

Her smile was still a little sad as she raised her eyes to meet his.

"I wish her parents could be told the truth. She wasn't just another victim."

Zane's muscles tensed so much his entire body felt coiled. "It's dangerous to you to have guessed as much as you have."

"I have no intention of letting anyone else have a clue I figured out a little of the truth." She wiped at both of her eyes and gave a soft laugh. "I don't even know enough to have it tortured out of me."

"Don't talk about things like that." Zane ground his teeth and reached for her hand as he drove with his other.

Willow interlocked her fingers with his and squeezed. "I understand, Zane. Just know that with me you don't have anything to be afraid of."

"I have everything to be afraid of," he said quietly.

They remained silent the remainder of the way to Zane's house, their hands joined and resting on the padded console as he drove.

Their conversation played through Willow's mind as she thought about Stacy and the dangerous life she must have led. And that Zane lived now.

When he came to a stop in front of a colonial-style home, he parked, climbed out, then went around to her side and helped her out of his big truck. When her feet were firmly on the sidewalk, Willow found herself meeting Zane's gaze, his hands resting on her waist.

His eyes were shadowed in the darkness that was relieved only slightly from a nearby streetlight. He looked at her for a long moment before she kissed him. At first he seemed hesitant, almost like he was afraid she would break. But then she drew him into the kiss, and his hunger and the strength of his need flowed through her.

He needed her.

She needed him.

Not in the sexual sense, but in the soul-deep sense.

Although the sex was a must.

Zane drew away, his expression as dark as the night and just as easy to read.

The doors locked silently as he used the remote before he took her hand.

Willow said, "It looks like a nice street."

"I'm not home a lot, but the neighbors watch out for one another." Zane continued to hold her hand as they went up the front steps. "It's a good community."

When they finally made it into the house, Zane didn't give her much time to take in his living area and kitchen. She only caught a glimpse of hardwood floors, leather furniture, and granite countertops because he immediately flipped on a light that illuminated the stairs and began leading her up.

Three open doors led off the upstairs hallway and Zane took her to the farthest one. She caught a glimpse of a darkened weight room and a small tiled bathroom on the way. He turned on another switch and soft light illuminated the room from either side of what was definitely a master bedroom. It was entirely masculine. Thick rough natural pine furnishings and a stone fireplace with a pine mantel, along with wood blinds and wood flooring gave it a rustic look. The colors suited him, too. Forest-green bedding and throw rugs by the fireplace and bed.

"This is not what I'd call messy," she said as she looked up at him.

He shrugged. "I have a cleaning service come in once a week so it's not too bad all of the time."

The covers on the bed were pulled back, and her heart started beating faster as he led her to it. He maneuvered her so that she was sitting on the edge of the bed while he knelt and eased off each of her heels.

She thought he was going to take off her dress, but instead he guided her so that she was on the bed lying on her side and watching him watch her.

"God, you're beautiful, Willow." Zane looked almost helpless. "And not just on the outside."

"Whether or not you believe it, Zane Steele," she said softly, "so are you."

She didn't take her eyes off of him as he removed his boots before slipping out of his overshirt. He put his shoulder holster and handgun into the drawer of the nightstand next to the bed.

Then he slid onto the mattress so that they were both on their sides, fully clothed, and looking at one another. Not touching, just being.

Her gaze traveled over his powerful body, his defined biceps, corded forearms, and strong hands. His thick black hair was a delicious contrast to his green eyes, which held fire and warmth, danger and excitement—and fear.

It was the fear that tore at her heart.

After a few moments his muscles shifted in his shoulders and arm as he brought his fingers to her face and traced her jawline. His expression was serious, pained. "I'm scared to death, Willow."

She brought her hand to his and felt his warmth beneath her palm. His callused hand was rough over her cheek as she turned her head just enough to kiss his palm before meeting his gaze again. "Don't be," she said.

Zane brought her hand to his chest, over his heart, and she felt the strong rapid beat through his shirt. "Feel that?" His throat worked as he swallowed. "It would break if I fell for you and anything happened that would take you away from me."

7

Willow's own heart jerked at Zane's words and she felt his fear for those he cared about and his loneliness straight to her bones.

An unexpected sensation twisted deep in her belly and she realized it was her feeling the same fear for him—that something might happen to him like what had happened to her cousin. She pushed back those thoughts and concentrated on the man she was with. The man she wanted to soothe and make love to.

Willow moved her hand to his powerful shoulder and felt the ripple of muscle beneath her palm as he let her slowly push him onto his back. She eased herself up and onto him so that she was straddling his trim hips, her short dress hiked all the way up her thighs. She wasn't wearing panties and his jeans felt rough between her thighs. She could feel the bulge of his erection pressed against her folds.

They looked at each other for a long moment before she brought her lips to his. The kiss was slow and more erotic and sensual than any of their rough and demanding kisses. This one held no demands, only the gentleness of two people learning about each other.

Zane ran his fingers up and down her bare arms, making her nerve endings feel alive, on fire, and she wanted to feel those incredible hands all over her body. She grew almost dizzy from his touch, his kiss. His rugged scent filled her, his taste drugged her, the warmth of his body wrapped around her.

Willow drew away and smiled before she reached behind for her zipper and eased it down. The dress was silky on her skin as she pulled it over her head, the material soft yet causing her nerve endings to tingle even more. The dress slid from the sheets like a dark waterfall that shimmered to land on the floor.

He looked up at her with an expression that might have been something like wonder.

"How many times can I say how beautiful you are?" He reached up and cupped her breasts in his palms. "Everything about you."

"Shhh." Willow eased down his body so that he had to release her and she was low enough to unfasten his jeans. She brought his zipper all the way down. Good, he didn't have on any boxers or briefs. She hadn't noticed in the restaurant's bathroom. All she'd been able to concentrate on then was the feel of his thick, long erection inside her.

She released his cock and balls from his jeans and he almost seemed to sigh with relief that the rough cotton wasn't strangling him anymore. But then he groaned when she ran her fingers up and down his erection before cupping his sac and lightly squeezing.

Willow shimmied just a little bit farther down and Zane groaned again. Then he sucked in his breath when she licked his erection like she'd been licking the ice cream cone when they first met.

"Christ." Zane reached for Willow and ran his fingers through the strands of her hair before catching his breath as she sucked the head of his erection.

He looked at Willow as she knelt between his thighs and he groaned as her lips slowly went down his length and back up again. Watching her go down on him was so erotic he had a hard time breathing, much less holding back one hell of an orgasm.

"I don't want you to stop, honey," he said in a voice that sounded rough and raspy. "But I want to be naked and feel your soft skin."

Willow smiled around his cock and he groaned again as she rose and let his erection slide from her mouth. She licked her lips. "You're asking an awful lot by making me stop," she said with a teasing glint in her eyes.

Zane let out a low rumble as he grabbed her by her upper arms and dragged her to him at the same time he sat up. He had to lose the jeans. In a hurry.

He kissed her first before maneuvering her so that she was sitting on the edge of the bed. Then he was stripping out of his socks, jeans, and T-shirt. Before he had a chance to do a damned thing, Willow knelt on the throw rug by the bed, her fingers wrapped around his erection.

"Now where were we . . ." She smiled as her eyes met his. "Oh, yeah," she said before she took his cock into her mouth.

His knees threatened to give out as she licked and sucked his cock. He'd never experienced anything like this before. It wasn't just sex.

What the fuck was it then?

Zane concentrated on Willow as she wrapped her slim fingers around the base of his erection and took him as far as she could.

The feel of his cock in her wet, warm mouth was one of the most incredible experiences he could think of. Plenty of women had given him head, so what was the difference?

They weren't Willow.

Zane slipped his hands into her silky sun-streaked hair and caressed it as he watched his cock slide in and out of her mouth. Her breasts jiggled as she moved her head up and down his erection, her nipples and areolas dark pink. He wanted to be sucking those hard nipples, but at the same time he didn't want her to stop what she was doing.

Because what she was doing was going to blow his fucking mind.

Willow made soft sounds of pleasure when she was the one giving *him* pleasure. She closed her eyes, and even as sensation gathered in his groin he could see her enjoyment in going down on him.

"I'm about to come in your mouth unless you stop." He watched her face and she stayed in the moment and only increased the friction of her mouth and hand. "Open your eyes." His voice sounded so damn rough. "Look at me."

Willow did, her sea-blue gaze meeting his.

That was all it took to slam him over the edge.

Zane gave a shout from the intense sensations of pleasure that were so good they were almost painful. Willow continued sucking his cock until she'd swallowed every drop of his semen and he couldn't take any more.

Warmth flowed through Willow as she looked up and into Zane's green eyes. By the expression on his features, she saw how much pleasure she had given him.

"Come here." He reached for her upper arms, drew her up, and wrapped her in his embrace so that they were skin to skin, her head resting on his shoulder. "Thank you," he said in the same raspy voice. "Now I'm going to return the favor."

Willow looked into his eyes and saw a dangerous glint in them. Excitement swirled in her belly like a windstorm. With a growl, he grasped her in his arms and moved so fast her head whirled. The next thing she knew she was on her back on the cool sheet, her head resting on a pillow, and Zane's head was between her thighs.

A gasp escaped her as he ran his tongue up her folds to her clit, catching her by surprise. He slid his hands under her and raised her legs so that they were over his shoulders. She felt the powerful play of the muscles in his back and shoulders beneath her thighs and calves. The roughness of his callused hands beneath her sensitized her skin even more.

But it was his tongue and mouth that had most of her attention. The way he licked her folds and teased her clit with his tongue could easily drive her out of her mind.

Willow barely realized she was gripping the sheets so tight with her fingers that her knuckles ached. Her cries grew louder the harder he worked her with his tongue. She almost screamed when he plunged two fingers into her channel and then again when he added a third. They were such a tight fit—like he was—and it felt so incredibly good.

She squirmed from pleasure that tingled everywhere possible on her body and she knew that when she came there was no telling what would happen. She might explode for all she knew.

Willow gripped the sheet tighter in her fists and her thighs trembled as her orgasm started rushing toward her. "I'm so close, Zane. So close." Her words were almost cries as she said them. She could swear he was teasing her until she shouted, "Please!"

Zane thrust his fingers in fast and hard then sucked her clit.

She lost it.

The scream that had wanted to escape her when he'd taken her at the restaurant tore loose this time. Her body vibrated and trembled, and she felt sparks in her mind and body. Thought wasn't even possible. Only feeling.

Willow gradually came down to earth, back to the room, and looked at Zane, his head still between her thighs and the corner of his mouth curved into a smile.

"Damn, you do scream loud, honey." He glanced over his shoulder as if looking around the neighborhood before he brought his gaze back to hers. "Just wait until they hear you when I fuck you."

8

"I love the way you say that." A thrill tingled within Willow that went beyond her orgasm as she watched Zane slip her legs off his shoulders.

"Makes you hot?" His hard sculpted lips curved in a dangerous way as he moved up her body and braced his hands to either side of her. "When I say I want to fuck you?"

"Yes." She looped her arms around his neck and looked into his green eyes. His thick black hair was ruffled and his muscles shifted beneath his golden skin from his shoulders down to the hard slab of his torso. "Just hearing your voice does funny things to me."

He cocked one of his black eyebrows. "I'm not so sure I like the idea of being funny when it comes to sex."

Willow grinned. "You know what I mean."

Zane's answer was to lower his head and capture her mouth

with his firm lips. He took possession and kissed her with hunger and need. Since the moment she met him, his masculine scent never failed to seep into her pores and capture her. Now her musk was mixed with his scent and his taste. Breathing wasn't easy when he drew away. Everything about him stole her breath.

"You are addictive." Willow lowered her eyelashes and moved one hand to his shoulder and trailed her fingers over the power of his biceps that flexed beneath her touch before she slid her hand back to his shoulder. She met his gaze again. "I think it would be hard to get enough of you."

She'd wondered if he might back off, if her words scared him, as if she was demanding some kind of commitment.

"You say exactly what you think, don't you, honey?" He teased her lips with his, letting his stubble brush against her chin. When she didn't answer, he added, "I like that in a woman. Opinionated and decisive—just be sure you remember to be careful."

His expression remained dark and predatory as he kissed her again.

Willow savored his warm masculine taste then pulled back enough to say, "I'm careful. Usually." Zane gave her a yeah-sure look, and she smacked her palm against his arm. "I am careful."

"You lead with your heart, not your head. Believe me, it's not a bad thing. It's sexy as hell. But hanging around somebody like me, that could get you killed." The look on his features was so much more dark and dangerous that it gave her a little shiver.

To erase the train of worry going through his head, she trailed her fingers down his taut abs and neared his cock. She didn't go any farther as his expression changed to one of want and need.

"Yep." She sighed. "It's definitely going to be impossible to get enough of you."

So, there.

She'd said it again. Now what would he do?

His expression remained half-hunger, half-worry, but his eyes burned into her as if he might be trying to see exactly what lay in her heart. "I know exactly what you mean, honey."

"You feel good over me like this." She explored the corded strength of his shoulders and arms that were taut from holding himself above her. At the same time she kept her gaze fixed on his, wanting to read his thoughts and his feelings in his eyes as easily as he seemed to read hers. "And earlier . . . I don't think I've ever felt anything like the way you felt inside of me."

He looked as if he was reliving what they'd done in the restaurant. "It was better than I'd dreamed of how good it would feel to be with you. And it was goddamned sexy taking you in that restroom."

She traced one of her fingers from the center of his pecs and moved her hand slowly down, all the way to the hard ridges of his abs. Zane's body tightened beneath her fingertips as she let them travel to his erection again, and she skimmed her fingers along its length. She watched his jaw clench and the burning fire in his eyes that seemed to flame hotter as she started stroking his cock.

"Goddamn it, Willow." He closed his eyes for a moment as she lightly ran her nails along his erection. "I want to go slow with you, but you make me want to just drive into you and take you hard and fast like at the restaurant."

He groaned as he watched her run her tongue along her bottom lip. She brushed her moistened lips over his. "What's stopping you?"

"You deserve better than just a hard fuck." His voice came out in a deep rasp. "I'd like to make love to you for hours. Taste every part of your body, your smooth skin. But right now all I can think about is taking you."

"We can save the slow for later." She hooked her arms around his neck so she could draw him closer. "We have all night."

"Neither one of us is going to get much sleep if I have my way, honey."

She smiled against his lips. "I don't mind you having your way with me."

Zane's growl was low and primal as he pressed his erection against her folds, rubbing it over her sensitized clit. She couldn't have held back the soft moan that rose in her throat if she'd tried.

"I love how tall you are." He lowered his head and licked one of her nipples, causing her to gasp. "You're the perfect height. And your legs are so damned long. Let me feel them around me."

His hips were firm between her thighs as she crossed her ankles behind him, over the smooth skin of his taut backside.

"That's it." His voice sounded harsh, pained, as he rocked back and forth, rubbing his erection along her folds and over her clit. "The first time I saw you, I imagined this."

"I could see it in your eyes." She raised her own hips so that he was pressed tighter against her. "And it made me want you in every way possible."

"You were a goddamned tease with that ice cream cone."

She grinned. "Yup."

"Like they say, paybacks are a bitch." Zane ran his tongue over one of her nipples and then the other.

Willow moaned and arched her back, wanting him to lick and suck them. She wanted to shout how much she wanted him. *Right. Now.* But she knew he needed to feel he had at least this much control.

"I can't take this anymore." Zane reached down and put his erection at the entrance to her core before he braced himself again.

She caught her breath as he waited two heartbeats and then slammed his cock inside her and she cried out. "Oh, God. You're so long and thick."

"Is that a good thing?" he said as he moved in and out in slow, torturous strokes.

"Uh-huh." With every stroke she felt how big he was and she raised and lowered her hips in time with his thrusts so that the curls of his groin pressed tight against her. "No vibrator on Earth could compare."

Despite the fact sweat was rolling down the sides of Zane's face and he was nearly in pain from holding back from driving in hard and fast, he almost laughed. "Better than a vibrator, huh?"

Willow wiggled beneath him. "Even the ones with the little ears."

Zane snorted from trying to hold back a laugh and then one escaped him anyway. He pressed his forehead against her collarbone. "You are something else, honey."

"Yeah, well, I'm someone who wants you really bad." She squirmed beneath him. "I think I'll pass out if you don't get to—get to—"

"Fucking you?" He raised his head and looked down at her with a grin before he stated, "Can't say it, can you?"

"Just do it!" Willow looked like the sweat rolling down the sides of her face were actually tears of pleasure and pain.

Zane decided to have mercy on her—and himself—and began driving in hard and fast, so hard his balls slapped against her ass.

"Yeah. Oh, God." Willow tilted her head back and her chest rose and fell in harsh breaths. "That's what I want. Don't you dare stop or I'll show you that I'm capable of violence."

Zane almost snorted again and choked back a laugh. Who knew great sex could be so much fun, too? But he couldn't stop if he wanted. He kept up a steady pace, ramming into her as deep as he could go and enjoying the feel of heaven as her slick, tight core gripped him.

Willow had thought nothing could be more exciting, more intense, more fabulous than that restaurant sex. But this—this was blowing everything she'd ever imagined out of the water.

As Zane took her, she felt like heat was rushing up and down her skin in waves. He was so big that the walls of her core felt every thrust, every movement he made.

He wasn't moving fast or hard enough as far as she was concerned even though he was pounding in and out of her. She raised her hips up to meet his every thrust and wriggled to feel even more friction in her canal.

She met his gaze and her body started to vibrate. His green eyes focused intently on her, like she was the only thing that mattered to him in the world.

That look, the depth of passion in his eyes, made her orgasm rush toward her in an even hotter wave that burned her as she climaxed.

Willow let loose a cry that had to be heard for miles—one that would have the neighbors calling the police because they thought someone was being murdered.

As she came close to passing out and everything grew darker, she now knew what the French meant by "le petit mort," an orgasm being a "little death."

She fought to remain conscious as she experienced the most amazing thing she'd ever felt. Waves and waves of heat washed over her body as she shook. She gasped as she became fully conscious, her entire being trembling as Zane continued his relentless thrusting in and out of her.

Then he shouted, "Oh, shit!" before pulling his cock out of her.

At first, confusion sparked in Willow's orgasm-fuzzy mind until Zane fisted his hand around his cock and milked it. His semen spurted onto her belly in warm streaks until he was finished.

"Tell me you're on the pill," he said at the same time he collapsed and rolled them both so they were on their sides, facing each other.

She smiled as she saw the concern in his eyes while he used the sheet to wipe her belly. "I am."

"I've been tested and I've always used a condom—until right now." He looked up from what he was doing. "So you don't have to worry about that. Should have thought to tell you before you went down on me."

"I just donated blood a couple of months ago." Willow couldn't help a grin. "But I haven't been with anyone for a very long time. It's pretty much impossible to contract anything when you haven't had sex for a couple of years."

"What the hell?" Zane stopped wiping her belly. "You've gone *two years* with no sex?"

"At least." She shrugged. "I just never met the right person who remotely interested me."

"And then you have sex with a man you don't even know on the same day you meet him." He let the sheet drop back onto the bed and he moved his hand up to caress her hip. "That's awfully dangerous, honey. Like I said before, you lead with your heart."

"Okay, okay, you're right." She trailed her fingers over his jaw, his stubble rough beneath her sensitized fingertips. "But I also knew my instincts were dead-on when it came to you. I didn't have a single doubt in my mind that you're a good man, and that this would be right."

"Thank you." Zane cupped the back of her head and drew her to him for a hard kiss. "But you're not allowed to pick up strange men ever again."

Willow raised her brows. "Oh? And who's going to stop me?"

"I'll figure out a way," Zane said before he rolled her onto her back and took her again.

9

"Aunt Becky, really, it was okay." Zane had dropped Willow off five hours ago, at three in the morning, but she was wide awake and exhilarated. She crumpled a paper napkin and made an easy shot into the kitchen waste can. Two points, easy. "Zane's a nice guy and—"

"But you didn't know him." Becky set a plate on the breakfast bar with scrambled eggs, sausage links, and toast, which smelled so good Willow's mouth watered. She climbed onto a bar stool and swiveled on it as she lost a little steam under her aunt's gaze.

Becky put her hand on one of her portly hips. "Staying out until three A.M. with any man the first day you meet him isn't safe."

If she truly had an idea of exactly what Willow and Zane had been doing until two-thirty in the morning . . . Willow wasn't sure she wanted to know how her aunt would react. No, make that she *definitely* didn't want to know.

"Well, now I've met and had dinner with Zane. And we spent a lot of time talking and getting to know one another." Well, some of the time. Willow folded her arms on the breakfast bar. "And I know he's a good guy."

Becky sighed and adjusted the clip at the back of her silver-streaked blond hair. "Secret Service, right? That's what you said?"

Willow swallowed back the desire to tell Becky that she'd learned that Stacy had died for her country. Everyone thought it was a random act of violence. It was so unfair that no one outside of whatever agency Stacy worked for could know the truth.

Becky straightened and Willow met her aunt's hazel eyes. "You've been an angel to stay with us these past few months and helping out like you have with your job at Macy's." Becky reached up and put her hand over Willow's. "But you have a life to get back to."

"I'm enjoying being here with you." Willow said, and meant it.

Becky squeezed her hand. "For the Lord's sake, child, you've done everything but defend your dissertation to get your doctorate. You keep putting it off to stay with us. You need to go back to NYU, take care of it, and start applying for a position doing what you're so good at. Helping people."

Becky drew her hand away and her smile showed she was proud, sad, and frustrated with Willow. "Just imagine the lives you'll be touching. The positive impact you can make on so many futures."

"I want to be here for you right now." Willow glanced around the large, eclectic living area that she could see from the breakfast bar.

A place that would never have the grandchildren running around that Stacy and her fiancé would have had. Stacy and Barry had planned to start a family—she was going to be quitting her job as "an interpreter" to start her new life with her future husband.

Now that future was gone. No grandchildren would be terrorizing this house or their grandparents' cranky poodle.

Willow met her aunt's eyes. "Would you rather I leave?"

"Lord knows I love having you here." Becky's eyes grew a little watery and she busied herself wiping down the kitchen counters. "But you're putting your life on hold when you need to be living it."

"Right now I'm where I need to be." Willow picked up her fork but her hand shook for some strange reason. "I need to start preparing again to defend my dissertation anyway, and I can get busy on that in the mornings while I work in the cosmetics department in the afternoons."

"Then promise me this." Becky carefully folded the cloth she'd been wiping the counters with and set it beside the stainless steel sink. "After your daily morning run, you *will* go to the library every weekday morning with your laptop and do whatever polishing up you need to on that big paper, the dissertation. *And* schedule a date to go to New York City and be done with it." Becky's gaze was firm, determined. "No more keeping me company in the mornings before you go to work. I'm fine."

Willow gave her aunt a faint smile. "Can you and I still have Saturdays together as our day?"

"Until it's time for you to move on." Becky looked so much younger when she smiled. "Absolutely."

"Good." Willow looked at her plate and back to her aunt. "How about breakfast? Can we still chat over your wonderful dishes?"

"Of course." Becky reached up and stroked Willow's hair over her shoulder before letting her hand drop away. "I want you to promise me one more thing."

Willow tilted her head to the side. "What's that?"

Becky gave Willow "the eye" that said she wasn't fooling around.

So many times that look had scared the crap out of Willow and Stacy when they were kids. Willow had to fight the urge to squirm on the bar stool.

"No more picking up strange men in the Common," Becky said in a firm tone.

Willow smiled as she thought of Zane, who'd actually never left her thoughts at all. "I've heard that somewhere before."

Zane hadn't managed to get much sleep after he'd dropped off Willow and he'd forgotten to shave this morning. One glance at the glass wall of his office and seeing his reflection told him he looked like shit.

He couldn't get images of her off his mind: Willow looking fresh and pretty while she sat on a park bench in the Common eating ice cream; then supermodel-stunning at the restaurant; and best of all, how she looked after she'd just been fucked. Her features flushed, her lips parted and swollen from his kisses, her hair messy on his pillow, and her sea-blue eyes looking at him with pleasure and trust.

Trust. Zack looked out through the glass wall and toward the Command Center and its rush of activity with agents working on cases. The hundred or so monitors and screens gave the whole floor a blue glow. Goddamnit, Willow was too trusting and it was going to get her into trouble.

What are you going to do about it, Steele?

Zane rubbed his temples with his fingers. That was a question he wasn't ready to answer even though that answer hovered at the edge of his mind.

Why'd he agree to have lunch with Willow today?

Because she deserves more than a one-night stand, fuckhead.

And because he had to see her again. Her smile, the honesty in her clear blue eyes, the fact that she said whatever was on her mind, and her unpretentious beauty . . . *damn.*

Last night, before he'd dropped her off at her aunt and uncle's home, they'd agreed to take it a little slower.

Now he was regretting that agreement like hell.

"Knock knock."

Zane looked up to see Georgina Rizzo at his door. The agent showed every bit of her Italian ancestry in her striking looks. Those looks had gotten her a long way undercover. She was not only beautiful, but a damned fine agent.

"Are you all right, Steele?" Rizzo wore what looked like an incredibly expensive red silk blouse along with a tailored black skirt that came to mid-thigh. Her long dark hair hung in waves around her shoulders and she wore large hoop earrings that were obviously pure gold. She was the poster girl for the perfect Italian mafia girlfriend.

She tossed her hair back in a way that was sure to grab a man's attention. "I wanted to stop by and give you a report before I headed back out into the jungle."

"Everything okay?" Zane pointed to a chair in front of his desk.

Rizzo gracefully sat in the chair, crossed her legs at her knees, and casually draped her arms on the armrests. "At least Albano Petrelli is a gorgeous bastard of a mafioso, *Capo Bastone*."

"So you're in good with the underboss?" Zane reclined in his own chair. He didn't have to worry about Rizzo being followed—she was too good of an agent for that.

"Of course." Georgina held out her hand and examined her red nails before putting her hand down and giving Zane an amused look. "Albano didn't know what hit him once I got a hold of him."

"So what's up with the arms deal?" Zane said.

"The arms the Petrellis are selling?" Rizzo said. "They're Barrett 82A1 .50 cal. Armor piercing."

High-capacity semiauto rifles. Shit. Zane rubbed his temples again. "Okay, we've got specs on the shipment. But I still don't have time, location, and who they're selling weapons to."

"Oh, but I do," Rizzo said with a wicked smile. "One A.M. Tuesday morning at the Klein warehouse." She got to her feet. "Albano's totally in lust with me so he doesn't worry if I'm around when he's talking business." She frowned. "And get this. They're selling the weapons to a terrorist faction led by a man named Hisham Nasri."

Zane ground his teeth. "Since when did the Italian mafia start trading arms with terrorists?"

"When the terrorists offered more cash than the Petrellis make pushing dope, they went for it," Rizzo said.

"I doubt any of the other families are going to be happy about this if they find out."

Rizzo nodded. "We might want to leak that info."

Zane studied Rizzo for a moment as he thought of what she had to do to get this intel. "You're still okay with this op?"

Rizzo winked at Zane. "Like I said, Albano's *hot*. I can handle him." She shuddered. "It would be worse if I had to snort coke or if he shot me up with that designer sex drug, Lascivious, and tried to share me."

"If we're looking for a positive, that would be it," Zane said. "Excellent work, Rizzo. Just watch your back and your front."

Georgina Rizzo gave Zane a sultry look as she put her hand on her hip. "Baby, you're the only one for me," she said in a way that would send most men to their knees. Then she laughed. "Gets Albano every time.

"He thinks I'm out shopping." She held up the red purse that matched her blouse and looked even more incredibly expensive than her clothing. "Just wait until Wickstrom gets a load of my expense report for this purse and the clothes I had to buy before I got into Albano's graces." Rizzo opened the clasp of her purse. "Check this out." She tilted her purse so Zane could get a good look and he shook his head at the enormous roll of hundred-dollar bills. "Baby, I love to shop. No hardship here."

Dick Wickstrom was the ASAC, Assistant Special Agent in Charge, for the narcotics and weapons department, and a tight-ass if there ever was one.

Rizzo managed to make Zane smile at the same time he shook his head. "Get to shopping then. And be careful."

"I'll be in touch next time I have something to report." She turned and looked over her shoulder. "Otherwise I'll be out shopping."

By damned, they got what they needed. Now he just had to prepare teams of RED agents to come down on the warehouse to make the bust.

After having watched Georgina Rizzo walk out the door of his office, it hit him like a hammer to the gut. Rizzo's undercover assignment made him remember just how dangerous his occupation was. He withdrew his personal cell phone. He should call Willow and cancel their lunch date.

Then he remembered that of all things, Willow didn't carry a cell phone. She'd said it was because she didn't believe in them. He'd have to change that, too, so she'd have one for emergencies.

Zane pinched the bridge of his nose. *Christ.* The more he thought about her, the more possessive he felt.

Not a good path to head down, Steele.

If only he could get whatever it was in his chest to agree with him every time he thought of Willow.

10

Friday, three days after they'd met, Zane sat across from Willow at a deli on School Street. She was a lot like his sister—unapologetic when it came to eating in front of men. No prissy girl picking at her food to look like she didn't eat much. Willow ate with enthusiasm and enjoyment.

She was so pretty with her sun-streaked hair, her smooth, heart-shaped face. Every movement she made was graceful. Taking her to bed was what he thought of every time he saw her. Hell, even when he didn't see her he fantasized about her long golden legs wrapped around his hips, her slender arms linked around his neck when she brought him down for a kiss.

No, pretty didn't describe her. Beautiful wasn't enough, either. So much about her made it difficult to explain just how special she was.

And he loved to watch her no matter what she was doing.

"What?" She looked up from her thick barbeque pork sandwich. A touch of barbeque sauce was at the corner of her mouth.

"A little sauce." Zane reached across the table and wiped the sauce away with his thumb, just to skim his fingers over her face. She always smiled when he touched her, and every time her smile did something to his chest. An ache, a longing that told him he was in deep shit.

She moved her lips just enough to draw Zane's finger into her mouth and suck. He nearly groaned out loud.

Willow let his now wet finger slip from her mouth. "Don't want to waste any," she said with a wicked glint in her sea-blue eyes.

God, he wanted to take her now. But they'd agreed to slow things down and they'd only had lunch together every day since that incredible dinner and night afterward. Because Willow spent Saturdays with her aunt, she would spend this Sunday with him and his family, then him alone.

It was the alone part he was looking forward to.

Zane leaned back in his chair. "How's the preparation to defend your dissertation going?"

"You remind me of my aunt." That was something Zane wasn't so sure he liked hearing. "Every day she presses to make sure I'm preparing and not off doing something 'impulsive' like she says I do a lot."

"Like meeting me?"

Her lips quirked. "Yeah, she wasn't too crazy about me going out with a man the same day I met him and not getting in until three A.M. Even though you are Secret Service."

"I wouldn't have approved, either." He narrowed his brows. "And you promise to never do it again, right?"

She gave a mock salute. "Yes, sir!"

"About that dissertation."

"I've been going to the public library every day and making my last revisions on my laptop." Willow pointed at her purse, which was resting by her feet. It was large enough to hold her laptop, which was both slim and small.

With his memory for details, Zane wasn't surprised he remembered the design was something his youngest sister, Rori, was into, a brand called Coach. Not something his sister Lexi would go for—she wouldn't be caught dead with something designer if it wasn't part of her undercover work.

Willow took another healthy bite of her barbeque pork sandwich. "Can't wait to meet everyone in your family on Sunday," she said after she finished chewing. "I just have my younger twin sisters, so it'll be fun to be around a really big family."

"Well, now you'll get almost the whole experience." Zane held his own barbeque pork sandwich, ready to take another bite. "Almost the whole bunch. Our brother Ryan is Special Ops in the Marines and who knows where he is right now."

"Eight, nine, still big either way." Willow sipped some of her lemonade through a straw in her Styrofoam cup. She glanced at her watch before setting her lemonade on the table. "Hey, gotta run. I'll be late for work if I don't get going."

Zane stood at the same time she did and caught her by the shoulders before he kissed her long and hard as she kissed him back. He wanted to do more than kiss her, damnit.

When they parted, she picked up her purse and gave him one of her smiles that always punched him in the gut and made him wonder what the hell he'd gotten himself into.

"Now I'm *really* in the Land of the Friggin' Giants." Five-foot-four Lexi Steele planted her hands on her hips as she looked from the five-eleven Willow to her three over-six-foot-tall brothers. The diamond piercing at her belly button winked in the sunlight and Willow wondered what the Chinese symbol meant that surrounded Lexi's belly button.

By the spark in Lexi's green eyes, Willow could tell Zane's sister was comfortable with her shorter height and wasn't serious as she glared at everyone around her.

Now Willow could report back to her friend at work, Linda, that Zane *did* have older brothers almost as sexy as he was.

"But I'll take you each on one-on-one," Lexi was saying, and it was obvious she meant it. From what Zane told Willow, Lexi was a small package but she "kicked ass."

"How about we go three-on-three?" Zane's brother Troy said.

Willow tried to keep a straight face as she rubbed her damp palms on her jean shorts. The afternoon sun and humidity had her pulling her hot pink tank top away from her chest, too.

"Okay." Lexi looked around at her three older brothers, and their twelve-year-old brother who was already taller than she. "I'll take Zane and Willow over you buffoons."

Willow high-fived Lexi as she said, "These boys will go down fast."

She wasn't kidding. She'd played ball from junior high through four years of college and was even asked to try out for several WNBA teams as point guard. But for Willow, basketball was meant to be fun, challenging, and her break from studying. It hadn't been her life's ambition.

Within fifteen minutes, after several jump shots, easy passes, layups, and three-pointers, all three of the huge Steele brothers, including Zane, stared at Willow as if she'd come from another planet.

"You've got a ringer." Troy shook his head as he looked from Willow to Lexi. "We should get a handicap."

"I want to be on *her* side," the twelve-year-old shorter brother, Sean, said to Zane. "Trade ya."

Zane studied Willow and said, "Not on your life," as if he wouldn't trade her outside of basketball, either.

Heat flushed Willow's cheeks as she stood on the three-point line and palmed the ball. She glanced at Lexi who was grinning.

"Oh, you boys are so going to die," Lexi said with an evil laugh.

Lexi might be five-four, but she weaved around the men with ease and made several of her own jump shots as they started another game of three-on-three. Zane was just as good as Lexi.

The two men and younger boy on the opposite team held their own pretty well, but they never stood a chance.

After destroying the brothers five games to zero, everyone was pouring sweat except for Willow who wasn't really winded, just damp from perspiration, mostly from the heat and humidity. She'd never lost her endurance after so many years of playing one of the most demanding sports out of all athletics that required extensive cardio training. The five miles she ran every morning was barely challenging. It was mostly to help keep her fit.

Zane put his arm around her shoulders and Willow noticed that everyone around them just about dropped their jaws. Zane didn't seem to notice as he said low enough for only her to hear, "You're full of one surprise after another."

"Lemonade and whiskey pie," Mrs. Steele called from the front door.

Everyone picked up their jaws and bolted for the house. "Dibs on the biggest piece!" Sean yelled as he beat his older brothers up the steps and onto the porch.

Willow wanted to lean into Zane, but that might have been pushing it in front of his family. Apparently bringing home a date was something Zane had never done before—which didn't surprise her in the least.

She looked up at Zane. "Whiskey pie?"

He gave her one of his heart-melting smiles. "An Irish dessert, of course. Mammy grew up on Irish cooking and that's what she serves from appetizers to desserts." They reached the steps. "And not one of us complains."

Including Zane's parents, the eight members of the Steele bunch sat at the incredibly long table. The only one missing was the brother who was in the Marines. Willow sat between Zane and Lexi.

Mrs. Steele must have spent at least a couple of days cooking due to the amount of food that had been piled on the table both times they'd sat down that day. Now there had to be enough desserts for each person at the table to have his or her own pan or platter full.

"Cool," Lexi said as she reached for a platter with what looked like battered and deep-fried lumpy somethings. "Apple fritters, too."

Ah.

The way the whole family dug in, Willow figured she'd have to jump in if she wanted a taste of the apple fritters and whiskey pie. But Zane slid a slice of pie onto her plate, winked and smiled when she looked at him.

Melt.

God, he was so devastatingly handsome when he smiled like that. He made her feel like warm chocolate and she wanted to pour herself all over him.

Tonight.

Definitely tonight.

11

"I love your family." Willow interlocked her fingers with Zane's as they entered his home.

"You loved kicking their asses at basketball, that's why." Zane brought her flush against him as they stood in his front room. "You wouldn't say a word as to how you learned to play so well. What, were you with the WNBA?"

"Almost." Willow smiled as she slipped her hand from his and wrapped her arms around his neck. She leaned even tighter against the hard ridges of his body. He was so warm and he felt so good and smelled so fabulous. "A few teams tried to recruit me at the end of my four years at NYU. But I opted for concentrating on graduate school instead."

He kissed the corner of her mouth. "What other secrets do you have?"

"You'll just have to find out." Willow reached up and kissed him.

Thrill after thrill started rolling through her belly as Zane grew more demanding in his kiss and his hands roamed her body.

"I need you so goddamned bad right now." Zane kissed her ear, her jaw, her chin as he unfastened the button to her jean shorts. He pushed her shorts and panties down to her thighs. Zane took her by her shoulders and turned her so that she was facing the stone fireplace in his living room. "On your hands and knees, on the throw rug."

The excitement running through Willow had her senses on fire as she obeyed. She felt the brush of Zane's jeans as he knelt behind her, heard the zipper—

Then felt the sudden thrust of Zane's cock inside of her.

Willow gave a shout of surprise as he entered and started taking her hard and fast. "You've been teasing me all week." He leaned over her while sliding his hands beneath her tank top and pushing her bra up over her breasts. "Now it's time to get even," he said as he pinched her nipples as hard as he was driving in and out of her.

"I like the way you get even," Willow said, hardly able to get the words out. She might not get winded at basketball, but Zane somehow managed to steal her breath every time they were together.

"This isn't anything, honey," Zane said as he moved one of his hands down and rubbed her clit.

Willow gasped and almost climaxed. It was one of the most erotic things they'd done. Being on her knees with her thighs spread only as far as her jean shorts would allow her to felt delicious. Zane took her from behind while still clothed, his rough jeans rubbing her soft skin and stimulating her even more.

All of this combined with the feel of his erection inside her, the way he was stroking her clit while using the other hand to pinch first one nipple, then the other—she could barely hold on.

"I've wanted to be inside you every damned day this week." Zane's voice was a rough growl. "And now I'm going to take you until you're too weak to stand."

"I'm already too weak," Willow moaned as he continued his hard thrusts. "You're going to wear me out."

He pinched one of her nipples hard and she moaned even louder. "You weren't even breathing hard after five games of three-on-three. I think you can handle several good fuckings."

Willow began to tremble as her orgasm came closer and closer.

"Feels so good to have my cock inside your tight, slick pussy with no rubber between us."

"Yes. Good." Willow was almost dizzy from breathing so hard and all the sensations rolling through her body. She couldn't begin to get out a coherent sentence if she tried.

"That's it, honey," Zane said as she trembled harder and nearly crossed her eyes from the power of her oncoming orgasm. He rubbed her clit harder. "Come for me now."

This time her cries were like choking sobs as her climax broke through her. She felt as if her body fractured, with pieces flying and scattering into shards of glass that glittered all over the floor.

Her arms gave out while he was still taking her and her face pressed against the soft throw rug, her arms above her head. It was a wonder she didn't turn into a pool of hot melted glass.

Willow's body kept throbbing and she jerked with every spasm of her core.

Zane pulled out. "Turn over."

She struggled to move with her trembling arms. As soon as she was on her back, he jerked her shorts all the way off, leaving her socks and running shoes on.

Not even giving her a chance to catch her breath, much less absorb what he was doing, Zane lifted her legs so that her knees were over his shoulders. He had her backside raised off the floor before he thrust deep.

Willow made sharp, gasping sounds. After that incredible orgasm she was so sensitive inside that she could hardly take any more.

"Oh, you can take more," Zane said and she wondered if she had spoken the words aloud. "Especially after all of your teasing since I had you in my bed the first time."

"You mean several times."

He groaned as his own body started to tremble against hers. "And you're going to come again."

"What gave you the first clue?" she said between harsh breaths, and his grin seemed almost devilish as he looked down at her and pressed his thumb against her clit.

Willow shouted this time when she climaxed, and she twisted and turned almost without realizing it.

"That's it, honey," Zane said, and a few strokes later he gave a hoarse groan and she felt his cock throbbing inside her as he climaxed.

He eased her legs from his shoulders and settled on top of her without putting his whole weight on her, his cock still in her channel. His body burned hot, the smell of sex and his masculine scent heavy in the air.

Even as she lay there limp and exhausted, Zane hardened inside her.

"Let's try the table next," he said, and she smiled as she found her second wind.

If Georgina's intel was good, they were just about to make one hell of a bust.

An hour before, Zane's teams had taken their positions around the dimly lit warehouse. They intended to make sure they arrived be-

fore the Petrelli mob turned over the weapons to the faction of terrorists led by Hisham Nasri.

No way in hell was Zane going to let the Petrellis sell the Barrett 82A1 .50 cal armor-piercing rifles to terrorists. Where the hell
had the Petrellis gotten their hands on the weapons to begin with?

If anyone could find out, Rizzo could. She'd have to dig deeper.

Zane checked his watch, pressing a button that allowed the screen
to be so slightly illuminated that it wouldn't glow bright enough for
anyone but him to see.

Inside and outside, the warehouse was wired with RED's high-
tech cameras, and bugs so that every word would be easily heard.
RED's techs were the best.

As far as legality for whatever they did, RED had a blanket warrant on this op from the judge who handled all of RED's cases.

Ten minutes to one. The Petrelli family and Nasri faction should
be arriving any time now.

It wasn't long before a couple of big dark-colored Cadillacs
pulled up followed by what looked like a refrigeration truck.

A few more minutes and three black Mercedes arrived.

Why not terrorize in style?

In moments, several men climbed out of each car and walked
toward each other. It was almost comical. The men postured and
looked like gunslingers from the Wild West.

Two men, one from each group, met beneath one of the pale
warehouse lights. Zane moved his binoculars to his eyes and got a
good look at the men. From their intel and the photos they'd
pulled up on each man, one was Enzo Petrelli and the other man
was definitely Hisham Nasri.

Adrenaline began to fire through Zane's system harsh and hot
as they got closer to busting the sonsofbitches. And they'd get the

head of this terrorist faction—Zane hadn't been sure he'd show up himself.

Enzo's voice came through Zane's comm as clear as if the member of the huge mafia family had been standing right next to him.

Zane wasn't sure if he was relieved it wasn't Albano Petrelli because Rizzo would lose her "in" with the Petrelli family if it had been. On the other hand, he could have pulled her out if it was Albano and they busted him.

Enzo was saying, "We've got the goods if you've got the green." He gestured toward the white truck. "Check the merchandise and we'll take a look at the cash."

The terrorist had a hard, angular face and a cold, calculating expression. His accent was strong when he spoke. He mentioned the amount they were paying was in the case they'd brought.

Nasri then inclined his head to one of his men to check the truck. The back door rattled, the sound loud in the night as it rolled up to show crate upon crate.

Zane and his teams just needed to make sure what was in those crates . . .

Enzo had one of his men go through the briefcase of cash while he and Nasri had a stare-off.

The teeth-grinding sounds of nails screeching against wood cracked the stillness, then the hard thump of a wooden lid. One of the men shouted to Nasri and held up one of the illegal rifles.

Nasri and Enzo shook hands.

"Go!" Zane said into his comm and RED agents began swarming the area with shouts of "Police!"—the universal word for law enforcement.

It became obvious in a hurry that Enzo's and Nasri's men didn't intend to go down without a fight.

Zane joined his teams and fury roared through him as he picked off one of Enzo's men who'd shot a RED agent.

Enzo, Nasri, and a few of the other men raised their hands while the others now lay on the ground, around them, dead or injured.

It was only moments before the men were cuffed and all weapons and cash confiscated.

Two RED agents were down.

Zane shouted orders to team members, telling them what to do while he and three other RED agents ran toward those who'd been shot. Two RED ambulances had been waiting not too far from the warehouse and drove up at the same time Zane reached one of the agents.

He dropped to his knees and carefully removed the agent's helmet.

By the wide, unblinking eyes, the pale skin, and the stillness of her body, Zane didn't have to be told that Peters was dead. The bullet that pierced her throat had probably severed her spinal cord, and by the amount of blood covering her neck she'd probably died from both injuries.

"Fuck!" Zane shouted. The RED paramedics were at his side in a second and Zane probably didn't need to say it, but he did anyway. "Peters is gone."

Goddamnit but he could blow a hole through the head of every one of those assholes who were cuffed and now being shoved into vehicles as they were taken into custody.

"Jacobs took a round, but he'll live," Yanov called to Zane. "He got hit full in the chest, but they weren't using armor-piercing bullets."

Thank God for that. Still, Zane's hand shook as he closed Peters's eyes and let the paramedics take her away.

He stood and watched for a moment as his teams efficiently

cleared the site of any remaining evidence. That included taking down cameras and listening devices.

RED operated solo and through incredibly strong channels and people in high places, and it kept off the radar of any other law enforcement. RED had ways of warning off local police from their ops, and RED agents "took care of business" in smooth, quick, and exact precision.

It wasn't long before all the bodies and blood were taken care of and the site was left looking like it had before the transaction and the raid.

Tires crunched over gravel as an agent drove the now-closed refrigeration truck to HQ to be processed. The ambulances and body wagons followed.

A few moments more and all RED agents had cleared out and were headed back to HQ.

As Team Supervisor and operation leader, Zane was one of the last agents to leave the scene. He gave one final appraisal then headed off to the location he'd left his RED-issued Trailblazer.

12

"Double caramel venti frappuccino up for Willow!" a barista called out.

Yum. Willow went to the Starbucks pickup counter and grabbed her drink, the plastic cup instantly chilling her hand. She hitched her purse higher on her shoulder. It was heavy, as usual, with her small laptop weighting it. As soon as she finished drinking her frap she'd head to the library and work on her dissertation defense.

A pair of women vacated a small round table in the corner of the crowded coffee shop and Willow plopped into one of the chairs the moment it was empty. *She scores,* she thought and almost laughed then rolled up the sleeves of her white button-up blouse. She unwrapped and plunged her straw into her frappuccino.

Before she had a chance to take one sip, a man said, "Anyone sitting here?"

Automatically Willow shook her head as she looked up. The place was crowded and she was lucky to have grabbed a chair, so she didn't mind sharing.

The man smiled when she met his gaze. She started to smile in return but a prickly sensation sent goose bumps rising on her arms. Something didn't feel quite right about the way he looked at her with his dark eyes as he took the opposite seat.

He had beautifully carved features and night-black hair. He extended his hand. "Filippo," he said. His accent was clearly Italian like his name.

Willow didn't want to take his hand but she forced a smile and let him take hers. His was hot and dry, and more prickles rolled up her arm. He didn't take his gaze off of her and she had to tug to get her hand away from his.

"What is your name?" he asked in his smooth, accented voice.

Then she noticed the man didn't even have a cup of coffee.

Zane's and Aunt Becky's words echoed in her head at the same time, telling her not to be too friendly with strangers. She'd always followed her heart and her gut, and both were telling her to get the hell out of here.

"Oops!" Willow faked another smile as she wrapped her fingers around her frappuccino cup and pushed back her chair. "I forgot I'm supposed to meet up with my trainer. He's a former football player and he's *so* tough. He'll probably make me do extra reps."

She was on her feet and pushing her way through the crowded coffee shop before he had a chance to say a word.

As she opened the glass door to let herself out, she caught a reflection—the man was following her.

Willow's heart lunged into her throat. She tossed the frap that she hadn't even sipped into the black waste can beside the door and swung around the door as fast as she could without running.

You're imagining things, Willow. There's not some man following you. But she looked over her shoulder and she saw he was near and his long strides were taking him closer to her.

Oh, my God. He *was* following her. Willow glanced around and saw a large group of tourists on the Freedom Trail and ran straight into the middle of the crowd.

Immediately she realized she had a new problem. At five-eleven she towered over the group that was mostly comprised of foreigner visitors who were at least five inches shorter than she was.

The Italian joined the crowd and before she could move ahead, the man cupped her elbow with his hot, dry hand. "Where are you going in such a hurry, Willow?" he said in his smooth voice. He wrapped his fingers around her arm and jerked her to a stop so that the crowd parted around them, leaving them behind.

The sound of her name—which she hadn't told him—coming from the Italian sent cold shooting through her.

Bravado. Confidence. Don't let him know you're scared as hell.

Yeah, right.

She jerked her arm as she whirled and glared up at him. "Let go of my arm or you *will* regret it."

He smiled and tightened his grip as he moved behind her. "You're going to come with me."

She hadn't spent eleven years playing basketball without knowing how to intentionally foul someone.

With all her strength, Willow rammed her free elbow into the man's gut. At the same time she hooked her ankle around his and jerked him off balance.

A shout of obvious surprise came from him as her other elbow slipped from his grasp. She whirled on one foot like she was holding a basketball and looking for a good pass. Instead she let her heavy purse drop from her shoulder, slide down her arm, and into her grasp.

She gripped the straps of her purse in both hands and swung right at the man's face.

Score.

"Fuck!" the man shouted as she nailed him in the face, the side of her laptop slamming into him with the power of her swing. Blood immediately started flowing from his nose and it was bent at an odd angle now.

At the same time he'd dropped to the sidewalk, something metal with a dull shine flew from his hand and skittered across the concrete.

She ran.

It hammered at her mind that the man had been holding a gun and that's what had spun away from him. He could have shot her. Why would some strange man want to shoot her?

Willow's heart pounded like mad and adrenaline spiked in her veins, giving her more speed. She rounded a corner, her breath coming in harsh gasps from the fear racing through her. The squeal of tires came from around the corner.

She ducked into a clothing store filled with high racks of dresses and low circular racks of blouses and slacks. The salesperson was busy and at that moment all Willow could think about was hiding. The man had a freaking gun and she wasn't about to remain in the open.

Willow dropped to her knees and crawled under a rack of shirts and was relieved to see it wasn't a rack with an open center. It had a flat surface above that held a mannequin bust.

When she was under the clothing, she scrunched up with her jean-clad knees drawn tight to her chest and her purse clutched against her. She bit her lip to keep herself from breathing too loudly.

"Can I help you?" a woman said from somewhere across the store. The salesperson.

Then came that smooth Italian voice, only now it sounded not so smooth, like he was having a hard time talking—probably because she'd broken his nose. Every word he spoke held a bite of fury. "Did a woman come in here? Very tall. Blond."

The woman hesitated. "How long ago?"

"Now." It sounded like the Italian was also having a hard time not sounding like he was pissed. "Within the last two minutes."

"Definitely not." Willow almost let out a gasp of relief that the woman hadn't spotted her—or at least was covering for her.

The man said nothing in response and she heard his footsteps heading toward the door. He started speaking in a one-sided conversation and she realized he was talking to someone on a cell phone.

"She got away," the man was saying as his voice grew more distant. "No, I don't know where the hell she went. She wouldn't have escaped if I did." Then the faint words came, "cop . . . girlfriend."

And then nothing.

Willow slumped against the metal support at the center of the rack. He was gone.

She almost screamed when someone parted the clothing in front of her. Relief flooded through Willow again when she saw the salesperson.

"Are you all right?" the woman asked as she extended her hand. "I'm sure that man is gone. Should I call the police?"

"Thank you for not telling him that I came in." Willow let the woman help her up. Her head felt a little woozy as she stood. All that adrenaline and being scrunched like she'd been before getting up made for one dizzy blond.

Willow shook her head, more to clear it than to say no. "I'm dating a cop. I'll call him," she said when she began to think straight again. She needed to talk to Zane. Somehow she knew only he could help her. "Can I use your phone? I don't carry one."

The woman reminded Willow of Aunt Becky with her motherly air as she ushered Willow to the back of the store. "You should have a phone for emergencies." The woman glanced over her shoulder. "I don't know what this was all about, but that man looked dangerous. Not to mention all that blood on his face and his shirt."

"You bet I'm going to get a phone now just as soon as I find a store that sells them." Willow swung her purse onto her shoulder as she tried to think of the closest phone store. Her thoughts were pinging all over the place. "I could have been calling for help while I was hiding. Or when I first noticed that man following me."

"Why was he following you?" The woman went behind the sales desk and handed Willow a corded phone. "Did you hit him or something? Blood was practically pouring from his nose."

"Honestly, I don't know who he was." Willow's hands shook as she punched in the number for Zane's cell phone. "He just grabbed my arm and I let him have it with my purse." She glanced at the purse and shook even more when she saw the blood on the corner of it.

"Good job," the salesperson said. "You must have nailed him good." Then the woman moved away, obviously to give Willow some privacy as she made her call.

Willow almost cried with relief when Zane answered, "Steele."

"It's Willow," she said, doing everything she could to keep her voice from cracking. "Something just happened. I'm scared. I have to talk to you. I need to see you."

His voice sounded tight, concerned. "Where are you?"

"I'm—" She tried to focus as the adrenaline rush started to leave her. "Near King's Chapel." It hit her that the man had tried to kidnap her right in front of the centuries-old cemetery next to the chapel.

"Are you someplace safe?"

Willow looked at the salesperson. "What's the address?" she asked the woman, then repeated the address to Zane.

"I'll be right there." He sounded as if he was forcing himself to remain calm. "Don't move."

Willow swallowed. "Okay," she said right before he ended the connection.

"Thank you." She looked at the salesperson as she set the phone on the receiver. "My boyfriend, the cop—he's coming to get me."

The lady nodded. "You'll be safe here."

Willow stayed in the back of the store. The moment Zane walked through the door, she ran to him and threw her arms around his waist and started shaking.

"What happened, honey?" Zane's throat was tight as he put his arm around Willow's shoulders and guided her outside the store and into the sunny morning.

Zane had parked his work SUV illegally in front of the chapel's burial grounds, but had his placard in the window indicating that his vehicle was there for law enforcement purposes.

"Some man." Willow's shoulders were trembling and that scared the shit out of him. It had to be something bad. "He—I think he tried to kidnap me."

"What the hell?" Zane's mind churned as he stopped in front of the gate to the King's Chapel Cemetery. He took Willow by the shoulders and she met his gaze. She didn't look like she'd been crying but the fear was still in her eyes. "Tell me exactly what happened."

A shot pierced the quiet morning.

Willow gave a cry of pain and surprise and he barely caught her as she collapsed and blood began to spread, brilliant red against her white shirt.

262

13

Zane's system went on instant overdrive. Heat burned his skin and adrenaline pumped through his body.

He grabbed Willow by the waist and flung them both through the cemetery gates to the ground, causing her to cry out again even as he tried to cushion her with his body. He didn't know how badly Willow was hurt, but he had to get her out of the line of fire.

Zane had his Glock out in a second. With one hand holding his weapon, he kept a tight hold on Willow and scooted behind several ancient headstones.

At the same time he drew his handgun, Zane pressed a button on his holster for emergency extraction.

The moment Zane pressed that button, a RED extraction unit was notified and they had already honed in on Zane's location via a satellite link even more accurate than GPS.

Bullets pinged on the metal fence from the direction of the shots. People screamed. An ancient headstone exploded nearby as another bullet missed them.

Zane's whole body vibrated and he prayed Willow hadn't been seriously shot.

His gut clenched. All of that blood on the left side of her chest made it look like she'd been hit damned close to her heart. He glanced at her and saw blood coating her fingers and staining the shoulder of her blouse as she pressed her hand to a wound.

On her shoulder, not her chest.

She sounded like she was talking through gritted teeth as she laid flat on her back on the ground. "Don't worry about me. Just get him."

More shots rang out.

More people screamed in the street.

Fuck.

Zane stayed low as he held his Glock and looked through a pair of headstones. Anger burned through him as he spotted the shooter, a man with a bloody nose, peering around the side of the chapel.

The man swung around and used his handgun to shoot toward the stones where they were hiding. Another ancient headstone exploded and hard chunks rained down on Willow and Zane.

From his prone position, Zane held his Glock in a two-handed grip and sighted the shooter. The fury boiling inside him made him want to kill the sonofabitch. But he didn't know why the hell they were being shot at and he wanted to take the man in for questioning. RED would be there any second.

With two rapid shots, Zane put a bullet through the man's right shoulder, then his left. The screams that followed gave Zane only a little satisfaction as the shooter started to drop and his handgun slid into the street, at least ten feet away from him.

For good measure Zane shot the man in both thighs. More screams before the man fell on his bloody face.

He hoped there was only one shooter since the bullets had come from one direction and the shots had stopped the moment the man was down.

He jerked his RED cell phone out of its holster and pushed a speed-dial number. He could already hear tires screeching to a halt on the other side of the fence. "One shooter down," Zane relayed. "He could have another weapon on him. Take him alive for questioning. Not sure if there are any more perps."

He jerked his gaze to Willow and his heart nearly stopped beating. "I've got an injured civilian," he added before he clicked off and shoved the phone into its clip.

Willow's eyes were closed and her bloody hand had fallen away from her shoulder wound, which was bleeding so badly most of the top half of her blouse was soaked with blood. How close was the wound to her heart?

With the sound of RED agents swarming the area of the park they were in, Zane set his Glock close to him.

"Willow!" he shouted as he patted her face with one hand and pressed his other hand against the wound.

Fear spiked through him. All that blood—*shit*. He couldn't let her fall asleep. "Wake up, Willow. Stay with me."

Her eyelids fluttered, and of all things she gave a slight smile. "Guess I'll be calling in sick to work."

Zane's temples ached and the sick sensation in his gut grew even worse as he paced the waiting room. Willow had been taken to

RED's infirmary because he hadn't been sure whether or not the shooting was RED-related and the organization had to take special precautions.

What was taking so long? How badly was Willow hurt? There had been so much goddamned blood. He admired her spunk, the way she challenged him, and her fresh honesty and easy confidence. He loved how she constantly surprised him, like she had with her basketball skills and every dare she made.

Everything about Willow was special and his chest hurt even more, as if he'd been the one shot.

Why would anyone go after Willow?

To get to me.

"Zane!"

He snapped his head up and saw Georgina Rizzo and Lexi practically running into the waiting room.

"How is she?" Lexi asked, her green eyes bright with concern. "Is your girlfriend going to be okay?"

Zane barely registered that Lexi had referred to Willow as his girlfriend. "They haven't told me a goddamned thing."

"It's only been an hour since you arrived, so this isn't a bad sign. Just hold on." Rizzo was still decked out as a mafia girlfriend, wearing tight jeans but holding her high heels in one of her hands. "I heard about it the moment you called for extraction—I was in the department." She swallowed. "I couldn't go to the scene because of what I'd overheard from Albano, so I knew a Petrelli would be there."

Fire raced through Zane's entire body. "This was a mafia hit?"

Rizzo nodded. "All I overheard was that they were after whoever was responsible for the bust. I found an excuse to leave and went straight to HQ. Then everything went to hell."

"It was Henry, your mafia informant." Lexi said. Zane rounded on her and even his ears started to burn. Henry had been the snitch Zane had had a meeting with the same day he'd met Willow on the Common. "The information recovery specialists used RED's truth serum on Filippo Petrelli as soon as they brought him in."

"I was there when Lexi got the report," Rizzo said. "Thanks to the serum, Petrelli spilled everything about how they found out Henry was a snitch. The Petrellis tortured Henry the day following the takedown and broke all of his fingers until he told them 'the cop' who'd been responsible for the bust. Then they blew him away."

"They wanted blood—several of the Petrellis went down that night." Lexi touched Zane's arm. "The Petrellis have been following you and Willow the past two days since Henry gave you up." She glanced at Rizzo before looking at Zane again. "They were waiting for a chance to grab her to hurt you."

"Fuck!" Zane almost slammed his fist into a wall in the waiting room. This was exactly why he didn't get into relationships. Someone he cared about could get hurt because of *him*.

And Willow had been the one to pay for his stupidity. "I shouldn't have gotten involved with her." Zane went to a different wall and pulled his arm back, ready to put a hole through it.

"Don't." Lexi caught him by the elbow and he cut his gaze to her and almost growled. "You didn't do anything wrong," she said.

"Like hell." Zane was about to say more but the door to the infirmary slid open and Dr. Kelly walked through.

"She'll be fine." Dr. Kelly went straight to Zane and sheer relief made him weak.

"How bad is it?" Zane said in a gravely voice filled with so much he wanted to say along with so much anger he could explode.

"She was shot in the shoulder and the bullet chipped bone and tore ligaments, so it will take the injury some time to heal." Dr.

Kelly continued, "She's going to be wearing an arm brace and then a sling for a while."

"Goddamnit." Zane couldn't think of enough swear words to express himself right then. "When can I see her?"

"We're moving her to a private room now." Dr. Kelly started to turn to the infirmary doors. "About thirty minutes."

It was the longest ninety minutes of Zane's life—from the time they reached the infirmary to the moment he followed Dr. Kelly to Willow's room.

When they reached the door he almost didn't want to walk in. He sucked in his breath as Lexi said, "Go," and Rizzo added, "We'll wait here for you."

Zane swallowed and entered Willow's private infirmary room and he wanted to drop to his knees and beg for forgiveness when he saw her pale face, the dark circles beneath her closed eyes, the IV, and the huge brace on her arm.

Even though his feet didn't want to move, he made himself go to her and sit beside the bed. He took her hand and squeezed it. "Honey? Are you okay?"

Hell no she wasn't okay.

Willow opened her eyes. She smiled but it was weak, like she was too tired. "They gave me Demerol," she said. "I don't know how long I'm going to stay awake."

"I'm so sorry." Zane pressed his forehead against her hand. "I should never have—"

"Shut up." Willow sounded angry and he looked up and met her beautiful sea-blue eyes. Anger sparked there, too. "I knew *exactly* what I could be getting into. Don't you dare insult me by saying you never should have dated me."

Tingles prickled Zane's skin as a strange feeling rolled over his skin. "Willow—"

"I said *shut up*." She looked angry enough to come out of the bed. "You are *not* going to dump me because of this. Maybe for some other reason, but not because of your feelings of guilt that I got in the way."

Words wouldn't come to his mind or his mouth. If he said anything, she'd probably come out of that bed and after him in a flash.

"I'm a big girl, Zane." Color had returned to Willow's face. "I may not always do the right things or make the right choices, but with you I have. If you're going to leave me then it better be a damned good reason because this sure as hell isn't."

"Christ—"

"Do I have to knock some sense into that thick head of yours?" She started to rise out of the bed. "Because I will, Zane Steele. How do you think that creep got his broken nose? I'm not above bodily injury."

To his surprise, he almost smiled as he got up and pushed on her good shoulder to get her to lie back down.

"I can't help but love you." The words came to Zane so easily it surprised him. "Everything about you. But it scares me. *This* scares me."

Willow's features relaxed and she smiled. "I know."

"You've said that since the first time we met." Zane found himself starting to smile. "Do you know everything?"

"Of course," she said. "And I'm never going to let you forget it."

He bent over her and stroked her hair from her cool forehead. "Never?"

"Nope." She shook her head on the pillow. "I intend to kick your brothers' asses at basketball for a long time to come."

Zane was almost grinning now. "Are you asking me to marry you?"

Her smile was so brilliant it made his heart thump like crazy. "Is that a yes I see in your expression?"

He moved his knuckles across her cheek. "One thing."

She raised her brows. "Watch it . . ."

Zane had never smiled so much in his life as he did around Willow. "*You* haven't told *me* that you love me."

"Oh, that." She reached up her good arm and caught him by his shirt, bringing him down for a hard kiss.

God, she tasted sweet and womanly, warm and incredible. She only allowed him to draw away slightly. "I love you, Zane Steele. Now say you'll marry me. I promise to get a ring and do it right when I get out of this place."

Zane laughed at the image of Willow on one knee presenting a ring to him. She'd do it, too.

"Yes." He kissed her again. "When?"

"Before I defend my dissertation." Willow smiled. "Then instead of Dr. Randolph, I'll be Dr. Steele." She captured his gaze and held it.

"'Dr. Steele' has a nice ring to it," he said.

"Yup."

"I think I've found a way."

She raised an eyebrow. "A way for what?"

"To keep you from picking up strange men in the Common."

Willow smiled and drew him down to her again. "I think you have."

Wanted: A Real Man

by

Heidi Betts

This story is dedicated to one of my very best friends, Joanne Emrick, who passed away very unexpectedly just before I started this story. She loved romance, and had hopes of seeing her own writing published one day. It breaks my heart to know that will never happen now, and I only wish there were some way to bring her back so she could complete her journey to success.

I think of you often, Joanne, and miss you more every day, in a million different ways. I miss your laughter and wit; the long e-mails and even longer phone calls; closing down restaurants with our all-day gab/plotting/critique sessions; turning to you for *everything*; and even more, I miss knowing that you're there, no matter what.

(With much thanks to Kalen Hughes and Candice Hern for the research help!)

1

Claire Cassidy Scarborough entered the Pittsburgh U.S. Marshals Service building with her heart in her throat, her palms damp, and every cell of her body screaming for her to turn around and run in the other direction.

She *did not* want to do this.

But she needed to. Had to, for her daughter's sake.

Breathing in time with her rapid pulse, she made her way across the gray, institutionally tiled floor. Her heels clicked with every step, their echoes sounding like gunshots, at least to her ears.

She stopped to ask the first person who looked as though he belonged there where she could find Deputy Marshal Lincoln Rappaport and was pointed toward an elevator off to the right. Riding up to the third floor, she tried not to let her thoughts or anxieties spin out of control.

Deputy marshal. She still couldn't believe it. Couldn't picture the good ol' boy son of a mechanic she'd known since they were kids leading a successful career in law enforcement.

And not just any branch of law enforcement. Not just a small-town sheriff or state trooper, but a U.S. deputy marshal.

She'd read up on them, knew that their duties spanned everything from courthouse security and asset seizures to witness protection and hunting down fugitives. He was one of the big dogs.

That knowledge both comforted and terrified her. She needed him—his training and connections and expertise—but wished to God she didn't.

If there had been anyone else, any other way to solve her problem, she would have jumped at it.

Anything to avoid seeing him again.

No, that wasn't quite true. A part of her had always wanted to see him again—had never wanted to walk away in the first place. But knowing how he would react after so many years had kept her from ever trying to contact him.

The elevator doors slid open and she stepped out into a short hallway. To her left was a cluster of nondescript metal desks, each cluttered with computer screens, telephones, and sheaves of loose papers. Typical office noises met her ears—ringing phones, tapping keyboards, muted voices.

Inhaling sharply, she swallowed and steeled herself as best she could while her insides went liquid, then turned and headed into what she quite literally considered the lion's den.

Standing at the edge of the grouping of desks, she scanned the faces of the men and women busy doing their jobs. She didn't stumble for even a moment over any one of them.

It might have been ten years since she'd last seen him—ten long years, in which she was sure they had both grown and changed substantially—but as soon as her gaze landed on him, she knew. If her eyes hadn't sent the message to her brain loud and clear, the thumping of her heart inside her chest would have.

For a second, she couldn't breathe, and couldn't move even though she very much wanted to spin and run in the other direction.

But she couldn't afford to be a coward. Not today.

Stepping forward, she made a beeline for his desk, stopping just before she could have reached out and touched the cool metal surface. He was on the phone, turned slightly away from her, but knew she was there because he held up a hand to gesture that he'd be one more minute. She waited patiently . . . almost too patiently, considering that her gut instinct told her these few brief seconds were merely the calm before the storm.

Finishing his call, he hung up and twisted in his seat to face her.

"Yeah, what can I do for you?" he asked, speaking before he'd gotten a clear view of who was standing beside his desk.

As soon as their eyes met, as soon as he got a good look at her face, any hint of warmth in his expression vanished. His mouth thinned and he stared at her as though she was something he needed to scrape off the bottom of his shoe.

A shiver went through her. Of dread. Of regret. Of fear that his hatred for her would keep him from helping her.

But also of desire and a gut-level attraction that not even a decade apart could dispel.

He'd been a gorgeous teenager. Tall and lean, with hard muscles in all the right places. Wavy brown hair and eyes an indistinguishable color somewhere between light brown and hazel; she'd always thought of them as sort of a stormy, sexy shade of gray.

Popular, a star football player, and one of the boys who had all the girls swooning. They'd all wanted him, flirted with him, chased after him, but Claire was the one who'd landed him.

Not through any adolescent attempts at seduction, but because they'd been neighbors, grown up together, and because innocent childhood games had developed into something overtly sexual right along with their prepubescent bodies.

Memories rushed over her, sending tingles of awareness to all the right places.

As handsome as he'd been in high school, it couldn't hold a candle to his appearance now. His rich, dark chocolate brown hair was cut almost military short. His body had gone from lean and mean to built and rippling with muscle.

If there was an inch of fat anywhere on his solid frame, she would be hard-pressed to find it. Not that she—or any other woman on the seven continents—would mind searching.

His black, nondescript T-shirt clung to his chest like a second skin, showing every curve of his pectorals and the plane of his abdomen. His biceps, which were so big around that she doubted she could span them with both hands, flexed as he moved, showing the strangely erotic flow of the thick, black barbed-wire tattoo that circled his right arm.

She swallowed hard, wishing the mere sight of him didn't set off firecrackers in her bloodstream and send a sharp shock of heat directly to her womanly core.

"Linc," she said, forcing his name past her arid throat and stiff, dry lips. There was an empty chair next to his desk and she slowly lowered herself onto its seat before her legs gave out.

"What are you doing here?" he asked in a voice that blew over her like an Arctic wind. His jaw was clenched and a muscle ticked at the back of his cheek.

There was no point in beating around the bush. Nothing that she could say would alter his opinion of her or thaw his ice-cold demeanor.

It was just as well; she didn't have a lot of time to waste.

"I need your help."

He gave a loud snort and pushed away from his desk, arrogantly leaning back in his chair until the springs squeaked.

"What makes you think I give a shit?" he bit out.

Since she didn't have an answer to that—nothing that would appease him, at any rate—she chose to ignore the question. Instead, she pulled a sheaf of papers from her Coach handbag and spread them out in front of him . . . not that he took them or bothered glancing in their direction. She started talking, anyway.

"I'm in the middle of a divorce. Even though my soon-to-be exhusband comes from a very wealthy family, things have been amicable enough. His family was concerned I would try to take half of all his assets, but I signed a prenuptial agreement before we married, and I'm happy to stick to that, regardless of California being a community property state."

She held his gaze, refusing to look away no matter how cold, how angry, how distant his stare became. This was too important. She needed him to listen and understand.

"The one bone of contention between us is my daughter. He's fighting me for full custody, even though he has no biological claim to her. And now . . ."

She paused to take a breath, to calm her racing heart. Her throat grew tight and tears pricked behind her eyes.

"Now, he's taken her. He picked her up from school last Friday and neither of them has been seen since."

Linc's face remained impassive, looking for all the world like the countenance of some striking but lifeless stone statue. Nothing she said seemed to have any effect on him. Nothing she did, not even the emotion in her voice or the moisture gathering along her lower lashes made a dent.

When he spoke, his voice was flat and brittle. "I repeat: What makes you think I give a shit?"

Nothing, Claire thought. Not a thing. There was absolutely no reason he should care about her, or her daughter, or her divorce, or anything that was going on in her life. Any interest he might have had in her had withered and died ten long years ago.

Reaching into her purse, she removed a photograph and laid it flat on the desk.

"No reason," she replied calmly, slowly removing her fingers to reveal her daughter's long, dark hair and nine-year-old, gap-toothed grin. "Except that she's your daughter, too."

2

If raising his head and finding Claire Cassidy seated in the chair next to his desk had felt like a sucker punch to the gut, hearing her say he had a daughter felt like she'd put his balls in a vise and given it a good, hard twist. Stale air caught in his chest and his lungs refused to function to draw in fresh.

Their eyes stayed connected, and she never flinched, never looked away. Her crystal-blue gaze held only sadness and regret and a touch of fear.

He'd been a deputy marshal long enough to know when someone was lying or telling the truth, and there wasn't a bone in Claire's body that didn't believe what she was saying.

Not that he was going to just roll over and take her at her word. He hadn't seen her in ten years—not since she'd walked away from him and whatever future they might have had together. Damned if he was going to let her waltz back in and start spinning tales designed to . . .

To what?

Lure him back? Blackmail him?

If that was the case, then the joke was on her. He wouldn't take her back now if she came dipped in diamonds, and he didn't earn enough to make anyone think he was worth blackmailing.

But whatever she was up to would only work if he actually believed he had a child. Which he didn't. There was no way, at least not with her.

Curiosity, though, was a powerful thing. Breaking their gaze, he let his attention slip from her face to the photograph lying flat on his desk. He picked it up with two fingers and studied the little girl pictured there.

The long brown hair with bangs cut straight across her brow and a pink plastic headband holding back the sides. The slightly crooked front teeth, visible in her wide smile, that foretold the need for braces. The tiny rhinestone studs in her ears and a small flower necklace lying against the pink of her sweater to match the giant yellow-and-peach daisy knit at its center.

But it was her eyes and facial structure that clutched at his diaphragm. Looking at this little girl was like looking at a picture of his mother when she was young, and there were aspects of her that he saw in the mirror every morning.

Narrowing his eyes, he glanced back at Claire. She was still watching him, waiting patiently for his reaction . . . or for him to fall into her trap.

His chair scraped across the floor as he got to his feet, grabbing Claire's arm to drag her to hers. With the photo in one hand, Claire in the other, he headed out of the bullpen, calling back, "Hey, Keegan, I'll be in Interview One. Cover for me, will you?"

Not waiting for a response, he stalked down the hall, Claire's heels scrambling behind him as she struggled to keep up with his long, angry strides. Pushing her into the room ahead of him, he slammed the door behind them, kicked a chair out from the table, and barked, "Sit."

She did, taking a moment first to smooth her light blue skirt and straighten the sleeve of her matching designer jacket.

A muscle in Linc's cheek twitched as his molars began to grind. He could feel tension pulling at every muscle in his body, fury struggling for release.

He wanted answers, and he wanted them now, but that didn't keep him from noticing how much Claire had changed over the past ten years.

For one thing, she was wearing a tailored designer suit that probably cost more than he earned in a month. When they'd been in high school, she hadn't known clothing designers even existed. Like everyone else in their small town, her clothes had come from Kmart, and getting dressed up usually meant wearing black jeans instead of blue ones and a tee that *didn't* advertise the name of a rock band.

She'd looked hot in jeans, though. He still remembered the way her ripe, round bottom had filled out worn Wranglers, and how warm the denim would become when he slipped his hands into her back pockets to tug her close for a long, slow kiss.

A decade could change a lot of things, but apparently it couldn't completely eradicate sexual attraction. Not judging by the throb of his cock as it grew and hardened behind his fly.

Disgusted with himself and his errant dick, Linc frowned. Turning his attention *away* from his memories of the old Claire and what they'd done together in the backseat of the cherry red Trans Am he'd rebuilt in his dad's garage, he tried to focus on her current appearance.

In addition to the expensive outfit and demure choice of accessories, her hair was smooth, short, and bobbed—a far cry from the wild mane of curls she'd fought with all while growing up. He remembered her frequent complaints about tangles and frizz—not to mention the massive amount of hairspray she'd used while teasing the locks to greater and greater heights—but he had always loved absently twisting individual curls around his index finger or fisting her hair in his hands while he'd tipped her head back to devour her mouth.

It was obvious to him, even after only a few minutes in her presence, that she was no longer the fierce, uninhibited girl he'd known. She'd grown into a sedate, elegant woman who looked more like the wife of a politician than the daughter of a steel worker.

He scowled, not sure what to think—or how to feel—about the new Claire Cassidy. And then he reminded himself that he didn't need to think or feel anything about her. It didn't matter and he didn't care. What he cared about was getting to the bottom of this photograph.

Slapping the picture on the long metal table in front of her, he fixed her with his sternest spill-the-beans glare.

"Explain," he bit out from between tightly clenched teeth.

Her gaze flicked to the picture, then back to him. "Her name is Sara, and she's your daughter."

She said it so calmly, so point-blank, while Linc's insides were turning upside down.

Sara. His mother's name. Claire had attended the funeral with him after his mother had been killed in a car accident when he was sixteen.

Linc prided himself on keeping his emotions under control, of never letting anything show, at least not on the job. But even here, in one of the USMS's interrogation/meeting rooms, with a woman he *shouldn't* have any feelings about one way or the other, his knees were weak and his heart was pounding so hard, he was surprised it didn't break through his rib cage.

"Why Sara?" he asked, unnerved when his voice came out as little more than a cracked whisper.

Her blue eyes sparkled up at him. "You know why."

He did, if the kid truly was his. After his mother's death, after he'd broken down in Claire's arms and she'd held him until the worst of his grief had passed, she'd told him that when they got married and started a family of their own, they would name their first daughter Sara, in memory of his mom.

He reached around the corner of the table for a second chair and dragged it closer, letting the noise cover the fact that he had to blink to clear his vision and swallow hard to move the lump from his throat.

"I'm going to need more than that," he told her, dropping into the cold metal seat and draping an arm on the table.

Her lashes fluttered as she took a deep breath, set aside her purse, and began an abbreviated version of what had taken place in the past ten years.

"I was pregnant when I left, though I didn't know it at the time. And I married Jonathan Scarborough when I was three months along because he promised to take care of me and the baby. I needed that at the time, more than you can know."

Her cheeks colored slightly, but her apparent unease had no impact on Linc. She'd apparently been pregnant with his child, so why hadn't she come back to Butler and let him know? *He'd* have taken care of her. Of both of them.

But he still wasn't convinced, not just yet.

"And then . . . ?" he prompted.

"He was good to us. To both of us, and he treated Sara like his own."

A shaft of hatred for the man who had taken his place and raised his daughter while he hadn't even known of her existence stabbed through Linc, and he curled his fingers into his palms to keep from hitting something.

"But now that we're separating, he's decided he wants full custody of her. He knows he has no legal or biological claim to her, but his family is powerful in the San Francisco area and has more money than God, so he doesn't intend to let that stop him."

Linc's brows knit. "All you need is a simple DNA test. That should clear things up." He was certainly going to have one of his own run as soon as possible to see whether Claire's assertion that Sara was his daughter was true.

"That's just it," she said, a hint of desperation slipping into her expression as she leaned forward and grasped his forearm. "I think that's exactly what he's planning—an altered DNA test that will prove Sara *is* his."

"Isn't that a bit of a stretch?" he asked, skepticism clear in his tone.

"Not with the amount of money and influence Jonathan has," she insisted, her voice growing more urgent with each word. "All he has to do is pay off a private laboratory to fabricate the results, take them to a judge who's in his or his father's pocket, and they'll take her away from me."

Genuine panic shone from her eyes and tugged at the corners of her mouth while her nails dug into his arm. It was the first time since she'd sat down beside his desk that he was beginning to believe her story and that she might actually have cause for concern.

"And that's why you think he's taken . . . Sara and disappeared."

"Yes. I'm afraid that if we don't find her—*soon*—he'll falsify those documents and I'll lose my daughter forever. Our daughter."

She moved even closer, bringing up her other hand to grip his where it rested on the tabletop. Moisture glistened on her lower lashes, not yet spilling over, but close.

"Please, Linc. I need your help. I don't know what I'll do if you turn me away."

For a moment, he didn't reply, letting everything she'd said sink in. If she'd come to him for herself, he'd have had no problem refusing. They wouldn't even be here because he'd have kicked her out of the building two minutes after she'd arrived.

But this wasn't just about her, it was about a nine-year-old girl who could very well be his daughter. And if there was any chance another man might try to take her away before Linc found out for sure, before he could have his own DNA tests run and get to know his child . . .

If she really did turn out to be . . .

Not going to happen.

Pushing to his feet, he collected Sara's photo and handed Claire her purse, not bothering to shake off the grip she had on his wrist. "Come with me."

"Where are we going?" she wanted to know as he opened the interview-room door and headed back down the hall the way they'd come.

"To find our daughter."

3

Balancing the strap of her purse on one shoulder and dragging her wheeled carry-on behind her, Claire hurried through the Pittsburgh International Airport toward the gate where she was supposed to meet Linc for a 9:00 A.M. flight back to San Francisco.

To say she was nervous about returning to the city she'd called home for the past decade was like saying the Golden Gate was *kind of* a long bridge. Not because she might come face to face with Jonathan or his family, or because of what lay ahead in the search for Sara, but because of the man she would be traveling with.

Being near Lincoln Rappaport was like having lightning strike only inches from where she stood. Any time she was within arm's length of him, her skin tingled, her blood turned hot and threatened to boil, and she wouldn't have been surprised to look in a mirror and find her hair standing on end.

She didn't remember that. She remembered being head over heels in love with him, moon-eyed in the way only sixteen-year-old girls could be, but she didn't recall having such a visceral physical reaction whenever she got close to him.

Was it new, or had she simply forgotten?

She didn't know how anyone could forget something so intense, so compelling, something that literally took her breath away. But the mind was a powerful thing. Maybe she'd subconsciously buried the memory as a form of self-preservation. Lord knew she could use a bit of protection from him now.

Or maybe she'd blocked the memory because it was simply too painful to think about. To know there was a man out there who could make her elbows sweat while she was married to someone else and keeping his child a secret.

A twinge of guilt squeezed her heart. She'd made so many mistakes. Things she didn't think she could ever put right, even if Linc was willing to let her try. From his demeanor with her so far, she doubted that was a possibility.

He was so angry with her, hated her so much. Not that she could blame him.

She'd come to him for help because she didn't know what else to do. She'd looked for Sara on her own, done everything she could think of to get her daughter back.

She'd gone to Jonathan's attorney to first demand and then beg to be told where her daughter was. They'd turned her away, claiming they didn't know what she was talking about and that she'd be better off going through her own attorney. As though she'd been complaining that Jonathan had walked off with her favorite vase instead of her *child*.

She'd gone to the local police, who'd told her that until her divorce was final or it was clear something untoward was going on,

Jonathan had equal custody of their child and there was nothing they could do. Frankly, Claire thought they were afraid to make waves or do anything that would put them on the wrong side of the Scarborough family.

She'd even spoken with a private investigator but had gotten the feeling he would take too long, and that any money she put into one would be wasted. Before the divorce, she could have afforded to hire an army of investigators, but thanks to her prenuptial agreement and the fact that she didn't particularly *want* Jonathan's money, she thought that what little money she had on her own could be put to better use.

As frantic and desperate as she'd been, Linc still hadn't jumped immediately to mind. Her family—who knew about their past, knew Sara was his daughter, and didn't bother to hide their disapproval of her choice to marry another man and keep his daughter a secret—had kept her up-to-date over the years about Linc's whereabouts and activities. Her mother filled her in during their weekly phone calls and sent newspaper clippings of things she thought Claire might find interesting.

So she'd known when Linc had suddenly enlisted in the Marine Corps right after high school—right after she'd left Butler County for California—instead of taking a job at his father's garage. And she'd known when he'd come back and moved to Pittsburgh to join the U.S. Marshals Service.

But it hadn't occurred to her that he might be any help at all with the situation she currently found herself in until she'd been talking to her mother on the phone—crying, really, because she'd been so frustrated and frightened that she might never see her daughter again—that her mother had mentioned U.S. marshals *did* track down fugitives for a living, and then surreptitiously added that it was a shame she didn't know one she could ask for help.

Claire had gotten the hint. She wished she hadn't, but at this point, she wasn't sure she had much of a choice. If she wanted Sara back, she had to find her before Jonathan could do anything to forge his parentage and cut her out of her own daughter's life. And if that meant flying back to Pennsylvania to face down the one person in the world who had no reason to help her, no reason to even stay in the same room with her for more than three seconds . . .

But then, he did have a reason to help her. He just hadn't known it until she'd slid Sara's most recent school picture across his desk and said, "Surprise! You're a daddy!"

Her chest grew tight at the memory, and she slowed as she neared her gate. The look he'd given her had sliced her to the soul.

Not that she didn't deserve his anger, his derision, his punishment. When he'd reached for her arm after her monumental pronouncement, it had taken all her strength not to flinch. She'd thought he was going to strangle her, or at the very least shake her until her teeth rattled.

Then when he'd dragged her down the hall to that private interrogation room . . . well, she'd been more than a little relieved to have made it out alive.

But he hadn't killed her or strangled her or yelled himself hoarse about her betrayal, even though he may have wanted to. Instead, he'd pulled her out of the room, sat her back down at his desk, and proceeded to put into action a plan for tracking down Jonathan and Sara.

He'd barely spoken to her as he'd moved around the room, recruiting his friends to help him. She'd been both surprised and relieved at how quickly the other deputies had dropped what they were doing to look up maps, files, records—everything they thought might be useful in their quest.

Linc, in the meantime, spoke to her only when he needed information, and otherwise pretended she wasn't there. Which was fine with her. As long as he knew what he was doing and helped her find her daughter, she didn't care how he treated her.

Pulling her carry-on out of the way of other travelers, she stopped at her gate and scanned the crowd of waiting passengers. It wasn't hard to spot Linc. At six foot two and pushing nearly two hundred pounds of pure muscle, he tended to stand out. Then again, with the slow dip and roll her stomach seemed to take every time she saw him, he could have been in the center of a room full of giants, and Claire suspected her attention would have zoomed right in on him.

He had his back to her now, standing at the bank of floor-to-ceiling windows overlooking the tarmac, and she took a moment to study him. He was wearing a black leather jacket and jeans that fit him to perfection, his hands stuffed into his pockets as he stared straight ahead.

She wondered what he was thinking, and then decided it was better she didn't know. Chances were, it had something to do with her and either a firing squad or a vat of boiling oil.

Moving closer, she arranged her bag beside the small black duffel at his feet, then stood just behind him. She didn't have to say anything; he knew she was there. She could tell by the sudden tensing of his tall frame and the small jump of the muscle along his jaw.

If he kept that up, she thought, he was going to break a molar. It was also going to make for a very long trip back to San Francisco.

"You're late," he said after a couple of seconds.

She cleared her throat. "Sorry. I had to go home to my parents' place last night to pack, and then there was traffic getting back. They haven't started boarding yet, have they?"

She'd checked the monitors when she first arrived and knew they hadn't, but she was trying to be polite, straining for any wisp of conversation that would get him to put an end to the silent treatment. But when he didn't respond, didn't so much as glance in her direction, she knew it was going to take a lot more than small talk to break through the thick wall of betrayal and resentment between them.

And sure enough, he didn't speak to her again—at least not voluntarily—until well after they'd landed at San Francisco International. They were standing at the Hertz car rental counter, waiting for the clerk to finish with Linc's paperwork, when he turned to her and asked, "Do you have a private place to stay here, or were you still living with Scarborough?"

After spending such a long stretch of time with him, with absolutely no interaction, it took a second for Claire to realize he was talking to her. He was even looking at her, though his gray eyes were just as cold and vacant as they'd been back at USMS headquarters.

She shook her head, partly in answer to his question and partly in an attempt to toss off her shock and regain her equilibrium. "No. I moved out right after I filed for divorce. We stayed with friends for a little while at first, but ever since Jonathan disappeared with Sara, I've been staying at a hotel."

He gave a sharp nod, turning his attention back to the Hertz employee as she handed over a set of keys and his copies of the rental contract. "We'll do the same while we're here."

Heading for the rental car parking lot, he strode ahead, leaving her to follow at her own pace. On the way, he flipped open his cell phone, hit a number on speed dial, and waited for the person on the other end to pick up.

"Keegan. Yeah, it's Linc. We just landed in San Fran and are going to check into a hotel. I'll call you again when we get settled."

He unlocked the doors of a large black SUV just like the ones she'd seen parked outside the U.S. Marshals building and stowed his duffel bag on the backseat. Since he was still on the phone, paying little to no attention to her, Claire did the same with her own carry-on, then climbed into the front passenger seat.

Sliding behind the wheel, he started the engine and fiddled with some of the knobs to adjust the air and vents, all the while listening to the other deputy and offering the occasional "okay," "uh-huh," or "gotcha."

A minute later, he disconnected, pocketed his phone, and put the Suburban in gear. Claire waited, expecting him to fill her in on what Noah Keegan—whom she'd met briefly back in Pittsburgh—had said.

She knew from watching them in action just the day before that Noah and a few of the other deputy marshals who worked with Linc were supposed to be investigating Jonathan's past; alerting the San Francisco USMS office that Linc was going to be in town on personal business, but might call on them, if necessary; and looking for any clue that might lead them to Sara. But if there had been progress in any of those areas, Linc didn't seem eager or willing to share.

Finally, as they were exiting the maze of airport roads and merging with traffic onto 101, she couldn't take it anymore.

"Well?"

"Well what?" he said. Rather than look in her direction, he checked his side-view mirror and moved into the next lane.

It took a second for her to unlock her teeth and school her breathing. She was normally a fairly patient person. If being a mother hadn't taught her tolerance, then being Jonathan's trophy wife these past ten years certainly had.

And there were any number of things she was willing to do or put up with to find her daughter. Walking over hot coals, submitting to Chinese water torture, even tucking her tail between her legs and crawling home to beg for help from a man who hated her.

But she was quickly *losing* patience with Linc. His attitude toward her was understandable and probably even deserved. She'd known it would be this way if she came back. She was relieved, actually, that it wasn't worse.

What she didn't deserve, however, was his stony silence where his plans to find their daughter were concerned. Personally, he could treat her as badly as he liked, but when it came to Sara, she had a right to know what was going on, what his strategy was, and what progress he and his friends were making.

Hands in her lap, fingers curled, she said calmly, "What did your friend say?"

He took so long to answer that her diaphragm grew tight and her nails dug half-moon gouges into her palms.

"He alerted the local marshals that we're here in case we need them, and found some out-of-the-way properties that the Scarboroughs own."

His voice was low and clipped, and he reported the information as succinctly as possible, as though he didn't want to spend any more time than necessary speaking to her.

This was good. It wasn't a definite location for where they might find her daughter, but it was more than she'd had when she'd gone to Linc in the first place.

"Is that it?" she pressed, barely noticing when he flipped on the turn signal and pulled into the parking lot of a dingy, single-story motel.

She watched his hands flex and release, his knuckles going as white on the steering wheel as hers were in her lap.

"What more did you expect?" he bit out, angling into an empty spot near the manager's office and cutting the engine. "This isn't a television show, sweetheart. Clues don't conveniently pop up every five minutes leading us to the bad guys and a pat conclusion at the end of the hour."

Before she could say a word in response, he pushed open his door and climbed out.

Claire stayed where she was. For a minute, her head throbbed, her heart pounded, and her blood pressure rose to near-skyrocketing levels.

And then suddenly, she began to relax. Like air leaking slowly out of a balloon, the knot of tension at the base of her stomach loosened and the lion's share of stress she'd been carrying around all day washed out of her. It was almost as though her subconscious had finally realized there was little to no chance of getting through Linc's rock-hard skull and had decided to cut her body a break. No sense developing an ulcer because of something—or someone—she had no control over.

With a sigh, she pushed her door open and moved to stand alone beside the SUV, waiting for Linc to check them in to the small, run-down hotel.

In the ten years she'd been married to Jonathan, she'd gotten used to frequenting much nicer establishments than this. Five-star luxury hotels all over the world. *Penthouse and presidential suites* of five-star luxury hotels all over the world.

But she'd been born and raised in small, rural Butler County, Pennsylvania, where Wal-Mart was the norm and driving into Pittsburgh to hit the mall could be considered a luxury. Growing up, she'd slept in the woods, on the floor, and occasionally in the small, cramped backseat of Linc's Trans Am. No matter how shabby or run-down this motel might be, she would have no trouble making it her home until Sara was found.

Linc came out of the manager's office a few minutes later, his loose-hipped swagger eating up the pavement. He had a key in his hand—one of the old-fashioned kind with a giant, numbered key chain attached—and ignored her completely as he strode to the Suburban and removed his duffel from the rear. Without a word, he slammed the door and headed farther down the parking lot, apparently to where their rooms were located.

Or room, Claire thought, judging by the single key she'd seen. Swallowing the nerves that threatened to take up residence in her belly once again, she gathered her own luggage and followed after him.

Sure enough, he'd unlocked the door to only one room and already had his duffel open on the single round table near the window.

At least there were two beds—a fact she noticed when she stepped in behind him.

"So, we'll be sharing a room?" she said, making it more a question than a statement, just to be sure.

"Got a problem with that, princess?" he all but snarled, still facing away from her as he unloaded items from his duffel onto the tabletop.

"Not at all," she replied, falling back on the lessons she'd learned over the years about comportment and deflecting conflict.

"I suppose you're used to staying in fancier places than this. Places with complimentary bathrobes, turndown service, and mints on the pillows."

If he was trying to hurt her, he'd missed the mark. He was right about how she'd lived over the past decade, but wrong about her being a princess. So very wrong.

Closing the door behind her, she deposited her small suitcase on the bed nearest the bathroom, then turned in his direction, where she had an unobstructed view of his broad, spectacular back beneath the tight cotton of his black T-shirt. She stared him down, anyway, half wishing she could look him in the eye, and half glad she didn't have to.

Crossing her arms beneath her breasts, she said, "You forget that I grew up the same way you did, Linc. In a small town, with a middle-class family, not in the lap of luxury. My sheets over the past several years may have been satin and silk, but I'd sleep on a bed of nails if it meant finding my daughter."

At the mention of Sara, he went perfectly still. The muscles in his upper arms rippled as his fists clenched and released at his sides. And then he spun around, his body vibrating with resentment, his eyes flashing with barely leashed fury.

"Don't you mean *our* daughter?"

4

Linc balled his hands into fists and gritted his teeth. He wished Claire were a man so he could deck her. As it was, it took every ounce of willpower he possessed not to take the six steps it would take to reach her, grab her neck, and shake the life out of her.

Anger poured over him like a tidal wave, blurring his vision and clouding his senses, and he couldn't seem to stop it.

Ten years ago, he'd been madly in love with Claire Cassidy. He'd have done anything for her, thought they would spend the rest of their lives together—marry right out of high school, start a family, end up out on the porch swing in fifty years, still holding hands like teenagers.

And then she'd left him, walked away from all the hopes and dreams he *thought* they'd shared, and never looked back. He'd known she was afraid of a future that wasn't big enough, wasn't special enough. Of becoming the simple wife of a simple mechanic, since he'd planned to go to work in his father's garage full-time after graduation. Of living from paycheck to paycheck in a small town where nothing ever happened and no one ever got out.

He'd known it, but because he was content with the idea of living that sort of life and didn't share her concerns, he hadn't worried about it. He'd assumed, albeit foolishly, that once they married, her trepidation would pass and she'd be happy—as his wife, as the mother of his children. As happy as he'd anticipated being with her.

Then she'd gone and fucked it up.

It had taken him a good, long time to get over her betrayal.

And that's exactly how he thought of it. She hadn't just taken off to follow her dreams, dreams she'd shared with him and that he'd supported. She'd left in the middle of the night, without warning, leaving only a short note to explain her desertion.

He remembered every word. *I'm sorry. I can't stay. Please understand.* And she'd had the audacity to sign it, *Love, Claire.*

Yeah, like she had the first clue what the word meant. Love didn't take off without warning and run all the way across the country to get away. Love didn't say one thing and do another. Love didn't hide true feelings and keep secrets.

It had taken Linc a hell of a long time to get over Claire. To pick himself up and move on. To stop wanting to drive to California and track her down. Drag her back, or maybe even stay out there with her, as long as she said she still loved him.

The idea that he'd ever been that weak, that pathetic, that pussy-whipped made him want to puke. Thank God he'd joined the Marines and sweat that shit out of himself.

But the anger, the sense of betrayal was still there. Only now, it was compounded by the fact that she'd lied to him again, kept secrets again, *betrayed him* again.

He had a daughter, and Claire had kept that fact from him all these years. If that wasn't cause for justifiable homicide, he didn't know what was.

Before he could kill her, though, he had to find that daughter, and he needed Claire to help make that happen. Otherwise, there wasn't a power in this universe or the next that could have gotten him onto a plane, into a car, and now into a motel room with her.

"You're right," she said, breaking into the taut silence of the small, dingy room. The sound of her voice, however soft, however low, grated along his nerve endings like nails down a chalkboard.

He'd tried, God knew he'd tried, to tamp down on his emotions, to push the fury, the resentment, even the unwelcome sexual attraction he still felt for her down, down, down deep beneath his professional veneer. Stay focused. Do the job. Ignore the fact that the subtle scent of her perfume had had him walking around with half a hard-on for the past thirty-six hours.

"I'm so used to thinking of her as *my* daughter," she continued in that same gentle, agreeable tone, "but you're absolutely right that Sara is your daughter, too. I'll try to remember that in my phrasing from now on."

One corner of Linc's mouth ticked up in a sneer. She sounded like Dear-freaking-Abby. When had she turned into such a snooty, upper-crust debutante with a ten-foot stick up her butt?

"If you're even telling the truth about that," he spit out.

Her eyes widened for a split second, stunned hurt flashing across her face before it was replaced with calm resignation.

"Why would I lie to you about something like that?"

He snorted and turned back to his duffel, removing the bits and pieces of equipment he'd packed in with the bare minimum of clothes and personal items.

"Why not?" he retorted. "You've lied to me about everything else."

Behind him, he heard Claire shift, maybe unpacking her own suitcase, maybe simply fidgeting nervously. Whatever the case, he didn't bother glancing over his shoulder. He didn't care enough to check on her.

He was just setting his laptop aside and reaching for a folder of printouts when something hit him in the center of the back, hard and without warning. Pivoting on the balls of his feet, he lifted one arm to fend off a second blow, the other going automatically for the gun that would normally be in a holster at his side. Since he wasn't flying on official business that required him to remain armed, he'd been forced to pack his weapon to get through airport security.

Good thing, otherwise his Glock would be pressed point-blank into the center of Claire's forehead.

Before he could open his mouth to ask her just what the fuck she thought she was doing, she hit him again, this time in the center of his chest.

"What have I lied to you about?" she demanded, her voice rising with growing annoyance. Her palm slapped him again and he had to brace himself to keep from rocking back with the impact.

She wasn't that strong. He could have easily subdued her. Hell, he could have picked her up and carted her around one-handed. But the shock of having her lash out, verbally as well as physically, when she'd been so quiet and docile until now kept him frozen in place.

Plus, he sort of wanted to see how riled she'd get and just how daring her frustrations would make her.

"I came to you for help," she raved on. "I told you about Sara. I told you everything I know about Jonathan and his family that might help us find her, answered every question you asked to the best of my ability. So what, exactly, have I lied to you about?"

Her voice and body language grew more agitated with every word, and at the last, she smacked him again. Not with quite as much force as the first two strikes, but enough to snap what little restraint Linc had managed to hang on to up to this point.

Grabbing her wrist, he twisted her arm aside and held her in an iron-tight grip. She leaned away from him, the first signs of fear glimmering in the depths of her crystal-blue eyes.

Towering over her, he moved in until they were nearly nose to nose, his voice a low throb of rage and resentment as he grated, "You lied when you said you loved me. You lied when you said you wanted to marry me. And you lied when you kept my daughter a secret from me and passed her off as another man's child."

A whisper of hurt played across her features . . . the smooth, pale skin; the high cheekbones; the button nose and heart-shaped lips that had gotten him so hot and bothered as a teenager. He soaked up that pain, reveled in it, let it warm the dark, cavernous part of him that had spent a decade wanting to punish her for her disloyalty.

His enjoyment of her suffering lasted only a few brief seconds, however. Not nearly long enough to satisfy his long-standing desire for revenge.

But in its place came memories, snapshots of the history they shared and the deep-rooted feelings attached to them. The first time he'd started to notice her as more of a girl he might want to kiss than just another one-of-the-guys neighbor who climbed trees, skipped rocks, and helped him sneak toads and snakes into his sister's bed. The first time he'd kissed her behind a tree at a church picnic, after working up his courage for almost four months. All the times they'd gone out—for a burger, to the movies . . . parking at Lookout Point. The first time they'd made love, and all the times after that.

His diaphragm squeezed, cutting off his air. And lower, behind the tight confines of his zipper, his cock hardened even more, going

HEIDI BETTS

from the semi he'd been sporting since looking up from his desk to find Claire standing beside him, to full-blown, undeniable arousal.

He didn't stop to think, didn't *want* to think; he simply dipped his head and took her mouth. He kissed her like a starving man falling upon a feast. The way he'd dreamed of kissing her over the past ten years, on those lonely, endless nights when the anger faded away and there was only longing and regret.

The way he had when she'd been his world.

For a moment, she struggled, going tense and trying to tug her wrist out of his grasp. He didn't let her go, but instead tightened his hold on her right arm and grabbed for the left.

Wrenching them both behind her back, he tugged her flush with his body, pinning her in place and opening his mouth wider over hers. The tip of his tongue slipped past her closed lips, and inside their tongues brushed, tangled, fought a sensual duel that caused a heartfelt groan to roll up from his solar plexus.

He pulled her even closer, pressing the straining bulge of his erection into the vee of her thighs. Using one hand to manacle her arms at the small of her back, he brought his other around to her hip, her waist, and up to cup her breast through the soft knit of her watermelon-pink sweater.

His thumb searched for her nipple, but her bra must have had some sort of padding because all he could feel was a smooth roundness. With a growl, he reached for the hem of her top and drove his fingers under, skimming the soft, bare flesh of her torso until the satiny material of her underwire impeded his progress.

He wasted no time pushing it up and away from her breasts. The rigid point of her nipple bit into his palm, just as he'd known it would.

The knowledge that she was turned on, that she wanted him as

302

much as he wanted her made him growl. He nipped at her mouth like a wolf with its mate—biting, claiming, marking her as his own.

But still the bitterness of a thousand sleepless nights plagued his soul.

Breaking the kiss, his chest heaved as his lungs strained to refill themselves with fresh oxygen. Tucked into him like a second skin, Linc felt Claire struggling to do the same.

He'd relinquished her mouth, but he didn't relinquish her body. His thumb and fingers toyed with the pebbled tip of her breast while the rest of his hand palmed and kneaded it.

"Is this what it was like with your husband?" he grated. He couldn't bring himself to say the man's name, not while he was the one feeling her up. Bad enough that he was picturing the man on top of Claire—kissing her, stroking her, fucking her brains out.

"Did he stroke your tits? Did the thought of having him inside you make your nipples hard, the way they are right now?"

She'd begun to relax in his hold, but now she tensed again. Her lashes fluttered, her eyes going wary and slightly damp. "Don't, Linc. Please."

He ignored the weak pleading in her voice, and relinquishing her breast, his rough knuckles trailed the back of his hand down the line of her belly to the waist of her slacks. With a deft flick of his fingers, he had the button open and the zipper half down, burying his hand inside.

He didn't bother touching her through the lacy slip of her panties, but went underneath and straight to the slick, swollen folds of her pussy. His wide palm cupped her while his long middle finger skimmed the sensitive bud of her clit and circled her opening.

"Did you get this wet for him?" Her internal muscles gave a tiny, involuntary spasm, and his dick twitched in response. "Did he make you come with just a touch?"

She opened her mouth to answer—or maybe to beg him again to stop this cruel line of questioning, judging by the growing moisture at the corners of her eyes—but he cut her off by thrusting his finger deep into her sex and rubbing his thumb against her clit. The action did exactly as intended, though with much less effort than he'd thought would be necessary. Her pussy tightened around his finger, pulsed in his hand, and she came with a strangled scream.

Seeing her climax, feeling the shudders as they rippled through her body, rocked him to the soles of his feet. It hit him so hard, he nearly came himself—without a touch, without even freeing himself from his pants.

He wanted nothing more than to rip open his jeans and thrust inside her. Or rip open his jeans and jerk himself into blissful release. Either way, it wouldn't take more than a nanosecond to bring him off.

Locking his jaw and fortifying his stance, he fought for control, fought to keep images of touching her, tasting her, listening to her whimper as he pounded into her out of his head. She lay limp in his arms, eyes closed and breathing ragged as tiny aftershocks rolled through her.

Throat raw, words sandpaper-rough, he asked, "Did your ex-husband ever make you come like that?"

5

No, Jonathan had never made her come like that. Not remotely. Not even close.

She wasn't sure she'd ever felt anything like the orgasm Linc had just given her . . . even when they'd both been horny, oversexed teens, taking every chance they could get to roll around naked. It was almost as though his hatred for her, his brutal treatment, made the situation even more erotic and added to her level of arousal.

Her guilt and the fact that she hadn't had sex in recent memory might have helped, too.

But she would be damned if she'd answer a single one of Linc's malicious, insulting questions. First, her intimate relationship with Jonathan was none of his business. And second, she refused to play into his me-Tarzan-you-Jane Neanderthal behavior.

She was through with letting her remorse for past mistakes give him carte blanche to treat her like a doormat, to allow him to punish her again and again with his words and deeds. If he wanted to stay angry with her, so be it. But if he thought stuffing his hand down her pants and finger-fucking her into oblivion was going to adequately punish her for what she'd done to him oh, so long ago . . .

Well, since when was having an orgasm that made her eyes roll back in her head and see the face of God any sort of punishment at all?

Her shoulders ached from having her arms pinned behind her for so long, and there was a crick in her back from being bent almost in half, but none of that seemed to matter when Linc slowly began to remove his hand from her crotch. His hold on her wrists loosened, too, and he started to step away.

Oh, no, you don't, she thought. He wasn't going to strip her bare—figuratively, if not yet literally—and then walk off as though nothing had happened, with ammunition he'd most likely lob at her later in a continued attempt to penalize her. At the very least, on the sexual battlefield, she wanted them to be on equal ground.

She rolled her shoulders and flexed her hands to return the blood flow to the slightly numb limbs. Then, before he could put too much distance between them, she reached out and grabbed the waistband of his jeans.

The heat of his flesh beneath his T-shirt burned the backs of her fingers. If she hadn't been deprived of oxygen from her recent ravishment, she might have sucked in a breath.

At her touch, Linc froze. She could feel his rigidity in the stone-hard flatness of his abdomen. And then his head tipped down, his simmering gaze going to the spot where she held him in place.

"Do you really care?" she asked quietly, referring to his earlier, double-edged demands. "Do you really care what another man did or didn't do to me when you're here with me now? When you're the one who just rocked my world with the mere stroke of your hand?" She gave a small tsk. "I'm surprised at you, Lincoln Rappaport. I would have pegged you as a man who had his priorities a little more in order."

Her taunt had the desired effect. He growled low in his throat, snagged the nape of her neck with one hand, and dragged her mouth to his.

The kiss threatened to melt her from head to toe and turn her into just another discoloration on the stained motel room carpet. It took all of the strength and lucidity she could muster to get her fingers working between them and open the button of his jeans.

His erection pressed against the snug denim, making it hard to get him out without hurting him. Slipping one hand inside to cup his impressive length, she used the other to lower the zipper . . . slowly, deliberately, while she stroked and squeezed his rigid cock.

He moaned, the sound rumbling from his lips through hers as his hands ran down her spine, inside the loose fabric of her already open slacks, and over her buttocks. Fingers flexing in the soft, round globes, he lifted her nearly off her feet and tighter to his chest.

Mouths still locked together and devouring, they made short work of undressing each other. She pushed his pants and plain white briefs past his hips as far as she could reach, and then changed direction to slide his T-shirt up and over his chest.

He helped her along, kicking off his boots and stepping out of his jeans before reaching behind his head to yank the T-shirt over his head. He released her only long enough to toss the shirt aside, then grabbed her again and did the same with her clothes.

Buttons flew when he grabbed either side of her blouse and ripped it open. She tried to step out of her shoes, but he toppled her backward onto the bed and took care of them himself.

A second later, she was crushed beneath him in only her bra and panties, the former caught above her breasts from the first time he'd had his hand under her shirt.

She'd forgotten how this felt . . . the firm press of a man atop her; her breasts flattened by a strong, planed chest; the burning heat of male arousal prodding her feminine mound.

Of course, she'd never had a man like Linc on top of her. When they'd become sexually active in high school, he'd been much thinner and more gangly. Healthy and athletic, but not nearly as buff and amazingly well-built as he was now.

And as far as Jonathan was concerned . . . well, he'd never measured up to Linc, anyway, physically or otherwise.

Linc's mouth fastened on her throat, the light dusting of crisp hair on his chest abrading her sensitive nipples as he shocked her thoughts back to the matter at hand. She tipped her head back, giving him more room to lick and nip, and to send her senses reeling.

His mouth alone threatened to spiral her into a dead faint, but she refused to lie there passively while he did to her. She wanted to do to him, too. She had a decade's worth of long-buried fantasies about him clawing to get out.

His arms mesmerized her, and she let the pads of her fingers trail over his massive shoulders; around his hard, rounded biceps; down to his equally strong forearms; and back up. She lingered at the black of his tattoo, her tongue darting out in anticipation of licking that long, sexy line of barbed wire.

He must have noticed the impromptu flick of her tongue, because the next thing she knew, he gave a low, animalistic growl and took her mouth with a ferocity that thrilled her to the tips of her toes.

Inside her veins, her blood pounded hot and heavy. Her heart beat like a kettledrum, and that spot deep between her legs hummed with anticipation unlike any she could ever remember feeling before, reminding her in no uncertain terms that she was a woman who deserved a man who could satisfy her body's urges and needs.

His hands cupped her breasts, kneading once on their way downward. He skimmed her waist, her hips; then his wide hands circled the tops of her thighs and his thumbs sneaked in on either side, brushing over the tight triangle of curls to pry her legs apart.

"I can't wait," he panted against her mouth, positioning himself between her knees. "I want you right now."

She wanted him, too. So much, she burned with it. So much, her limbs were shaking.

But she was still rational enough to remember what was important.

"Condom," she breathed, breaking away from his kiss. "Do you have a condom?"

"Shit." He dropped his head until it touched her own, his chest heaving for air as his eyes squeezed shut.

And then he pushed himself up and off the bed, sending those mouthwatering muscles rippling all along his arms.

For a split second, she wanted to grab him, say to hell with protection, and beg him just to take her. Hard, fast, *now, now, now.*

But before the thought had fully formed in her brain, he'd grabbed a shaving kit from his duffel, yanked open the zipper of the leather case, and pulled out a string of small plastic packets.

Tearing one off, he let the rest drop to the floor. On his way back to her, he ripped open the square with his teeth, removed the condom, and rolled it carefully over the generous thickness of his long, hard erection.

Claire felt strange staring at that portion of his anatomy, yet she couldn't look away. He was like some delectable morsel she wanted to both gobble up and savor at the same time.

He'd grown there, too, and not only because he was aroused. She didn't remember him being nearly this large, this commanding, and wondered if it was another delightful side effect of the extensive weight training he must have gone through to grow all those other magnificent muscles.

Whatever the cause, she liked it. She wanted to reach out and touch him, hold him, stroke him first with her fingers and then with her mouth.

From the heat blazing in his eyes, though, she knew she wouldn't get the chance. Not yet.

He was covered now, completely protecting them both. Lying flat on the bed, simmering beneath his intense scrutiny, she felt like a very small, very defenseless animal being stalked by a large and dangerous jungle cat.

A shiver went through her, and as he approached, grabbing her ankles to spread her legs, she let herself go limp. He might be twice her size and possess twice her strength, he might even hate her, but he wasn't going to hurt her. Not tonight.

"This won't take long," he gritted out, climbing onto the bed and lifting her legs so that they rested vertically along his chest. "Not the first time. I'll make it up to you later."

She had no doubt that he'd be true to his word, but there was no need to make up anything. Her ankles crowned his shoulders— not the most ladylike position, she was sure—as he situated himself at her opening, but the minute he entered her with a single, brutal thrust, explosions went off behind her closed eyelids.

It had been forever since she'd been with a man, and she was primed well beyond ready. Not only from the amazing orgasm his hand had given her, but from the thought of being with Linc again. Her first love, her first lover, the boy she'd thought to spend the rest of her days with.

Despite his enormous size, he slid right in, her body stretching and molding around him until he filled her to overflowing. He hit her in all the right places almost immediately. So deep, he wasn't just grazing her G-spot, but her H-, I-, and J-spots, as well. So tight against her clit, her hips arched off the bed and she nearly came again.

He hadn't moved, hadn't stroked, hadn't even begun to give her what she knew lay ahead, but already she was teetering on the razor-fine edge of a world-class orgasm.

Her legs slipped down to hook in the bends of his arms as he leaned close, pressing his chest to hers while he nipped at her mouth. He used his lips and teeth and tongue to tease, but it was what he was doing farther down that had her lungs coiling in her chest.

She would have liked to blame her light-headedness and the tingles running through her arms and legs on the lack of oxygen reaching her brain, but knew it came from Linc's touch alone. The raw scrape of his chest against her breasts; his mouth tracing lines of electricity along her jaw and throat; and most of all, the thick, rigid length of his cock throbbing inside her.

Hands snaking down her sides, he gripped her hips and canted her where he wanted her to be. He sat up slightly, lips peeling back from his teeth while he yanked her forward, then pushed her away.

Forward, back.

Forward, back.

His eyes drifted closed and a muscle jumped in his cheek as he moved her faster, then started thrusting his own hips to meet her so that the friction built and built and built.

Her breath came in gasps, her fingers curling into the bedspread beneath her, but she didn't look away from him. She couldn't, not when she'd waited so long to have Linc back in her life. Not when this might be the only memory she had to carry with her through the *rest* of her life.

A second later, Linc's eyes snapped open. Their gazes met and held.

"Tell me what you want," he grated.

His voice was gravel-rough, scraping across her nerve endings, and the incredible tension spiraling through her belly and lower tightened another notch.

She'd never been one to talk dirty, even in the most intimate of circumstances, but for a moment it flashed through her mind to give him what she knew he wanted. To tell him to fuck her. *Fuck me, Linc. Take me hard. Take me fast. Fuck me like you mean it.*

The thought sent her that much closer to climax and her inner muscles quavered around him like the ripples of a pond after a rock had been skipped across its surface.

But as quickly as the notion came, it disappeared in the knowledge that that wasn't what she wanted, not truly.

Holding his gaze, she licked her lips and whispered the one thing she craved most of all. "You," she told him. "I just want you."

For a split second, the world seemed to halt. Linc stopped breathing as hunger and a hint of surprise raged behind his storm-gray eyes. And then he moaned—an earnest, almost frantic sound that went straight to her soul—and fell on her, kissing her until she thought her lips would ignite and turn to ash.

She kissed him back, wrapping herself around him with her arms and legs. As best she could, anyway, in her current position.

He embraced her as well, pulling her tight against him and levering her at an angle for the deepest access, the longest strokes, the most pleasure.

His hips pistoned between her legs as he thrust into her, pumping so hard that the rough fabric of the cheap motel comforter chafed—scraped—her bare skin as he drove her inch by inch across the bed. But the slight discomfort only heightened her pleasure, drew every glimmer of her attention to the indescribable sensations rocking through her system.

Linc's chest buffeted her own, his breaths doing the same against her mouth as he refused to break their kiss. Insinuating one of his large, warm hands into the almost nonexistent space between them, he slipped two fingers into her slick folds in search of her clitoris.

She was already so close to meltdown that at the first touch, she went off like a rocket. Her skin prickled, tiny dots of color burst behind her closed eyelids, and wave after wave of pure, unadulterated ecstasy rolled through her.

Back arching, nails digging into his broad shoulders, she opened her mouth to scream, only to have Linc cover her once again and swallow any ear-shattering noises she might have made. He continued to drive into her, his thrusts growing shorter and harder, even as her snug sheath convulsed around his still-rigid cock.

"Yes," he huffed, his rough cheek brushing hers, his face turned into the curve of her neck. "Yes, yes, *God, yes.*"

And then he came, erupting inside her with a hoarse bellow. The sound echoed in her ears and through the small, dingy room. As thin as the walls of this place probably were, she wouldn't have been surprised if all of the other motel guests had heard him, too.

Not that she cared. At the moment, she was too relaxed and felt too content to care about much of anything.

Linc's weight pressed her into the worn mattress, making it difficult to catch her breath. But instead of shifting or asking him to move, she wanted to stay this way as long as possible. Wanted to luxuriate in his heat and blatant masculinity, in the sensation of him still filling her, still making her feel like an attractive, desirable woman.

All too soon, however, he started to roll away. But before she could heave a sigh of regret, he circled her waist and pulled her with him.

He arranged them so that his head rested on one of the pillows near the headboard and she was draped atop him like a warm, boneless, and completely sated blanket. The now dreadfully wrinkled and dislodged bedspread tickled beneath them, but neither moved to cover themselves.

Just as she was beginning to drift off on a cloud of satisfaction she hadn't experienced in a very, *very* long time, his chest rumbled beneath her cheek and his chin dug into the crown of her head.

"Don't get comfortable," he murmured. "I'm not finished with you yet."

6

A glutton for punishment, that's what he was, Linc thought as he lay there with Claire's soft weight covering him from neck to shin.

After the pounding he'd just given her, he should have been wrung out. Lord knew it had been a hell of a long time since he'd come that hard, if ever. Even his toes tingled with the intensity of orgasm he'd found in her willing, welcoming body.

He should have been satisfied, replete, down for the count. So it came as a surprise to find that his system still hummed with yearning, still blazed with an unquenchable hunger. Deep inside her, where his wayward cock remained buried, he twitched and began to stir back to life.

Unheard of. With any other woman, he'd have taken one good fuck, then rolled over and called it a night. Or gathered his clothes and made a hasty retreat before she could start weaving the web of a future that didn't exist.

He certainly hadn't been celibate since Claire had picked up and run off, leaving him brokenhearted, confused, and thoroughly pissed. But neither had he ever found another partner who rocked him to the bottom of his soul the way she did.

He supposed that made him the love-'em-and-leave-'em type. When he got an itch for female company that couldn't be alleviated with his own right hand, he went out and found someone to scratch it for him. No ties, no pretty words, no promises.

But just like the first time he'd kissed Claire's lips, stroked her smooth skin, lost himself in the warmth of her sweet body, she sucked him in and wouldn't let go.

He wanted to curse the air blue, put a hole in the wall, and maybe throw a couple of the dive motel's shit-ugly lamps across the room. The *last* thing he needed was to get drawn in again—to lower his defenses when it came to Claire Cassidy Scarborough.

If anything, he should be strengthening his resolve. Running through a mental list of her transgressions and working up a good mad that would help him once again put an ocean's worth of distance between them.

Yet here he was, lying with her on a cheap motel bed that was so old and well used it sagged in the middle with their combined weights. His arm circling her waist. Her head pillowed on his chest. His cock still covered in latex and buried in her soft, wet folds.

He needed his fucking head examined. He needed an antidote to whatever virulent virus she'd infected him with. He needed a Hummer or tank or Gulfstream jet to carry him away from her as far and as fast as possible.

But was he going to move? Was he going to push her off of him, get dressed, and go back to the job he'd come here to do?

Not if the devil himself reached up and grabbed him by the tea bags.

He knew he'd regret it, and he might even burn for it later. But for now, Claire was in his arms, in his bed, and he intended to keep it that way. At least until whatever sick obsession he seemed to have with her ran its course. Maybe then he'd be able to put her out of his mind and move on.

He didn't let himself think about the little girl who was most likely his daughter, or the fact that if Claire's claims turned out to be true, he would be tied to her for the rest of his life through Sara.

That would come later. There was only so much a man could handle at any given time, and at the moment the only thing he wanted to handle was Claire's hot bod and his once again aching dick.

She stirred above him, adding to the pressure gathering in his groin. It would have been nice to roll right into another round, but he knew better than to test the limits of a single rubber. If he wasn't almost rigidly safety-conscious by nature, yesterday's revelation that he was likely a father would have hammered home the need for care.

Giving her lush rear a little slap, he said, "Lean over the side of the bed and grab the rest of those condoms."

She sat up a bit, her blue eyes meeting his with a trace of wariness shimmering around the irises.

"Do you think that's a good idea?" she asked softly.

"I think it's a great idea." Freaking fabulous. Better than the creation of electricity or cross-country telephone lines.

Turning her head, she glanced toward the heavy, closed drapes that covered the room's single window that faced the parking lot.

"It's the middle of the day," she murmured, as though the time had just now occurred to her. Pulling her bottom lip between her teeth, she worried it lightly, tiny wrinkles appearing above her nose. "Shouldn't we be . . . working or something?"

Bringing a thumb to his mouth, he licked the pad and reached out to stroke it across the tip of her breast. The nipple immediately beaded and elongated at the damp touch.

"Not a lot we can do until Noah gets me some more information on your ex," he told her, his focus firmly rooted on the evidence of her mounting arousal. "And when he has that, he'll call."

She still seemed undecided, the corners of her mouth drifting down in a frown, but he had no intention of giving her time to debate or overthink. Not now, when he had her naked and at his mercy.

Later, maybe. Later, they could both regret their actions and swear never to darken each other's doorsteps again. Later, they could play the blame game or claim temporary insanity. Whatever made them feel better and erased the guilt and shame that he suspected would eat at both their bellies.

But until then, just for a while, he wanted to pretend there was no bad blood between them. No betrayal or resentment or ten years of secrets and lies. Only hot, jungle sex that stripped him of every ounce of energy and desire.

The very thought of having her again, of riding them both into exhaustion, turned him poker stiff. That, if nothing else, caught her attention, and she turned back to him with a moan.

Still worrying her lower lip, she said, "I thought men needed more time than this to recover."

"Guess that depends on what kind of woman they have straddling their lap." He lifted his hips a fraction, driving his point home—quite literally.

And then suddenly, she was gone. Up off his lap and off the bed, leaving his latex-covered erection bobbing unceremoniously in midair. He jackknifed into a sitting position, ready to follow her, but before he could so much as swing his legs around, she was back. The mattress slumped under her weight as she crawled toward the center—toward him—on her knees, the string of condoms in her hand.

"I remember that you used to be this randy when we were teenagers, too," she remarked, swinging one of her legs to the other side of his to seat herself over his knees this time instead of over his groin.

"Randy?" he questioned, quirking a brow at her odd choice of description. He stretched out his arms, then ground his teeth in annoyance that she was beyond his reach.

She shrugged a bare, sloping shoulder, causing her breasts to jiggle enticingly. "Randy, horny, insatiable. Call it what you will. We would no sooner finish doing it than you were ready to go again."

He remembered. He hadn't been able to get enough of her then, either.

"I didn't hear you complaining," was his noncommittal reply.

She shook her head, sending her brown hair floating around her rosy face. The stylish, perfectly coiffed 'do she'd started the day with was nothing more than a memory, leaving a passion-mussed tangle in its place. He much preferred the tangle.

"No, I never complained," she murmured, her fingers trailing down the plane of his chest, her gaze following close behind. "I loved you. I loved making love with you, being with you whenever and however I could. If I could have crawled inside your skin and lived there forever, I would have died a happy woman."

Her words, more than her featherlight caress, snaked through him and began to twist. The uncomfortable sensation began in his gut and crawled upward, coming disturbingly close to his heart.

Oh, no, he wasn't going there. He wasn't letting *her* go there. A few honeyed words and flashbacks from his past weren't going to knock down his walls and make him vulnerable to her again.

He was in this for the sex, plain and simple. He was in San

Francisco for the little girl who might be his daughter. But he was *here,* in this bed, for straightforward, down and dirty, no-holds-barred s-e-x. He didn't need memories or her reminders of the past to get off . . . or more to the point, to *keep* him from getting off.

He started to sit up again, in order to grab her and kiss her, or roll her onto her back, or whatever it took to shut her up.

Instead, the air rushed from his lungs as her fingers curled around the base of his dick and gave a little squeeze. He fell back against the pillows, every muscle but the all-important one in her hand going slack with both shock and pleasure.

With two fingers, she slowly rolled the used condom up and over the head of his cock, then leaned far enough away to drop it into the nearby trash can. It didn't take her long to return and take up where she'd left off.

"I remember something else about you, too," she said barely above a whisper.

His vocal chords felt frozen in his throat. He wasn't sure he could speak until he opened his mouth and a rough "Oh, yeah? What's that?" grated out.

"How much you used to like my mouth on you."

With that, she leaned over and licked the hard length of his shaft. The stroke of her tongue sent a lightning bolt of ecstasy shuddering up his spine and out to every extremity.

He was surprised he didn't erupt at that alone, but he was glad he somehow found the restraint to hold back when she swirled around the tip, then closed her lips over him and began to suck . . . gently at first, then with more pressure as she found her stride and fell into a rhythm that nearly caused his eyes to roll back in his head.

He curled his fists into the sheets, hoping the action would keep him anchored to the bed when what he really wanted was to shoot to the moon. And then, when he couldn't take it anymore, he reached up to comb his fingers through her soft, silky hair, and to aid her movements.

Not that she wasn't doing fine all on her own. Any better and she'd have him on his knees . . . begging, pleading, writhing. Ready to say anything, do anything, promise her anything.

It was a slippery slope, and he was entirely too close to utter stupidity as it was.

"Claire," he ground out, trying his best not to hurt her by clutching her scalp too tightly or forcing her farther down on his engorged member than she could comfortably handle. "Claire. Stop now or I'm going to come."

She released him just long enough to meet his eyes, but kept her lips near the head of his dick, lightly brushing back and forth, left to right to maintain his arousal and remind him of what she'd been doing, what she could do.

"That's the idea," she told him with an angelic smile, though with his cock that close to her mouth and her body starkly, lusciously naked, she looked about as far from being an angel as it was possible to be. Unless it was the naughty, fallen-from-Heaven variety.

Her tongue darted out to moisten a particularly sensitive spot near the base of his cock and her fingertips slipped down to toy with his balls.

"Ah, Jesus!" His hips lurched off the bed and he knew he only had a few seconds left before any protests he might have made turned into whimpers and the pathetic ramblings of a desperate man.

"You taught me well, remember?" she said softly.

Before he could answer, before his addled brain could even begin to *process* the words, she took him into her mouth again, swallowing him whole.

Holding back his climax would have been like trying to hold

back the tide with a barrier made of Popsicle sticks. There was no way he could have stopped the rising pleasure, the sharp-edged need, the fist that reached into his gut and jerked. Everything that was in him ripped free and spun out of control until he was shaking with the power of his release.

She moved with him, rising and falling to meet the thrust of his hips, taking all he had to offer until he was wiped out. Drained. Very possibly on the verge of a coma.

Never before had a single orgasm caused him to go almost literally cross-eyed with pleasure or a woman left him feeling so turned inside out.

He chose not to contemplate that last too closely. Not now, while his bones were liquid and Claire was stretching out along his side to settle in as though she belonged there.

And maybe she did.

Maybe she did.

7

"Tell me about Sara," Linc breathed quietly just above Claire's ear. The scratchy, nondescript sheets were pulled up around them and she was cuddled up to him so close, even air didn't have a chance of slipping between them. Or maybe he was cuddled up to her, his chest against the smooth line of her back, his groin pressed to the soft, round cushion of her delectable ass.

He hoped she was right about their daughter not being in any danger from her ex-husband, and the fact that it was a weekend would work against Scarborough getting falsified DNA documents together, because he sure as hell wasn't holding up his end of the bargain in tracking down the little girl.

Oh, what he'd told Claire was the truth—he was waiting for Deputy Keegan to get them more information about Jonathan

Scarborough and his family's holdings, but that didn't mean Linc couldn't have been working on other leads in the meantime.

So instead of hitting the streets or working the computer like the marshal he'd trained to be, he was holed up in some random, run-down motel room having more creative, spine-tingling sex than a porn star. He couldn't seem to get enough of Claire . . . and she didn't seem to be in any rush to put an end to things, either.

Earlier, between bouts of rolling around on the bed, the floor, and a couple of hot and heavy sessions in a chair and the bathroom doorway, he'd run out to a nearby fast-food joint to pick up some burgers and drinks. Partly because they hadn't eaten much during the flights and layovers that had brought them there, and partly to keep their energy up for whatever would take place throughout the rest of their night alone together.

He didn't share that last point with her, but putting the hours between dusk and dawn to good use was definitely at the top of his list.

At the moment, however, he was thoroughly sated—at least temporarily—and his mind had returned to its normal calm and logical functions instead of sailing south and taking up residence between his legs. He was here—in California *and* this motel room—with only one concrete goal: to track down Jonathan Scarborough and retrieve the child Claire claimed was his daughter. The sex was a nice, but not necessarily productive, sideline.

And though his heart gave an awkward lurch at the thought of how Claire would choose to respond to his less-than-subtle prompting, or being subjected to details he might prefer not to hear, he *needed* to know about this little girl he'd supposedly fathered.

He'd felt Claire's body go tense along his at his softly spoken command, probably expecting the topic to quickly dissolve into a heated confrontation, and she hadn't relaxed as the seconds ticked by in edgy silence. Finally, in a voice as quiet as his own, she asked, "What do you want to know?"

Everything! his mind screamed. If Sara was indeed his daughter, he'd missed everything from her birth to her first time riding a bike without training wheels. That loss curdled his insides and made him want to punch something. But since violence—no matter how justified—wasn't likely to get him anywhere, he schooled his breathing and focused on collecting as much information as he could while he had the chance.

Something Claire told him in the dark, with their recent intimacy swirling around them, might prove helpful in tracking down Sara. Or it might simply fill in some blanks and help him come to terms with the events of the last ten lost years of his life.

"Tell me how you met Scarborough," he said, trying not to let his derision for a man he didn't even know but despised all the same seep into his tone, "and when you discovered you were pregnant."

Her chest hitched as she took a deep breath. "I'd been in Los Angeles about a month when the morning sickness started. At first, I just thought I had the flu, but when it seemed to last forever and I never got any better, I knew something was wrong. I couldn't afford a doctor and was too embarrassed to go to a free clinic, so I bought one of those cheap over-the-counter pregnancy tests. And sure enough, the stick turned blue."

Slowly, as she talked, her muscles started to loosen and she began to relax again within his embrace. Her head rested on his thick bicep, the featherlight strands of her coffee brown hair brushing against his skin, his cheek, his chin.

"I was frantic. I didn't know what to do. A part of me wanted to run home—to you, to my parents, to a world I was familiar with and knew would accept me." She paused for a moment and her chest hitched as she inhaled deeply. "But I knew if I did that, I would end up living exactly the kind of life I went to Los Angeles to escape."

"Would it have been so bad?" he murmured into the darkness, his voice graveled with suppressed emotion. No matter how sensible her past decisions seemed to her, it hurt to know that she'd chosen moving across the country, marrying another man, and keeping his child a secret over staying in Pennsylvania to build a life and raise a family with him. He'd taken less painful kicks to the crotch.

"I thought so at the time," she admitted after a beat. "I wanted so badly to be someone, to have bigger and better than was possible in our tiny little town. I know that sounds terrible, and realize in retrospect that my decision was probably a huge mistake. At the very least, it was incredibly selfish of me and horribly unfair to you. But I was young and scared, and I just didn't know what to do."

With conscious effort, Linc unlocked his jaw and posed another question he wanted an answer to. "So when did you meet Scarborough?" *The man who stole my girl, my kid, and my life.*

"He was a regular customer at the coffee shop where I was working just off Sunset Boulevard. I'd seen him several times, and we'd made small talk when it was my turn to wait on him. And then the day after I found out I was pregnant, I couldn't stop crying. I'm sure I looked a mess, and the people I served probably feared for their lives from the crazy waitress having an emotional breakdown in the middle of Java Juice. The other girls tried to get me to go home, but then I would have spent the day alone, crying in my rat-infested apartment. And I knew I needed to save up as much money as possible if I had any hope of supporting a child."

She shifted slightly, drawing the covers a few inches higher over her bare shoulders. "Jonathan was one of my customers that day, and he asked what had me so upset. At first I didn't say anything, but when he pressed, I . . . I guess I needed to tell someone, to get it off my chest and not feel so *alone* anymore. So I sat down at his table and spilled my guts. He came in every day after that, asking how I was holding up, inviting me to sit and chat with him for a bit. And one day while I was talking to him on my break, he asked me to marry him."

A noise somewhere between a snort and a chuckle vibrated up from her diaphragm. "I thought that was the most bizarre thing I'd ever heard. Crazier even than the day I'd spent trying not to drip tears into people's cups. But he was serious, and launched into this big speech about coming from a wealthy family that was pressuring him to settle down, how marrying him would solve all my problems and more than a few of his own. He promised to take care of me and the baby, and said it didn't have to be a real marriage, just something to help me out of the jam I'd found myself in. We'd give it a try for a couple of years, and once I was back on my feet, if I wanted to leave, we'd simply go our separate ways."

Clearing her throat, she started to tense again in his arms, and he tensed with her, bracing himself for whatever she might say next. "It all sounded so good, and I was so desperate. He caught me at a weak moment, I suppose, and it seemed like a solution to all of my problems. Not the perfect one, maybe, but better than anything I'd come up with on my own. So I agreed, and he took me home to San Francisco to meet his parents and plan a wedding."

Linc was glad she was turned away from him, because he didn't think he was a decent enough actor to keep his feelings from being visible on his face. The anger, the sorrow, the frustration—and other things he couldn't put a name to.

"We fell into a companionable relationship, and after a while, what had begun as a marriage of convenience turned into a marriage in truth. We had Sara by then, and Jonathan was wonderful with her. I didn't love him the way I loved you, but I cared for him."

"You started sleeping with him, you mean," Linc couldn't stop from spitting out.

Claire remained silent at first, but then said quietly, "Yes. He was my husband, and a good man, a good father. We fell into it naturally, and being a real wife to him was the least I could do after everything he'd done for me."

After a second, she added, "If it makes you feel any better, sex with him was never like it was—or is—with you."

"Is that supposed to be a compliment?"

She gave a short, lighthearted laugh, almost as though she couldn't help being amused, despite the severity of their conversation.

"Definitely. Jonathan was a nice man, but he made love the same way he did everything else—stuffily, seriously, and with a decided lack of emotion. He had about as much passion as a piece of wilted lettuce."

For the first time since he'd introduced the topic of her ex, a smile stole across Linc's lips. It took all of his self-control not to push back his shoulders, straighten his spine, and preen as best he could on the horizontal. But down below, his penis stirred, unwilling to fall in line with fake modesty like the rest of his anatomy.

"So I take it you gave up on the idea of becoming a big movie star."

"Yeah," she sighed. "That was kind of a silly dream to begin with. I think I just needed something to aspire to that would get me out of Butler County. Of course, it took being away and being turned into a vapid, useless trophy wife to make me realize that living in a small town where everyone knows everyone else and can be relied on to help you out in a crisis wasn't as bad as I'd made it out to be."

"A trophy wife, huh?" He gave her a small squeeze with the arm he had draped around her waist.

"Oh, yes. As safe and comfortable a life as Jonathan provided, it came with a price. That price was letting him—or more precisely, his mother—mold me into the perfect, socially acceptable wife. Etiquette lessons, tennis lessons, ballroom dancing lessons . . ." She ticked them off on her well-manicured fingers before adding, "I've been coached more than a gymnasium full of Olympic hopefuls. They made sure I knew how to dress, how to sit properly, which utensil to use when, and supplied me with a list of acceptable topics for dinner party conversations. My friends were women from the country club whom Jonathan and his mother approved of, and no one else."

"It worked for you for ten years," he felt compelled to point out, though his comment didn't carry the same accusatory tone as it might have before.

In a low, almost imperceptible voice, she said, "Do you have any idea what it's like to be completely transformed? To have your entire personality modified to fit someone else's preferences? I hardly noticed it at first; I was just so appreciative of all the Scarboroughs had done for me that I was willing to do whatever I could to repay them. But after a while, I started to feel like a Barbie doll. Or maybe a paper doll they kept stripping down and redressing to fit their image of the perfect wife, the perfect mother, the perfect daughter-in-law."

She shook her head, sending the silk of her hair gliding back and forth across the flesh of his inner bicep. "There was no giant fight or infidelity or anything else that broke up my marriage. I simply woke up one day and realized I couldn't live that way anymore."

"How did Scarborough react when you asked for a divorce?" Linc wanted to know.

"He was okay with it," she responded carefully. "I don't think it came as much of a surprise to him, really. Or maybe he was as unhappy in the marriage as I was by then. He even offered to have his lawyers draw up the divorce papers. I'd signed a prenuptial agreement before we married, so there wasn't much question of what I would get from the split and what I wouldn't. But then . . ."

Her voice grew thick and broke for a minute, and she had to swallow before she could continue. "Then he informed me that I was welcome to leave, but I'd be leaving Sara behind. *That's* when things turned ugly and the fighting began. There was no way I was going anywhere without my daughter, but I knew he had the money and influence to take her from me if he really wanted to."

"Not going to happen," Linc said immediately, a thread of steely determination running through the words. He didn't care how rich or powerful Jonathan Scarborough was, the bastard wasn't going to get custody of *his* child. Not while he had breath left in his body and a round left in the chamber of his Glock.

"You don't know that," she protested shakily.

A shudder of pain and fear rolled through her and he tugged her even closer, using his body to offer comfort, strength, and warmth. He thought it was helping until he felt something damp touch his arm and realized it was tears.

"Hey," he said, his own voice growing rough with emotion as he pressed a kiss to her temple. "Don't cry, it's going to be all right."

"You don't *know* that," she said again.

"Yes, I do," he told her with conviction. "We're going to find Scarborough and get Sara back. I promise."

"You promise?" she repeated.

"I promise. Now go to sleep," he ordered softly. "We have a lot of work to do in the morning to bring our daughter home."

Hugging her tightly against his chest, he closed his eyes and started to drift off. He tried to hang on to his anger, his bitterness, to the hatred that had driven him for so many years. But for the first time in as long as he could remember, he couldn't seem to work up a bad thought about Claire or what she'd done to him.

Instead, he thought the ice around his heart might have begun to melt, and found himself feeling almost . . . content. Like maybe now that she was back in his life, he shouldn't let her get away again.

8

Even with the need to get to work and track down his daughter weighing heavily on his mind, Linc made a conscious decision to put that on a side burner and make the most of his night with Claire. Maybe his only night with her.

They made love over and over, dozing only briefly before waking up and turning to each other again. If they kept this up, he'd have to make a run for more rubbers. But he was reluctant to leave again, even for a short while, for fear it would destroy the comfortable, idealistic bubble they'd managed to erect around themselves—however temporary.

Of course, that bubble would burst soon enough all on its own, he thought with a sigh, glancing at the digital clock on the nightstand. The glowing red numbers showed it was almost six o'clock, and the hint of daylight peeking through the heavy green and brown drapes warned that they would have to get up soon and put their attention back on what had brought them three thousand miles across the country to begin with.

But they still had a *few* minutes left, he thought wickedly, snuggling into the soft pillow of her bottom where it was nestled against his groin. His slowly stirring, rearoused groin.

Sliding one hand up the flat plane of Claire's waist, he cupped her breast and fondled the nipple until she began to wiggle in his arms and let out a sexy, low-throated moan. He kissed the side of her neck, letting his tongue moisten a trail of soft skin up to her ear, then nipping at the sensitive drop of her lobe.

"Wake up, sleepyhead," he murmured, slipping his free hand down over her hip and into the warm, inviting vee of her legs. "I've got a little morning delight for you."

She moaned a second time, longer and with more feeling as her thighs parted to give him better access. "Is that anything like afternoon delight?" she wanted to know.

Her voice was rusty not just from sleep, but from all the times she'd screamed in his ear throughout the night when he'd brought her to orgasm. He'd be lucky if he didn't require a hearing aid by the time he got back to Pittsburgh.

"It's better," he replied, using his fingers to part her already slick folds and tease all the sweet spots he'd discovered the day before . . . and a few he remembered from a decade ago.

She gasped as he grazed her swollen clit, then thrust two fingers deep into her waiting sheath. "Why?"

"Because we get to do it now instead of waiting until later."

Her strangled laugh went straight to his solar plexus, and it was all he could do not to take her right then and there. He wanted to spread her legs just a little bit more and slide into her from behind while still holding her snug against him, still cradling her full, round breast in his hand.

He needed a condom and he needed it *now*. Before he did something stupid like driving into her bare. It might feel like Heaven on Earth while he was inside her, and he would have given his eyeteeth to be skin to skin with nothing between them but pure, unadulterated lust, but it just wasn't worth the risk. Not after what had apparently happened the last time they weren't careful enough.

With that harsh reality planted firmly in his brain, he nudged her slowly across the bed until he could reach the last of the condoms on the battered nightstand. He ripped off one of the cellophane squares, tore it open with his teeth, and quickly covered his raging erection.

He was one second, one breath, one centimeter from burying himself to the hilt when his cell phone rang. For a heartbeat, he seriously considered ignoring it. Nothing could be more important than feeling Claire's hot, wet body enveloping him, clutching him, milking him dry.

Finally, though, his law enforcement instincts won out over his overactive libido. Or maybe it was the knowledge that his daughter was out there with another man who planned to do whatever he had to do to claim her as his own.

With a groan of regret, he slapped Claire's butt to get her moving and off the bed ahead of him, then grabbed up his phone from where he'd left it on the table with his duffel and laptop, and flipped it open.

"Rappaport," he barked, his brows pulling down in a scowl when Claire started to shuffle away from him.

Grabbing her wrist, he yanked her back into the circle of his arms, holding her snug just the way they'd been in bed—her back to his chest, her ass to his groin.

He listened as Keegan filled him in on what he'd found out about the Scarboroughs while at the same time nuzzling Claire's temple. She put up a token struggle, but settled when his teeth closed on the long tendon running down the side of her throat and the same two fingers that had begun teasing her only moments ago snaked through her silky curls to wreak havoc once again.

Her mouth opened on a silent pant and she arched her bottom into his throbbing cock.

Shit, this was hot. It gave new meaning to the term "phone sex," and if Keegan didn't wrap up his report soon and hang up before things got out of hand, his fellow deputy was going to get an earful of something he'd probably rather not hear.

"Okay, good," Linc said roughly, doing his best to sound as though he wasn't as hard as a rock and just about to fuck the most rockin' woman on the planet. "Give me a minute to boot up my notebook, then send it on through. Thanks, man, I owe you one."

Clicking the phone closed, he tossed it to the table, then stretched an extra few inches to snag his computer. Thank God the thing was wireless because he *really* didn't have the patience or inclination right now to screw around with cords and connections.

That done, he pressed Claire forward a couple of steps. "Bend over," he told her. "Grab the arms of the chair."

She did as he instructed without a qualm or a question, and a surge of power, of want and need, roared through him. He stroked a hand up and down her spine, centered himself, and lunged forward, filling her with one long, strong motion.

She whimpered and he felt it in his balls, which were already drawn up tight to his body in anticipation of what was to come. Clenching his teeth, he fought for control as he slowly began to move.

Every stroke was like a lighted match to his cock. He could feel every muscle clasped around him, every fleshy fold and spontaneous ripple of her lush, welcoming sex.

"Christ," he swore, not sure he could hold himself in check, not sure how much more he could take.

But Claire was right there with him, just as she'd been all yesterday and all last night. She pushed against him, reaching an arm back for him even as her head drooped toward the seat of the chair, sending her hair to fall in a curtain around her face.

"Harder, Linc. Take me harder, please."

A muscle ticked in his jaw at the shudder of near-orgasm that rolled through him. He took her hand, twining their fingers together and giving her a squeeze. Then he slipped their linked hands beneath her, into the thatch of curls between her thighs, and used both of their index fingers to roll and pinch her tender clitoris.

Only when she was shaking with pleasure and so close to the edge he knew he could push her over with the slightest touch did he do as she'd asked and take her hard. As hard as he could. As hard as he dared. So hard, the chair skidded thrust by thrust across the carpeted floor.

The end, when it came, was like an atomic explosion, annihilating everything in its path. She screamed. He shouted. And they both nearly collapsed where they were standing, their sagging, half-draped bodies catching on the low-backed chair instead.

Slipping out of her, he lowered her onto the seat, where she sort of slumped with a low hum of pleasurable exhaustion. He grinned, feeling a bit like humming himself.

Heading for the bathroom, he disposed of the condom, then took a quick shower and shaved off a day's worth of beard stubble. When he reappeared into the main room with a too-small, threadbare towel tucked around his waist, Claire was still slumped where he'd left her. She'd readjusted herself and pushed the tangle of her hair away from her face, but otherwise hadn't moved.

He smiled again, a little less lecherously this time. Knowing he'd had a hand in zapping her energy and leaving her languid enough to stay in one place for twenty minutes, too exhausted to move any farther, filled him with masculine pride. But he was also filled with a sense of wonder that she was here with him at all.

Ten years. Ten long years when his emotions had run the gamut. He'd loved her, he'd longed for her; he'd worried about her, he'd missed her; he'd felt betrayed by her, he'd hated her; and there for a while, he'd thought he'd forgotten her. And now they'd been thrown together once more, almost as though some invisible hand was reaching down to play with them like giant chess pieces.

At first, he'd been thoroughly pissed at her for showing up again just when he'd gotten her out of his system and had his life back on track. But how could he stay angry with her after she'd given herself to him so openly, so freely, all through the night?

Even the reminder that she'd kept their daughter from him for so long didn't bring the same wave of fury as before. Instead, he found himself eager to find Sara and bring her to safety, to see her with his own two eyes . . . to start being a father to her, if she would let him.

There were a lot of things still up in the air, a lot of things he wasn't quite sure of, maybe couldn't even put a name to.

What he did know, however, was that he had a solid lead on tracking down Sara and Scarborough, and that was at the top of his list.

The rest . . .

He crossed the room, scooping a naked Claire into his arms and carrying her back to the bathroom.

The rest he would deal with later.

Setting her on her feet on the mat just in front of the tub, he gave her fanny a light smack and said, "Get cleaned up, then meet me back out there. We've got work to do."

He turned to leave, making it about two steps before stopping in the doorway to risk a last glance over his shoulder. The long line of her slim, bare body, even from the side, had the air going stale in his lungs and his fingers itching to grab her up again and forget about the rest of the world outside the four paper-thin walls surrounding them.

"Make it snappy," he ordered, his voice rough but carrying no real censure. "Or I might be tempted to join you, and then we *really* won't get anything done today."

9

Where a minute ago, Claire had been so pleasurably drained, she didn't care if she never moved again, Linc's reminder that Sara was out there, waiting for them to find her spurred her back to full-blooded awareness. She rushed through her shower, jumping out to dry as best she could with the single remaining towel, then headed into the main room, where Linc was dressed and seated at the table with his laptop open. Papers and maps were spread out around him, and he seemed deep in concentration.

Wrapping the damp towel around her and tucking the ends just above her breasts, she took a moment to study him before he realized she was there. Or maybe he already knew. Lord knew the man didn't seem to miss a trick.

He looked so darn handsome, with that wide, strong, newly shaved jaw and the smoky, sultry gray eyes. His short, almost black hair was still wet at the ends, combed through with his fingers to leave it looking casual and unkempt. Much like the day before, he was dressed in faded blue jeans and a black cotton shirt that molded to his impressive chest and arms like a second skin.

Sexy, that's what he was. And she caught herself thinking, wondering, wishing . . .

Was there a chance? Could he forgive her enough to put the past behind them and work to build a future together?

She didn't know if she could ever be so lucky, but she sure did hope.

Without a word, she moved around the room, gathering clothes and toiletries and getting dressed. She didn't bother drying her hair, deciding that for once since becoming Mrs. Jonathan Scarborough, she would let it go and deal with the consequences. She was beginning to think she could stand a new hairdo, anyway; she was tired of the stiff, formal style that had become so much a part of her life in recent years.

She was equally tired of her wardrobe, she thought as she dug through her suitcase and saw—with new eyes, it seemed—her sorry lack of choices. Though every item bore a designer label and cost more than everything in the cheap hotel room put together, they still looked as though she was getting ready to pose for page sixty-two of a mail-order catalog.

As soon as this was over and her daughter was back with her safe and sound, they were taking a girls' day out to go shopping and fill Mommy's closets with all new clothes. She may not have the funds to shop the way she used to, but she would rather dress in thrift store chic and feel like herself again than be covered in Donna Karan from head to toe and feel like a terrible fraud.

Doing her best to go for casual, she put on a pair of tan slacks and a lavender blouse, added small gold hoop earrings, a small gold cross necklace, and slipped into light brown pumps.

Stepping back into the bathroom with her toiletries case, she quickly brushed her teeth and washed her face, then returned to the table and pulled the free chair up beside Linc's.

"So where are we?" she asked.

He slanted a glance in her direction, and for once his expression toward her wasn't hard and frosty. It must have softened sometime during the night, while they'd both been sweaty and frantic with need, but it had been too dark for her to tell. She saw it now, though, and hope once again flared low in her belly.

"We've got maps and deeds to a cabin Scarborough's parents own up in Auburn. Noah had some guys from the district U.S. Marshals office here in San Francisco run by some of their other properties to look around. The closer, more well-known ones. No luck. Noah also cold-called Jonathan's house and office, pretending to be a business acquaintance and, when he pressed, someone—a secretary, most likely—let it slip that he'd gone to the mountains for a while. So I think there's a pretty good chance this is where your ex-husband is hiding out with Sara."

Claire leaned over the map, studying it more closely. "I didn't know anything about this property. He never mentioned a cabin in Auburn that I can recall."

"Maybe it's where he took his mistresses or something," Linc replied flippantly.

For a second, she was startled by the remark and thought it might be another of Linc's digs about her past choices, her marriage, the woman she'd become. But then she realized there was no venom in his tone. And on top of that, she didn't *care* anymore. Not about anything Jonathan may or may not have done while they were married.

The only thing she cared about was her daughter . . . and the man sitting only inches away from her in this cramped, dingy motel room.

With a chuckle, she said, "You're probably right. I never considered infidelity on his part but, for all I know, he may have been having affairs from the day we met. And if I'd found out about them, been able to prove he'd been unfaithful, then he'd have been guilty of breaking his part of the prenuptial agreement and I *would* have gotten half of everything."

She shook her head. "I feel like such an idiot. That's probably exactly what was going on, and he had everything planned from the very beginning to make sure I'd leave the marriage with nothing." Taking a deep breath, she blew it out on a sigh. "I think I'm glad I got out when I did. I wouldn't have wanted to stay married to a man like that."

Though his lips thinned slightly, Linc didn't reply. Then he inclined his head in what could only be taken as a nod and returned his attention to the matter at hand.

"While you were in the shower, I called the local Marshals office and talked with one of the guys Noah's been working with. A couple of off-duty deputies are going to accompany us up there and help us check it out."

His eyes clouded and, to her surprise, he reached over to cover her hand with his own. His big, tanned fingers covered her smaller, paler ones, and the electric zap of sexual awareness that had always been there, *would* always be there, she suspected, sizzled through her.

"If you want me to, I'll ask them to send guys who are on duty so that if Jonathan and Sara are there, Scarborough can be taken into custody for abducting Sara without your permission. I don't have that authority, since I'm out of my jurisdiction and am personally involved, but I can make sure someone who does is there, if you want Scarborough arrested."

She swallowed, holding Linc's gaze while she considered her options. Part of her wanted very much to punish Jonathan, punish *anyone* who would dare take her daughter from her. But another part of her just wanted Sara back and then to be done with the whole, sordid mess.

Shaking her head, she said, "I just want Sara back. If we can get her away from Jonathan and prove you're her father before he concocts proof that *he* is, I'll be happy."

A beat passed in tense silence, and then he nodded. "Fair enough. I've got everything lined up," he added, pushing back from the table and beginning to gather his things. "It's a two-hour drive up to Auburn, and we're meeting the other marshals outside their headquarters in one, so pack up and get ready to leave. We'll stop for breakfast on the way."

Several hours later, as the SUV bumped along a muddy, rutted dirt road with thick woods on either side, Claire's stomach was in knots. She could feel the slight tremor in her sweating palms as she clenched and unclenched her hands in her lap.

On the drive to the USMS headquarters, while they'd eaten a quick breakfast out of fast-food bags, Linc had filled her in on a few more details of the plan to check out the mountain cabin. And when they'd reached the office building, she'd overheard even more while he'd conferred with his fellow deputies.

This wasn't a raid or a takedown. Linc and the other two men following behind them in a second equally large, equally black SUV were all armed and dressed as though they were expecting trouble, but Linc had assured her it was merely their version of a uniform and acted as more of a precaution than anything else.

She hoped he was right. If this turned into some kind of stand-off . . . if Jonathan was crazy enough to think he could keep Sara away from her or survive a confrontation with U.S. Marshals and someone got hurt . . . she didn't know what she would do. Even if it was more likely that Linc would be the one doing the hurting instead of the other way around.

"You all right?" Linc asked.

His voice came out of nowhere, startling her and making her jump.

She took a deep breath, laying her hands flat on the tops of her thighs in an effort to settle her nerves and put an end to her fidgeting. "I just want Sara back, and for this to be over."

Surprising her more than his gruff voice in the earlier silence of the vehicle had, he reached over to thread his fingers with hers. Heat suffused her at that small touch. Not the heat of sexual attraction—though that was there; with Linc, it was always there—but of comfort and support and solidarity. They were in this together, she thought, and for the first time since she'd discovered her daughter was missing, she truly believed everything would be okay.

"If they're at the cabin the way we suspect, then it won't be long now. When we get there, though, remember that I want you to stay back. Stay in the car, or stay *by* the car, until we know who's inside and get a feel for how things are going to play out."

His hand tightened on hers and she squeezed back, grateful for the contact.

"We've done this a thousand times before and know what we're doing. Everything's going to be fine."

Both her chest and her throat began to close on her, but she quickly got herself back under control. She nodded and turned her head to face him. For a brief second, before he had to return his gaze to the heavily potholed path of the road, their eyes met and a thread of understanding passed between them.

"I trust you," she said softly.

"Good. That'll save us some time down the road," he replied.

She opened her mouth to question him about that cryptic comment, but just then the thick copse of trees they'd been driving through for the past half hour started to thin until they could see a small but well-built cabin tucked off to the right. Claire's heartbeat accelerated as Linc took his foot off the gas and slowed to study the cabin and the surrounding area.

"That's one of Jonathan's cars," she murmured in a near-whisper. Linc's hand had left hers as they closed in on the cabin, but now she reached out to grip his solid forearm.

With his free hand, he flipped open his cell phone, muttered a low curse, then tossed it down again. "No reception."

Instead of turning into the short drive that led to the cabin, he pulled off the side of the road and cut the engine, checking the rearview mirror to see that the other SUV had done the same. He opened his door and stepped out, closing it again with barely a sound. Following his lead, she climbed out, too, meeting Linc and the other two marshals at the rear of the first vehicle.

"I'm going to walk straight up to the front door and knock, see what kind of response I get," Linc told Deputies Warren and Quintaro. "You guys go around the sides, peek in some windows. Signal if there's anything I need to know before I go in there."

Both men nodded.

"You," Linc said, focusing his attention directly on Claire, "*stay here*. Don't move until I give you the all-clear. Got it?"

She nodded, even though she wanted to be the one running, not walking, up to the cabin door. It took all of her restraint to keep from grabbing on to his belt and making him drag her along, whether he liked it or not.

The other two marshals started forward, moving toward either side of the building. They glanced inside Jonathan's car as they passed, but must not have noticed anything of interest, because they kept going.

Linc watched their progress for a second before turning back to her. Grabbing her chin between his thumb and index finger, he tilted her gaze up to meet his.

"Hold on to the tail pipe if you have to, but do *not* move from this spot. Got it?"

She was getting a little tired of being treated like a recalcitrant three-year-old. "I've got it," she snapped, being careful to keep her voice low. "Now why don't you stop worrying about me and go do your job, *Marshal*. Go find our daughter."

Instead of being offended by her remark, a wicked half-grin flashed across his already too-handsome face.

"Yes, ma'am," he murmured. Then he leaned in to press a fast, hard kiss to her lips before turning on his heel to follow his partners.

Claire held her breath while Linc approached the cabin. She might not have been a trained law enforcement officer, but it didn't take a genius to figure out what the other two marshals were saying when they used their hands to signal: There were two people inside, as far as they could see. A man and a little girl. No weapons were visible.

Her lungs burned from lack of oxygen and she seriously considered digging her nails into something to keep herself rooted to the spot. If not the tail pipe, as Linc had suggested, then maybe the metal bumper at her hip. Her lips began to move in a silent prayer—several silent prayers—for Sara, for Linc, for all of them.

At the other end of the small clearing, Linc climbed the porch steps and crossed to the door, lifting a hand to knock on the solid pine door. She could imagine Jonathan's surprise at having someone show up out of the blue when she was sure he thought they were alone, practically untraceable up here in the mountains at a cabin even his wife of ten years hadn't known existed.

A minute later the door opened, but only a few inches. Linc flashed his badge and starting talking, but Claire wasn't close enough to hear what was being said.

She had noticed, however, that Linc very wisely closed the distance between himself and Jonathan, slipping his foot into the crack between the door and its frame to keep Jonathan from shutting him out. The other two marshals stood on either side of the porch, out of sight, but close enough to spring into action if they were needed.

Whatever Linc was saying, it was clear Jonathan wasn't happy. Even from her position by the Suburban, she could see his face turning red and hear his angry, raised voice.

Rather than raising his own voice in kind, Linc seemed to become more stoic, his tall, muscular frame straightening and growing larger to tower over her ex, who had always been quite tall and imposing himself. A second later, Linc put one wide hand to the door and gave the wooden panel a shove, forcing Jonathan back as he stepped inside. Almost by invitation, the other deputies came around, following behind in an added show of manpower and support.

Claire's lungs felt as though they'd been frozen in her chest for ages, but now they were working overtime, sending her dangerously close to hyperventilation. The butterflies in her stomach were doing cartwheels and her blood pressure, she was sure, was shooting well into the red zone.

And then Linc reappeared, coming through the door with her daughter in his arms, and her whole world shifted, righting itself on its axis and going back to being a glorious, wonderful place to be once again.

10

"Sara!"

Linc and the little girl balanced easily on his hip both shot their gazes to Claire as she shouted her daughter's name. Despite her earlier promise to stay put, Claire ran toward them, and Sara wiggled against him until he lowered her to the ground and let her go.

A lump formed in his throat as they ran toward each other and the child leapt into her mother's arms. He wondered what it would have been like to see that sort of display of affection on a regular basis, from the time Sara was a baby just learning to toddle around on her own two feet.

He'd missed a lot, and he couldn't say the anger and bitterness over *why* he'd missed out was completely gone, but he realized he'd give a hell of a lot to see more of this type of mother-daughter interaction. And maybe experience a bit of father-daughter inter-action, as well.

"Oh, baby, I missed you," Claire said, kissing Sara everywhere she could reach—her cheek, her ear, her hair—and squeezing her until he was surprised the little girl could still breathe.

"I missed you, too. Daddy said you were coming, but then you never did, and I wanted to go home, but he said we had to stay." Pulling back, she framed Claire's face with her small hands, a frown marring her perfect mouth. "There's no TV or computer or video games or *anything* here. I had to read books and play cards with Daddy, and I was *soooo* bored. Can we go home now?"

Hearing Sara call another man "Daddy" set Linc's teeth on edge, but he tried not to let it bother him—or at least not to let it show. What did he expect? Jonathan Scarborough had raised her; he was the only father she'd ever known. But if Linc had anything to say about it—and he damn sure had something to say about it—that would soon change.

Claire had said she'd explained things to Sara when she'd sat her down to tell her about the divorce. Explained that Scarborough wasn't her real father, and that another man was. That should make Linc's entrance into her life smoother, right?

He returned his attention to the two females who were currently the center of his life. And with any luck, would be for a long time to come.

Claire chuckled at Sara's animated recap of her stay at the cabin. "Yes, sweetheart, we can go home now. Remember the talk we had about Mommy and Daddy's divorce, though. We aren't going back to the big house you're used to. I think we'll go visit Grandma and Grandpa Cassidy in Pennsylvania instead. But don't worry, they've got television, and a computer, and video games, and everything."

Sara nodded, wrapping her arms around Claire's neck and snuggling in once again.

Over their daughter's head, Claire met Linc's gaze, her blue eyes glistening with tears. "Thank you," she whispered.

Feeling his own emotions teeter precariously, he inclined his head, then cleared his throat and said, "Why don't you take Sara to the car and get her settled. I have a few things left to deal with in the cabin, then I'll be out to drive you back to the city."

"Okay," she agreed softly.

He started to turn away, but she reached out to grab his wrist and tug him back. Moving closer and standing on tiptoe, she brushed her lips across his cheek and flashed him a smile like the ones she'd given him back in the motel room when he'd had her under him, over him, in front of him, beside him. . . . It promised things, things he wasn't sure he could define, and reached deep inside him to tie him up in knots.

"We'll talk when this is all over, right?"

"Yeah," he said roughly. "We'll talk."

He watched her walk off, Sara tucked tightly against her chest, then returned to the cabin where his fellow deputies were keeping Jonathan Scarborough busy. Linc hadn't wanted to risk a confrontation between Scarborough and Claire in front of Sara, not after everything they'd already been through.

Quintaro met him at the door. "He's singing like a jaybird." The deputy chuckled. "He didn't even give us a chance to tell him he isn't in custody."

From the sounds of it, Scarborough was squawking more than singing. He'd apparently passed the point where he was confessing all and had moved on to threatening to call his lawyers and have them charged with everything under the sun.

"We found this," Quintaro added, handing him a manila folder.

Linc flipped it open and glanced at the papers inside. Letters, memos, handwritten notes, and medical records for both Scarborough and Sara. At the bottom of the pile was Sara's birth certificate, and his heart flipped over in his chest, threatening to beat through his rib cage when he noticed his name at the bottom of the page.

His name, not Scarborough's. Claire may have married Scarborough, may have let the man play father to her daughter all these years, but she hadn't denied Sara's parentage.

Closing the file, he tucked the entire folder into his jeans at the small of his back. Nothing seemed to have been falsified yet, but with the information currently balanced in his hands and enough money to grease the right palms, Linc could definitely see how new, fake DNA documents could be produced.

"Great, thanks. I appreciate your help." He shook Quintaro's hand, then started toward Warren to do the same.

"Mind leaving me alone with Mr. Scarborough for a couple of minutes?" he asked politely, but both men knew it was more than a request.

"No problem," Warren replied, the corner of his mouth tugging up in a grin. "We'll be outside. Yell if you need anything."

"Will do, thanks."

As soon as the other two men stepped onto the porch and closed the door behind them, Scarborough went back to squawking.

"I don't know who you think you are . . ." he began.

But Linc cut him off. Leaning down so that he was almost nose to nose with the man sitting in a chair beside the round oak table in the center of the kitchen nook, Linc pulled his lips back and gave Scarborough a feral, wolfish smile.

"My name is Lincoln Rappaport," he said in a tone sharp enough to cut glass, and was pleased to see Scarborough blanch.

"I'm Sara's biological father. The man you tried to cut out of her life."

Straightening, he dragged a second chair over with the toe of his boot, turned it around, and straddled the seat to face Scarborough.

"So here's the deal," he continued, keeping his voice low and menacing. "You're going to forget about Sara. Forget about trying to prove you're her father, when we both know you aren't. And you're going to forget about Claire. You might rethink the divorce settlement, give her a little chunk of your millions to thank her for her devotion over the past ten years—especially since we both know that if she'd caught you at one of your affairs, she could have taken you for half of everything. California is a community property state, after all."

He removed his hands from the back of the chair to cross his arms over the thin, curved line of wood instead. "Either way, you're going to forget the two of them ever existed. You won't call them, you won't write to them, you won't even breathe their names at one of your tight-assed dinner parties. Otherwise, I'm going to come back here and make you very, very sorry."

Scarborough opened his mouth, and Linc thought he might actually have been working up the courage to retort. Linc didn't give him the chance.

"Very. Sorry." He carefully stressed each word, as though they were separate entities. "Do I make myself clear?"

The other man didn't reply.

"Yes or no, Mr. Scarborough?" he asked, relaxing slightly on the chair, letting his voice turn more amicable and less threatening. "In case you hadn't noticed, I'm armed, and so are the other two marshals out on that porch. They also happen to be close friends of mine, who wouldn't mind swearing to any story I asked them to about what might have happened here today. And Claire and Sara are out in the truck, so they don't know what's going on."

He reached to his side to unsnap the holster at his hip and fondle the butt of his Glock. "Accidents happen all the time, Mr. Scarborough. Especially in the woods, when guys go up to their cabins to get away and do a little hunting."

Scarborough's eyes narrowed. "You're threatening me?" he asked through tightly pursed lips.

"I'm telling you how far I'm willing to go to protect my family." The word slipped out before he thought about it, before he realized what he was about to say. But it felt right. More than right.

And he meant what he'd said—to protect Claire and Sara, he'd do anything, go anywhere, give up his badge, his principles, his very life.

The truth of that must have been plain on his face, because any fight Scarborough might have had in him seemed to disappear. His jaw clenched and a flush started to creep into his cheeks. "Fine," came his gritted reply.

"Good." Linc slapped the back of the chair and pushed to his feet. "We'll leave you to the rest of your little mountain retreat, then. Have a nice weekend."

He left the cabin whistling, and had a good laugh with the other two marshals, who had heard his entire conversation with Scarborough, despite their subdued tones. Shaking both men's hands, he wished them well at their vehicle before heading back to the rented Suburban.

Claire and Sara were both in the backseat. Sara was playing with a travel-size Gameboy, which Claire must have had packed away for when she was back with her daughter—*their* daughter—and Claire had her arm around the little girl's shoulders, stroking her hair and kissing the top of her head as though she couldn't stand not to be touching her after such a long, stressful separation.

The sight tugged at his heart, and he knew he didn't want to let them go. Either of them.

Opening the driver's side door, he climbed in, then twisted around in the seat. "You girls ready to go home?"

Sara lifted her gaze from the video game and looked at him with eyes the same color as his own. She grinned, showing a gap in her teeth. If he hadn't already been head over heels in love with the kid, just knowing she was his, he would have fallen at that moment, and fallen hard.

"Ready!" she singsonged before returning her attention to her game.

Claire rested her cheek on Sara's head before meeting his gaze with her own. "Take us home, Linc."

Epilogue

Loud voices, laughter, and childish shrieks filled her parents' large backyard as just about every member of Claire's and Linc's families gathered for a late afternoon Fourth of July picnic. A few friends and neighbors were thrown into the mix, too. And later, after the sun went down and the fireworks came out, things would get *really* noisy.

Sara ran past, two young male cousins hot on her heels, while she squealed at the top of her lungs. Claire watched her race away with a smile.

Sara had always been a happy child, but since they'd moved back to Pennsylvania, she'd begun to grow and thrive and learn what it meant to be part of a happy, close-knit family. Once in a while, she would beg for the latest toy or throw a temper tantrum because she didn't have the newest gadget, but otherwise her transition from the lap of luxury to middle-class nonluxury had gone fairly smoothly.

The transition Claire was most pleased with, though, was Sara's quick acceptance of Linc as her real father. After leaving Jonathan's cabin, Linc had driven them back to San Francisco, where he'd checked them into a higher-price hotel than the place the two of them had stayed in the night before—although she had some rather fond memories of that ratty old motel room—until they could get a flight back to Pittsburgh.

Linc had told her she didn't need to rush anything, that he was willing to wait for the official introductions to be made. But she'd seen the longing in his eyes and etched into his face, and hadn't wanted to add any more time to the decade he'd already lost with his daughter.

So, with Linc right there to hear every word, she'd sat on the hotel bed with Sara and explained everything over again, making sure Sara knew who Linc was and that he was going to be in her life from now on.

At the time, even Claire hadn't known just *how much* a part of Sara's life—or her own—Linc would become.

But, as precocious a child as Sara was, she'd taken the news in stride, climbed onto Linc's knee—which Claire thought had probably left the big, bad U.S. marshal speechless for the first time ever—and proceeded to play Twenty-Thousand Questions until she knew everything from how Linc and Claire had met to what his favorite color was.

At first, Sara had called Linc "Daddy Linc" or "Daddy Number Two," with Jonathan being "Daddy Number One." While Claire knew Linc liked having Sara call him Daddy, he hadn't been fond of the "Number Two" moniker. But lately, Jonathan's name had come up less and less, and Sara had taken to calling Linc simply "Dad."

"Wanna sneak off and neck until the fireworks start?"

The question, whispered in a low hush just above her ear, brought back warm memories of all the times as a teenager he'd lured her away to neck or pet or make out. And the same as it had back then, the suggestive invitation sent shivers skating down her spine.

Despite the hot summer sun blazing overhead and raising the afternoon temperature into the high nineties, goose bumps broke out along her arms and legs. The wide palms slipping seductively into the pockets of her shorts to cup her bottom didn't help matters, either.

Tipping her head back, she met Linc's warm, laughing eyes. "Would those be the actual fireworks or the ones you hope to get started after we sneak off?" she asked quietly enough that no one else would hear.

"Both," he responded, the corners of his mouth turning up in a lascivious grin.

The prim and proper woman she'd been while married to Jonathan Scarborough never would have agreed, but she'd changed a lot since the divorce had been finalized. She was feeling more like her old self every day.

Pushing up from the picnic-table bench, she climbed out, took the hand he offered, and followed him away from the festivities. He led her off to the side of the yard, where a small wooded area separated her parents' property from the neighbors'.

As soon as they were out of sight, he yanked her behind a tall, wide-trunked tree, pinned her against the rough bark with his equally imposing body, and took her mouth in a hot, searing kiss that rocked her all the way to her toes.

When they came up for air—which wasn't for several long, very enjoyable minutes—they were both sagging and gasping for breath.

"Mmmm. You taste like grape Kool-Aid," he murmured, sliding his hands over her hips and pressing the proof of his desire into her belly.

"It's your daughter's favorite," she replied.

His eyes lit up, as they always did at the mention of Sara, and Claire's heart swelled. He'd taken to fatherhood like a bird to flight. He doted on Sara, and though there had been a few heated arguments over the past and the secrets Claire had kept from him, for the most part he'd come to terms with that, too. They'd worked things out and gotten to know each other again over family dinners and trips to the park or the movies or the mall.

In the beginning, Claire and Sara had stayed at her parents' house in Butler, and had either driven in to Pittsburgh to visit Linc, or he'd driven out to see them. The closer they got as a family, the more time they spent together, and now that Sara was out of school for the summer, they'd all but moved in with him.

She liked it, and at times it felt as though they'd never been apart, as though she'd made the right decision all those years ago instead of the wrong one—staying in Butler, marrying Linc, and starting a family the old-fashioned way.

"We should get back," she nearly panted, feeling her nipples pucker inside the cups of her bra as his hands wiggled beneath the hem of her sunflower yellow top to graze her stomach and inch ever higher. "People will get suspicious if we disappear for too long."

He toyed with her mouth before trailing his lips along her cheek to nibble at her ear. "They won't be suspicious," he said. "They'll know exactly what we're up to."

Too true, considering anyone with the gift of sight would find it hard to ignore the almost spontaneous combustion that occurred whenever she and Linc were within shouting distance of each other. His gaze smoldered, and he rarely bothered to keep his hands off of her, while her entire body went hot and damp and needy whenever they were in the same room together.

"If you promise to be good until after the picnic, when our families are no longer watching our every move," she murmured, running her hands up and down his firm, muscled back, "I promise to be *very good* when we get back to your place."

He let out a low growl, gently biting the pulse point at the side of her throat.

"I've been thinking about that," he said, mumbling the words against her skin as he continued to nuzzle her neck and shoulder.

The more he touched her, the fuzzier her thoughts became, but she managed to follow along enough to ask, "About what?"

"My place." He kissed her collarbone, then started back up toward her mouth. "I've been thinking it should be *our* place. Or that we should look around for a bigger apartment or maybe a house that we could make a real home, for ourselves and for Sara."

He pressed his mouth to hers, then pulled back, meeting her gaze. She blinked at the sudden lack of his sensual attentions and noticed the serious expression on his face.

Gathering her wits, she said, "You want us to move in together? Officially?"

"Yeah." His lips quirked up in a grin at her choice of words. "It's not only the living arrangements I want to make official, though."

Reaching into the front pocket of his jeans, he pulled out a small, square box. A jeweler's box just the right size for a ring.

Claire's chest tightened as her breathing sped up and tears prickled behind her eyes.

He opened the box and a beautiful, princess-cut diamond sparkled in the dappled sunlight.

"Will you marry me, Claire?"

Lifting her gaze from the ring to his handsome, precious face, she saw the sincerity in the question, his trepidation that she might say no.

"I love you, baby," he went on in a rush, his voice thick with emotion. "Have since we were kids. Even when I hated you, I still loved you so much, it ate me up inside. It's time to put things right and do what we should have done ten years ago. I want you to be my wife, to help me make us a real family for Sara. Maybe even give her a little brother or sister one of these days," he added with a sexy waggle of his dark brows.

Swallowing hard, she tried to slow the desperate pounding of her heart beneath her rib cage, but couldn't stop a wide smile from breaking out across her face.

"I love you, too," she told him in a watery voice. Taking his hand, she kissed the knuckles, then placed his palm over her heart and covered it with her own. "I wish so much that I'd never gone away and we'd married straight out of high school the way I know you wanted to. Our lives would have been so much different if we had, and I know we both would have been happier."

"Probably," he agreed, "but that's water under the bridge. I'm talking about now, about our future. So are you going to finally let me make an honest woman of you, or what?"

"Yes." She laughed and threw her arms around his neck, hugging him tight. "Oh, yes. Just try to get rid of me."

"Not a chance." He pulled away only long enough to remove the engagement ring from the case and slip it on her finger, then yanked her back into his arms. "Now that I've got you, I'm never letting go of you again."